"Set in the very near future, Anthony Gardner's second novel is a gentle, engaging and topical satire on our surveillance society and on British subservience to the Oriental superpower . . . Gardner is a natural storyteller who writes with great skill, nuance and wry humour. Highly recommended"

The Mail on Sunday

"A deeply satisfying plot that has shades of *The 39 Steps* sprinkled with Tom Sharpe-style wackiness that pitches in into that rare and difficult-to-carry-off genre, the comedy thriller"

Country life

"A plot that fizzes like PG Wodehouse mixed with John Buchan"

The Tablet

"The pace is fast but Anthony Gardner's fluid and euphonious style keeps it on the right side of hectic . . . as a satire on the reality of ever-encroaching mass surveillance it has a passionate vein of seriousness running through it"

The Irish Times

"Part thriller, part satire, part farce, and wholly brilliant."

The Church Times

About the Author

Anthony Gardner is an Irish writer and editor based in London. *Fox* is his second novel; his first, *The Rivers of Heaven*, was described by Selina Hastings as 'An amazing novel, so moving, so hauntingly imaginative, so quietly funny and so wonderfully well written'. He has also published a collection of poetry, *The Pool and Other Poems*. He was the founding editor of *The Royal Society of Literature Review* and is a trustee of the Keats-Shelley Memorial Association. He has written for a wide variety of British, Irish and American magazines and newspapers, and his poems have appeared in *The London Magazine*.

FOX

ANTHONY GARDNER

ILLUSTRATIONS BY
NICOLA AND ROSANNA REED

Scotland Street Press

Paperback edition October 2018
Published by Scotland Street Press (SS Press Ltd)
100 Willowbrae Avenue
Edinburgh EH8 7HU

A CIP catalogue record for this book is available from the British Library

First published in hardback in 2015 by
Ardleeven Press

ISBN: 978-1-910895-29-0

Typeset by Hewer Text UK Ltd, Edinburgh
Printed and bound in Poland

For my wife Rosanna

PROLOGUE

As dawn broke over London, the sound of a horse's hoofs echoed along Oxford Street. In a few hours, the pavements would eddy and spill with shoppers, and the roadway become a garish procession of buses; but for now the only competing noise was the whine of a dustcart as it laboured from lamppost to lamppost, while four men in Dayglo jackets tossed black plastic sacks into the back. The six hounds keeping pace with the horse padded silently, noses to the ground, tails erect.

The man in the saddle wore pristine jodhpurs and a scarlet fleece with the initials HPH across the back; the polished leather of his boots and saddle gleamed in the early light, a shade darker than the holsters cradling his handgun and rifle. Under the peaked riding hat his blue-grey eyes scanned the street for a flash of fur.

He had been up at 3am to draw the alleyways behind Marble Arch's fast-food restaurants. It was the devil's own work with so many food smells mingling on the air. Now, just as his hounds seemed to have picked up the fox's trail, here was this bloody great rubbish van filling the street with its stench.

'Hey, Frank!' shouted one of the bin men over the noise of the truck. 'What you doing down here? Bit early for the sales, ain't you?'

'Morning, lads,' said the huntsman. 'Looking for a big dog fox. Anyone seen him?'

'I seen *a* fox,' said one of the other men. 'Headed down towards Selfridges. Probably in the food hall by now.'

'Cheers!' shouted the huntsman, urging his horse into a fast trot.

The hounds raced ahead, their dark reflections flickering across the windows of Marks & Spencer. A hundred yards further on they spotted their prey. Giving tongue, they darted across the road, hurtling into the streets of Mayfair. Frank wheeled his horse to follow them.

Cutting a corner of the pavement, its hoofs slid on a manhole cover. Frank felt the animal lurch forwards; for a moment he thought he was going to be thrown headfirst to the ground. But the horse, police-trained, was well used to the uneven terrain: with Frank clinging to its neck, it found its balance and hit a steady canter, allowing its rider to right himself and gather the reins.

He swore with relief. The last time he'd taken a fall on a pavement he'd been hospitalised for six weeks. But there was no point in complaining – it went with the territory.

Glancing at his watch, he saw that he had thirty minutes before the West End opened to traffic. With luck that should be enough.

He put his horn to his lips and blew.

CHAPTER ONE

Fox flu was at the top of the agenda as the British Prime Minister began his state visit to China. A concerted international response to this new and deadly disease was something that required much discussion. At least, that was what he had told the newspapers. If his mission had a more personal side, the public was not privy to it.

'So, Mr PM, welcome again to the People's Republic,' said the head of the reception committee as their limousine left Beijing Airport. 'It has been too long since your last visit.'

'Thank you, Mr Vice President.'

'You like my car?'

'Very much.'

'The interior was designed for me in Milan. Ostrich leather throughout.'

So that was why the back seat felt like a cheese grater. 'Magnificent,' said the Prime Minister.

'I hope you noticed the dashboard: I chose it myself. Rosewood from the heart of the Brazilian rainforest. I bet you have never seen the like in Britain.'

'No, I can't say I have.'

'You should come and live in China!' The Vice President laughed heartily. 'Best of everything here!'

'Perhaps when I retire you could find a job for me.'

The Vice President laughed again. 'Very funny! Would you like a whisky?'

'It's a bit early in the day for me.'

'Never too early for Glenfiddich twelve-year-old malt. Let me show you something.'

The Vice President pressed a button on the arm of his seat. A section of panelling behind the driver slid down to reveal a small bar. At the touch of another button, whisky glugged from the mouth of an upturned bottle on to a pile of ice cubes in a cut-glass tumbler.

'Sure you will not change your mind?'

'No thank you.'

The Vice President reached for the glass. 'Waterford crystal,' he said. 'I have Baccarat in my other car.'

The Prime Minister pursed his lips. He'd known this would happen: his only time alone with Zhou Zhi in the five days of his visit – his only chance to find out what he really needed to know – and all the old roué wanted to do was brag about his new toys.

'A snack from the on-board microwave maybe?' offered Zhou.

'Thank you, no.' The Prime Minister prided himself on his trim figure, which, together with his boyish grin and full head of hair – silver now, but still proudly bouffant – had brought him a commanding share of the female vote. Compared to the short, portly figure beside him he was the King of the Beasts, a lion lording it over the veld.

'There is something I'd like to ask you,' he said, as his host drained his tumbler and sucked noisily on the ice cubes.

'Ah-hah! I think perhaps I can guess. You want to know if we have developed a vaccine against fox flu.'

'It wasn't that, actually. This surveillance programme of yours – the Mulberry Tree . . .'

'Mulberry Tree!' Zhou almost dropped his glass, his jocularity suddenly dissipated. 'What do you mean, Mulberry Tree?'

The Prime Minister smiled inwardly. It wasn't often that he managed to discomfit the Chinese.

'We might as well be frank,' he said. 'You gather intelligence on us; we gather intelligence on you. And last week my people brought me news of a very interesting project – so interesting that at first I couldn't believe it. It seems such a fantastically ambitious undertaking – to keep tabs on every single member of your population . . .'

'You want to lecture me on bloody human rights? Well, you can forget that, Mr high-and-mighty PM.'

'I only wanted . . .'

'Who you think you are, anyway? You introduce Twitter tax, laptop licences, stop-and-swab DNA testing! You torture people for traffic offences!'

The Prime Minister winced. The water-boarding of recalcitrant motorists in the basement of the Ministry of Parking had been the first major scandal of his tenure; four years later, the headlines still haunted him.

'You're getting me wrong, Mr Vice President. There was a time, I know, when Britain failed to sympathise with China's internal problems. But have I ever questioned the need to maintain a firm grip?'

Zhou grunted and activated the whisky bar again.

'And I don't intend to,' the Prime Minister went on. 'Because we live in an enlightened age where the old differences are being worn away. You have come to share our aspirations, and we have come to share your political wisdom. The people of London and Beijing wear the same clothes and support the same football teams; we in Westminster and you in the Great Hall of the People are pitted against the same destabilising influences. And it is because of those influences that I'm asking you about the Mulberry Tree.'

A smile broke across the Vice President's face.

'You are a very cunning man, Mr PM!' he exclaimed. 'You want our technology to keep tabs on your own citizens. You think if you can keep all troublemakers under surveillance, maybe you will win next election in spite of embarrassingly low ratings in opinion polls!'

Had his years in high office not entirely eroded the Prime Minister's sense of shame, he might have blushed at this crude but accurate summary of his ambitions. He had long ago reached the conclusion that Britain could not be governed effectively except by a small élite: a cabal of invisible, like-minded men whom he dubbed 'the Ruling Few', paying only lip-service to Parliament. But to achieve this goal was harder than ever in the age of social media: if he was to keep control of the cyber-loving citizenry, access to their emails and phone records no longer sufficed – he needed weapons like Mulberry Tree. It was fortunate that MI5 were desperate to have it for their own purposes – and that the head of MI5 was one of the Few.

'It's not quite like that,' he said.

'Oh, but I think it is. You take a tip from me – easier not to have elections in the first place.'

'I'm afraid that's not really an option at this stage.'

'No, because you still pretend to be a democracy. Big mistake, my friend: you give people votes, you make them unhappy with what they got. No votes, they just get on with it.'

'In China, perhaps; but yours is a more stoical race than ours.'

The Vice President considered the ice melting at the bottom of his glass.

'So you want Mulberry Tree, eh?' he said at last. 'Maybe it is possible. But now you tell me, Mr PM: what are you going to give us in return?'

II

The following afternoon the Prime Minister stood gazing at row upon row of grey-jacketed officials seated at desks divided by low partitions. Each was equipped with a computer terminal and a CCTV monitor, so that the constant flicker of images – repeated as far as the eye could see – gave the impression of a world in flux, struggling in the electric twilight to take a definite form, only to relapse into tentative, inchoate fluttering.

'So,' he said. 'This is where it all happens.'

'Not all,' said the Vice President. 'Mulberry Tree is too big to contain in a single room – even a room as large as this one. This is merely the Beijing Central Monitoring Station.'

At a dozen points along the walls were larger screens where groups of three or four men – many in police uniforms – stood in excited conversation, pointing at enlarged figures moving in jerky, marionette motion above them.

Their guide, the station's supervisor, led the way to the nearest group. The policemen moved quickly aside, bowing apologetically.

'If you will allow me,' said the supervisor, 'I will give you a demonstration. Mr Prime Minister, would you care to choose an area of the city?'

The Prime Minister hesitated, reluctant to admit that his knowledge of Beijing's geography was almost non-existent. 'How about Tiananmen Square?'

The supervisor frowned. 'There will be many visitors from outside the city. They may not be on the system.'

'Try,' said the Vice President sharply.

The supervisor's fingers danced over the control keys. An aerial view of the square, divided into dozens of rectangles, appeared in front of them.

'Now, Excellency, please choose a grid reference.'

'Let's have G18,' said the Prime Minister.

The camera zoomed in to show an area of featureless pavement, largely occupied by a Western tour group and its guide.

'Ah, not so good,' said the supervisor. 'I was going to ask you to choose a single person, Excellency – and most of these are foreigners.'

'How about the man walking past them with the white shopping bag?'

The fingers danced again. An outline appeared around the chosen figure, glowing red, as the camera followed him into the next rectangle; then a sidebar appeared on the screen, filled with Chinese script.

'So,' said the supervisor, smiling with relief, 'here are many useful things to know about this man. His name is Wang Ye; age 38. He was born in Xian, and graduated from university there with a degree in economics. Now he works as a salesman for the Sun Automobile Corporation, and is married to a fellow employee. Five years ago he was arrested on suspicion of handling pirated DVDs, but released without charge. He is taking evening classes in calligraphy, and – ' the man added triumphantly – 'he is cheating on his wife.'

'Cheating on his wife? How do you know that?'

'Because here' – the supervisor indicated the last lines of the sidebar with a laser pointer – 'is a list of items he purchased half an hour ago with his debit card, including a packet of condoms.

But we know from his medical and travel records' – the laser travelled upwards – 'that he and his wife recently visited a clinic in Germany specialising in fertility treatment. So it must be that the condoms are for use with another lady.'

'Amazing,' said the Prime Minister. 'Really.'

'Now,' said the supervisor, 'we can set the computer to track him indefinitely if we want to. Or' – he pressed another button – 'we can go backwards and find out where he has been in the last 72 hours.'

The figure on the screen went into reverse, hurrying back across the square, reboarding a bus, clutching again at one of its straps, waiting at the stop where he had hailed it.

'But perhaps,' the supervisor continued, 'it would be more interesting for Your Excellency to know where Mr Wang's wife is. In order to do that I just need to cross-reference her name and ID number and –'

The screen went blank for a moment, then blossomed into a series of abstract tessellations before resolving itself into a picture of a woman standing in a railway station. She held a large brown envelope in her hand, and was deep in conversation with a tall, good-looking, grey-haired man.

'Hm,' said the supervisor. 'Who is she talking to? Maybe she has a lover of her own.' He highlighted the stranger, and a new sidebar appeared. 'Very interesting – very interesting indeed. This man is managing director of Grade One Auto Parts, an important supplier to the Sun Automobile Corporation. But why are they meeting on a railway platform? Perhaps their relationship is to do with more than business; or perhaps that envelope contains something it should not. We are indebted to you, Your Excellency. I think perhaps we will keep an eye on the Wang family.'

'Amazing,' said the Prime Minister. If he hadn't chosen the passer-by himself, he would have thought the whole exercise a set-up. 'But

– how? To track a suspected terrorist is one thing – but any one of 1.3 billion people, selected at random? What's the secret?'

The Vice President smiled. 'That, Mr Prime Minister, is for us to know and you to guess. I take it that you are still interested in purchasing Mulberry Tree?'

'Oh yes,' said the Prime Minister. 'Very interested indeed.'

III

The Vice President's villa stood high on Jade Spring Hill, with a magnificent view of Beijing across Lake Kunming. So lavish was its interior that the Prime Minister wondered whether he shouldn't upgrade Chequers. The tables groaned with gold and silver *objets de vertu*, the gifts of grateful dictators who had found a place under China's wing. The exquisite figures around the swimming pool had been looted – so the British Embassy's cultural attaché reported – from Tibet's most sacrosanct monasteries. As for the military statues in the marble entrance hall, why leave ten members of the Terracotta Army mouldering underground when they could be displayed to such advantage?

It was two o'clock in the morning. Their aides had been dismissed, and the two politicians sat alone in the gilt-pillared banqueting room smoking Havana cigars and cradling balloons of cognac in front of an open fire. From time to time the Vice President leant forward to help himself to a Charbonnel & Walker truffle, popped it into his mouth and gave a sigh of satisfaction. Outside, a full moon glinted on the lake, giving the night a poetry which seemed to touch even Zhou's stony heart. He began to declaim rhythmically in what his guest took to be Mandarin.

'Do you know the works of Tu Fu?' Zhou asked when he had finished. 'The poet says that dew gives way to frost, but the moonlight does not seem as bright as it did in his old home.'

'Beautiful.'

'I will see to it that you receive a presentation copy. Now, as I was saying . . .'

The Prime Minister braced himself. What was he going to be asked for now? He had already promised more than he was confident of delivering in exchange for the secrets of Mulberry Tree. But Zhou – the man who had made his name by cajoling, threatening and browbeating a host of international dignitaries into accepting Beijing's bid for the Olympic Games – was known to be a negotiator without equal. He might drink like a fish, but he always seemed to get exactly what his government wanted.

'The Brothers of Light,' said Zhou, pausing to draw on his cigar. 'They are causing us many problems.'

'So I've heard.'

The Christian splinter group, condemned by China's government-approved Church, had been engaged in underground evangelism for more than two decades. Believers were trained to carry their message to parts of the country where Christianity had never before taken root, establish churches there without the local authorities having any idea of their existence, and move on.

It was a tall order in a country so heavily policed, and progress was slow at first; but then the government became distracted by another religious movement. While the members of Falun Gong were hounded and imprisoned, the Brothers of Light worked undetected, establishing footholds throughout the country. By the time the Party leadership recognised them as a threat, their hidden congregations were growing at an astonishing rate. In some remote regions, where the local officials were already more of a law unto themselves than Beijing liked to admit, there had been large-scale demonstrations demanding freedom of worship and speech.

'You are not of their faith, I think?' asked Zhou.

'No.'

'Good. I wanted to be certain.'

'But I don't know how I can help you. The Brothers of Light have no presence in the UK.'

Zhou frowned. 'I am surprised to hear you say such a thing. They may not have an office in your country, but they have friends in high places – that is beyond question. In particular, a Dr Hardy has come to the attention of our intelligence services.'

'The name means nothing to me.'

'It is of no consequence – we expect to neutralise him shortly. But some very senior figures in the Anglican Church have recently been recruited to the cause of these dissidents. They have been agitating against the People's Republic. There is talk of a United Nations resolution.'

'I'm sorry to hear it.'

'Sorry is not enough. China cannot brook interference in its internal affairs by reactionary clergymen hiding behind the skirts of your government.'

'The Church of England doesn't take orders from me. Its leaders are a bloody-minded lot at the best of times.'

Zhou shook his head. 'You disappoint me, Prime Minister. Of course, if you do not want Mulberry Tree, that is fair enough. But if you do . . . I suggest you think along more expedient lines.'

'Meaning?'

The Vice President rose and placed his glass on the mantelpiece. For a moment he considered its golden brown gleam, then turned to his guest with a look of fury.

'Meaning this, Mr bloody PM. Bring me the balls of the Archbishop of Canterbury.'

CHAPTER TWO

Father Chang's congregation never met in the same place twice. Tonight two dozen of its members had assembled at the top of a dilapidated warehouse in the Chongwen district of Beijing. The floor was thick with dust, showing white in the light of a single electric bulb hanging from a bare beam; the blunt shapes of abandoned packing cases piled to the ceiling could just be discerned behind the worshippers. A smell of damp sacking filled the air.

Father Chang was a thin, elderly man with a bald head and a wispy white beard. His bushy eyebrows, jutting dramatically, suggested the outstretched wings of a bird of prey. Years of imprisonment and beatings had left him badly stooped, but his presence was an impressive one, and he had no need to raise his voice to command his audience's attention. A clerical collar peeping above the black jacket of his threadbare suit was his only badge of office.

'This evening,' he said, 'we are joined by a friend from England who is going to say a few words. And when I say friend, I mean not only to me personally – though he has been that for many years – but to all the Brothers of Light. Our movement is much indebted to him.'

Christophe Hardy smiled and rose carefully to his feet. He was a good twelve inches taller than Father Chang, and his hair brushed the low beams. His audience watched him intently, as though good money had been staked that he would have a sore head before the meeting was over.

Christophe knew how entirely foreign he must look to them, with his fair hair, blue eyes, angular face and aquiline nose; but after two decades of visiting China he was used to that. He felt privileged to be standing next to the old priest; privileged, too, to be addressing these adherents of a dissident church, whose mere presence here could earn them a death sentence.

'I won't keep you long,' he said. 'When I told my son I was going to speak at a meeting in Beijing, he said, "Dad, is that really fair? These people have spent their lives listening to three-hour speeches by the Party leadership. The last thing they need is a Westerner bending their ears about all the human-rights conventions he's been to." '

Christophe paused. Had he got the right phrase for 'bending their ears'? Though his Mandarin was fluent enough after a year with the biochemistry faculty of the university, it was by no means perfect. But the laughter which echoed through the room showed that they'd got the joke.

'Of course,' he said, 'teenagers are almost always right – but in this instance I think he was wrong. I think you do need to know that three years ago, when I went to an Amnesty International conference in Sweden, hardly anybody I met had heard of your Church, or of the extraordinary work being done by the Brothers of Light to encourage freedom of thought. And you also need to know that in the past month I have met groups in Paris, Vienna and Seattle who could talk of little else.

'I explained to them what was happening here. I told them that China was a country caught between the excesses of Communism and of capitalism, but thanks to the Brothers of Light it had a chance of following a different path. That a movement had started here which was gathering momentum every day, from Beijing to Guangzhou and from Chengdu to Shanghai.'

There was a sudden movement in the corner of the room. Looking round, he saw a young man jump away from the single smeared window which looked down on to the street.

'Police! Everybody out!'

The congregation leapt to their feet. Two men began dragging heavy sacks on to the hatch Christophe had entered through; the others made for the far end of the room.

'This way!' Ying, the girl who had acted as his guide earlier in the evening, tugged at his arm and hurried after them.

From below there was the sound of a door being broken down; shouts and police whistles; dogs barking; running feet. A moment later the hammering on the underside of the hatch began.

'Down there, quick as you can!' hissed Ying.

She pointed behind a pile of battered cardboard boxes. The top of a ladder protruded through a small trapdoor; Father Chang was being helped down it by a bald, muscular man in a leather jacket. Christophe followed.

He found himself in a low-ceilinged, windowless space lit only by a torch flashed across the floor. The rafters were thick with cobwebs which tugged at Christophe's jacket as he pushed through them. Up ahead was another trap door; behind him, Ying closed the one they had come through. The shouts of the police were suddenly fainter.

The second ladder brought them down to ground level. The light of another torch picked out the fugitives' faces as they lined a dank brick wall; at the front, the bald man was wrestling with a length of timber which barred a tall pair of wooden doors.

'It's jammed!' he gasped. 'It won't give!'

Christophe hurried forward to help him. Together they shoved with hands and shoulders; but try as they might, the beam seemed immovable. In the darkness someone started to pray aloud.

Putting their shoulders to the beam once more, Christophe and his companion heaved.

Suddenly it gave. The doors swung open and they stumbled out into the night air.

They were in a concrete yard surrounded by tall fencing and illuminated by a pair of street lights. At the far end, twenty yards away, a pair of ramshackle gates stood open. Between them was parked a police van, with six armed men in riot gear on either side of it. They pointed their guns at the fugitives.

'Raise your hands and stay where you are,' said a voice through a loud-hailer. 'Anyone who moves will be shot.'

II

Christophe and his companions obeyed. The voice shouted an order, and half the policemen hurried into the warehouse to search for stragglers.

'Kneel!'

They knelt. One woman, slower than the others, was pistol-whipped to the ground.

The officer in charge handed the loud-hailer to a subordinate and strode into the midst of his prisoners. He was a young man with cropped hair dressed in a captain's uniform.

'All of you,' he said, 'have been taking part in an illegal gathering. You are also –' he stooped to pick up a bible, which he held above his head – 'in possession of seditious literature. This means that you are plotting against the People's Republic and may be summarily shot.'

He paused. The woman felled by the pistol groaned.

'But,' the captain continued, 'you are very lucky people. Because every time I shoot somebody, I have to fill out a form – and I do not like filling out forms. In fact, I can never bear to fill in more than two at a time. So tonight I am only going to shoot two of you. Let's see which ones.'

He looked around theatrically. The prisoners pressed their faces to the ground, praying for deliverance, hoping to avoid his gaze. At length he clicked his fingers and shouted to his men.

'Take the old man inside! And –' he paused again – 'the *gwailo.*'

Christophe felt strong hands grasp his arms and collar. A moment later he was being dragged across the concrete.

This isn't right, he thought as he struggled in vain to free himself. This is the land of show trials and public executions, not police murder squads; a land where attacks on foreigners carry harsh penalties.

The two men who had seized him threw him to the ground beside Father Chang. He heard the echo of their boots grow fainter on the floorboards. The double doors creaked as they were pulled to.

Christophe lifted his head a fraction. The captain towered over them, a torch in his left hand and a pistol in his right. Then he raised the pistol and fired two shots.

III

Lying in the half darkness, Christophe wondered why he could feel a soft, dry trickle upon his neck. If this was death, it took an unexpected form.

'Sorry,' said a voice which sounded like the police captain's. 'It was necessary. You OK?'

Christophe pressed his arms against the floor. It felt hard and rough, as it should to a living person. Twisting round, he saw the captain squatting beside him, torch in hand.

'Yes,' he said. 'I seem to be.'

'Father Chang, you OK?'

'Yes, yes, thank you.' The old man's voice came from the darkness behind them.

Running his fingers across his neck, Christophe found that it was covered with a pale, dusty deposit.

'What happened?' he asked.

'I fired into the ceiling. There is an informer among your fellow worshippers: it is important that she thinks you have been dealt with.'

'I see.'

'Thank you,' said Father Chang. 'Brother – ?'

'It is better that you do not know my name. And, Father, you must go into hiding. Two of my men are also Brothers of Light. They will take you to a safe place.'

He helped the old man to his feet.

'My congregation,' said Father Chang: 'what will happen to them?'

'They will not be charged. But I will warn them that they must not meet again like this.'

Christophe stood up gingerly. 'How can I thank you?' he asked.

The captain bowed. 'It is a privilege to help a man who has done so much good work for the Chinese people. But there is something you can do for me.'

'If I can, of course.'

'What I have to ask of you is dangerous. One of our associates is very sick, but it is not safe for her to visit a hospital here. We would like you to escort her out of the country.'

Christophe whistled. He hadn't expected anything like this. But he'd given his word and there was no going back.

'I'd be happy to,' he said. 'But is that a good idea? Won't she be more likely to attract attention if she's travelling with a foreigner?'

'No – you will see.'

Christophe shrugged. 'If you say so. Do you have a route in mind?'

'Everything is in hand. You will be taken to a safe house – a different one from Father Chang's – and contacted when the necessary arrangements have been made. I must rejoin my men.'

He clicked off his torch and was gone.

IV

The safe house – or rather, apartment – was clean and sparse. Except that it was on the west side of the city, Christophe had no clue to its location. His police driver had followed a labyrinth of back streets before parking in front of a tower block like a thousand other tower blocks and leading the way up six flights of stairs.

'I will leave you here, brother,' said the policeman. He looked very young, and used the word 'brother' hesitantly. 'Someone will come later with food for you. They will knock on the door but you must wait for five minutes before opening it.'

'Will I see you again?' asked Christophe.

'No. But you will receive a message in a few days. Then it will be time for you to leave Beijing. You must not go out, or telephone anybody, or let anyone see you.'

'Where will I go after Beijing?'

'I cannot tell you that.'

'I see. Well, thank you for everything you've done.'

'One more thing.' The policeman produced a small camera. 'I need to take a photograph of you.'

'A photograph? Why?'

'We must issue you with a false passport. It may not be safe for you to travel on the one you have.'

'It could be even less safe for me to travel on forged documents.'

'You must allow us to be the judges of that. Please stand against the wall.'

Christophe did so. The policeman raised his camera.

'Thank you,' he said. He turned and left.

The flat consisted of a bedroom, a living-room-cum-kitchen and a tiny bathroom. It was disconcerting to be in a place without any stamp of human personality – no decorations, no mementoes. Christophe emptied the contents of his jacket on to the kitchen table: mobile, wallet, keys to his flat in Oxford, sunglasses, passport, pocket edition of the poems of Victor Hugo. But instead of making the room more homely, they made it more forlorn. 'Besides,' he thought, 'I might have to leave in a hurry.' He put everything back in his jacket except the poems.

He turned on the mobile and looked at the half-dozen photographs in its memory: three of his wife Sara, dead now for five years, and three of their son Ben. Sara outside their weekend cottage in Gloucestershire; Sara on the beach in Brittany; Sara as he'd first seen her, halfway up a mountain in Serre Chevalier. They'd shared a table in a crowded café; she'd left her sunglasses on her chair and he'd raced the cable car to the bottom, arriving with a minute to spare to hand them back to her. That was the kind of thing he did in those days; now Ben was a better skier than he was, leading his friends from the Sorbonne headlong down the slopes with all the fearlessness of a nineteen-year-old. Suddenly Christophe felt an aching need to call him in Paris; but he knew that his escort had been right – nothing was easier to trace than a phone call.

The knock on the door came at eleven o'clock. Christophe waited for five minutes as directed, then peered out into the corridor. A blue holdall had been left on the floor.

In it he found a large bag of rice, tea bags, two dozen eggs, a loaf of Western-style sliced bread, a jar of plum jam, a larger one of pickled vegetables, a bottle of soy sauce and three cans of processed meat. There were toiletries too, and a change of underwear. At the bottom was a bible in Mandarin.

It was a new edition, better printed and more compact than the ones he had smuggled into China in his youth. Nowadays, of course, you could carry the whole thing in a memory stick; but back then not even Westerners had possessed PCs. He'd had to wrap the bibles in his clothes and hope that no one would search the depths of his suitcase.

His first visit has been as an undergraduate. He had come hoping to feast his eyes on poetic landscapes where neat paddy fields gave way to quaintly shaped mountains topped by smudges of trees. Instead he wasted days trying to organise the simplest journeys, struggling like a fly in the web of a bureaucracy deeply suspicious of lone foreigners. For a while it looked as if he would never get past Guangzhou; then, exploring the streets by the Pearl River, he met Father Chang.

The river was busy that day with steamers, barges and sampans. Christophe crossed it by bridge and found himself in what had once been the European quarter. Inaccessible to traffic, it seemed almost forgotten, its neo-classical buildings dilapidated and converted into tenements. A church – the first he had seen in China – stood shuttered and locked.

At least, that was how it appeared. When he came closer, he found a padlock unfastened. He pushed the doors open.

The air was stale, and he expected to find the floor as dusty as the pavements outside. But the tiles beneath his feet were clean, and ahead of him, by the altar, he saw a middle-aged man hard at work with a mop.

The man looked startled; then, noting Christophe's Western appearance, relaxed.

'Hello,' he said in English. 'Welcome.'

'I was expecting to find this place closed down.'

'It is, officially; but I managed to obtain a copy of the key. I come here when I can to clean up. One day, God willing, it will be full of worshippers again.'

'Are you the priest?'

'No, he is in prison. I hope one day to be ordained, but it is very difficult now. Most of the bishops only do what the government tells them.'

'Could you be sent to prison for what you are doing here?'

'Yes, of course. But I will go where God sends me.'

Impressed, Christophe had picked up a large brush made of rushes and started to help him. It had been the beginning of a friendship which still endured a quarter of a century later. Chang had helped him to buy his ticket to Shanghai; Christophe promised to return, bringing the bibles that Chang desperately needed. It was exactly the kind of challenge that appealed to him; but what had begun as a simple adventure had become a deepening commitment. When the research laboratory where he worked began an exchange programme with the University of Beijing, he found himself with an excuse for visiting on a regular basis, smuggling money, literature and letters from Western Churches to the beleaguered Brothers of Light.

Over the last year he had become one of the Brothers' principal conduits to the world outside China. When Church councils or human-rights organisations met, Christophe was there behind the scenes to plead the cause of the Brothers – the only body, he argued, that could effect a peaceful change in China. He raised money, liaised with Chinese expatriates and helped Brothers who had had to flee their homeland.

Now it looked as if his own luck was running out.

Who had betrayed Chang and his congregation? The police captain had said that the informer was female. Of the twenty people who had met in the warehouse, only two – to Christophe's knowledge – were expecting him to be there: Father Chang and the girl Ying. Had it been her?

Christophe considered the little he knew about Ying. She was a student at the university, which was why she had been chosen to take him to the meeting. There was nothing remarkable about her appearance, with her plain face and spectacles, tartan skirt and duffle coat; her manner was quiet but efficient, and she had led him to their rendezvous as if in charge of a child, negotiating a bewildering succession of buses. Chang had greeted her fondly; at prayer she seemed as devout as anyone.

There was nothing to suggest that she was working for the government – but then, that was the mark of a good spy; and the captain had told him that the informer in their ranks was female. He thought of her guiding him towards the secret exit: had she been trying to save him, or to lead him into a trap?

He stood up and walked to the window. It looked out on to other tower blocks, some with white lights, some with amber, some with blue; their silhouettes were those of armoured warriors, shoulders hunched, brooding. And below were more lights – the red tail-lights of thousands of cars moving slowly along an expressway. Sometimes it overwhelmed him, this city: he felt the cars dragging him with them as they disappeared from sight, pouring away into blackness. He was a small meteorite adrift in a vast galaxy, and only one thing could lift him upwards.

They shall mount up with wings as eagles;
he murmured,
they shall run and not be weary.

Would he be able to come back to Beijing? It seemed unlikely. He would have to find new ways of doing the Brothers' work.

Then he realised that he was getting ahead of himself, because there was one thing he had to do first: escape with his life.

CHAPTER THREE

'It could be worse,' said Sammy.

'Oh yeah,' said Jake. 'Meaning what, exactly? That I might have been eaten alive instead of being banged up in here? Very consoling that is. I can't say I've noticed champagne on the prison menu, but if it comes up, I'm definitely cracking open a bottle.'

They sat in the visiting room, separated by a table wide enough to make physical contact awkward, though not impossible. Sammy thought of childhood games of table tennis, and the knack he'd developed of dropping the ball just over the net so that his opponent couldn't quite reach it. Few things in adult life had proved as satisfying.

He and Jake looked an odd pair at the best of times; more so here, surrounded by couples with young children attempting something akin to family life in these sterile surroundings. Jake was tall and well-built, but a slow, unthreatening presence; Sammy, slight and furtive, like a rodent seeking an exit. Jake's newly shaven head did nothing to diminish his good looks; Sammy's wispy blond moustache did nothing to enhance a face which seemed too thin even for his thin body.

'What I meant,' said Sammy, lowering his voice so as not to be heard by the warder, 'is that the government has this new thing about not radicalising animal-lovers. It was on the radio this morning. They're trying to make a distinction between people who simply want to help animals and people who are prepared to hurt humans in the process. So as far as they're concerned, you're one of the good guys, because you decided to spring a bear rather than blow up a scientist who experiments on rabbits.'

Spring a bear. It was the ungrateful grizzly at London Zoo that had proved Jake's undoing, knocking him unconscious with a single blow of the paw as it was lured into the back of Sammy's van. Jake had awoken to find himself in handcuffs while Sammy chauffeured the liberated animal swiftly out of the sleeping city.

Sammy was nothing if not ambitious. He had first made the Animal Lovers' Army front-page news by abducting a giraffe from Longleat. The failed attempt to smuggle it back to Africa in the stairwell of a double-decker bus had in no way dented his perception of himself as a combination of Oskar Schindler and Noah. Soon afterwards he had recruited Jake through a radical website masquerading as a chat room for alpaca enthusiasts, and together they had embarked on a series of daring rescues. If a wolf roamed free in the Welsh Marches, or a lynx on Bodmin Moor, the chances were that it owed its liberty to these two men.

'So they might drop the charges altogether?' said Jake.

'The lawyer doesn't think they'll go quite that far. They don't want to be seen as soft on crime, he says. But he does think you might get bail after all, and very probably a suspended sentence – which is better than a slap in the face with a wet fish, eh?'

'I suppose so.'

' 'Course it is. Don't worry about it: he's a top man, he'll see you all right. And in the meantime, there's one very happy bear making himself at home in the Borders. That's got to be worth something, hasn't it?'

'I suppose so.'

'That's the boy. You keep your pecker up – it'll be over before you know it. And don't think it isn't appreciated, your keeping stum about your comrades. Soon as you're out of here we'll have a bit of a party.'

Back in his cell, Jake wondered why he always found himself being talked round. Of course Sammy had the gift of the gab: there was no denying that. But next time someone tried to tell him that a bear's freedom was more important than his own, he wasn't going to be persuaded. That much he had promised himself.

He turned on the television. Someone was interviewing Frank Smith, 'the people's MFH'. Sadistic git and class traitor more like, thought Jake; and he promised himself that if their paths ever crossed, the Master of the Hyde Park Hunt would regret it.

II

Frank Smith dismounted beside the timber clubhouse in the centre of St James's Park and handed his reins to the groom.

'Morning, Tommy,' he said. 'I suppose I'm last as usual.'

The boy grinned. 'Just about. Everyone's here except Mr Akibo, but the word is he took a nasty fall in Wapping High Street, so chances are he won't show.'

'Poor Bill.' Frank took his rifle from its holster and emptied the bullets into his pocket. 'I don't envy him that country. Give Dostoevsky a bit of breakfast, yeah?' He gave his horse a pat. 'He's had quite a morning. Chased a big bastard of a fox twice round the Serpentine before we killed.'

Inside, Frank locked his rifle into the gun rack and pushed through the double doors into the meeting room. A cheer went up from the two dozen figures already seated on battered wooden chairs.

'Hi, Frankie!'

'Better late than never, Frankie!'

'Watching yourself on TV again, Frank?'

Frank mimed blocking his ears and took the nearest chair. This sort of banter was *de rigueur* in the clubhouse, though he'd been getting more of his fair share since becoming a television personality. *Frank Rides Forth*, the early-evening feature which followed him and his hounds twice a week, had proved a surprise hit since its introduction six months ago; there were even bookmakers offering odds on how many kills he would make in the next show. Frank had no particular desire to be famous, but anything that taught the public about fox control had to be a good thing – besides which, the extra income came in useful. Running a pack of hounds was an expensive business, and government grants only went so far.

He glanced around the room. There was Tip Cassidy, the rough-and-ready whiz-kid recruited from the Scarteen in Ireland to run the Wandsworth Hunt; gloomy, stuck-up Martin Frobishire, whose country was the Hackney Marshes; Mary d'Abo, a battleaxe if ever there was one, owner of London's poshest kennels up in Holland Park; Davy Prideaux of the Highbury and Holloway, looking like a Regency dandy in his red coat with eau-de-Nil facings.

Only two years ago, such a gathering would have been unthinkable. The law against hunting with hounds had seemed destined to remain on the statute books for ever; meets were monitored not just by anti-blood sports activists but by undercover police. All that had changed with the threat of fox flu.

The obvious question was why no one had seen it coming. Here was a wild, cunning beast without natural predators which had been allowed to roam and breed freely; finding easier pickings among the refuse sacks of the city than in the countryside, it had lost its fear of humans, who continued to regard it as a picturesque curiosity. By the time its raids on barbecues and kitchens began to cause concern, the urban fox population had become so enormous as to be almost ineradicable; the collapse of dozens of London streets as a result of basement excavations had furnished it with limitless boltholes. A virulent disease could not have asked for a better carrier.

The term 'fox flu' – invented by journalists with a professional weakness for alliteration – was a misnomer. The disease was more akin to rabies, though its incubation period was far shorter; transmission to humans was commonly through a bite or close contact with the animal. As yet no cure had been found.

It had been a bitter humiliation for the politicians, going cap in hand to the huntsmen they had long inveighed against. But what choice did they have once the virus – first detected in Kazakhstan – reached continental Europe? In Germany it seemed to stall, only to reappear in Frankfurt at the city's annual book fair, where the sight of a mangy vixen running through the exhibition halls had sent the world's publishers leaping with shrieks of terror on to their tables. The following week the French authorities announced a state of alert near Strasbourg. Optimists argued that the disease could never jump the Channel, but as each new outbreak brought it nearer, the public became less convinced.

Asked to devote its expertise to a clearance of the cities, the Masters of Foxhounds Association played its hand cleverly, securing an immediate repeal of the laws against field sports. Then, rebranded as Fox Control UK, it deployed dozens of huntsmen in the metropolitan centres; and here were London's finest now, assembled for their weekly briefing by the Association's head. A small, brisk man, Nick Llewellyn reminded Frank of one of those robotic dogs which could make their own way across a room, tail wagging, legs marching indefatigably forward.

'Morning, ladies and gentlemen,' he said as he took the podium at the far end of the room. 'Can everyone hear me? Yes? Good. One point of housekeeping to start with: not everyone's been updating their online tallies as often as they should. Unless every kill is posted within twenty-four hours the whole system will go up the spout – remember that.

'As the figures stand for this week, Martin Frobishire is in pole position with twenty kills. Any advance on that? Let's hear it for Martin.'

There was a burst of applause. A faint suggestion of a smile passed across Frobishire's face.

'Before I go on, I'm pleased to announce that we have a guest delegate with us. Some of you have already met Anna McCormack of the Birmingham and Edgbaston, but for those of you who haven't – Anna, will you make yourself known?'

A fair-haired young woman in the front row stood up, smiling a confident smile.

'Anna has come down to see how we go about things in the Big Smoke, so please share with her whatever you can. It would obviously be helpful for her to ride out with a couple of different packs – but I'm sure there'll be no shortage of offers for a pretty girl like her.'

The MFHs laughed obligingly.

'Let's get down to the main business of the day, which I have to tell you is extremely serious. I've just come from a meeting with the Deputy Prime Minister, and the latest news from France is not good at all. A teenager has been attacked by a fox within twenty miles of Coquelles in the Pas-de-Calais. And Coquelles, in case you don't know, is where the Channel Tunnel begins.'

A murmur ran through the room.

'The Channel Tunnel,' Llewellyn continued, 'is of course very heavily guarded. But it is guarded against terrorists and illegal immigrants – not against foxes. The security services have agreed to increase the number of dog patrols, and that will obviously be very helpful. But we have to face the very real possibility that a diseased fox will make it through to this country sooner rather than later.

'I've agreed with the Deputy PM that Fox Control UK will do whatever it can to bolster those packs of hounds based in Kent. If we can eliminate as many foxes there as possible, the chances of the disease spreading beyond the tunnel will be greatly reduced. But even if we can create a firewall in the south-east, London remains a dangerously soft target. So I'm afraid I must ask you to redouble your efforts.

'I need you each to be realising a kill figure of thirty, forty or even fifty foxes a week. If that means hunting from dawn to dusk seven days a week, so be it. Because remember, if fox flu does become embedded, every hound that sinks its teeth into a diseased animal will have to be put down, and it won't be long before all the kennels in the land are empty.'

Tip Cassidy raised his hand. 'Any more news on the railways, boss?'

'Negotiations are still ongoing, but it looks as if the Mayor will agree to more closures on Sundays, and a few on Saturday as well.'

'Tell him from me he'd bloody well better. If I can't draw those coverts around Clapham Junction without my hounds being run down by a f–ing train, I might as well f– off home to Terryglass.'

'We all appreciate that, Tip; and we know that any fox coming out of the Channel Tunnel is likely to follow the tracks. But I'm hopeful that the news from France will get everyone singing from the same hymn sheet. Any other questions?'

When the meeting broke up, Frank found himself buttonholed by Mary d'Abo.

'Never mind the railways,' she said. 'How about getting the bloody parks closed at weekends? Not to hunt supporters, of course, or members of the Pony Club, but everyone else. That way we could make some serious progress.'

'Love to, Mary. But is that going to keep the public on side, depriving them of their pedalos and ice-creams? I don't think so.'

'Come on, Frank. If anyone can persuade them, you can. You've got them eating out of your hand with that television programme of yours. Give them a touch of "Fight them on the beaches" and pack them all off to the Science Museum.'

He laughed. 'Chance would be a fine thing.'

'Sorry, Mrs d'Abo, may I interrupt?'

Anna McCormack was standing beside them. She was short and busty, and Frank couldn't help glancing down the front of her shirt. From what he could see of her lingerie it was lacy and expensive.

'I just wanted to ask Mr Smith if I could join his hunt one day while I'm here. People at home are much more likely to listen to me if I can say I've ridden forth with Frank.'

Her voice had a note of mockery which was inescapably flirtatious.

'Hm,' said Frank. 'I don't know. Strictly speaking you should wait for the next Help A London Child auction and bid for the privilege. But seeing as you come with the chief's seal of approval, we might just stretch a point. What do you think, Mrs D?'

'I think, Anna, that you're in danger of giving this young man a swollen head,' said Mary d'Abo. 'But if you want to see how a city hunt should really be run, you're welcome to visit the Holland Park. Goodbye, Frank – think about what I said.'

She moved off.

Anna giggled. 'Don't tell me she's jealous of your great fame.'

'No, she just thinks it's infra dig for an MFH to pander to popular culture. But she's a decent old bird underneath – gave me a lot of good advice when I took over the Hyde Park, and judged me on the results, pure and simple.'

'Unlike some?'

He shrugged. 'You know how it is – there's some toffee-nosed types think you've got no business hunting hounds unless you're the Duke of bloody Whatsit.'

She reached up and ran her fingers along his shoulder. He caught a warm scent of lavender drifting from her hair.

'Am I mistaken,' she said, 'or do I detect a bit of a chip?'

He laughed. 'Not on me you don't. The only chips around here are in the canteen. I'm going to grab some breakfast and then, if you fancy, we can do some hunting. That suit you?'

She smiled again. 'Yes,' she said. 'It does.'

III

Frank and Anna's day was one of mixed fortunes. They chased a great brute of a fox down to Chelsea Harbour, finally cornering it in the underground car park, though not before several of the residents had been reduced to hysterics; then they were called to the other end of the King's Road, where a vixen had slipped on to a bus, bringing the traffic to a standstill as the passengers poured out on to the road. The vixen had escaped in the confusion; by the time Frank and Anna appeared on the scene, she had vanished with a chicken stolen from the Cadogan Rôtisserie.

'Call yourself a huntsman?' the manager shouted at Frank. 'That's the third fox I've had in here this week.'

'Give them customer loyalty cards, mate,' Frank replied cheerfully, 'and don't forget to ask for their addresses. We'll catch them, roast them with some parsnips, and your clientele won't know the difference.'

Finally, with the hounds exhausted, they returned to the hunt's headquarters.

'This is it,' said Frank. 'Not a bad gaff.'

'It's beautiful,' said Anna. The low, elegant building stood in the middle of the park, close to the Serpentine. 'Prime residential property, I'd say. How did a country boy like you get his hands on a place like this?'

'They wanted to palm me off with one of the little gate lodges. That was a laugh – there was hardly room to swing a cat. And like I told them, they'd have had to build new kennels adjacent. Whereas here it was a straightforward conversion. I'm round the front, hounds and horses round the back.'

'What was it before?'

'An art gallery. They used to have some great piss-ups here – Lord and Lady Muck turning out for charity. Then the bottom dropped out of the Britart market and its number was up. They had so much tat on their hands they couldn't give it away – you wouldn't believe some of the rubbish the builders found.'

Anna followed Frank inside. The tack room was steeped in the smell of saddle soap; steel bits and stirrups glinted in the electric light. Frank unloaded his pistol and rifle and laid them on a large pine table. Anna followed his example.

The sitting-room was dark and homely, though the furniture had seen better days; familiar hunting prints lined walls where once bold abstracts in human excreta had hung, and a bronze figure on horseback dominated the mantelpiece. An old hound which had been sleeping by the fire struggled to its feet and limped towards them.

'This is Captain,' said Frank, handing Anna a mug of tea. 'He had a nasty run-in with a taxi last Christmas. The vet was for putting him down, but I was sure we could get him back on his feet. Help yourself to some toast – I recommend the strawberry jam.'

Anna tasted it. 'Delicious.'

'My nan makes it. And do you know where she lives? Tiptree – I'm not kidding. There's a bleeding great jam factory down the road, and she goes out every summer to pick her own strawbs – well, used to until the arthritis caught up with her – so she can fill her kitchen with pots for her nearest and dearest. Oh, and for the Russian Orthodox monks next door.'

Anna burst out laughing. 'Russian Orthodox monks in Tiptree – what are you talking about?'

'It's God's own truth. A whole bunch of them fetched up there years ago – probably after the Russian Revolution. And my nan's best friends with them. Not that she's a churchgoer, but she's a devil for those huge great Russian novels: *War and Peace, Crime and Punishment* – you name it, she's read it. That's why I called my horse Dostoevsky, in her honour; the next time I get two good dog pups from the same litter, they're going to be the Brothers Karamazov. Anyway, I reckon that's why she likes the monks: says they've got Russian soul. Which I suppose they must have.'

'She sounds like quite a character.'

'Yeah, she is.'

'And is Tiptree where you grew up?'

'That part of the world. My dad was a terrier man with the East Essex. Soon as I was old enough, he'd take me with him as spade-carrier. I tell you, for a kid growing up on a council estate, it was magic – being out in the open air on a frosty morning, seeing the sunshine on the hedgerows, hearing the hounds yelping in the distance. I couldn't understand why my mates would rather stay inside sniffing glue and watching the telly.

'Only thing I didn't like was some of the hunt members. The way they talked to my dad, like he was some kind of slave – if they bothered to notice him that is. Not the old-style toffs, mind you – they always gave him respect – but the nouveaux riches who thought they could lord it over everyone. So I said to myself, "One day I'll show you." And I did. The day I came home in my first pink coat, my dad had tears in his eyes. His boy, a whipper-in: you'd think I'd been asked to play for England. I wish he'd lived to see me make MFH.'

'You were young, weren't you? Twenty-five, I read somewhere.'

'Near enough – twenty-six. I had a lucky break. There was a big barney over the hunt funds – turned out the Master was a bit too keen on the ponies and had gambled away a season's subscriptions; so he had to go, and the treasurer and half the committee along with him. The huntsman had broken his leg, and no one else could be found at short notice, so there I was as Acting Master with ten weeks of the season left to run. At the end they told me it was the best ten weeks anyone could remember, and if I wanted the job permanent it was mine. So of course I said yes.'

'Brilliant.'

'It was at first. But some of them never liked the idea of the terrier man's son taking over, and after a while they got together and started making trouble – questioned my expenses, said they couldn't afford a Master who didn't have a private income, that sort of thing. In the end I decided I couldn't be arsed; so when I was offered the Hyde Park I gave them the finger and said goodbye.'

'That's me. What about you?'

'Nothing as impressive as you. Rich daddy, Pony Club, decided hunting was the next best thing to sex, here I am.'

He looked at her. Was the reference to sex a come-on?

'Give us a break, Anna,' he said. 'I know it's not that simple. How many female MFHs are there? A dozen? And most of them are tough old birds like Mary d'Abo. It can't have been any easier for you than it was for me.'

'You're right – I wouldn't be an MFH at all if hadn't been for the urban hunts. There were never going to be huntsmen queuing up to take a pack of hounds through the Bullring at rush hour, and I got my grant application in at just the right moment. And do you know what? I like it. OK, I've had the odd beer bottle thrown at me in the dodgier parts of town; but most people are glad to see someone who knows what they're doing drawing a covert in a public park. It makes them feel safer, and it makes them feel in touch with things they'd forgotten or come to take for granted – tradition, the animal kingdom, all of that.'

'That's what I tell myself too. But . . .'

'But what?'

'It's not what we became huntsmen for, is it? Drawing shitty alleyways with half a dozen hounds, and making most of our kills with a bullet – it's not exactly sport. The urban fox may be public enemy number one for now – but if that flu gets across the Channel the government is going to want every fox in the country culled. It won't just be them that'll end up extinct – it'll be us as well.'

'So we can't let it happen.'

'No,' said Frank, 'we can't.'

'And in the meantime . . .'

'And in the meantime what?'

'There's one thing I've never done.'

'What's that?'

'Kissed another MFH.'

It's too good to be true, thought Frank as he knelt in front of her and placed his lips on hers, closing his eyes, feeling the softness of her hair under his fingers and the warmth of the fire on his back. And indeed he was right, because no sooner had they paused for breath than Anna got quickly to her feet and pulled on her jacket.

'Got to go,' she said. 'Sorry. Thanks for the tea. The jam was first class.'

'Posh totty,' Frank muttered to himself after she had gone. 'Frankie boy, you should have known better, you stupid bastard.'

CHAPTER FOUR

Matt Dunstable sat in the dripping ruins of his great aunt's house singing Buddy Holly:

The sun is out, the sky is blue,
There's not a cloud to spoil the view
But it's raining – raining in my heart.

'Sunshine and showers' the forecast had said. The showers were now firmly in control, peppering with raindrops what had once been the kitchen ceiling; several leaks had appeared in the protective plastic sheeting, allowing the water to stain the new roof beams. Even so, it was the only room that provided a modicum of shelter, which was why Matt had made it his headquarters, furnishing it with a camping stove and two old wooden chests stencilled with the words 'GOOD TEA IS BETTER VALUE'.

He was a gangling, handsome young man with sandy hair and a freckled nose. His eyes were somewhere between grey and green

– though exactly where was impossible to say, for they seemed to change with the light. His face was generally amiable, and his smile was an engaging one; but as his gaze fell upon the letter lying beside him, he suddenly looked very serious and very displeased.

The letter was from the local council.

Dear Mr Dunstable

it read

> *With regard to your letter of 17th April, I must inform you that continued refusal to pay the County Tax due on your property will have serious consequences.*
>
> *As the owner of the second home known as Stooks Farm, you are obliged by law to pay a contribution to the many services provided by the Council, including road maintenance, schools, the fire brigade and the police service. The extent to which you personally benefit from these services is not relevant.*
>
> *Unless payment in full is made by the end of this month, you will inevitably receive a court summons.*
>
>
>
> *Yours,*
> *Jennifer Pettifer (Ms)*
>
>

'Second home'! Given that the house had neither roof, floors nor windows, and could only have been considered habitable by an easy-going rat, the description was plain lunacy.

As for the council's so-called 'services', wasn't it the fire brigade's complete failure to find the house that had led to its incineration? The police were nowhere near catching the thieves who had stolen his tools six weeks ago; the potholed track which led to the farm scarcely deserved to be called a road; and what use were schools to someone with no children (and little prospect of acquiring any, unless his career-minded girlfriend had a change of heart)? The council should be refunding his money, not charging him more.

Matt had been working on the house for four months now, and there were times when the project threatened to overwhelm him. But however bad it got, it was still preferable to the tedious career as a shipping broker that he had left behind. His great aunt, bless her, had lived just long enough to collect the insurance money owing from the fire; rather than pay expensive contractors, he had chosen to do the work himself. He had learnt carpentry as a boy and bricklaying in his gap year, and few aspects of the work were unfamiliar. When extra manpower was needed, he had a pool of casual labourers to draw on: Jason, his neighbours' taciturn teen-age son; Mitch, a perpetual student writing a thesis on Taoism; and Ifor, a bearded gypsy whose appearances coincided strangely with the full moon.

The first tax demand he had assumed to be a mistake. He had written to explain that he had no hope of occupying the property in the next twelve months; in the meantime, he was dutifully paying tax on the small house he *did* occupy twenty miles away. And that, he assumed, was that.

But he had reckoned without Ms Pettifer. Though 'bitch' was not a word he often used, it came to his lips now. He pictured her as a plump, red-faced harridan in shapeless knitwear and ortho-paedic sandals.

In his weaker moments, Matt was tempted to give in. The sum involved was not enormous – better, surely, to pay up than lie awake night after night seething with disproportionate rage.

But Matt was a man of principle, and to ignore such flagrant injustice went against the grain. In what other situation could you be expected to pay good money and receive absolutely nothing in return? Not in the most ramshackle North African souk; not in the least regulated of Irish horse fairs; not in the sleaziest Balkan speakeasy.

He thought of the Bostonians who had filled their harbour with tea chests – identical, perhaps, to the one he was sitting on now – in protest against an exploitative British government. They had sparked a revolution: could he not do the same?

And so, as the rain rattled above his head, he composed a letter to Jennifer Pettifer informing her that he despised the council's tyranny and would rather rot in jail than pay her a red cent.

From San Diego up to Maine,
In every mine and mill –
he hummed,
Where working men defend their rights
It's there you'll find Joe Hill.
It's there you'll find Joe Hill.

II

Sitting in her office at County Hall, Jennifer Pettifer considered Matthew Dunstable's letter coldly. The insolence! What right had he to question the council's decision? Jeffrey Crusham would not have stood for it – not in a thousand years!

Jennifer Pettifer was a thin, pallid woman whose delicate appearance belied her professional tenacity. Indeed, her nickname in the department was 'Boots': not because she often wore them – although she did, generally of black suede – but because of a supposed affinity with the hobnailed kind.

Ms Pettifer had dark, shoulder-length hair cut across her forehead in a fringe whose severity echoed that of her sharp nose and wire-rimmed spectacles. She wore a grey suit with a knee-length skirt, and though the council's buildings were invariably overheated, prided herself on never removing her jacket; her white blouse was fastened at the top with a bow. She disapproved of jewellery in the workplace, but did permit herself the lapel badge of the Civil Service Soft Toy Collectors' Club. One of her bears, Reginald, was propped against the computer terminal, wearing a red and yellow striped cardigan of Jennifer's own design.

Jennifer gazed at the photograph above her desk and brushed it with her fingertips. Three similar ones hung in her flat, the most treasured bearing a handwritten message:

To Jenny,

Best wishes, Jeffrey

They had worked together for two years at Wandsworth Council: two years which Jennifer considered the happiest years of her life. She still remembered the day that Jeffrey Crusham had arrived to take over his office: it was as if the gates of heaven had opened above her dull world and a chariot descended to the sound of a celestial choir.

It wasn't simply his good looks or his formidable intelligence: it was the way he brought enthusiasm to the least inspiring tasks. She had ceased to be a drudge and become an evangelist, spreading the good news of Jeffrey Crusham wherever bureaucrats met. She still kept the T-shirts he had handed out at their twice-yearly team awaydays. 'NOT MY DEPARTMENT, MADAM,' read one; 'TRY THE NEXT DOOR ON THE RIGHT', another. There was no denying his wonderful sense of humour.

His philosophy was both dazzlingly simple and startling in its audacity. The councillors, he explained to her, had hamstrung themselves by making promises to the electorate that they could not hope to fulfil. Every department was in thrall to a vacuous mission statement and a so-called 'contract' with its 'customers'. Who had dreamed up this airy-fairy nonsense? What mattered was to get the job done; and the best way to achieve that was by dispensing with targets and shifting the responsibility – so subtly that the adjustment went unnoticed – from the council to the men and women in the street.

'When I was a boy,' he said, 'the council came to dig a long trench in our road. Trouble was, a lot of people had parked their cars where the trench was going to be. It was no good just putting notices on windscreens, because sometimes the owners didn't go near them for days on end; so some poor soul had to go knocking on people's doors and asking them to shift their vehicles. I was only twelve at the time, but I thought, "They've got it all wrong! It shouldn't be *him* asking *them* to move their cars – it should be *them* checking that their cars are *still allowed to be there.*" So I wrote to the council and suggested changing the procedure – and do you know what? Within a few months that's exactly what they did! I knew then that I could make a difference.'

Jennifer thought of his triumphant smile and sighed. What heady times they had shared! What magic had filled the air of the town hall! Before they knew it, Crusham's mantra had spread to the highest echelons of government: the public, not the public servants, must serve. No longer would the taxman waste his time calculating bills: the taxpayers must work them out themselves. Nor would railway ticket-sellers be obliged to sell tickets: the traveller must find a way of buying them. Oh brave new topsy-turvy world!

Crusham had not, in those early days, received the credit that he deserved. Nor had he been recognised as the formulator of the first great cliché of the 21st century, 'putting measures in place' – that phrase so redolent of good intentions, so altogether lacking in commitment. Nevertheless, he had gradually begun to get noticed; and Jennifer had realised with awful certainty that he would one day be called to higher things. When the news came that he was moving to the Mayor of London's office, she had locked herself in the ladies' lavatory and wept like Dido for Aeneas; if she did not burn herself on a pyre of spreadsheets, it was only because the rules of the building forbade the striking of matches.

He had had a ruthless side, of course. She remembered the suggestion of a parking meter that refunded money for unused time: how Jeffrey had ridiculed its designer! But, as he had so often reminded her, you couldn't make an omelette without breaking eggs.

Years had passed since then; every Christmas she had sent a card, without ever receiving a reply. Yet still she carried a torch for him – and when members of the public questioned the principles he had established, her heart filled with indignation. She imagined sacrificing these ingrates in his temple – she clad in the diaphanous robes of a priestess, he presiding as a naked god anointed with precious oils.

She leant forward to stamp the words 'FAST-TRACK PROSECUTION' on Dunstable's file.

CHAPTER FIVE

'And where do you think *you're* going?'

Matt looked at the warder blocking his path.

'I thought I'd get myself a cup of tea,' he said.

'Get yourself a cup of tea? What do you think this is – the self-service cafe at the London Dungeon?'

'I saw the urn sitting there, and I assumed –'

'You don't assume nothing. You don't assume that you can blow your nose, clean your teeth or scratch your arse – because you can't, not without my say-so. Next time you fancy a cuppa, you say to yourself, "Am I a free man who can wander down to Fortnum & bleeding Mason any day of the week and order a pot of their finest Assam Breakfast Blend, or am I scum doing time until the parole board has mercy on my miserable hide?" Got it?'

'Yes,' said Matt. 'I don't think you've left much room for ambiguity.'

'Then go and f–ing sit on that bench until you're told to do otherwise, or you'll find yourself in f–ing solitary.'

The rest of the work party chuckled. To them Matt was just another wet-behind-the-ears newcomer – not that that worried him. The knowledge that he had given up his liberty for the sake of the nation would sustain him, as it had political prisoners across the centuries. If he had been thrown off balance, it was simply because everything had happened so fast.

The dawn raid had come only three days after he'd posted his letter of defiance to the council. Not content with arresting him, fingerprinting him and taking a DNA sample, the police had ransacked his rented house and taken away his computer.

'Surely they're not allowed to do that?' he said to his solicitor.

'I'm afraid the new tax-enforcement legislation means they are.'

'What do they think they'll find on my computer – downloads from a bombmaker's website?'

'They're probably just marking your card. But if you ever get it back, I advise you to wipe the hard disc. They often like to plant some kiddy porn, so they can put you away for that if all else fails.'

This had not proved necessary. The magistrate listened sympathetically to Matt's statement, but explained that his duty was to uphold the letter of the law, not to be drawn into questions of common sense. He had no alternative but to sentence the defendant to six months in prison, unless the money owing to the council was produced.

'For God's sake, Matt, pay up,' urged his girlfriend on her mobile from a stockbrokers' conference in Moscow. 'You don't want a stretch behind bars on your CV.'

'I'm self-employed. I don't need a CV.'

'Maybe not at the moment. But one day you'll go back to a proper job.'

'You may not have noticed, Nikki, but there are tens of thousands of people who make a good living as builders.'

'Not what *I* call a good living.'

'No, but you're in the top one per cent of UK earners, which makes you one of the few women in the country unable to rush to her boyfriend's side and give him moral support.'

'There's no need to be like that. You know I'd be there for you if I could.'

'But you can't be, can you? That's the point.'

'You're being *so* unreasonable. Look, the moment this meeting's over I'll call whoever's in charge and pay your tax on my credit card.'

'But I don't *want* you to pay my tax. I want you to understand why I'm doing this. I want you to be on my side.'

'Got to go, darling. But the offer's there. I'll be back on Tuesday. Ciao.'

And that had been that. Did he and Nikki have any future together, he asked himself? And did he care?

The task he had been given in the prison workshop – fitting plastic nozzles on to plastic tubing – was so simple that the novelty wore off in twenty minutes. The one compensation was the grumbly camaraderie among the eight men around the table. What the others were inside for he had no idea: his instincts told him it was better not to ask. He was certain, too, that being able to pay his way out if he wanted to was unlikely to make him popular.

He was surprised, therefore, when he returned to his cell to find a stranger in residence who introduced himself with full details of his criminal activities.

'I'm Jake,' he said. 'Maybe you read about me in the papers – that business with the bear in London Zoo. ' "Bear-faced cheek" the *Sun* called it; the *Mirror* was even better: "Trouble is Bruin!" Breaking and entering they're charging me with, and theft. Makes me sound like a burglar, dunnit? Like I'm going to steal a bear and sell it to the highest bidder.'

'Sorry,' said Matt. 'I don't read the papers much any more. What did you want with a bear?'

So Jake explained.

'That's me,' he said when he'd finished. 'How about you?'

So Matt explained.

'Top man,' said Jake. 'Power to the people, eh? We're prisoners of conscience, you and me.'

'How long are they likely to keep you on remand?'

'Three or four months my lawyer reckons.'

'That's a long time if you haven't been found guilty of anything.'

'Yeah. I got the sack from work, of course – said they couldn't hold the job open. Ten years I was in that post room. But Sammy says he'll find me something when I'm out.'

'What, like feeding the lions at Whipsnade? I'd steer well clear of him if I were you.'

'He's all right. I mean, you got to take a few risks, ain't you?'

'Poor sucker,' thought Matt. 'With friends like Sammy, who needs enemies?'

But as he lay in bed that night, trying to sleep despite Jake's snores and the harsh, avant-garde symphony of metallic noises which characterised the restless cell block, it occurred to him that compared to Jake's headline-grabbing antics his own protest was voiceless and futile. Which of them, then, was the sucker?

II

In the year since his son had left for university, Christophe Hardy had grown used to life on his own: used to going home to an empty flat, to cooking supper for one, to settling down afterwards with a glass of Bordeaux to watch a film or a documentary. But even to him, passing the days in an anonymous Beijing apartment without so much as a radio for company presented a challenge.

He knew that he needed to exercise, and forced himself to do hourly sit-ups and press-ups. Then he remembered his Uncle Jacques – a Marxist historian of the circus who had spent a summer holiday in the Dordogne teaching Christophe to walk the tightrope. Perhaps this was the moment to dust off those skills.

A search of the flat produced a length of electrical cord which Christophe ran from one leg of the kitchen table to a chair jammed into the doorway. After a couple of hours the knack of balancing began to come back, though the pain in the soles of his feet reminded him why he would never have made a professional.

He was setting up the chair for his morning practice when, on his sixth day in hiding, someone finally came for him: a skinny, unsmiling youth who stared at him through thick spectacles.

'Time to go,' said the visitor. 'Please come with me double quick.'

Christophe gathered his possessions. The stranger went through the fridge and kitchen cupboards, emptying the remnants of food into a black rubbish sack.

'You have the holdall?' he asked. 'Bring it. You will look suspicious if you travel without luggage.'

Out on the street the noise was so overwhelming that Christophe had to stop for a moment to get his bearings. His guide looked at him in alarm.

'You OK?'

'Yes – just a bit disorientated.'

'No time for that. Come on!'

There was a bus stop ahead of them. The youth pressed a ticket into Christophe's hand.

'I will wait further down the street,' he said. 'When the bus comes, you will get on and I will follow, as if I do not know you. Get off at the last stop.'

There were a dozen other people waiting. Christophe felt their stares as he joined them. Foreigners were no longer the curiosities they had been when he first visited Beijing, but the presence of one was always registered.

The bus took an age to arrive. When it finally did, Christophe saw that its destination was Beijing West railway station.

What did that mean? He guessed a train to Shanghai. From there he could be smuggled out by boat; but if that was the plan, why did he need a false passport? If only he could question his escort – but that was clearly out of the question. They remained at opposite ends of the bus, carefully ignoring each other.

At the final stop the passengers surged so frantically from the doors that an old woman was almost trampled underfoot. Christophe heard a voice in his ear:

'Follow ten paces behind me. Someone will greet you. Go with them.'

The station was on the far side of the road. Christophe had forgotten its immensity: it loomed like a fortress, its two wings separated by a monumental arch, its brutalist façade implausibly prettified by a series of pagoda roofs.

His escort led the way towards a footbridge past street vendors selling boiled eggs and roast chicken for the journey. The throng of people hauling suitcases seemed impossible: the escalator giving access to the bridge had failed, and those ahead were having to labour up the steep, narrow slope as best they could. Christophe was hard pressed to keep sight of the figure in front of him. The young man pushed on through the crowd, never stopping to look back.

The girl who intercepted Christophe seemed to come from nowhere. She stepped out of the throng and grasped him by the arm. 'Quickly,' she said. 'You have only a short time to catch the train.'

He didn't immediately recognise her. Then, suddenly, he placed her as Ying, the girl who had taken him to the prayer meeting. Was she to be his travelling companion – and if so, could he trust her? Was this a trap?

'Which train?' he asked.

'The train to Kowloon. This is your ticket' – she passed him a small slip of paper – 'and your passport. You are Mr Charles Brown, a film producer.' Kowloon: in other words, Hong Kong. Christophe was astonished.

'That means going through passport control twice,' he said: 'here and in Hong Kong. And the train journey is what, 24 hours? There must be a safer way.'

But the girl was giving nothing away. 'There are reasons – you will see.'

The entrances to the station were as packed as the escalator had been; indeed, the queues seemed hardly to be moving. As Ying led him down to street level, an English voice on the Tannoy announced that train T97 to Kowloon was ready to depart. 'Perhaps I'll miss it,' Christophe thought. 'And perhaps it'll be just as well.'

But the entrance marked 'Immigration' led into a relatively empty room. There were only a few people in front of him, queuing to put their luggage through an X-ray machine.

'I will leave you now,' said Ying.

'You're not coming with me? Then who . . .'

'You will see. Quick – you will miss the train.'

She turned and was gone.

He passed through security, showed his ticket, and walked unchallenged past two customs officers. Ahead lay passport control.

Before approaching it he had to fill in a departures card. He examined the passport the girl had given him. It looked convincing enough – but what would an immigration officer make of it?

He queued behind a young couple. The booth ahead was staffed by a plump woman in a surgical mask, the eyes above it a study in impassivity. A panel by her window invited passengers, incongruously, to rate her performance in terms of a smiling or frowning face.

Christophe handed her the passport and card. He tried to focus on her police number, displayed in red electronic figures: 4-6-8-1. What might come next in that sequence? Add two, then two more, divide by eight . . . She seemed to be having trouble scanning the passport: was there something the forger had got wrong? He mustn't stare or look worried: 3,5, 5/8 – or should they all be integers? Try subtracting seven instead of dividing . . .

'Thank you.' She handed the passport back.

'*Xièxiè.*' He pressed the smiley face.

The door ahead of him led straight on to the platform. Beyond its marble pillars the train stood waiting. Inhaling the fresh air, he paused for a moment, wondering how he had got this far. Then he noticed three figures in police uniform standing by the engine. He climbed quickly aboard.

His compartment had four berths. That meant that he and his companion would be sharing with two other passengers – possibly talkative, inquisitive ones. It was a problem he could have done without. But so far the compartment was empty and the bunks with their freshly laundered linen were undisturbed. Everything was much as he remembered it from the last time he had done this journey, the lace covers and the pot plant on the small table by the window giving the impression of a British seaside boarding house circa 1950. He was wondering whether there might be a volume control for the muzak on the PA system when a woman appeared in the doorway.

She was dressed in an elegant green raincoat with black trousers and shoes; a yellow silk headscarf and dark glasses all but obscured her face. She was tall and thin – too thin.

'Mr Brown?' She spoke with an American accent.

'Yes.'

She smiled. 'I'm Mrs Brown. Do you mind if I join you?'

'Please do.'

She laid a small suitcase on one of the bunks and slid the door shut. Even this seemed an effort for her. She sank on to the couch opposite him.

'I don't know if they told you my real name,' he said. 'It's Christophe Hardy.'

He held out his hand. Hers, in a white glove, felt as delicate as a leaf.

'My name is Amy.'

He didn't press her for a surname. 'Can you tell me, Amy, why we're going to Hong Kong? It isn't the easiest route out of China.'

'It was the only possible one for me. I have an illness which means I'm not allowed to fly.'

'What about Shanghai? Wouldn't it have been easier to pick up a ship there?'

'Too risky. The World Trade Fair is opening in ten days. There are police everywhere.'

'And when we get to Hong Kong?'

'Someone will meet us at the Star Ferry terminal, Kowloon side.'

'And then?'

'Arrangements have been made. That's all I know.'

He wasn't sure whether to believe her.

'It's very frustrating not having the whole picture,' he said. 'Especially when you're taking the risks we are.'

'I'm sorry. But you know as well as I do how the organisation works.'

The train began to move.

'It looks like we've got the compartment to ourselves,' said Christophe.

'Good.' She reached up and removed her dark glasses and headscarf.

Christophe found himself staring at a beautiful woman in her mid-thirties. She had large, dark eyes, fine features and short, platinum blonde hair. But while her face was unmistakably Chinese, her skin was so preternaturally white that she might have been sculpted from marble.

He tried to conceal his surprise, but made a poor job of it.

She laughed. 'Didn't anyone explain to you?'

'Nobody explained anything.'

'I have a genetic condition which affects the pigmentation of the skin. It's not as extreme as albinism – we don't have pink eyes – but we certainly stand out in a crowd. People use the same nickname for us as they do for foreigners – *gwailo*. So when this journey was being planned it seemed safest to pretend that I was a foreigner, married to a fellow European. That's why you got dragged into it. '

'*Gwailo* – white ghost.'

'That's it. In a lot of places I've been to, beyond the tourist routes, they've never seen anyone with pale skin, so they don't know what to make of me.'

'That must have complicated your work.'

'Sure, in some ways. But in others it helped.'

That made sense. Christophe had never known a nation as superstitious as the Chinese. There must have been plenty who thought of her as belonging to another world.

'How long have you been with the brotherhood?' he asked.

'Four years – nearly five.'

'How did they recruit you?'

She frowned. 'You need to know that I grew up in a town in the middle of nowhere. There was nothing there except a school and a factory, and they were the beginning and the end of people's lives: you went to school to learn what the Party wanted you to be taught, and then you went to work in the factory until you got too old or too sick from the chemicals to work any more. Every night you went home to a small flat in a block which started to fall apart almost as soon as it was built. In summer it was like an oven and in winter it was so cold and damp you might just as well have been living in a ditch.

'A few people got rich – the local Party bosses, the people who ran the factory – and if they had any sense they moved away. Everyone else just staggered on, trying to keep body and soul together. Occasionally, when people couldn't take it any more, there'd be a riot: they'd throw bricks at the houses of corrupt officials, torch a couple of police cars – but nothing ever changed. What kept my family going was our faith in God. I don't know how other people got by.

'Then one day a man I'd never seen before arrived to stay with us. He looked perfectly ordinary, but there was something about him that stood out, like a fire blazing in a field at night. And when he spoke about his faith, you felt life wasn't just to be endured – it was suddenly full of possibilities. He could talk to anyone – the guy sweeping the street, the old lady selling vegetables – and they felt it. I can't tell you how amazing it was. So I said to him, "I want to do what you do." And he said, "In two months' time I will come back this way. Be ready to go with me."

'So that's what I did. He took me to a place hidden away in the north, where they trained students – usually for a year, but because my eyesight is bad for reading I was slower and stayed for two. Then they decided I was ready.

'To begin with I worked in the big cities, where my appearance didn't attract quite as much comment; then I moved out into the countryside. That was more stressful – keeping out of sight, never travelling by day, talking to small groups in houses. But the rewards were great.'

'And you were never caught?'

'Once, in a town in Hunan Province. Fortunately there was a member of the congregation who had a lot of influence: he persuaded the chief of police to let me go.'

'You were lucky.'

'I realise that. Anywhere else it could have been prison, torture, execution – they warned us of that at the seminary. Two of the missionaries who trained with me are dead.'

'That doesn't surprise me. I've helped to make arrangements for priests who've had to leave the country. Some of them had very narrow escapes.'

'And how did you become involved?'

He told her.

'So here we are,' she said. 'Two fugitives together.'

The noise of an argument came from the corridor; a moment later the door slid open. There was just time for Amy to replace her scarf and sunglasses.

Two middle-aged women glared in. Behind them was the carriage attendant in her militaristic blue uniform and red-banded cap.

The women, it seemed, had paid for a two-berth compartment, but had been given tickets for a four-berth one. They were not pleased to be sharing – particularly with a man.

The attendant was not sympathetic. 'You should have examined your tickets at the time of issue,' she said. 'There are no other berths available, unless you want to go hard sleeper.'

'Hard sleeper!' exclaimed one of the women. 'I pay for de luxe soft sleeper, and you expect me to lie with my head in the corridor with bad-smelling students!'

'It is your choice.'

Still grumbling, the women dragged their suitcases into the compartment. Christophe helped to stow them in a space above the door.

'That pig of an attendant!' exclaimed the older of the women.

'Pig,' agreed the second. 'They get worse every year.'

'Maybe some people will get off at Wuchang,' said Amy. 'It might be possible to rearrange things then.'

'Wuchang!' said the younger woman. 'We won't get there until midnight – if we're lucky.'

Christophe decided to take a walk along the train. At one end was the restaurant car; next to it, a de luxe carriage of two-person compartments, their doors all firmly shut. The following three carriages, which included his own, were the next class down: 'soft sleeper'. Each had an attendant's room, a washroom and a lavatory. He glimpsed a group of men playing cards, and two families who had already climbed into their beds.

The remaining carriages were hard sleeper, with tiers of three bunks and no doors to separate them from the corridor. One was dominated by Western students – Canadian, judging from the maple leaves on their luggage tags – who were still trying to stow their rucksacks. Overseeing them was a tall, moustachioed man of Christophe's age whose voice resounded along the corridor.

'Richard! It is *not* going to fit. What did I tell you about packing sensibly? Stack it in the corner and sit down.'

Christophe returned to his own compartment. 'I'm afraid the attendant was right,' he said. 'The only spare berths I could see were in hard sleeper.'

The two women grumbled again. They were laying out a picnic on the small table by the window. The sight of their food made Christophe suddenly very hungry.

'Shall we see if we can get some lunch in the restaurant car?' he asked Amy.

'Sure.'

They found seats by a window. The same old-fashioned aesthetic was in evidence here: checked tablecloths, net curtains, the waitresses in frilly white aprons. Outside, the showy skyscrapers of the city centre had given way to run-of-the-mill apartment blocks and industrial estates.

Christophe and Amy ordered from a laminated menu with a 'warmth warning' which asked them not to outstay their welcome ('As the seats here are limited, please be going back to your own seat after dinner'). To Christophe, after a week of basic rations, the dishes read like a gourmet's fantasy.

'Christophe.' Amy leant forward to whisper across the table. 'I want to thank you for doing this. It would have been hard for me to make this journey on my own: I tire very easily. And it is much safer for me to be travelling as part of a Western couple. But I'm afraid it may be more dangerous for you.'

'I've been in worse situations. Crossing the road in Beijing, for instance.'

She smiled. 'You have the famous English self-deprecating sense of humour. But Christophe's a French name, isn't it?'

'My mother was French and my father was English. They were both self-deprecating, but in my mother's case it was actual modesty. My father had a rather high opinion of himself, but we were brought up to believe that nothing was worse than boasting.'

'There was no boasting in my family. My parents were deeply ashamed that their only child should be a girl who looked like I did – it was very difficult for them.'

'I'm sorry.'

'Oh, I was lucky. A lot of parents would have got rid of me at birth. Mine took the view that God had sent me as a punishment which they must endure.'

'And that didn't put you off Christianity?'

'No. It made me want to show people that Christianity was about love, not punishment.'

'How long have you been ill?'

'On and off, all my life. It goes with the way I was born: exposure to sunshine, for example, can damage my skin and my eyes. But recently I began to feel sick in a way I never had before. The doctor told me that I needed hospital treatment – but that would have meant registering with the authorities, which I couldn't risk. That's why I have to go abroad.'

Their food arrived.

'This is good,' said Christophe, taking a sip of chicken broth. 'The food on these trains used to be appalling. The rice came in cold, hard lumps like specimens of quartz from the Natural History Museum.'

'You've done this journey before?'

'A couple of times, many years ago – when it took thirty-six hours instead of twenty-four. And of course you couldn't go straight through to Hong Kong: you had to change at Guangzhou. The view from the window was different too.'

They were passing the outskirts of a satellite town with factory chimneys belching smoke. Christophe leaned forward to watch children playing basketball in a playground; then he glanced across the carriage. Suddenly he reached for the menu and held it firmly in front of his face.

'Is something wrong?' asked Amy.

'At the far end of the carriage there's a man in a grey suit, name of Professor Li. Someone I know from the university.'

'He's coming this way.'

Out of the corner of his eye, Christophe watched his acquaintance pass, followed by a man he had never seen before.

'I'll go after them,' said Amy, 'and see what compartment they're in.'

Christophe cursed his luck. What were the chances of one of the few people in Beijing who knew him by name being on the same train? And how aware was Professor Li of his situation? Had he and his colleagues been questioned by the police?

Amy returned a moment later. 'They are in the next carriage. I think that the second man may be an escort or bodyguard. Is that probable?'

'It's certainly possible. Professor Li is an important man.'

'Do you work in the same department?'

'No, but our work is closely connected. I am a virologist; he is one of the world's leading experts on inoculation. If you ever need a state-of-the-art hypodermic syringe, he's the man to go to.'

'But why does he need a bodyguard? Maybe if he was a nuclear physicist . . .'

Christophe shrugged. 'Perhaps he's worried about industrial espionage. If you think how many syringes the world uses, it has to be big business.'

'I suppose so.'

'The other question is how far he's going. It surely can't be all the way to Hong Kong. Why take a twenty-four-hour train journey when you can fly?'

'The train makes three stops before Hong Kong: Zhengzhou, Wuchang and Changsha. He could be getting off at any of those. But Hong Kong is also possible. Internal flights get booked up a long way in advance.'

'How far is Zhengzhou?'

Amy looked at her watch. 'Another five hours.'

Christophe frowned. He would just have to keep his head down, and hope.

CHAPTER SIX

Back in their compartment, the two women were hunched over a laptop. Amy took out a book; Christophe watched the country-side – if it could be called that – flash past. He remembered this journey for its picturesque landscapes – geometric paddy fields, abundant lakes, Willow Pattern hills, Dr Seuss trees. Instead he found himself looking at mile after mile of industrialisation: newly built factories and high-rise tenements; old factories with sagging roofs; vast warehouses; shacks with dusty satellite dishes; vacant lots piled high with rubbish.

He thought of the one visit he had made to China with Sara. It had been soon after they were married; they had done this journey in reverse, boarding the train in Guangzhou and clanking off into the moonlit night.

The trip hadn't been a success. Sara's initial enthusiasm for the country had been worn away by freezing weather, depressing accommodation and vindictive officialdom. Overshadowing it all had been the incident with the bibles.

Christophe had insisted on taking a dozen of them. It was his third delivery to Father Chang: after the previous two he felt that it was expected of him. In addition, he now admitted to himself, he had become hooked on the excitement of it.

But in Beijing everything had gone wrong. Their taxi had been involved in a minor collision, bringing them to the attention of a suspicious traffic policeman; if Christophe hadn't had the presence of mind to slip the bibles under the front passenger seat, he and Sara could easily have ended up in prison.

'How could you?' she asked him afterwards, shaking with anger and fear. 'This isn't a *Boy's Own* adventure! This is our lives.'

She could have left him there and then. But she had loved him, and though she had never again travelled with him to China, she never tried to dissuade him from going, even after Ben was born.

Jesus, of course, demanded that you leave your loved ones to follow Him. But it seemed to Christophe, after five dark years as a widower, that in failing to cherish his wife he had also failed his God. Was she not as precious as the souls Father Chang saved? Had he not sworn to care for her in sickness and in health? And yet when she had most needed her husband, he was nowhere to be found.

Only after her death had he realised how much one person could need another. He had seen bereavement often enough, but convinced himself that the moment of loss was by far the hardest part: a moment which, with the passage of time, became dulled, assimilated, eventually almost forgotten. He remembered a photograph of a tree in a scrap yard, slowly encroaching on the rusty wreckage all around until even a bicycle disappeared inside it. Life went on; anything could be absorbed.

So it had come as a surprise to find himself cast adrift. All that had seemed absolute was now merely relative: his work, his ambition, his survival. His place in time had shrunk, and he saw himself as history must see him – a blade of grass, a fleck of foam on the ocean; just one of the millions upon millions of souls that lived, and had gone before, and were yet to be. Everywhere he went he felt his wife's absence, and her beckoning.

And this, he realised, was what was meant by losing the will to live. It was not a desire for non-existence, but the hearing of a call from the other side, and a longing to be there – to know again what he had once possessed. The divide between life and death had become less defined.

Bereavement had strengthened his faith rather than diminished it. But it had also given him what he had never felt before: a sense of inadequacy. He had not been worthy of his quiet, thoughtful, selfless wife – so how could he be worthy of God's love?

As he watched the foreign fields rush by, his forward path was as unresolved as ever. His son was all he had left to him – and here he was, half a world away. He would do things differently when he got home.

II

The *Frank Rides Forth* team were huddled around their outside-broadcast truck waiting for the sun to rise. It had been a cold night, and the steam from their mugs of coffee hung over them like the ghosts of huntsmen past.

'Hello, Frank. Good morning for it.'

'Hi, Vanessa. Yeah, I fancy our chances. Thought we'd start up in Kensington Gardens.'

'With the statue of Peter Pan in the background, maybe?'

'Whatever you like, Van. You're the producer.'

Standing next to them, Anna McCormack wondered what the sport's great heroes would have made of the media age. Would

John Peel have consented to being miked up, or Nimrod to having his cheeks rouged?

'Are you going to introduce us, Frank?' she asked. She disliked this producer woman, with her air of long-suffering superiority, and had no intention of being ignored.

'Sure. Anna, this is Vanessa. Vanessa, this is Anna from the Birmingham and Edgbaston. She's going to be whipping in for me today.'

Vanessa examined the newcomer, wondering whether she and Frank were lovers. Her instincts told her not; but how else to explain Frank's discomfiture?

She computed the effect on the show. A love interest might play badly with Frank's female admirers. On the other hand, Anna – who looked undeniably sexy in her jodhpurs and hunt jacket – could hardly fail to attract young men; feminists and lesbians might buy into her too. Vanessa decided to be as friendly as she knew how.

'Pleased to meet you, Anna. If you could just keep a bit of a distance between you and Frank while we're filming, that would be great. He's the star of the show, after all. We'll pick up some shots of you and the dogs at the end if we've got time.'

The lights of a Parks Police car came into view.

'Morning, Frank,' said the driver.

'Morning, Sergeant.'

'Hope those hounds of yours are up for it. I've got £50 at the bookies says you'll make thirty kills this week.'

'I'll let them know, Sarge. I'm sure they'll do their best for you.'

'Before we move off, Frank,' said Vanessa, 'I wanted to ask how you'd feel about maybe filming out of London. It's good to have an occasional change of scene – and it would help our figures in the provinces.'

Frank shrugged. 'OK by me, as long as it's just the odd day here and there. I'm all in favour of spreading the word.'

'You'd have to be careful not to tread on any toes,' said Anna. 'Some of the MFHs might not like you stealing their thunder.'

Frank grinned at her. 'You talking about the master of the Birmingham and Edgbaston?'

'Maybe.'

'Actually,' said Vanessa, 'I thought we might start by the seaside.'

III

Christophe woke with a start to find himself sprawled across the bunk. He must have nodded off – but when? He squinted at his watch: almost five o'clock.

He was suddenly aware of three women looking at him with broad smiles on their faces.

'You slept like a baby,' said Amy.

He grunted, still half asleep.

'Miss Ma and Miss Chen are very excited to hear you are a film producer.' She nodded to the two women.

'A film producer?' It took him a moment to remember his cover. 'Yes, of course.'

'Miss Ma and Miss Chen work for a television production company. They have a series which they would like to sell to the West. They would welcome your opinion.'

And so Christophe found himself watching a Shanghai soap opera on the women's laptop.

'What do you think?' asked Miss Chen after three episodes. 'Please tell us frankly.'

'Very good,' Christophe lied. 'A bit over the top, but the plot is strong.'

'Over the top?'

'Exaggerated.'

'And British audiences do not like such programmes?'

'Quite the opposite. They like them very much.'

Satisfied, the two women disappeared to the restaurant car. Amy went with them to buy some water. A moment later the train began to slow: they must be coming in to Zhengzhou.

Christophe stood up to stretch. As he did so, he heard a voice behind him.

'Dr Hardy!'

He turned. Professor Li was standing in the doorway – drunk as a skunk by the look of him. His tie was skewed and his hair dishevelled; in his hand he held a bottle of beer.

'I thought it was you, Dr Hardy! Even from behind I thought, "This is a man I know!" '

Christophe forced a smile. 'What an amazing coincidence. But please, call me Christophe.'

'No, no,' said Li, shaking his head emphatically. 'That would not be respectful. You will always be Dr Hardy to me.'

Christophe winced. The last thing he needed was Li identifying him to the world. Why hadn't he been quicker to shut the compartment door?

'The thing is,' he said in a low voice, 'I'm not travelling alone.'

Li stared at him uncomprehendingly for a moment. Then he broke into a wide smile.

'I get you!' he said. 'You have a lady friend!'

'That's right. One of the students from the university, as a matter of fact. So I'd rather people didn't know I was an academic.'

'I get you! Rumpy-pumpy in the department! Professional misconduct!'

'Exactly. You'd be doing me an enormous favour if you didn't mention it to anyone.'

'Naughty boy, eh?'

'Yes.'

'Dirty weekend?'

'That sort of thing,'

'Don't worry, Dr – '

'Christophe. Call me Christophe. Or even better, Christo. That's what my British friends call me.'

'Christo.'

'Yes.'

'OK, Christo. You like a drink?'

He proffered the bottle of beer.

'Not at the moment, thanks. Are you travelling far?'

Li laughed. 'Everyone on this train is travelling far.'

'I mean, all the way to Hong Kong.'

'I am going to visit my grandmother. How old do you think she is?'

'I don't know. Seventy?'

'One hundred and two.'

'That's quite something.'

'And my aunt?'

'Sixty-five?'

'One hundred and four.'

'Your aunt is older than your grandmother?'

'Different sides of the family.'

'Well, that's good. That means you have longevity on both sides. You must be the baby of the family.'

Li laughed heartily. 'You like cards?'

'I play a bit of poker.'

'You come with me. I will teach you soft-sleeper pelmanism. Very advanced – for people of superior intellect, like you and me, Dr Christo.'

'It's very kind of you, but I was about to take a nap. I had rather an early start.'

'You don't want to play cards with me? Afraid, maybe? Not want to be shown up by my advanced intelligence? You got a post-colonial hang-up about the People's Republic?'

Li was almost shouting. Christophe realised that he had to shut him up.

'Fine, I'll sleep later. Where would you like to play?'

Li was immediately mollified.

'You are a good sport, Dr Christo. We will go to my compartment.'

Christophe scribbled on a piece of paper and tucked it into Amy's book.

'OK,' he said. 'Let's go.'

It was only when he stepped out into the corridor that he saw Li's minder and realised that the man had heard the whole conversation. Did it matter, he wondered? Did the minder even understand English?

Li's compartment reeked of alcohol. Half a dozen bottles were lined up on the table; three more rolled on the floor. Li slid the door shut; the minder remained outside.

'Now,' said Li. 'I show you how to play advanced pelmanism.'

It was hard to see where he could lay out fifty-two cards: the table was certainly not big enough. But as Christophe watched, the professor started to distribute them over all the available surfaces – on both bunks, on the floor, and on the luggage racks.

'You see?' cried Li triumphantly. 'Much more difficult!'

'It's certainly a challenge.'

'Maybe we have some music. You like jazz?'

'Very much – but not too loud. We don't want to disturb the other passengers.'

Li activated an MP3 player. The sound of Fats Waller singing *My Very Good Friend the Milkman* filled the compartment.

'You start, Dr Christo.'

With a sigh, Christophe turned over two cards on the lower bunk: the three of hearts and the knave of clubs.

Li's enjoyment of the game was transparent. He shimmied up and down to the music, waving a fresh bottle of beer and flipping each card over with a flourish.

My very good friend the milkman says
That I've been losing too much sleep
He doesn't like the hours I keep

he sang. 'King of spades.'

Christophe found it impossible to reconcile this extravagant, inebriated figure with the man he had seen keeping his own counsel in a corner of the Senior Common Room. Was the professor's trip simply a family matter, or had he been sent by the authorities to dry out?

Whatever the answer, he must be humoured at all costs – first of all by letting him win. This was easy enough. Christophe turned the cards up at random, occasionally matching them by accident.

'Tell me,' he said, 'who's your friend outside in the corridor?'

'Not my friend.' Fats Waller had given way to Elisabeth Welch. *Stormy weather*
Since my man and I ain't together
Keeps raining all the time.

'No? Who is he then?'

'Government.'

'What, like a civil servant?'

Li found this very funny.

'No, no. *Can't go on, everything I had is gone* . . . bodyguard. Government got to protect Li – got to protect everyone.'

'I'm impressed. I hadn't realised your work was so hush-hush.'

'Oh yes. Queen of hearts, queen of diamonds. Pair!' Li took another swig.

'Then I'd better not ask you about it.'

'No, top secret. Ten of clubs . . .' he hesitated as the track finished and the Andrews Sisters came on. '*Don't sit under the mulberry tree with anyone else but me . . .*' he sang.

'Apple. It's an apple tree.'

'Not in my project – ace of hearts, pah! My project is Mulberry Tree.'

Christophe couldn't help feeling curious. What had Li been up to in that laboratory, two floors up from his own? His instincts told him not to press for details. He was in trouble enough without becoming the unauthorised holder of classified information.

But two games and two beers later, Li returned to the subject.

'Nanotechnology,' he said.

'What about it?'

'It is the future.'

'In what way? Are you talking about syringes?'

'I am talking about what can be delivered by syringes.'

'I don't understand.'

Li gave a little giggle. He kicked off his shoes and sprawled among the playing cards on the lower bunk.

'You virologists,' he said, spilling his beer on the pillow. 'You think that syringes are only good for vaccinations. Don't try to deny it, Dr Christo.'

'I don't deny it.'

'You are a good scientist, my colleagues tell me: a very good scientist. But I have to tell you that you lack imagination.'

'Explain.'

Li propped himself up on one elbow.

'You British love your dogs, correct?'

'If you mean that we keep them as pets rather than eating them – yes, we do.' Christophe thought of the carcasses he had seen in Chinese markets – Labradors split down the middle; disembowelled pi-dogs; neatly beheaded chows.

'You put silicone chips in their necks so you do not lose them.'

'Some people do.'

'But you don't do the same with human beings.'

Christophe laughed. 'I can't see that being very popular.'

'No. Nobody wants to line up and have foreign body stuck inside them, right?

'Right.'

'But very useful if you can do it.'

'I don't follow.'

'Suppose,' Li drained his bottle, 'that your government wanted to keep track of everybody in the country.'

'It pretty much does that already. You can't move in Britain without being recorded on CCTV.'

Li spat on the floor. 'Old technology. Horse and cart. All those man hours spent watching footage, trying to find somebody. How are you going to control your citizens like that? But Mulberry Tree – ' his voice sank to a whisper – 'Mulberry Tree is something else. Everywhere a person goes, he activates cameras, sensors, satellite tracking. With Mulberry Tree you can trace any member of the public at any time.'

Christophe stared at him. Could such a thing be possible? Or had the alcohol waging war on Li's brain cells created a wild fantasy?

'Amazing,' he said. 'And your syringes have something to do with this?'

'Exactly. Our scientists worked for years to perfect the tracking system, but at the end they still had a big problem: how to implant the chips that would activate it. So they came to me. "Professor Li, you are the world's number-one expert on the hypodermic syringe. We need you to invent a new kind: one that will embed a tiny silicone chip permanently in human tissue without the subject noticing."

'So I say to them, "You mean, a man goes to the doctor for inoculation, and he comes away with an armful of spyware? Not possible!"

'But they say to me, "Professor Li, for you anything is possible." And do you know what? They darn tooting! Six months later Li comes up with a blueprint for state-of-the-art syringe with surveillance capabilities. Twelve months later, the syringe is in production. Now anyone in China goes for an injection, he gets secret bonus.'

'I see,' said Christophe, 'so that mass inoculation programme in Tibet last summer, against the new strain of cholera . . .'

Li shouted with laughter. 'You got it! There was no new strain of cholera – just a whole lot of monks who need to mind their Ps and Qs! You seen photos of them all lining up? None of them have the faintest idea!'

Christophe struggled to contain his horror.

'Very impressive,' he said. 'All this must be keeping your compatriots very busy.'

'Not just my compatriots. At least, not for long.'

'No?'

'Guess who has just bought Mulberry Tree technology.'

'Russia?'

'No.'

'Cuba?'

'No.'

'Burma?'

'No,' Li giggled. 'Not even close.'

'Tell me.'

'I give you a clue. A Western country.'

Christophe racked his brains. France? Italy? Surely not the USA?

'I give up,' he said

'Your country, Dr Christo! Great Britain! Home of Kenny Ball, Johnny Dankworth, Mr Acker Bilk!'

Puffing out his cheeks and raising an imaginary clarinet to his lips, Li approximated the opening bars of *Stranger on the Shore*; and then, with another little giggle, he let the invisible instrument slide to the floor and fell fast asleep.

Christophe stepped out into the corridor. Li's minder was sitting on a jump seat talking to a man in a railway uniform. Christophe smiled at him, pointed into Li's compartment, and mimed sleeping. Then he went to look for Amy. It was time for supper, and a talk.

IV

Most of the tables in the restaurant car were occupied by the Canadian students. Christophe and Amy took the last one.

'So he didn't tell you where he was getting off?'

'No,' said Christophe. 'He could be going all the way to Hong Kong, which would give him sixteen hours to sleep it off, sober up, and say something to his bodyguard. I wonder if we shouldn't get off before he does: lie low in Wuchang for a day or two, then take another train on.'

'Maybe we should.'

'What about the people waiting for us in Hong Kong?'

'There are ways of contacting them.'

'And the delay to your hospital treatment – how serious would that be for you?'

'Not as serious as being arrested.'

'Then I think that's what we'd better do.'

A waitress came to take their order. The students were arguing noisily about ice hockey.

'I haven't told you what Li did tell me,' said Christophe when the waitress was gone.

He explained the nature of the Mulberry Tree project. Amy looked at him in consternation.

'This is a catastrophe for the brotherhood,' she said. 'Our lives are dangerous enough already.'

'It's a terrible thing for your people, and for mine. And I can't see any way of stopping it.'

'We could tell the press. The British press, that is. No one in China would publish such a thing.'

'Nor would anyone in Britain without evidence. It would be my word against the government's – and the government would dismiss me as a mad conspiracy theorist.'

They looked at each other despondently. As they did so, the noise at the adjoining tables died away. The Canadian students, whose food had just arrived, rose to their feet and stood in silence, their hands clasped in front of them. The teacher in charge paused for a moment, then said,

'For what we are about to receive, may the Lord make us truly thankful.'

'Amen.'

Amy turned to Christophe with a radiant smile. 'It's a sign. God will help us to find a solution.'

Christophe smiled back, wishing his faith was as strong as hers.

V

'You ever seen an alpaca, Matt?' asked Jake.

'I can't say I have.'

'Beautiful creatures. Not the same as llamas – a lot of people make that mistake. They're smaller, and they got much finer hair.'

'My aunt gave me an alpaca pullover once. Or was it mohair?'

'You'd know the difference. Mohair is prickly. Alpaca is as soft as – as angel's wings.'

Matt smiled. He had grown fond of his cellmate. Jake was not the brightest spark on the cell block, but he was well-informed – about animals, at least – and well-intentioned. He was also a useful person to have watching your back when one of the other prisoners tried to pick a fight.

'So these alpacas – have you ridden them?'

Jake shook his head. 'Their backs ain't strong enough to take a human. But they're excellent pack animals, long as you don't over-load them.'

Matt lay back on his pillow and imagined sauntering through the Andes at sunrise, his alpaca by his side. The tops of the mountains were hidden in mist; below, a rock-strewn river glinted. He thought of the Inca people who had walked this trail hundreds of years before him, their panniers chinking at every step with precious sea shells carried from the coast. The temptation to pay his fine, draw out his savings and take the next flight to Peru was suddenly acute. But the memory of the council's bullying letters hardened him against it. Would he be bound to the will of those preposterous bureaucrats – or, more precisely, Ms Jennifer Pettifer? Not while there was breath in his body.

And perhaps, after all, he was serving a useful purpose here. It had taken him only a few days to form a close-harmony group in the prison workshop; and though two of the warders had declared that there would be no such nonsense on their watch, others had been more sympathetic, turning – as it were – a deaf ear to the choruses of *Whispering Grass* and *Address Unknown* which cheered the daily nozzle-fitting sessions.

The sound of heavy footsteps brought him back to the present. A key turned in the lock.

'On your feet, Dunstable.'

It was Bentley, one of the less musical warders.

'What for?'

'Governor wants to see you.'

Matt followed reluctantly. The Governor was generally held to be a tough nut: not one of those enlightened types who wanted to set you on the right path, but an old-fashioned dispenser of retribution who would bang you in solitary as soon as look at you. A summons from him could only mean that life was about to take a turn for the worse.

The office to which Matt was led did nothing to reassure him. The carpet was thin and grey; the bare walls were painted a washed-out green; the only furniture was a Formica-topped desk with three plastic chairs and a computer. A bald man in thick-rimmed spectacles tapped at the keyboard, apparently oblivious to his visitors.

Bentley started to say something, but the Governor interrupted him.

'Not now, Bentley. I'll be with you in a minute.'

Matt wondered whether the Governor's house was similarly decorated. The prison's cells seemed cheerful in comparison.

'Very well,' said the Governor at last. 'This is Dunstable, is it?'

'Yes, sir.'

'Let him answer for himself, Bentley.'

'Yes, sir,' said Matt.

The Governor glared at him. 'Personally,' he said, 'I can't be doing with tax rebels. Look at this place – full to overflowing. Every prison I've run has been the same. And then people like you decide to add to our problems: never mind that the courts are setting bona fide criminals free because there's nowhere to put them.'

'I'm sorry,' said Matt.

'Sorry *sir*,' hissed Bentley.

'I'm sorry, sir, but it wasn't my choice to –'

The Governor gave him a look which stopped him in mid-sentence.

'I hear, Dunstable, that you've been singing.' He glanced at the screen in front of him. 'Singing in the prison workshop, and encouraging others to do the same. Is that correct?'

'Yes, sir. I thought it would be good for morale. In the tradition of the chain gang, if you like.'

The Governor raised his eyebrows. 'If I like? Well, I think I have your measure. You're a tenor, aren't you?'

'Yes, sir,' said Matt, surprised.

'Ever sung professionally?'

'No, sir. But I used to be a member of the Bach Choir.'

'I heard them sing the Verdi *Requiem* at Chester Cathedral a couple of years ago. Were you in that?'

'Yes, sir.'

'Well, let's hear you.'

'You want me to sing, sir?'

'No, Dunstable, I want you to stand on your head and balance champagne glasses on the soles of your feet. Now get on with it.'

Bemused, Matt cleared his throat. Tentatively at first, but growing quickly in confidence, he gave 'Una Furtiva Lagrima' from *L'Elisir d'Amore*.

The Governor removed his spectacles and polished them with his handkerchief.

'Here's the thing, Dunstable,' he said. 'My daughter belongs to a local glee club. They've reached the semi-final of the county singing championships, only to be let down by their president – ran off with the manageress of the local restaurant, last heard of singing Rodgers & Hammerstein in a bar in Biarritz. I promised to find a replacement, and as far as I'm concerned you fit the bill.

Help them win and you'll get time off for good behaviour; refuse and you'll spend the next two weeks in solitary.'

It did not take Matt long to make his choice.

'What are they singing, sir?' he asked.

VI

All along the train people were settling down for the night. Christophe lay down fully clothed on the bunk above Amy, setting the alarm on his mobile in case he should fall asleep before they reached Wuchang.

He need not have worried. The dangers that lay ahead surfaced and dived and resurfaced like sea otters, keeping him wide awake. Would Wuchang prove a haven or a trap? Would the authorities guess that he and Amy were still heading for Hong Kong? Might staying on board give them a better chance – indeed, their only chance – of getting there? Then he thought of Li in his drunken stupor: could that last for the rest of the journey? Surely not. And when he awoke – what then?

At last the amber lights of Wuchang came into view. He climbed down from the bunk; in the berths opposite, Miss Ma and Miss Chen were snoring in unison.

'Are you awake?' he whispered to Amy.

'Yes.'

'Let's go.'

The corridor was deserted. Christophe led the way to the door at the end of the carriage; through it, as the train eased to a halt, he saw a vast, hangar-like station, its girdered roof studded with lights, its stairways starkly delineated by steel railings. Ranks of trolleys stood idly at the end of the platform beside piled blue sacks of rubbish. Christophe zipped his jacket and waited for the door to open.

But it didn't.

Pressing his face to the glass, he realised that there was not a single passenger waiting to embark. The only people to be seen were a handful of uniformed officials positioned at intervals along the platform, staring at the train.

'What's the problem?' asked Amy.

'I don't know, but nobody's getting on the train, or off it.' He tried the door without success. 'People got on at Zhangzhou, didn't they?'

'I don't know – I didn't look. Did you?'

'No.'

A sense of panic took hold. He shoved at the door with all his strength, but still nothing happened. And even if it did open . . .

He peered out again at the line of officials. With a sinking heart, he realised that he and Amy were going nowhere.

'It must be a sealed train,' he said. 'When we went through immigration in Beijing, we were officially leaving China – so if we got off here, we would be sabotaging their procedures. No one can leave the train until Hong Kong.'

'Then why does it make four stops?'

'I've no idea. Perhaps they need to take on food, or water. They'd have to carry a lot to last the whole journey.'

'So we're stuck on board with Professor Li for another thirteen hours.'

'Yes,' said Christophe. 'I'm afraid so.'

CHAPTER SEVEN

It was early evening in London when the Archbishop of Canterbury was ushered in to see the Prime Minister. A thickset man – though barely five foot two without his mitre – he had been in his youth the embodiment of muscular Christianity, finding sporting fame as a forward for Harlequins before devoting himself to good works in Soho ('A hooker ministering to hookers,' the joke went). But the strain of overseeing a Communion divided against itself had taken its toll, till he had come to resemble a battleship rusting in the shipyards of a disenfranchised superpower. The Prime Minister, who had eyed him warily when they first shared high office, now scented weakness, and greeted him with the satisfaction of a bully in the ascendant.

'Good evening, Archbishop.'

'Good evening, Prime Minister.'

'All well at Lambeth Palace?'

The Archbishop shrugged. 'No better and no worse,' he said. 'All God's Creatures have agreed to suspend direct action until the next Synod, but whether a long-term solution can be found . . . I have to confess I do not feel optimistic.'

All God's Creatures, an American-based movement which held animals to be closer to the Creator than man, had grown increasingly militant over the past twelve months. Dogs, sheep, chickens and on one occasion a pet python had been brought into services by owners determined that they should receive the Eucharist.

These agitators were, in the view of the Archbishop, misled souls as full of devilment as the Gadarene swine; nevertheless, they had found friends in high places, including – it was rumoured – the chairman of the Republican Party. 'Among right-wing pressure groups,' declared the *Washington Post*, 'All God's Creatures is the cat's whiskers.' Financially, too, they were on a strong footing, with dedicated fund-raisers lurking opportunistically outside vets' surgeries and pets' cemeteries.

In Britain, the earliest reports of the movement had met with deep hilarity. But as so often, what began as a joke soon took on a dangerous reality. Intense young ordinands in theological colleges laboured through the night to find scriptural support for animal Communion; and when dispatched to their first parishes, they took their hamsters and budgerigars with them. Some were reported to hold clandestine services in cowsheds.

'Well,' said the Prime Minister with feigned sympathy, 'I dare say the guy upstairs will sort it out. Man proposes and God disposes, eh?'

The Archbishop inclined his head.

'What I wanted to talk to you about,' the Prime Minister continued, 'was another movement: the Brothers of Light. I understand you've been giving them a great deal of support. You are obviously not aware that they have recently been classified as a terrorist organisation.'

The Archbishop looked astonished. 'By whom?'

'By the Chinese authorities.'

'The Chinese authorities!' Something of the prelate's old fire returned to his eyes. 'Who are those godless criminals to call anyone terrorists? The Brothers of Light is an entirely respectable, non-violent organisation devoted to spreading the word of God by civilised means in extraordinarily dangerous circumstances. I am shocked that you should give credence to such slanders.'

The Prime Minister pursed his lips.

'I can understand,' he said, 'that you are reluctant to believe any such thing of your co-religionists . . .'

'*My* co-religionists?' said the Archbishop sharply.

'*Our* co-religionists,' the Prime Minister corrected himself. 'But I'm afraid that on my recent visit to China the Vice President showed me a file of very persuasive evidence.'

'What kind of evidence?'

'Photographs, video recordings, transcripts of telephone conversations. MI6 says it's all very convincing.'

'I don't believe it.'

'Nor did I at first. But who am I to quibble with the spooks?'

'You are the Prime Minister, are you not?' The Archbishop's blood was up now. 'It would hardly be the first time.'

His adversary forced a smile. 'Nevertheless, in this I accept their judgement. And since Britain is a major player in the fight against terrorism, I can hardly turn a blind eye just because a regime I dislike has been targeted. Which is why I want you to issue a public denunciation of the Brothers of Light, and ensure that they receive no further support from the Anglican Church.'

'Never!'

'Then I must ask for your resignation.'

The Archbishop gave him a look so furious that they might have been about to lock heads in a grudge match at Twickenham.

'May I remind you, Prime Minister, that I answer to God, not to you – and I would be failing in my duty if I entertained your request even for a moment. Now, if you will excuse me, I believe we have nothing further to discuss.'

He got to his feet.

'Before you go . . .' The Prime Minister reached across his desk for a thick dossier bound in red leather. 'I think you should consider this.'

'What is it?'

The Prime Minister read the title page: '*Report by the Health and Safety Executive on the state of churches and cathedrals in the United Kingdom.* I'm afraid it doesn't make happy reading. You might like to sit down again.'

'I'll stand, thank you.'

'Very well. A lot of work has gone into this, as you can see, but I'll just run quickly through the section headings: stone floors, slipperiness of; bells, hearing loss caused by; pulpits, climbing of by untrained staff; crypts, disabled access to; stained-glass windows, fragility of; candle-lighting, training of young persons in; harvest-festival offerings, application of sell-by dates to; straw in Christmas cribs, fire hazard of; lead roofs, risk of poisoning from; heating, inadequacy of . . . Would you like me to go on?'

The Archbishop shook his head.

'With what I have here,' said the Prime Minister, 'I could close down half the churches in Britain tomorrow, and put enough safety-improvement orders on the rest to bankrupt you within the year. That's before we even get on to diversity and what you're doing for members of other faiths. As for the additional risks posed by all these animals being brought along for services – it doesn't bear thinking about.'

The Archbishop clutched the chair in front of him for support.

His face had the pallor of a mediaeval wall painting whitewashed in an age of iconoclasm.

'You wouldn't dare,' he gasped.

'Try me.'

'God will punish your wickedness.' His voice was high and trembling. 'Your power is nothing compared to His.'

'And His is nothing compared to the Health and Safety Executive's. There is no institution in the land that it cannot bring to its knees. Is that what you want for the Church of England?'

The Archbishop shook his head.

'Then here's the deal. Either you publicly condemn the Brothers of Light or you resign. Which is it to be?'

The old man remained silent for a long time. At last he said quietly, 'I will resign. But don't imagine that my successor will be any more willing to betray our Chinese brothers.'

'We'll see about that.' The Prime Minister stood up and steered him towards the door. 'You know the way out, don't you?'

When his visitor had gone, the Prime Minister returned to his desk, cheerfully rubbing his hands. He quickly drafted a note to the Chinese Ambassador, and then clicked on the intercom.

'Send in the Archbishop of York, will you?' he said. 'And a bottle of champagne.'

II

The Chinese dawn brought another grey day. Raindrops clung to the train's windows, distilling the grudging light. But Christophe's spirits lifted at what he saw beyond them: tall hills, their scrub-covered slopes emerging from the morning mist, their summits mingling with the clouds; neat, emerald-green paddy fields; a broad river, its surface tinted a pale gold, blending with the russet trees around it.

On his way to the washroom, he found the Canadian schoolmaster in the corridor, studying a map.

'Managed to work out where we are?' he asked.

'A bit more than halfway between Changsha and Guangzhou, I guess, if the train's on time.' The teacher's finger traced a railway line. 'Should be just about here.'

'We left Changsha on schedule. There haven't been any stops since, so I think you must be right.'

The man lifted his eyebrows. 'You've been awake all night?'

'I had things on my mind. I'm Christophe Hardy, by the way.'

'Bud Wiseman. Good to meet you, Christophe.'

'Wasn't there a Cardinal Wiseman back in Victorian times? Any relation?'

'I wish I could say yes, but I don't think so.'

'Not that he would have had any direct descendants.'

'Certainly not.'

The two men laughed.

'Your first time in China?' asked Christophe.

'Second. I spent two months here a couple of years ago, travelling around. I'm with a party of students from a school in Toronto, and I wouldn't have liked to bring them here without some prior knowledge of the place.'

'Are they enjoying it?'

'I'd say so, on balance. I think it came as a bit of a shock to them – they mostly haven't seen another country apart from the US. But they're kids, they like an adventure. How about you? Been here before?'

'A few times. It's changed a lot over the years.'

'I'll bet.'

'If you'll excuse me, I'm going to grab the washroom while it's free. Nice to talk to you.'

'And you, Christophe. Catch you later.'

Filling the basin, Christophe wondered whether he had been too friendly. It had perhaps been rash to give his real name rather than his alias – but then, what did he have to fear from a Canadian schoolmaster?

Rather than risk meeting Li in the restaurant car, he break-fasted on biscuits from the catering trolley. Outside the rain had stopped and the sun was beginning to force its way through the clouds, brightening a tranquil lake; he glimpsed ducks and water buffalo, the first animals he had seen since leaving Beijing. Then he dozed off.

He was awoken by an official checking passports. Only after he had pulled his from his pocket did Christophe remember that it was false. But again it went unchallenged.

Ten o'clock: three hours of the journey left. They were approaching Guangzhou. A flyover and enormous billboards announced it as a more prosperous city than the ones they had passed, though the windows of the tower blocks had rusted grilles and balconies draped with washing.

The train halted at a platform full of hurrying passengers. Watching them stagger under the weight of their luggage, Christophe almost failed to notice Professor Li.

Li! How had he got off the train? Christophe hurried to the door of the carriage. As before, it was locked; yet there was Li below him, talking to some kind of official, his minder beside him. He looked as dishevelled as when Christophe had last seen him; in his arms he clutched a half-closed briefcase bulging with papers. All three men wore furious expressions.

The train started to move. Suddenly Li dropped to his knees and rummaged in his briefcase; he seemed to shout something and gesticulate at the line of carriages. The train shuddered as if it had changed its mind, then began to pick up speed.

Amy was at his shoulder. 'What's happening?'

'Li got off the train. I don't know why or how. And from his behaviour I think he may have left something important behind. I'm going to take a look.'

The air in Li's compartment was heavy with sleep and beer. The lower bunk was a tangle of sheets; playing cards were still strewn on every available surface, bottles lay on the floor. Christophe closed the door behind him and began to search.

It didn't take long to find the small padded envelope which had slipped down the side of the mattress. Christophe sat down to open it; but even as his fingers worked at its edges, he was sure of what he would find inside.

It was a hypodermic syringe sealed in cellophane. A label attached to it bore several words in Chinese and two in English: 'Mulberry Tree.'

He thrust the package into his jacket as the door opened behind him. Turning, he found himself face to face with Li's minder.

How the man had got back on the train was as much a mystery as how he had got off it. Christophe remembered the momentary slowing of the engine, imagined a door still unlocked.

'Hi,' he said in Mandarin. 'I think I dropped something here last night. I was just looking for it.'

The man pointed to the bulge in Christophe's jacket. 'I think you'd better give that to me.'

'I don't know what you mean.'

'Yes you do.'

Before Christophe knew what was happening, the man had pushed him sharply backwards. As he sprawled across the table and against the window, his head hit the glass with a crack which made him cry out in pain. His attacker stepped forward, reaching for the package which jutted from his inside pocket.

Off balance as he was, Christophe could do only one thing to defend himself. He brought up his right arm with all the strength he could find and hit the man across the side of his head. The minder fell to his knees.

Christophe hadn't been in many fights, but he knew that this was no time for half measures. An unopened bottle of beer stood on the table. He seized it and hit his assailant over the head.

The minder groaned and keeled over against the bunk. But still he wasn't finished: his fingers moved across the crumpled sheets, looking for purchase. Christophe hit him again. This time he lay still.

Christophe looked down, astonished. Recovering himself, he stepped quickly over his attacker and locked the door.

Was the man still breathing? Yes. How long would he remain unconscious? Impossible to say.

There was a stack of clean bed linen in the luggage space over the door. Seizing a sheet, Christophe tore it into strips and used it to tie the man's hands behind his back. Then he tied his feet and gagged his mouth. Heaving the unconscious form on to the lower bunk, he covered it with a sheet. That would do for now; but what would happen when they reached Hong Kong? If the minder was found and the alarm raised before he and Amy had got clear of the station, they would be in deep, deep trouble.

He looked again at the luggage space. There was room in it for a man of medium build, but Christophe knew he couldn't haul him up there on his own. He needed help, and his only ally, Amy, was obviously not the person to give it.

Then he thought of Bud Wiseman.

He found the schoolteacher in the restaurant car.

'Just getting a little peace and quiet,' said Wiseman. 'Keeping an eye on those kids in a city like Hong Kong isn't going to be easy, so I'm recharging my batteries.'

'Mind if I join you? I have a favour to ask.'

Christophe outlined the situation as briefly as he could. He explained his involvement with the Brothers of Light, the danger he and Amy faced from the authorities, and his encounter with Professor Li. He made no mention of the Mulberry Tree project or the syringe in his possession.

'I wouldn't ask for your help,' he said, 'if Amy and I weren't in a real fix. But we are.'

Wiseman looked anxious. 'I'll help if I can,' he said, 'but I have a duty of care toward the students. I couldn't get involved in anything that might put them in danger.'

'Of course not.'

'If this guy even sees my face I'm implicated.'

'He won't. I'll enter the compartment first to check that he's still out for the count. Then I'll blindfold him.'

'On those conditions, OK.'

'Thank you.'

Christophe found the minder exactly as he had left him. He pulled a pillowcase over his head, then slipped open the door to beckon Wiseman in.

'This isn't going to be easy,' said Wiseman, looking up at the luggage space. 'I suppose there isn't enough room under the bunk?'

'I'm afraid not.'

'Then we'd better get to work.'

The man was heavier than he looked. They hauled him upright and propped him with his back against the door; then, one on each side of him, they tried to manoeuvre him upwards.

The difficulty was getting enough height. It was only possible to stand on the lower bunk by gripping the side of the one above, leaving just one hand free. There was no ladder, merely a steel footrest at knee level, so narrow that it was of little help. Even a suitcase half the man's weight would have presented a problem.

'We'll have to lay him on the top bunk, then edge him across,' said Christophe. 'If you can hold him while I climb up there, and then take some of the weight, I'll try to pull him after me.'

The space between the top bunk and the ceiling left little room for manoeuvre. Christophe lay on his side and grasped the man under the armpits while Wiseman lifted his legs off the floor. By the time Christophe had managed to bring the unconscious bulk up to his level, he was gasping and sweating.

'If this guy wakes up,' he thought, 'it's going to be impossible.'

But the minder didn't wake up. Somehow the two men managed to inch him across the gap – twice almost dropping him – and fold him into the luggage space in a foetal position. All being well, he would not be discovered until the cleaners came through the train after everyone had disembarked. Wiseman used a rancher's knot to tie his hands to his feet and prevent him kicking to attract attention.

'There,' he said. 'A job well done.'

Christophe allowed himself a smile. 'I can't thank you enough. There's no way I could have managed on my own. Now, shall we get out of here?'

They stepped into the corridor, closing the door behind them. Christophe hoped that it would remain closed until long after they reached Hong Kong.

'You've been gone a long time,' said Amy when he reached their compartment.

'I met an old friend – and a new one. Come into the corridor and I'll tell you about it.'

They stood at the window watching bulldozers scrape grey earth in a slow, grim ballet. The mist appeared to be thickening into fog.

'How did Li manage to get off the train?' asked Amy.

Christophe shrugged. 'He's an important person – I suppose he, or his minder, knew someone who was prepared to bend the rules.'

'Do you think he will have reported what happened?'

'I doubt it . . . First, he must have an appalling hangover, and secondly he'd only be bringing trouble on himself. As far as he's concerned, his minder is sorting everything out.'

'You're OK after the fight?'

'A bit of a headache. It'll pass.'

'It's lucky Wiseman was prepared to help.'

'Very.'

'And you have the syringe – so you'll be able to prove to the British media that what you say about Mulberry Tree is true.'

'I hope so.' He smiled. He could see no benefit in pointing out that whatever the danger they had been in before, it had just doubled.

III

The next two hours were the longest of Christophe's life. His mind ran over the events of the last week: if only he hadn't accepted the invitation to the service in the warehouse; if only Li hadn't been on the train; if only . . .

But that was the wrong way to look at it. He had been given an opportunity – to help this remarkable woman, to expose the evils of Li's project: to do something to atone for his past failures. He had to be grateful, and make the most of it.

It was the familiar grey steel and glass façade of the Hong Kong Institute of Biotechnology that alerted him to the approaching end of their journey. The train glided under a flyover, past a high-rise primary school, and into the gloom of Hung Hom station. The fluorescent lights illuminated large pink murals of flowers and reflected off stainless-steel barriers.

Although they were among the first off the train, Amy could only walk slowly. By the time they reached passport control a queue had already formed, with a young couple at the front arguing with a frowning official.

'This is all we need,' thought Christophe. Any moment now the alarm would be raised, and they would be stuck on the wrong side of the barrier. He imagined the attendants going through the train, checking that nothing had been left behind.

Suddenly the argument was resolved. The couple moved through, the queue shuffled forward; there were four people ahead of them, three, two, one . . .

'How long are you staying in Hong Kong, Mr Brown?'

What was he to say – that he didn't know?

'Two days.'

'Purpose of visit?'

'Holiday.'

The official stared at his passport.

'I think you don't take many holidays.'

What was the man getting at? Christophe's heart began to race.

'Why do you think that?'

'Your passport. Two years old but good as new.'

How could he have missed that? He'd had twenty-four hours on the train to make it look travel-worn, and the thought hadn't even crossed his mind.

Relax, he told himself. Whatever you do, don't let him see your anxiety.

'When I was a child,' he said, 'my father used to say to me, "The most valuable thing you can have in the world is a British passport. Take good care of it." So that's what I've always done.'

'Better to have a Chinese one now,' said the official.

And he handed it back.

Outside they found a taxi without difficulty. As they climbed in, Christophe wondered whether the safest thing wouldn't be to go straight to the British Consulate. But the British Consulate was an arm of the British government – and the government was now his enemy.

'Star Ferry,' he told the driver.

The journey took only a few minutes. Looking out of the window, Christophe thought how little the city had changed since the handover of power – just a bit busier, if that were possible, a bit more conspicuous in its consumption. Yet everyone had expected to see it become regimented, puritanical. There was never any telling how things might turn out.

The Star Ferry terminal had never been part of Hong Kong's glittering brashness. The paintwork was still a dingy green, the floor still bare concrete.

'What now?' he asked Amy.

'Someone will meet us.'

'You don't know who?'

'No.'

Christophe scanned the quayside for candidates. Was it the tourist taking photographs of the grey skyline across the water? The pretty girl with the Louis Vuitton bag?

'Mr and Mrs Brown, if I am not mistaken.'

The speaker was a small, podgy man with a picnic basket at his feet. He wore a navy blue blazer with gold buttons, a pristine white shirt with a red and green striped tie, beige trousers held up by a black patent-leather belt, and a Panama hat. From his breast pocket spilled a blue and white spotted silk handkerchief, which he now used to polish his sunglasses.

He was not, to put it mildly, what Christophe had expected.

'You are . . .?'

'Gao Liang, at your service. You need a made-to-measure suit in twenty-four hours, I'm your man.'

'I don't think I do, thank you.'

'Just joking! In twenty-four hours you will be well away from here, God willing. Now, please follow.'

He picked up his picnic basket and headed off along the quay.

CHAPTER EIGHT

Gao Liang led them a few hundred yards to the Outlying Ferry Terminals. There he bought three tickets for Lamma Island.

'Our rendezvous is at Sok Kwu Wan,' he said. 'But not until this evening. It is better not to draw attention by waiting there too long, so we will take the ferry to the other side of the island and walk across.'

It was years since Christophe had been to Lamma. He remembered it as a small place, but even so . . .

'I don't know,' he said. 'Amy isn't well. It might be too much for her.'

'A gentle walk, that's all,' said Gao. 'Not very far. There is a good path; we can take it easy and stop for a picnic on the way.'

He held up the basket.

'What do you think, Amy?' Christophe asked. 'Are you up to it?'

'I think I'll be OK, if we go slowly. But there's my suitcase . . .'

'Don't worry, I'll carry that.'

'Better leave the suitcase,' said Gao. 'It will look strange on a picnic.'

Christophe frowned. 'I don't think this is a good idea. Surely there's a hotel in Sok Kwu Wan where we can lie low.'

'Unfortunately there are no hotels in Sok Kwu Wan.'

'It's OK,' said Amy. 'The suitcase is mainly clothes. If I can just put a few things in your holdall, Christophe, I'll manage fine.'

The upper deck of the ferry was half full. They took seats at the back, behind a couple reading local newspapers, while the other passengers clustered around the windows. Across the bay the skyscrapers on the mainland jostled for position. In the middle distance a pair of sampans pushed through the waves.

The crossing lasted half an hour. The islands they passed were vague shapes in the mist; the only flash of brightness was a welder's torch on a container ship. Their own boat carved a pale green wake. Christophe fell asleep.

He was woken by Amy's hand on his shoulder. She smiled down at him.

'I've never known anyone sleep like you do.'

He smiled back. 'I just closed my eyes for two minutes. Surely I'm allowed a nap?'

'We're nearly there.'

Through the windows he saw yellowish rocks and low hills covered with green vegetation. The noise of the engine died as the ferry nudged the quay. A tug with the nameplate *Smart Genius No. 1* rode at anchor beside it.

They disembarked. Beyond the rusting steel barriers of the terminal stood rows of commuter bicycles. The sails of a wind turbine turned slowly above the hills.

'We need to get rid of Amy's suitcase,' said Christophe.

'I have an idea,' said Gao. 'Take a room and leave it here.' He indicated a small concrete building advertising itself as a hotel. 'If anyone is following you, they will think you are coming back.'

'You think someone is following us?' asked Amy.

'I have no reason to believe that,' said Gao. 'But it is possible.'

In the hotel room Amy transferred a bundle of possessions to Christophe's holdall.

'Couldn't we just wait here until dark and then take a taxi to Sok Kwu Wan?' Christophe asked Gao. 'I don't think Amy should do more than she has to.'

'There are no taxis. No road – just a path. You will see.'

He was right. The only vehicles on the narrow main street were bicycles, pushchairs and tiny low-loading trucks. Once out of the town they found themselves on a well-kept concrete path over-hung by the giant fronds of banana trees. It was punctuated by street lamps and small fire hydrants, like dwarfs in early diving suits.

Though the going was easy and Gao set an undemanding pace, Christophe watched Amy anxiously. So far she was coping well enough – but what if it became too much for her later on? When they came to a sandy beach where a handful of children played in the shallows, he suggested a short rest.

They sat down at a picnic table. Gao stared at the few adults in the vicinity, then seemed to relax.

'Now it is safe to tell you more about the rendezvous,' he said. 'At Sok Kwu Wan we will be met by a fisherman. Once it is dark you will board his boat and he will take you out to meet a cruise ship bound for Europe. From there it should be, if you will excuse the expression, plain sailing.' He smiled at his own joke.

'It sounds straightforward enough,' said Christophe.

'What about patrol boats?' asked Amy.

'There may be some police boats. Or navy. Or coastguard.'

Suddenly it didn't sound so straightforward.

'What are our chances of meeting one?' asked Christophe.

Gao shrugged. 'We are in the hands of the Lord, are we not? There is providence in the fall of a sparrow.'

After the beach the path climbed upwards. To their left was a line of hills; to their right the view was dominated by the three thin chimneys of a power station. Beyond, towards the grey clouds of the horizon, lay a score of cargo vessels. Christophe wondered whether the cruise ship was already steaming towards them.

There were few other walkers on the path. It seemed that it was simply a tourist trail – which was all to the good.

After half an hour they came to a lookout point marked by a small pagoda. Below were two jade-green coves, waves foaming around their rocky promontories.

'We will have our picnic up there,' said Gao, pointing along a short, steep mud track which led to the brow of a boulder-strewn hill. 'If anyone is following, we will see them coming.'

The picnic he laid out seemed designed for an English river-bank rather than this rough, scrub-covered terrain. There were starched napkins, glasses in small wicker holders, plates with a cherry-blossom motif, and an apparently endless supply of mini-ature baskets containing spring rolls, dumplings, finely chopped vegetables and warm rice. To Christophe there was something surreal about sharing this al fresco banquet while he and Amy were fleeing from the whole might of the Chinese government. Around them the grass fizzed with the noise of insects, as if it were wired to the power station below. The sun pushed weakly through the haze.

He shifted his position, feeling his leg starting to go to sleep. As he put his hand down on his jacket, he touched the bulk of the packet containing the syringe. What would he do with it when he got back to England? Show it, ideally, to someone who could verify Li's claims and denounce the Mulberry Tree project: but who did he know with both the requisite scientific knowledge and the courage to take on the government?

'Stop it,' he thought. 'You're getting ahead of yourself again.' There would be time to think about such things on the journey home.

He was relieved when Gao began to pack away the picnic things.

'It is time to go now. I hope you are feeling revived, Amy?'

Before she could answer, a deeper sound cut through the insects' chatter. A helicopter swung into view as if from nowhere. It swooped over them, windows glinting; paused for a moment above the pagoda, then turned right-handed towards the power station. Amy sprang to her feet with a cry, then appeared to lose her balance. Christophe caught her just before she hit the ground.

'She's fainted,' he said.

'It must have been the shock of seeing the helicopter.'

'Either that or she's exhausted herself.' Christophe felt furious with Gao for getting them into this situation, and furious for himself for going along with the plan.

Slowly, Amy began to revive. Gao peered at her.

'Is she all right?'

'I hope so. We should never have bought her on this hike. We should have hired a boat to take us to Sok Kwu Wan.'

'The fewer people we deal with the better. It is dangerous to attract attention.'

Christophe was too angry to speak. How could he talk about not attracting attention, this absurd figure dressed for the Henley Regatta?

'How much further to Sok Kwu Wan?' he said at last.

'Forty minutes or so. It is mainly downhill. She should be able to manage.'

Amy gave a small groan and tried to sit up, but sank back on to the ground.

'Are you feeling sick?' asked Christophe.

'Not sick. Just tired – very tired.'

It was clear that she couldn't walk any further. There was only one solution. He would have to carry her the rest of the way.

She smelt of rosewater. Her hands locked around his neck with the little strength that they had. He thought of Sara – carrying her over the threshold of their first house, and years later up the stairs after her knee operation. But there was no time to dwell on the memory.

The path wound downwards for several hundred yards, then began to curve up again. On either side stood boulders graffitied with Chinese characters. The ground to their right dropped sharply towards the sea.

Little as Amy weighed, the going wasn't easy. Christophe felt himself breaking into a sweat. Ahead lay a line of trees which he hoped would give some shade. Behind them Gao laboured under the weight of the holdall and the picnic basket.

Suddenly they heard the helicopter coming back.

Christophe quickened his pace. They reached the trees just before the helicopter came into view.

'Do you think they're after us?' he asked Gao.

'Who can say?' He put down the picnic basket and wiped his forehead with his handkerchief. 'We must pray not.'

The shelter of the trees stretched for some way in front of them. A short distance ahead the path forked, one arm of the signpost reading 'Sok Kwu Wan: 30 minutes'.

'I have an idea,' said Gao. 'I shall walk ahead. If they have been looking for you, they will perhaps think you have gone the other way. After half an hour you follow me.'

Christophe looked at the sun. It was dropping towards the sea. 'Will that give us enough time?'

'Yes, enough time.'

Christophe hesitated.

'All right,' he said. 'Where will we meet you?'

'I will wait at one of the restaurants on the waterside. I will look out for you.'

Christophe set Amy down with her back to a tree. He watched Gao disappear from sight. The noise of the helicopter faded.

'How are you doing?' he asked Amy.

'Still very tired. Perhaps I'll sleep for a little.'

She dozed off almost immediately. It was a strange intimacy, the two of them alone in this quiet, dangerous place, killing time.

He heard voices in the distance. They were coming from the path ahead. Whoever they belonged to, it wasn't wise to stay here. Perhaps further along the track there would be a hiding place. He picked Amy up as gently as he could and began walking.

As the trees thinned, Sok Kwu Wan came into view. A mountain rose steeply behind it. In the centre of the bay was a cluster of rafts and boats, and on the near shore an enormous white silo with a steel jetty stretching into the water. A strong breeze blew from its direction, agitating the trees behind him.

There was a turning ahead, the signpost this time pointing to another look-out point a hundred yards away. Covering the ground as quickly as he could, he found a deserted pavilion. He left Amy stretched out with his jacket for a pillow, and stole back along the track until he had sight of the main path.

Two figures were walking up it, moving quickly, deep in conversation. Christophe recognised the couple who had sat in front of him on the ferry.

What were they doing? It was possible that they had walked to Sok Kwu Wan and started back again; but if so, they could only have spent a few minutes in the village. Day trippers would surely have stayed longer and taken the ferry directly back to Hong

Kong. He could only conclude that they were looking for something – or someone.

He waited until they were out of sight, then hurried back to Amy. No good could come of hanging around here: Gao might only have fifteen minutes' start on them, but it would have to do.

Amy had woken up. 'I guess I fell fast asleep,' she said. 'Not up to much, am I?'

'You're doing really well. There isn't very much further to go. I think we should press on if you can manage it.'

He gathered her to him.

'Christophe,' she said as she closed her arms around his neck.

'Yes?'

'You mustn't let me hold you back. If you have a chance to get away on your own, you must take it. You've done quite enough for me already.'

The idea of abandoning her hadn't crossed his mind; he felt touched, but also chastened. Touched that in her feeble state she could find the strength to worry about him; chastened by the idea that she had thought him capable of desertion. It was as if she saw a flaw in his heart that he had tried to bury – a propensity for failing those who needed him.

The path dropped steeply down towards the sea. Christophe concentrated on his footing, trying not to think about the couple and who they might be reporting to.

At the bottom of the hill the path skirted a small group of huts, their corrugated iron roofs weighted with rocks and driftwood. Beyond lay a grassy open space with a school on the far side of it. Christophe's eyes scanned his surroundings intently, looking for places to hide if necessary. For the time being there was no sign of life.

At last they came to the edge of the bay. A small, rough beach spread out at their feet. In the far distance the towers of Hong Kong rose into the haze.

Although Sok Kwu Wan lay directly ahead, the only way to reach it was to follow the curve of the bay all the way round, in clear view of anyone on the other side. Christophe set Amy down.

'Do you think you might be able to walk now?' He judged the distance to be about a quarter of a mile. 'It's just that we're likely to draw attention to ourselves if I carry you.'

'I'll try.'

She moved more slowly than he would have thought possible. Putting his arm around her waist to support her, he felt like a crab inching its way sideways along the strand.

'Sorry,' she said every few steps. 'Sorry.'

' "Never apologise, never explain". Who said that?'

'I don't know.'

'Someone with very bad manners, I imagine. But in this case – really, don't apologise.'

'Sorry.'

They laughed.

'Sizzling king prawns with ginger,' he said. 'That's what I'd like for supper.'

'Cherrystone clams straight from the sea. My grandmother cooked those better than anyone.'

From a distance, he thought, they must look like lovers, holding each other so close, talking so easily.

They came at last to a bridge where a small river ran into the harbour. The grey of the sky darkened into twilight as they walked; the lights of the restaurants, and Hong Kong in the distance, grew brighter.

On the outskirts of the village was a temple guarded by stone lions. An old lady watched them from an empty café as they entered the single street which ran the length of the waterfront.

The restaurants were much as he remembered them: a series of large, open-sided rectangles, divided by steel railings and distinguishable from each other mainly by the colour of their plastic chairs and tablecloths. The smarter ones had tiled floors, the rest concrete; the steel roofs were studded with ceiling fans and fluorescent lights which brightened the dark looking-glass of the bay. Clear plastic sheeting across the front protected customers from the wind. On the other side of the narrow street were the kitchens, with tanks of shellfish to tempt passers-by: bamboo clams; jumbo scallops; enormous red crabs, their claws bound pathetically with twine.

Christophe thought of the first time he had come here, on a junk with a party of spoiled young expatriates, long before the handover of Hong Kong. Where were they now, those girls called Debs and Hilary, with their turned-up shirt collars and their pearls? He wondered whether he would recognise them if he met them again; he wondered whether they would remember him. So much had happened since then – marriage, fatherhood, bereavement. But here he was again, in the company of another young woman, with the dusk gathering and who knew what in store for them.

'If you could just hold my hand,' said Amy, 'I think I'll be able to manage.'

They found Gao at the third restaurant along, drinking a beer. His face was shiny with sweat. From time to time he would give a vigorous rub to his left arm. He must have strained it carrying the holdall.

'You had no problems?' asked Gao.

Christophe told him about the couple from the ferry.

'I passed them,' said Gao, 'but their behaviour did not seem suspicious.'

'Then maybe we have nothing to worry about.'

'Maybe.'

'When will our contact be here?'

'Any moment.'

Christophe ordered a beer for himself and tea for Amy. As they waited, he noted the lay-out of the strange floating community which sprawled along the waterfront. At the corner of the restaurant, concrete steps led down to a narrow pontoon of weathered planks bolted together and weighted with concrete blocks. At the end of it lay a large raft of similar construction, divided into open squares – containing, presumably, the cages in which the fish farmers kept their stock. On each side of the raft were moored half a dozen dinghies with outboard motors, while beyond were two other small craft – a sampan and a miniature pleasure boat with a gaily striped awning. Further away, their outlines fading as the darkness thickened, were other rafts surrounded by similar clusters, the larger ones with huts boldly numbered in white paint. It looked like a chaos of flotsam and jetsam, but clearly worked to some kind of system which a stranger could not fathom.

His beer arrived. At the same time he noticed a young man making his way across the restaurant towards them.

He wore jeans, white trainers, a red polo shirt with a Lacoste crocodile on the breast, and white trainers; a watch with a strap like a tank tread weighed down his wrist, and a pair of sunglasses balanced on his slicked-back hair.

'Hi,' he said, giving Christophe a strong handshake, 'I'm Quentin.'

Christophe had come across plenty of Chinese who had adopted Western names for their dealings with the outside world, but none whose choice seemed as far-fetched as this one.

'Is everything prepared?' asked Gao.

'Sure. I got a full tank of gas. You say the word and we kick ass.' He grinned.

'Has our man on the ship sent confirmation?'

'One hour ago. Soon as we are outside Chinese territorial waters, a tender will come to meet us. No problem.'

'Very good. I suggest that we get going.'

'No need to hurry.' Quentin signalled to the waiter for an extra beer. 'No point in being early. Maybe I get something to eat.'

The chorus of an Eighties pop song sounded in his pocket. Quentin pulled out his mobile, checked the screen, and stood up to take the call, wandering towards the entrance of the restaurant.

Gao took an envelope from his jacket and passed it quickly to Christophe.

'This is money to give Quentin when you reach the rendezvous – not before. He has been paid half in advance. If he gives you any trouble, tell him you will drop it in the sea. I will accompany you as far as his boat.'

'So he's not part of the brotherhood?' said Amy.

'No, but he has helped us on several occasions. I think this is good business for him, so there should not be a problem. But you should be careful all the same.'

Christophe did his best to hide his annoyance. The coming hours promised to be difficult enough without a skipper who was only half trustworthy.

'I hope this is not your money,' he said. 'You must tell me how I can repay it when I get home.'

'Please don't worry. We have many contributors to our funds. I know you do important work for the brotherhood. It is right that we should cover your expenses.'

'You're very kind, but – '

He broke off. A police launch had appeared beside the furthest raft and was sweeping it with a searchlight.

'Is that usual?' he asked.

Gao followed his gaze. 'I have no idea. Perhaps Quentin can tell us.'

Quentin returned.

'Should we be worried about that police boat?' asked Christophe.

Quentin grinned. 'You leave the worrying to me, boss.'

Gao was rubbing his arm again.

'Are you OK?' asked Christophe.

'Just a bit of stiffness. I had an injection yesterday: an inoculation against hay fever. The strange thing is that I have never had hay fever in my life, so I don't know why the doctor insisted on it. But better safe than sorry, I suppose.'

Christophe stared at him. He felt the syringe in his pocket; then he looked across at the police boat, drawing slowly nearer, and was filled with a terrible realisation.

'Gao,' he said in a low, urgent voice, 'the police are following you. We have to split up. You finish your drink, then head back to the mainland. Amy and I need to get to Quentin's boat as quickly as possible.'

Gao looked bewildered. 'How do you know this?'

'It's something somebody told me on the train from Beijing. I've only just put two and two together. You need to keep your head down, and above all don't contact any member of the brotherhood. You'll only compromise yourself and them.'

He got to his feet.

'Thank you for all you've done,' he said. 'Quentin, we must get out of here.'

A white glare filled the restaurant. The launch was coming in to land.

'Let's go,' said Quentin.

He set off down the concrete steps on to the pontoon.

Christophe looked at Amy. There was no way she would be able to manage such a precarious journey.

'Leave me,' she said.

He shook his head. 'No, absolutely not. I'm going to give you a fireman's lift. Ready?'

He knelt to take her on his shoulder. As he straightened up, he took a last glance at the lonely figure of Gao Liang, nervously sipping his glass of beer.

In the minutes that followed, Christophe had reason to be grateful for his uncle's tightrope lessons. Even in broad daylight the obstacle course stretching ahead would have challenged his sense of balance; in the half-darkness it was a nightmare. There was nothing that amounted to an even surface: planks sagged or were nailed on top of each other in a manner apparently designed to trip the unwary. The yawning gaps could only be gauged by light glinting on the water. Prows of boats rose suddenly in front of him; ropes waited to entangle his feet. Quentin, meanwhile, moved easily and quickly, so that Christophe was forced to keep looking up in order to follow him. And all the time the raft and its makeshift walkways dipped and rose with the motion of the water.

More than once Christophe missed his footing and hung in space fighting to regain his equilibrium – only to find when he finally succeeded that Quentin had disappeared from view. Then there would be a moment of confusion as his eyes searched the dusk for his guide's silhouette, before the dangerous pursuit began again. He couldn't afford to think about what might happen if he slipped – Amy's delicate body crushed against a spar or her head striking a gunwale as she keeled into the water . . .

At last Quentin stopped beside a cluster of oil drums. He paused to let Christophe catch up.

'You wait here.'

Christophe watched as Quentin crossed to one of the floating huts. Then he eased Amy off his shoulder.

'You OK?' he asked.

'I'm fine. You'd make a first-rate fireman.'

Quentin was talking to a small figure who sat crouched on an upturned crate, working on a fishing net by the light of a hurricane lamp. He was an old man with cropped white hair and a beard that reached his scrawny chest; he wore a pair of shorts and black wellington boots. The two whispered together for what seemed to Christophe a very long time.

At last Quentin called them over. 'My friend says there are more police patrols than usual tonight.'

'Does that mean it's too risky to go out?' asked Amy.

Quentin laughed. 'Don't worry, you OK with me. Quentin can outsmart any policeman any day. But we got to time it right: got to wait for everything to calm down a bit.'

'How long do you think that will take?' asked Christophe.

'Maybe one hour.'

'Can we afford that? Suppose the police are interrogating Gao Liang now?'

'I think maybe they take him back to the mainland to do that. Maybe they not pick him up at all.'

'And how long will the ship wait for us?'

'It will be in reach for the next ninety minutes.'

'So we may only have thirty minutes' leeway.'

'It will be enough. Trust me.'

'And in the meantime,' said Amy, 'we wait here?'

'Best place for you to hide is in my boat.'

Quentin pointed to a tarpaulin-covered speedboat moored a short distance from the raft. It was so small that it was hard to see what hiding place it could contain.

The old man pulled it in with a boathook; Christophe read the name *Ocean Spirit* as it floated towards them. Quentin detached the tarpaulin and arranged it carefully over the back seat.

'You hide under there.'

Christophe looked at Amy. 'Are you all right with this?'

'We don't have much choice, do we?'

'I'll get in first. Then Quentin can hand you down to me.'

Once she was on board he lay down, arranging himself as best he could to protect her from hard edges. She settled herself against him, and Quentin drew the heavy, abrasive, salt-smelling tarpaulin over them.

'Are you comfortable?' Christophe asked.

'OK. Your elbow is digging into my back. You could maybe put your arm around me instead.'

So Christophe put his arm around her and held her as he had held no woman for five years. It wasn't the same as holding Sara: Amy was skinnier, less soft to the touch. And yet – to feel this woman's warmth, smell her scent, hear her breathing . . . all this was a reminder of things as they should be, a moment of normality after the strange days and nights of living as a fugitive.

He must have dozed, because when he next looked at his watch he saw that almost an hour had passed. He began to push the tarpaulin aside and struggle to his feet, only to be shoved violently back on to the seat.

'Stay down!' hissed Quentin's voice.

Christophe heard the noise of an approaching engine. A flash of light reached him through a gap in the tarpaulin; the engine slowed, and a shouted conversation took place above it, in words he was unable to make out.

'What's happening?' whispered Amy.

'I'm not sure,' said Christophe, though he was almost certain that the vessel was a police boat. There was nothing to be gained from sharing his unease.

The conversation dragged on. The throb of the engine seemed to fill his body and dismantle his bones, pulling him apart gradually, sinew by sinew. Just as he thought he could stand it no longer, the words stopped, the engine revved, and the *Ocean Spirit* was rocked by the other boat's wake.

'We give them five minutes,' whispered Quentin.

Christophe felt the little time left to them steadily seeping away. The consequences of missing their rendezvous didn't bear thinking about. The ship – wherever it was bound – was unlikely to come back for another try.

'OK, let's go.' Quentin pulled the tarpaulin aside and dragged it on to the raft, where the old man started to fold it. 'No point in carrying extra weight.'

He fired the engine, and the boat began to nose its way out from among the rafts. Someone shouted in Mandarin that it wasn't showing any lights; Quentin spat a curse in reply. He seemed well used to finding his way in the dark.

Once the way ahead was clear, Quentin opened the engine to full throttle. Its noise ripped at Christophe's ears as the boat shot forward.

The lights of Sok Kwu Wan shrank rapidly, until they were as tiny as those of the Hong Kong skyline far ahead. A strong following breeze helped the boat on its way. But beyond the shelter of the bay the wind took on a savage aspect. Christophe felt himself buffeted by one gust after another; sheets of spray engulfed him, soaking through his shirt and jeans. He reached out to put an arm around Amy. The moonlight showed high, white-peaked waves rising around them as the boat lurched and laboured from ridge to ridge.

'Force six, maybe force seven,' shouted Quentin. 'Good for us – keep patrol boats in the harbour.'

Christophe didn't share his verdict. The wildness of the sea might reduce the chances of pursuit, but it was also slowing the speedboat's progress. Would they reach the rendezvous in time? And if they did, how were they to board the ship?

'Life jackets!' he shouted to Quentin. 'Have you got any life jackets?'

'No life jackets – sorry! We need to bail! You take the wheel – I find bucket.'

Christophe's experience of small boats came mainly from holidays in Norfolk as a teenager. No craft he had come across there had been anything like as powerful as this one: the thrust from the engine pushed the speedboat's nose so sharply upwards that it all but blocked his view of the sea ahead. How Quentin had been able to stay on course he had no idea.

'OK – now you bail!'

Christophe stepped aside to let Quentin take the wheel; but at the last moment something glimpsed out of the corner of his eye made him think better of it.

The other boat loomed out of the spray without warning. Like the *Ocean Spirit* it showed no lights; if not for the moon, Christophe wouldn't have seen it at all. As it was, he had only a second to twist the wheel with all his might, wrenching it to starboard. The *Ocean Spirit* slewed sideways, missing the oncoming boat by barely a metre.

'What the hell was that?' he shouted.

'Coastguards!' Quentin seized the wheel. 'Bail! Bail or we f–ing dead!'

Christophe grabbed the bucket. Behind them the coastguard vessel – twice the size of theirs – had taken longer to react; now it too was turning. 'What's it doing here?' he wondered. 'Were we just unlucky, or was it waiting for us?'

There was no telling. All he could do was bail and hope that Quentin knew what he was doing.

A betting man would have put his money on the coastguards. The *Ocean Spirit* had a good start on its pursuers, and its skipper steered with confidence, hugging the ridges and leaping the troughs like a surfer; but the boat behind was heavier, and so better equipped to deal with the rough sea. Its searchlight glared brighter as the distance between the two started to shrink.

Quentin showed no sign of panic. 'We know where we going,' he shouted. 'They don't – so they got to follow us. Hang on!'

He threw the *Ocean Spirit* into a tight turn. As it veered away, skimming across the moonlit water, the coastguards' boat moved ponderously to give chase.

'Five minutes,' he shouted, squinting at the GPS monitor in front of him. 'Almost in international waters. Rendezvous boat up ahead.'

He pointed. At first Christophe could see nothing; then he made out a large, slowly moving ship, marked out by four long rows of lights.

But as he did so, he became aware of another ship taking shape in the darkness: a ship so colossal that his senses almost failed to register it. It was a tanker – and its course was taking it directly between the *Ocean Spirit* and its rendezvous.

The choice facing Quentin was clear. He could head across the bows of the tanker in the hope of outpacing it, or he could turn in the other direction and try to pass behind it. If he chose the first, and misjudged it, the *Ocean Spirit* would be crushed like a beetle under a shoe. If he chose the second, the tanker would become a steel wall between the speedboat and the open sea, giving the coastguards every chance to catch him.

Quentin chose the first. Changing course again, he turned the boat to port and sent it hurtling on a trajectory to cross the tanker's path.

Christophe's familiarity with tankers was slight, but he knew that if anyone on the bridge spotted the *Ocean Spirit* heading for a collision, there would be nothing on earth they could do about it. And if they didn't see it, they would be quite unaware of the vessel being carved in two beneath them.

As the great hulk came nearer, blotting out the world beyond it, Christophe's heart began to race at a speed which seemed unsustainable. Beside him Quentin, rigid with concentration, was unrecognisable as the laid-back figure from the restaurant. Behind them the coastguards had slowed their pursuit: their quarry's fate was now in other hands.

The tanker was fifty yards away when Christophe saw the hopelessness of their position. The great ship's momentum was carrying it faster than he had realised; the ground that the *Ocean Spirit* was gaining was inadequate, its angle of approach too narrow.

'Forget it!' he shouted. 'We haven't got enough speed!'

But Quentin made no reply. His hands clenched the wheel as if it had become part of him; he seemed not to see the vastness of the vessel ahead. It was as if he had reduced the danger of death to an abstract formula. The speedboat forged on.

'Do I jump?' thought Christophe. This was the moment to do it. But something he could never adequately explain – fear, reluctance to abandon Amy, or Quentin's overwhelming confidence – prevented him; and as he closed his eyes and prayed, the speedboat crossed the tanker's path with ten yards to spare, and carried them into international waters to make their rendezvous.

CHAPTER NINE

Shivering in the darkness of a copse in northern France, Ibrahim Kalil pulled out a torch and checked his few possessions. The old backpack picked off a skip was an improvement on the crude bundle he had brought from Morocco, but the stitching was beginning to give way and he worried about something falling out. So he arranged his two spare T-shirts – grease-stained but still serviceable – as an inner lining, and knotted the smaller items (cigarettes, soap, a bar of chocolate) together in a plastic bag. Then he stood up and slipped his arms through the shoulder straps. Having his hands free would give him an inestimable advantage.

He prayed that his attempt to reach England would be successful. His journey, begun six months before, had been a dangerous one. He had left his family tearfully in Fez, promising that when he found prosperity in Europe he would send for them to join him. On the north coast he had paid most of his savings to a surly, hard-eyed people-smuggler for the privilege of cramming on to a small, unseaworthy boat to make the crossing to Spain – a crossing which, though short, had seemed interminable. When, soaked and shaking, he had finally waded ashore, he had not given thanks for his deliverance but cursed himself for his folly.

He thought better of spending what remained of his money on a bus to the nearest city, where he was more than likely to be picked up by the police. Instead, falling in with two brothers whose information seemed more reliable than his, he found temporary work on a vegetable farm, tending tomatoes with chemical sprays in stiflingly hot polytunnels. The pay was poor and the conditions were atrocious: he soon developed breathing difficulties which prompted the farmer – horrified by the prospect of a death on his premises and the inevitable police enquiries – to drive him off his land in the middle of a humid, thundery night.

But Ibrahim had been there long enough to save the money he needed for the next leg of his journey, northwards across Spain as part of a lorry's illegal cargo, and then over the Pyrenees to France. To the men in the polytunnels Britain was the promised land: less stringent in its immigration policies than the Continental countries, astonishingly open-handed with its social welfare; and so Ibrahim had settled upon England as his final destination. Now, close enough to the Channel Tunnel to see the trains from Paris racing towards it, he felt himself almost at the end of his odyssey.

'Ten minutes,' said Habib, the big Tunisian who had befriended him, holding up ten fingers. Ibrahim nodded.

He had not been sorry to leave the makeshift camp nearby. In the two weeks he had spent there, he had seen terrible things. The police raids had been bad enough – the dazzle of headlights from heavy 4x4s, the barking of Alsatians, black shapes in riot gear wielding batons indiscriminately, people being handcuffed and driven away: all these were a chilling reminder that he was non-person here, outside the protection of the law. But the immigrants had wrought greater terror among themselves: a Nigerian had knifed an Albanian, who would have died but for an old man who'd once been a medical orderly; a girl had arrived one night and vanished before morning, leaving rumours of rape and abduction.

The attempted breakthrough to the Channel Tunnel was a nightly ritual. The tall fences – floodlit and energetically patrolled – were the chief obstacle; if you could get past those, you could hope to stow away on a train bound for England. A brave few had tried journeying into the tunnel on foot; none had been known to reach the other end alive and undetected.

Up until now Ibrahim and his friends had been unlucky: they had only had to approach the outer fence for a patrol to appear and chase them off. But tonight he felt optimistic. Habib and his cousin Walid had obtained the services of the Mesh Man.

The Mesh Man – nationality unknown, for he spoke half a dozen languages, none of them fluently – was even larger than Habib. He also carried a formidable array of equipment, including a pair of wire-cutters which he wielded with unrivalled expertise. If anyone could give you access to the Channel Tunnel, the Mesh Man could.

'Somebody once asked him why he didn't go through himself,' Habib had reported. 'He shrugged and said, "And do what? It's not like there are illegals trying to escape from Britain." '

It started to rain. 'Is that good or bad?' Ibrahim wondered. Perhaps it would make the perimeter guards less rigorous in their patrolling; perhaps it would make the Mesh Man's job harder, his cutters slipping on the wet wire. Allah would decide.

The Mesh Man muttered something to Habib, who turned and gave his two companions the thumbs up.

'Time to go,' he whispered.

The Mesh Man led the way. Habib followed, then Ibrahim. Walid brought up the rear. The field they had to cross was planted with a crop Ibrahim didn't recognise. It came up to his chest – alone, he would certainly have lost his bearings.

The dark vegetation rustled noisily against them as if intent on alerting a patrol.

'Perhaps they will mistake it for the wind,' thought Ibrahim. 'Please let them mistake it for the wind.'

The going was difficult, the ground uneven and invisible beneath their feet. Ibrahim stumbled more than once, almost bringing Habib down with him. It was a relief to reach the far side of the field; they stopped to draw breath on the edge of the flood-lit strip which separated them from the tunnel's fortifications.

The fences were not the only obstacle. First there was a belt of razor wire, so sharp and cunning that a man could slash himself to pieces on it. But the thickset figure with the wire-cutters applied himself confidently, severing one strand after another, the muscles in his arms and neck moving rhythmically in the glare of the lights. He made equally short work of the first three fences.

The fourth and last was a wire skeleton stretching as far as the eye could see. Beyond it railway tracks, arc lamps and cables defined a no-man's land wholly indifferent to the fugitives. But to Ibrahim they signalled a new world – one in which he would be free to live in comfort and prosperity.

Then, suddenly, they were spotted. They heard the shouting of guards and the barking of dogs; uniformed men were racing towards them along the open ground. The intruders had only a moment to make up their minds: they could go back the way they had come, or they could try to squeeze through the gap.

For their guide there was no such dilemma. Grasping his clippers, the Mesh Man turned and raced back the way he had come. Habib and Walid followed.

But Ibrahim was not ready to give up. He threw himself at the half-cut opening and began to wriggle this way through.

He moved quickly, but not quickly enough. Just when he thought he had made it, a pair of hands grabbed him by the ankles and began to drag him backwards. His attempts to kick free were in vain: a minute later he was handcuffed and dragged towards a van.

The patrol radioed for a repair team to come and make good the fence, which they did with commendable efficiency; but not before a mangy-looking vixen had slipped through it and disappeared into the depths of the Channel Tunnel.

II

The following morning, Christophe Hardy sat on the first Eurostar of the day as it began its headlong charge across the English countryside towards London. He had little enthusiasm for trains after his journey in China, but he couldn't have boarded a plane with the hypodermic syringe in his hand luggage, and he would not risk consigning it to the hold.

Since leaving Hong Kong he seemed to have stepped into a parallel universe. At one moment he and Amy had been fugitives, risking their lives in an open boat; at the next they had been helped aboard the most luxurious vessel Christophe had ever seen. The double-height lobby with its spiral staircase belonged in a Hollywood musical; the wall opposite it was given over to a silvery waterfall, tumbling from high above his head into a pool of exotic fish. As for his cabin, the sight of the enormous bed and marble-floored bathroom made him feel like a story-book knight inveigled by an enchantress with a flair for interior design.

Whoever had arranged his escape seemed to have thought of everything. A parcel of clothes had been left for him in his cabin; in the purser's safe was a sealed envelope containing a credit card and a letter which told him that he was booked on the ship as far as Piraeus. There was no signature, just an email address he could contact if necessary.

His first priority was to contact his son Ben, to whom he spoke – with a rush of joy and relief – on a surprisingly clear radio connection. Next he emailed his friends to reassure them that he was all right. And then he started to consider what to do with the syringe.

How could he alert the people of Britain to their government's plan? An Opposition MP was the obvious starting point, but Christophe was not inclined to trust politicians of any variety. The media, then – he had had dealings with a number of journalists over the Brothers of Light. But they were all religious correspondents, whose chief interest was in the Church of England's doctrinal cheeseparing. He doubted that they had the stomach for a difficult and dangerous fight.

It was Ben who came up with the suggestion of Tessa Traherne.

'The thing is, Dad, you know where you stand with Tessa,' he said on the evening of Christophe's arrival in Paris. 'She's obviously got a real nose for news, and apparently her editor thinks she's the best thing since sliced bread; but she's also got loads of integrity. If this story – whatever it is – can only be given to someone you trust, she's your girl.'

Christophe had wanted to tell Ben every detail of his adventures, but reckoned that the less he knew the better. So he had merely indicated that his work with the Brothers had attracted the attention of the Chinese authorities, and he had had to leave the country in a hurry; now he wanted to expose some underhand dealings between the governments in London and Beijing.

But if he was unwilling to compromise Ben, what about Tessa? He had known her since she was twelve years old; her parents were still neighbours in Gloucestershire. He didn't like to think of that charming, unusually friendly adolescent being pursued by those who enforced the will of the Establishment.

But Tessa was no longer an adolescent: she was a capable, ambitious young woman of twenty-four. Would she thank him for standing between her and the biggest story of her career? He didn't think so.

He wondered how safe his own situation was. If Li had told his superiors that a British citizen was aware of the Mulberry Tree project, and they had passed the news to London, the enforcers might already be looking out for him. The sooner he unburdened himself of his secret the better.

He wondered, too, about Amy. After a week spent gathering her strength under the care of the ship's doctor, she had been met in Singapore and taken to a private hospital. An email had reached him a few days later saying that she was being well cared for and undergoing tests prior to an operation. Since then there had been no word. Would he see her again? The distance between them made it unlikely. But to know that she was all right – that at least would have been something.

'Monsieur, excuse me . . .'

It was the woman sitting across the aisle from him. He had exchanged a few words with her husband when they boarded the train in Paris, and helped put their luggage in the rack; both recently retired, they were treating themselves to their first visit to England for twenty years.

'My husband . . .' There was panic, bewilderment, in her voice. 'My husband is feeling ill.'

Christophe looked at the old man in the window seat. His face was pale and his eyes were unfocussed. He seemed only half conscious.

'I'll fetch the guard,' said Christophe. 'I'll be as quick as I can.'

He found the guard examining his fingernails in a cubbyhole three carriages along. The man listened to Christophe's story, then followed him reluctantly to the scene of the emergency. The pensioner looked even worse than he had done a few minutes before.

An appeal on the train's Tannoy brought two doctors, who laid the old man on the floor and advised that he should be taken off the train at the first opportunity. The guard went to speak to the driver, returning with the news that an unscheduled stop could be made at Ashford.

An ambulance was waiting at the station. A team of paramedics came aboard and lowered the old man on to the otherwise deserted platform. The old woman followed; Christophe passed their suitcases down to her. As he did so, the pathos of the scene struck him to the heart. How terrible, he thought, to find yourself in a strange country with your loved one at death's door, not knowing who you could depend on for help.

Pulling his own bag from the rack, he hurried after them; and as a consequence, the two strangers waiting for him at St Pancras International scanned the faces of the arriving passengers in vain.

III

'And the Chief Medical Officer – what does he say?'

The Home Secretary read from the file in front of him. ' "Inasmuch as carrier foxes have been positively identified on the French side of the Channel Tunnel, there is every possibility of the disease spreading to these shores. It is my advice that the Government should implement a programme of inoculation as a matter of urgency, commencing in the south-east of England, with the aim of immunising all except infants and the elderly – who might suffer an adverse reaction to the vaccine – as soon as possible.'

'Except infants and the elderly,' repeated the Prime Minister.

'That's a saving anyway,' said the Chancellor of the Exchequer. 'It'll have to come out of the NHS budget, of course.'

'Really, Prime Minister, I must protest – particularly since, in my view, the clinical trials have been dangerously rushed.'

'Let the Secretary of State for Health's protest be minuted.'

'She's right,' said the Head of Communications. 'It won't play well after all the cuts.'

The Chancellor glowered at him. 'And what would you suggest?'

The Prime Minister clasped his hands and looked from one to another. He liked few of his Cabinet colleagues, least of all the Chancellor, whose hunger for the top job was ill-concealed. He suspected the Deputy PM of briefing against him, and the Secretary of State for Health of leaking sensitive documents. Any of them would sell their grandmothers for two pins. That, above all, was why he must have the Mulberry Tree technology: to protect him from his own side.

'Obviously,' he said, 'we must spend whatever is necessary to protect our citizens. At the same time, it would be wrong to abandon the principles of fiscal prudence. The estimate from Dedham Vale Pharmaceuticals for supplying the vaccine would make a severe dent in the health and welfare budget. But I am pleased to say that there is an alternative.

'As you know, on my recent visit to China I discussed the fox-flu epidemic with Vice President Zhou. He told me not only that Chinese scientists have developed a vaccine of their own, but they that have invented a new kind of syringe which makes delivery of that vaccine very much cheaper. The government of the People's Republic is willing to supply us with sufficient syringes and doses of vaccine to cover the present situation at a cost twenty-five per cent below that of Dedham Vale's.'

His words met with a murmur of approval.

'How quickly can the Chinese deliver?' asked the Home Secretary.

'The first batches can be here within five weeks.'

The Home Secretary looked perturbed. 'Do you think, Prime Minister, that that is fast enough?'

It was the Prime Minister's turn to glare. 'This can't be actioned overnight. Look, we're talking about millions of doses of vaccine, and millions of syringes. I'm very clear that five weeks is an acceptable target parameter.'

'But say that an infected animal made its way through the Channel Tunnel tomorrow, and that it travelled twenty miles a day thereafter . . . The disease could reach Scotland before the inoculation programme began. If we have a company in Essex which can supply the vaccine more quickly, surely we should go with it. It might be more expensive, but at least we'll know that we've taken the most stringent measures available – and it will boost our own pharmaceutical industry.'

The Home Secretary's gift for hitting the nail on the head was an immense asset in the House. Just now the Prime Minister could have done without it.

'What you're looking at, Jack,' he said, 'is very much a worst-case scenario. First of all, a fox is highly unlikely to breach the security in place around the Channel Tunnel. Secondly, foxes are territorial animals and rarely venture outside their established habitational zones.' He was not at all sure of this point, but – the Cabinet being short of countrymen – calculated that he could get away with it. 'Thirdly, Fox Control UK has agreed to create a firewall by doubling its activities around our end of the tunnel. Even if we were to go with Dedham Vale, the vaccination programme would take three weeks to get up and running. Under the circumstances, I feel that the savings to be made from the Chinese solution heavily outweigh the supposed risks. Any more questions?'

There were none.

'Right then. Item two: increased budget for the internal security services.'

IV

The finals of the county amateur singing championships took place on a warm night in a large, poorly ventilated Victorian hall whose architect had been torn between the Pre-Raphaelite movement and the orientalism of Sir Frederick Leighton. Thus, while the entrance was Gothic and the stained-glass windows told the story of Tristan and Iseult, the tiling was rich in Arab calligraphy and the roof owed something to the Blue Mosque of Istanbul. But Matt, thirsty for objects of beauty after his long weeks in prison, had no inclination to quibble. To his desiccated soul, the hall was paradise, and he intended to do it justice by inspiring the Brackthorpe Glee Club to a zenith of harmony.

He had rehearsed twice with the club, and found himself not only welcomed but deferred to. The Bach Choir, which he had joined on a whim five years before, gave him a cachet among these small-town warblers which he could not have guessed at. The scandal of his predecessor's disappearance was soon forgotten as they launched into *Tiptoe Through the Tulips* and *Mr Blue Sky* with new confidence.

None of them knew that Matt's days were spent in a prison workshop, for the Governor, aware of the fun the press might have with the situation – 'JAILBIRD TURNS SONGBIRD'

— had threatened dire consequences if this was discovered. The role of escort had been given to McBain, a loyal, easy-going warder who enjoyed any kind of outing.

'If you're asked, say you're Dunstable's personal assistant,' the Governor instructed him. 'And if they take that to mean body-guard, so much the better: they won't bother you with any more questions.'

Matt for his part delighted in the friendly, law-abiding people who made up the glee club. To be driven out of jail in McBain's Astra was like being gathered up by Jove's eagle and delivered to halls of Olympus; and when he took his place beside his fellow singers and mingled his voice with theirs, he could almost believe himself part of a heavenly choir.

These new friends went some way towards filling the void left by Jake. His cellmate's sudden departure a fortnight earlier, follow-ing a deal between the government and the Animal Lovers' Army, had saddened Matt more than he could ever have anticipated: they had embraced each other like brothers, and Matt had even scribbled down directions to Stooks Farm, in case Jake should ever happen to be passing. Jake's place had been taken by a fellow tax rebel, but this had proved a mixed blessing: the man's ceaseless complaints about the Inland Revenue had made Matt realise that even political martyrs could be bores.

Surprisingly, the only member of the glee club Matt could imagine doing time was the Governor's daughter. Selina was a Goth, with all that that entailed: black clothes, black nail varnish, long leather coat, heavy boots, pale face, silver chains and elabo-rate piercings. How this squared with her enjoyment of close-harmony singing was unclear, suggesting the same kind of artistic dualism as the hall in which they now stood. But the other members of the club seemed to accept her, and be grateful for her role in recruiting Matt.

If Matt expected her to show him gratitude, however, he was mistaken: at the first rehearsal she had not even introduced herself. He wondered whether she felt it beneath her dignity, or thought she owed it to her father to keep her distance.

'The others don't know where you're from, and that's the way it's going to stay,' she had whispered – or rather, hissed. 'You keep your mouth shut and so will I.'

Matt regretted this hostility, because when she smiled – as she very occasionally did – she was rather beautiful. In weak moments he fantasised about her dressed in fishnet stockings and a sequinned bustier: an outfit far removed from Nikki's sexless designer underwear. Ashamed of his disloyalty, he struggled to banish his phantom seducer.

Who, though, could blame him? He was young man with a healthy sex drive, exiled from the pleasures he and his girlfriend had shared. Prison's limited alternatives did not appeal: Selina had him at a disadvantage.

As for Nikki, he had seen nothing of her since his trial. Any inclination she might have had to visit him seemed to have dissipated. In their phone conversations she stressed the demands of her work, which took her from one European capital to the next as if in mockery of Matt's immobility. The offer to pay his fine had not been repeated. Underlying every conversation was the suggestion that this was a situation purely of Matt's making, and that sticking to his principles was an act of appalling selfishness.

As the glee club prepared for its moment in front of the perspiring audience, Matt thought of the one person who had always stood by him. Fifteen years older, with none of his father's coldness or his mother's fondness for alcohol, his sister had been his true parent. She had inculcated his love of music, singing to him softly as she put him to bed and patiently overseeing his piano practice. And when he was sent to boarding school it was she, more often than not, who came to take him out for exeats, although by then she had had a son of her own.

Now she was dead – too soon, too young. Not a day went by when his thoughts didn't turn to her; his parents troubled his memory less frequently, stirring ambiguous emotions with which he preferred not to engage. For a moment, as he and the other singers filed on to the stage, he felt a chasm in his heart; and then, just as quickly, he became aware of the audience settling in their seats, and knew that he owed it to her to sing in spite of it.

They launched into *Up, Up and Away*, and from the start it was perfect. For a few minutes Matt forgot the frustrations of his life and the ignominy of his current circumstances: not merely in harmony with his colleagues, but translated to a higher plane – at one with the music of the spheres.

'Well done, everyone,' said Sidney, the plump club secretary, as they left the stage to enthusiastic applause. 'That knocked the socks off the rest of them. We're home and dry, you mark my words.' And indeed, when the judges gave their verdict, Matt found himself remounting the stage to collect the trophy. As the cameras flashed around them, he could think of nothing in life that had given him greater satisfaction.

Afterwards, backstage, Sidney opened a bottle of Prosecco.

'Fancy some bubbly, Matt?'

Matt, who had almost forgotten the taste of wine, accepted gratefully. The bubbles played on his tongue as if dancing to the music of Vivaldi.

Suddenly, in that moment of happiness, he found himself over-whelmed by its evanescence. In a matter of minutes he must leave all this and return to prison, like Faust called from his life of vain-glorious indulgence to give the devil his due. The fetid air, the sarcasm of the warders, the stark corridors, the brutal clang of metal against metal, the lack of anything colourful or generous or uplifting – Matt contemplated all these and felt his resolve buckle. He would sign the cheque, pay the fine, leave the nightmare behind, and then . . .

Then what? How could he face his friends in the knowledge that his pathetic attempt at a moral stand had fizzled out so easily? What would he have to show for thirty years on this planet except a failed career in shipbroking, and a house without roof or windows – an apt symbol for his life? In despair he raised his glass and took another swig.

He felt a hand on his own. Turning, he found himself face to face with Selina; but instead of her customary sullen stare, she was looking at him with bright, smiling eyes.

'You did well,' she said – and much to his surprise, kissed him on the cheek.

'Thanks. So did you.'

'When I think that a couple of weeks ago we were on the verge of pulling out . . . It's awesome. A dream come true.'

'It's been great. The only trouble is that in half an hour I'll be back inside in a nightmare.'

'So that's what you think of Dad's prison.'

'I'm not saying that it's worse than any other. It may be the Hotel Cipriani of prisons for all I know. But compared to this – standing here with a glass of wine, talking to a pretty girl . . .'

'Another drop, Matt?'

Sidney filled his glass and moved on.

'So you think I'm pretty?'

He stared brazenly into her eyes. Nikki was elsewhere; he had a fleeting chance to flirt with an attractive woman. He would be a fool not to take advantage.

'That's what I said.'

'So what are you going to do about it?'

His instinct was to kiss her there and then, thrusting his tongue against hers for as long as he could, drawing out the sensation to remember in days ahead. But even at this dark hour his sense of propriety – something his father had passed on to him, perhaps in lieu of love – could not quite be ignored. So instead of causing a stir among the singers of the Brackthorpe Glee Club, he said,

'There's not much I can do while your father's heavy is waiting to take me back in chains.'

'My father's heavy is fast asleep.'

She led him back on to the stage. In the far corner of the room McBain – lulled by the warmth of the summer evening and the pint he had drunk in the interval – was slumped in a chair, the last remaining member of the audience.

'Dead to the world,' said Selina. 'Come on. My car's round the back.'

And Matt, too inflamed and fuddled by alcohol to think about the consequences, followed her outside.

V

'I still don't like it,' said Jake.

Sammy gave an exasperated sigh. 'I've told you,' he said. 'The risk is so small it's not even worth thinking about. We drive in, we spray the walls with the ALA symbol, we drive out – it'll be over in less than a minute. We wear balaclavas, so it doesn't matter how many CCTV cameras they got in there. The car will be stolen, so they won't be able to trace it to us; keep your gloves on and you won't leave any marks. Once we're clear we ditch the motor and walk away – end of story. Another publicity coup for the Animal Lovers' Army, and the Old Bill running around like the Keystone bloody cops.'

'It's all right for you, Sammy. You ain't seen the inside of the slammer. I tell you, once you been in there, you ain't in no hurry to go back.

'Sounds all right to me, sharing a cell with bloody Pavarotti: I wouldn't mind a touch of the Nessun Dormas sending me to sleep at night. But the point is, all that's academic, 'cos in a highly planned operation like this one nothing is going to go wrong.'

On the face of it, Sammy's scheme was simple enough. Compared to rescuing a bear from London Zoo it should present few difficulties. But Jake's faith in Sammy was not what it had been, and so he hesitated.

'You ever stolen a car?' he asked at last.

Sammy snorted. ' 'Course I have. You're looking at Mr Grand Theft Auto. I can hot-wire a motor in my sleep.'

Jake could think of no other objections.

'All right,' he said, 'I'm in. But if there's any sign of the Old Bill, we abort the mission. OK?'

'OK.' Sammy slapped him on the back. 'Stick with me – you'll be all right.'

CHAPTER TEN

'Morning, lover. How does it feel to be on the run?'

Matt woke with a start from a dream of his cell. It must be time for slopping out, he thought; then he opened his eyes and found himself sprawled on a comfortable bed in a room without bars, looking up at a half-naked woman.

'Jesus!' he exclaimed. 'Where am I?'

'In my bedroom,' said Selina.

'Jesus!'

Throwing aside the duvet, he hurried to the window. It looked on to an apple tree whose branches were old and gnarled, its bark so overlaid with moss of the darkest green and lichen of the lightest grey that the whole cycle of growth and decay seemed gathered together in a mosaic. Its leaves were shiny with early morning rain, and through them he glimpsed the red roof of a barn. He thought he had never seen anything so beautiful.

Selina, dressed in a black T-shirt which barely reached the top of her thighs, watched him with amusement.

'You'd better keep your head down in case Dad sends the filth here.'

'What?'

'You're probably OK. I told him I last saw you backstage at the concert hall. He's got no reason to think that I aided and abetted you. If they do track us down, I'll tell him that you took me hostage – tied me up and had your wicked way with me.'

Matt stared at her aghast. 'I don't believe this. What the hell have you done? Yesterday I was an innocent victim of government persecution; now I'm an escaped prisoner and kidnapper. I could spend an extra twenty years in that God-awful place.'

'What have *I* done?' Selina looked even more amused. 'You weren't exactly unwilling: in fact, I've never been given such a seeing-to in my life. Maybe I should remind you of what you got your hands on.'

She crossed her arms and began to remove her T-shirt.

'No, no!' Matt tried to restrain her, only to find himself sprawled on top of her while she nipped at his shoulder with eager teeth. It seemed very much as if things were going to get out of control again.

'No, no, no!' He struggled to his feet, located his trousers, and retreated into a corner to pull them on.

'You might as well make the most of it. It may be your last chance for quite some time.'

He glared at her as he tugged at his zip. 'You're really enjoying this, aren't you?'

She laughed. 'Lighten up, lover.'

'A *Goth* is telling me to lighten up! Give me a break. Is this how you get your kicks – persuading your father to let his prisoners into your clutches and then watching them squirm?'

'I can't say I make a habit of it. But it is kind of fun.'

'Where are we, anyway?'

'We're in the charming village of Cleafield, about two miles from your prison.'

'Two miles?'

'It's OK. We're actually five miles closer to the prison than we were in the concert hall. The pigs will expect you to head as far away as possible, so they won't look around here. When we're ready we can hit the road.'

'We?'

'I'm the one with the car, remember? I could lend it to you, I suppose, only you're a felon – definitely not to be trusted.'

Matt sat down on the bed and stared at her in bewilderment. At one moment she seemed to be taking a sadistic pleasure in his predicament; at the next, she was offering to compromise herself to help him. All that could be said for certain was that she liked playing games.

'Suppose the police come here to question you?'

'I'll tell them I don't know anything.'

'They might want to search the house.'

'It's a possibility. But I still think you're safer here than out in the open.'

Matt knew what he ought to do. Common sense dictated that he should walk the two miles to the prison and give himself up. But at this moment he simply couldn't face it. He had experienced the thrill of freedom more intensely than ever before, and he could no more hurry back to his cell than a bird could forget how to fly.

'It's not going to do your father much good, having a prisoner escape from his care.'

She laughed again. 'What is this? Men on the run are supposed to persuade people to help them, not bombard them with reasons why they shouldn't. Dad can deal with it – it's not like you're a murderer. And I like to think that I'm doing something to undermine the fascist regime he represents.'

Matt stood up and gazed out of the window again. He realised how much he had missed the countryside in that place of concrete and steel. He thought of Stooks Farm and its surrounding fields: the corn growing thick and high at harvest, the dark furrows in the earth at ploughing time, the rustling of invisible birds in hedgerows, the disc of the setting sun breasting the nearby hills. If he could just visit it briefly, he could get a proper perspective on things. Either he would find renewed strength for his prison ordeal, or decide that enough was enough and write a cheque for his fine. The Governor would surely prefer to forget this embarrassing episode and discharge him as soon as possible.

'OK,' he said. 'Do I get some breakfast?'

'Not yet,' said Selina, crossing her arms again.

And this time Matt made no attempt to stop her.

II

'Well,' said Frank, 'this is a first. I've never hunted hounds by the seaside before.'

'Nor me,' said Anna.

'My nan remembers donkey rides on the beach when she was a kid. I suppose this is the next best thing.'

'No candy floss, though.'

'Nor toffee apples neither. I've got some brandy in the hip flask though. Fancy a nip?'

'I wouldn't mind.'

The sky was grey over the Kentish coast, but the early sun was doing its best to penetrate the clouds, giving a soft glow to their edges as the breeze dispersed them over the sea. A lark rose towards them, carolling ever higher and more faintly.

The spot where Frank and Anna stood commanded a view both of Sandwich beach and of one of Britain's finest golf courses. The club secretary had reported an infestation of foxes to the local hunt ('Snatching balls right off the greens! The sheer cussedness of it!'), and the *Frank Rides Forth* production team had recognised a story too good to miss.

'Fantastic!' Vanessa had exclaimed. 'We'll give them the works. Frank, I see you teeing off with the secretary; then, if we're lucky, a fox grabs your ball and the hunt is on. At the end of it you're back in the clubhouse being clapped on the back by all the old farts. You let them buy you a gin and tonic, which you raise to the camera with a wink – then whisper to the viewers that you'd rather have a pint of bitter any day. Maybe we get the fox's head mounted and put up over the bar next to all their trophies.'

Needless to say, it had not proved that straightforward. The club secretary was not keen to be filmed playing with a non-member – particularly one who had never before held a golf club. Worse still was the suggestion that horses might be allowed to gallop across the club's carefully tended turf. Frank for his part flatly refused to pursue his quarry in a golf cart. In the end a series of compromises had been reached, including an undertaking that Frank and Anna would ride mountain bikes and stick to the rough, while the club secretary would be shown putting successfully for a birdie at the ninth.

'To your viewing figures,' said Anna, raising the hip flask and taking a swig. 'Next thing they'll have you up in Scotland hunting in a kilt, or riding naked through the streets of Coventry.'

'I think I'll leave the Lady Godiva bit to you, thanks very much.'

'In your dreams, Peeping Tom.'

Frank shook his head and gazed out to sea. Anna was a tease and no mistake. She hadn't let him near her since that kiss in front of the fire, but kept on flirting like there was no tomorrow. He told himself he didn't mind: he'd felt suffocated by his last relationship, and six months on was in no hurry to start another. If Anna decided she was on for a roll in the hay, he certainly wouldn't say no. If she didn't, he wasn't going to lose sleep over it.

And yet he had to admit that something about her had got under his skin. Anna was in a different league from the other girls he'd known: better spoken, better dressed, in every way more sophisticated. Could he be turning into a social climber? The idea that he, who had seen his father looked down upon by toffee-nosed hunt followers, should now be guilty of the same snobbery filled him with disgust. Was it, then, a hidden instinct for revenge? He remembered an old lady who ran a knocking shop telling him of an Arab prince who only ever wanted to go with Jewish girls. Maybe having an upper-class bird would chase away all those old humiliations.

He turned to look at Anna. As he did so the sun broke through to light the gold of her hair. He felt ashamed.

The sound of distant shouting brought him back to himself. A man in grey check trousers and a purple sweater was hurrying towards them across the fairway, waving a golf club.

'Hi!' he shouted. 'Hi you!'

The man was tall and lean, with greying hair combed over a bald patch; he hobbled slightly as he walked, but covered the ground with considerable speed. Frank and Anna exchanged glances.

'What the hell do you think you're doing?' He glared at them through gold-rimmed aviator's glasses. 'Don't pretend you don't know this is private property. No one is allowed on the course at this hour – not even members, which you're clearly not.'

'Keep your hair on,' said Frank. 'We're here with the club secretary's permission, to sort out some foxes been giving him aggravation. It's all kosher.'

'Kosher?' exclaimed the man, his face becoming darker. 'Are you making fun of me?'

'No,' said Frank, bemused. 'Simply stating the facts. We have been invited on to this course by Mr Drummond, who seems to be the closest person to God around here, and will be staying for as long as may be necessary to complete our business.'

'Closest person to God!' repeated the stranger, who was now the colour of his sweater.

'We're sorry if we interrupted your game,' said Anna, smiling sweetly. 'We were told there wouldn't be anyone around, you see. As soon as we've got the lie of the land we'll start hunting. We'll be out of everyone's way as soon as we can.'

'And how long will that take?'

'A few hours I should think.'

'A few hours! Do you imagine I've got a few hours to spare hanging around a golf course?'

'Well . . .'

But the man had returned his attention to Frank.

'You say you're a huntsman?'

'What does it look like?' said Frank, indicating his riding boots and breeches. His temper was wearing thin. 'I'm not dressed like this because I'm the Archbishop of Canterbury.'

'You're not . . . you're not . . .'

'The Archbishop of Canterbury.'

The man drew himself up to his full height. 'No,' he bellowed, 'you are *not* the Archbishop of Canterbury! *I* am the Archbishop of Canterbury – or at least the Archbishop elect. I am exercising the privilege of my office to play golf on this course without interference from anyone else, and I do not intend to be twitted by a jumped-up kennel boy. I will be having words with the club secretary. Is that understood?'

And with that he turned on his heel and marched away.

'Blimey,' said Frank. 'I wouldn't want to meet the Pope.'

III

Selina's car was an old but immaculate MG.

'It's beautiful,' breathed Matt. 'I don't think I've ever seen one in such good condition. Who looks after it for you?'

'God, you're a throw-back. Why do men always assume that women don't understand cars? I look after it myself, thank you very much. But you can give me a hand putting the roof down.'

This seemed a bad idea to Matt given the chill in the air, but in his embarrassment he could hardly refuse. Still wearing his borrowed polyester shirt and dinner jacket, he huddled as low as he could in the passenger seat as the car gathered speed. Bizarrely, he found himself yearning for the warmth of his cell.

But as the early mist began to lift from the landscape, and the dim outlines locked within it revealed themselves as trees and fields, he was filled with elation. The sunlight falling on the windscreen – this golden currency shared by all except the imprisoned and the bedridden – left him speechless: had he been driving, he would have pulled over and climbed out to open his arms to it. Instead, he raised a single hand in salute. To his left, as if in answer, a flock of gulls rose from a flooded meadow.

Despite its age, the MG raced along the road without complaint. Glancing at the young woman beside him, her breasts tight against her leather coat, Matt wondered whether he could truly bring himself to go back to prison – or to Nikki.

The countryside was now familiar. There was the river, straightening out as it approached the old mill; the steep pasture dividing two swathes of woodland; the rundown roadside inn with its banner advertising steak lunches; the isolated church which he could see from the top of his barn.

'It's the next exit,' he shouted above the noise of the engine. 'Just a couple of miles to go.'

He thought it unlikely that the police would be waiting for him – the address on their records was his town house, and twenty-four-hour surveillance was surely not something they could afford in the case of a non-violent escaped prisoner. If they were, he didn't intend to run for it; if they weren't, he would enjoy the farm's peace for a few hours at least.

The dual carriageway gave way to a country road. The farm track, when they reached it, was too rough for the MG, so they left it behind a hedge at the entrance to a field. The ground was dry underfoot as they walked down to the house, the cracked clay still rutted by the tyres of Matt's 4x4.

His fear was that the house might have been vandalised in his absence. Not that there was much to vandalise – but vandals had a flair for working with the most unpromising material.

A quick inspection showed nothing that had been interfered with, apart from the plastic sheeting which covered the new beams. Someone had been up a ladder repairing the leaks. Matt felt deeply touched.

'I suppose a cup of tea is too much to hope for,' said Selina.

'Leave it to me.'

One of the outhouses served as Matt's storeroom. He unlocked it with the ancient, ill-fitting key he kept under a stone in the disused pigsty. While the kettle boiled he swapped his dinner jacket for a set of working clothes. The jeans and sweatshirt were slightly damp, but comforting in their familiarity.

'Good of your great aunt to leave you all this,' said Selina, 'though she could have kept it in better nick. What was she like?'

'She was wonderful. She was one of those people who simply refused to give in to old age. She carried on doing what she wanted, and if some ailment slowed her up, she never complained – just worked around it as best she could.

'Did she have a husband?'

'No, but that didn't seem to worry her either. She was very independent. In the war she worked in factories and drove for the Army – things that a nice middle-class girl would never normally have done. Then when it was over she became involved in voluntary work – ended up running a charity for people with depression. She was interviewed by a magazine once, and the introduction said, "When you leave things to someone else to sort out, these are the people you leave them to." '

'And how come she took such a shine to you?'

Matt smiled. 'Well, I am of course extremely charming . . . And my family's very small, so she didn't have a wide choice of heirs – though I suppose she might have given the place to charity. She always liked being with young people; in fact, I think that was one of the ways she staved off old age. Instead of harking back to the past, she wanted to know what was happening now. I ended up coming here quite a lot; and if there was something she couldn't fix – which didn't happen often, because like all women she was incredibly practical – I'd sort it out for her. The real tragedy of the fire was that she lost her independence: she had to go and live in what they call "sheltered accommodation", which didn't suit her at all. She didn't complain, of course; but I think if it hadn't been for that she could have lived another ten years.'

'It sounds as if you miss her.'

'I suppose I do.' He took a sip of tea. 'And you? Do you have a large family?'

'No. I was only a child, and as soon as I left home my mum pissed off as well – now living in Yorkshire with a funny little man who restores old motorbikes. Dad just had this obsession with locking things up, and I suppose it got to her in the end: he was always repairing fences and putting bolts on doors and bars on windows – "heightened security" he called it, as if he didn't get enough of that at work. Mum found it very lowering. Now she's got a guy who takes her out in his sidecar every day, she must feel like a budgerigar that's been let out of its cage.'

'So how come you're living on your father's doorstep?'

'Someone had to keep an eye on him – he's not very good on his own. I didn't mind all the locking up; perhaps that's why I got into bondage.'

Matt raised his eyebrows. 'I think I've got some binder's twine. Fancy a roll in the hay?'

IV

In the back of his limousine, the Archbishop of York was suffering a rare moment of self-reproach. He regretted losing his temper with the two interlopers on the golf course, even though he had been well within his rights. There had long been an understanding that the incumbent at Canterbury could have the fairway to himself for an hour before it opened to club members, and he considered it essential to the dignity of his office – or rather, the office he was about to take – that such rights should be upheld. But when, on leaving, he had caught sight of the television crew in the car park, he realised that he had come close to a PR disaster. He must behave more circumspectly in future: above all, in the weeks that remained until his installation.

His years at York had been restless, as he eyed the top job with a covetousness which, had he been a Catholic, would have earned a string of penances at the confessional. Now he was taking over from a man widely considered to be a saint; but was a saint the best person to lead a 21st-century church? The answer had to be no. If Anglicanism was to survive these difficult times, it required a man who understood politics and was unafraid to make tough decisions: a man such as himself. So he had shown no hesitation when the Prime Minister sounded him out, agreeing to step into the breach if the see of Canterbury should, for whatever reason, become vacant.

When it did so rather more quickly than anticipated, he had risen to the challenge with his customary vigour. Only one other candidate had thrown his mitre into the ring – Bishop Blythe of Ely, a theologian of extraordinary intellect who could cut to the heart of any scriptural dispute. But Blythe had been too lost in his books to watch his own back, and carefully planted rumours of paedophilia soon put paid to him, leaving the field clear for his rival. The Church could not afford a long interregnum – particularly with the animal-lovers causing trouble – and the man from York had lost no time in assuming the senior archbishop's privileges and powers. All God's Creatures had been swiftly cowed (as he liked to put it) – its leaders arrested for misappropriation of funds, its junior members prosecuted under the Environmental Health Act for allowing animals into churches.

With regard to the Brothers of Light, he had followed the Prime Minister's wishes without demur. He would hold friendly talks with the Chinese Vice President on his imminent visit to London, and travel to Beijing in due course to declare his support for the government-sponsored Anglican Church. In his opinion, it was fractious foreigners who were chiefly responsible for his Communion's difficulties: if their own politicians could bring them to heel and send yes-men to the Synod, it would suit his purposes very well.

The silhouette of Canterbury Cathedral came into view. He thought of the great churchmen who had held sway there – Augustine, Lanfranc, Anselm, Thomas à Becket – and his heart rejoiced. Soon he, Justin Jones, would be numbered among them.

V

Jennifer Pettifer was feeling disempowered. She had spent the last few days training half a dozen new recruits classified as SBH (Sweet But Hopeless), and though she recognised their importance, she wished that she had been able to cut a few corners.

'The secret of a successful bureaucracy,' Jeffrey Crusham had confided in her, 'is to employ a small number of very intelligent people and a large number of rather stupid ones. The stupid ones act as a firewall, preventing the outer world from reaching the ones that matter, who can then get on with their work without danger of interference.'

Sweet But Hopeless had been a refinement of this, pioneered towards the end of his time at Wandsworth Council. 'We need *nice* people,' he had insisted. 'People who the public feel guilty about shouting at. We want our customers to forget what they're complaining about because they feel so sorry for the operative they're talking to.'

'You mean they should be educationally challenged?' Jennifer asked.

Jeffrey Crusham smiled. 'Precisely. You must remember that we are an equal-opportunities employer. Lack of intellect should not be a bar to success.'

Now, all these years later, Jennifer found herself in charge of a department with an unusually high quota of the Sweet But

Hopeless. She had argued for this on the grounds that county-council tax brought in more complaints than anything else; the automated telephone service, though programmed to cut off one call in three, could not keep every customer at bay. But even SBHs needed training, and there was no one else she trusted to enhance their evasion skills – which was why she had just spent two hours trying to drum phrases such as 'working on a partnership basis' and 'enriching customer experience' into their thick heads.

'But what does it *mean*?' they had asked.

'It doesn't *mean* anything,' she had replied in exasperation. 'That's the whole point! The crucial thing is to *sound* as if you're answering their questions, even though you're not.'

They would get the hang of it eventually, she told herself as she closed her office door and settled down to her packed lunch: cream-cheese sandwiches, a pre-sliced kiwi fruit, and – her daily treat – a chocolate truffle from Leonidas of Brussels. There had been a time when she had aspired to work in that great city, somewhere close to the heart of the European Union machine; now, in middle age, she was forced to admit that it was unlikely to happen. But though her fiefdom was small by comparison, she prided herself on running it with the stringency of an EU Commissioner. Whatever hand fate had dealt her, she was determined to play it well.

As she turned to her computer screen, an icon labelled 'Matthew Dunstable' caught her eye. She swore under her breath.

In the eighteen months since she had assumed her present role, no one had caused her quite so much annoyance as Dunstable. The fact that he was now behind bars did surprisingly little to assuage it. Certain phrases in his smart-aleck letters still had the power to torment her as she fidgeted under her duvet in the small hours of the morning. Not only had he insulted her and her department, but he had suggested that Jeffrey Crusham was ultimately responsible for his situation – a man whose shoes he was not fit to polish. Well, she would have the last laugh. She thought of the document she had assigned to one of the SBHs last week, and smiled.

She had passed his townhouse the previous day and rejoiced to see the front door still boarded up, the damage from the police raid as yet unrepaired. But what of his second property? She clicked on the icon and searched for its name.

Here it was: Stooks Farm. Surely there must be something about it that was not as it should be – a disregard for planning legislation or a failure to implement the health and safety rules. She had worked in enough different departments to feel confident of catching him out.

She consulted the map on her office wall. The farm wasn't that far away. She would go over later and take a look.

CHAPTER ELEVEN

'Ah, London! It may be the rotten heart of a discredited empire, but it still has the best shopping in the world. Don't you think so, Professor?'

'I'm sure you're right, Comrade Vice President.'

'Believe me, I am. Give me New York for culture, Geneva for quality of life, and Paris for the women. But for shopping – London wins hands down. Bond Street, Sloane Street, Burlington Arcade: those are the winning properties on the Monopoly board of life!'

'If you say so, Comrade Vice President.'

Professor Li did not feel comfortable with this conversation. He had the sense that he was being tested, and that whatever opinion he expressed would be wrong, exposing him as an undiscerning hick or a venal materialist. But then, he had never felt comfortable with the Vice President. As an academic he had witnessed a good deal of Machiavellian manoeuvring at first hand, but he recognised his colleagues as novices beside Zhou.

'Westbourne Grove,' said Zhou. 'We are almost there.'

Li peered out of the window at the stucco houses and wished that he could have gone straight to the meeting at the Ministry, instead of getting up an hour early to accommodate Zhou's lust for conspicuous consumption. He had slept badly on the plane and was still more than a little jet-lagged.

The car came to a halt outside a brand new shop front, consisting of an enormous pane of glass like the frozen surface of a swimming pool. A bodyguard opened Zhou's door while three others scanned the street. Zhou and Li were ushered into the shop, where the manager – a young man whose hair projected from his head in waxed corkscrews – was waiting to greet them.

'Good morning, gentlemen,' he said, smiling as if he had been looking forward to their visit for months, rather than being notified by the hotel concierge fifteen minutes before. 'Is there anything in particular I can help you with today?'

'Loafers,' said Zhou curtly.

'Loafers are over here, sir.' The manager led him towards some highly polished shelves. 'Perhaps with a tassel?'

Zhou shook his head. 'No tassels.'

While his superior examined the shoes, Li looked around him. He didn't need to inspect the price tags to know that this place was far out of his league. He would have liked to buy a little something for a girl he'd had his eye on at the university, but it was clear that little somethings around here cost a week's wages. When a highly made-up assistant came to hover beside him, he polished his spectacles and pretended to be interested in a rack of belts.

'Do you have a preferred colour, sir?'

Li opened his mouth to say no – but as he did so, the shop seemed to disintegrate around them.

The window went first, caving in with a terrifying crash and scattering through the air in bright knives of glass. Through it, to Li's amazement, came an enormous car, which slewed to a halt in the middle of the tiled floor, sending stands and racks and merchandising flying. There were screams of panic, cries of pain; the salesgirl next to him threw herself to the floor. But Li himself just stood there, shocked and bemused, as the doors of the car flew open and two men in balaclava helmets and army-surplus jackets jumped out.

II

'F—!' shouted Jake as he and Sammy surveyed the chaos in front of them.

This was not as it was supposed to be. The shop was not due to open for another hour – so what were all these people doing here? And not just any people. Jake's bewildered brain registered a number of men who were not only large and Chinese but armed with guns. Luckily for the intruders, two of the bodyguards were already down. One, apparently felled by flying debris, lay groaning and clutching his arm; Sammy, with great presence of mind, kicked him to make sure that he stayed there. The other was sprawled over an upturned table, apparently unconscious.

The two remaining guards were on Jake's side of the car – one just a few yards away. As the man raised his gun, Jake resorted to the only weapon at his disposal, an aerosol of paint for defacing the shop's walls. The man sank to his knees, his hands clutching his eyes.

That left just one, who might have done for Jake if he had not slipped on a carpet of broken glass. As he fell, his gun skittled across the floor towards Jake's feet. Jake stooped to pick it up.

He had never held a gun before, but the effects were instantaneous and gratifying. He didn't have to shout 'Don't move!' because everyone stopped moving anyway. They stared at him with open mouths and anxious eyes, looking – against the backdrop of the glass-strewn shop – like figures frozen by a sudden, unanticipated ice age.

'What do we do, Sammy?' he asked.

'What do we do? Get back in the f–ing car and get the hell out of here! And don't call me by my bloody name!'

But the raiders had reckoned without Zhou Zhi.

III

The Vice President was not a hero. He had been a bully at school, and had bullied his way to the top of the Party, being careful always to keep himself surrounded by thugs who could see off any physical threat. But sometimes, in the early hours of the morning, he would lie in bed sweating, imagining what his fate would be if one of his many enemies caught him with his guard down. The scenario of a kidnapping had more than once been played out in his mind, and he had long ago decided how he would behave: he would offer no resistance.

When Sammy and Jake came crashing through the shop front in their stolen SUV, it did not occur to Zhou that he might not be their target. Instead, he cursed himself for indulging in this unscheduled shopping expedition and leaving the hotel before his police escort arrived. How could he have been so stupid? The balaclavas, the army-surplus jackets – these were enough to identify the raiders as enemies of the People's Revolution. And when Zhou saw his bodyguards summarily overpowered, he knew that he was dealing with professionals.

'OK!' he shouted, raising his hands. 'You got me! I will come quietly! Professor Li, follow me.'

Sammy and Jake watched in astonishment as the two men climbed into the back of the car and lay down on the floor.

'What the f– are you doing?' exclaimed Jake. 'Oi, you two, get out of there!'

But the two Chinese only pressed themselves with even more determination to the carpet.

'What we going to do, Sammy?' asked Jake.

'Just get in the car. And don't call me Sammy!'

Jake did as he was told. Sammy threw himself into the driver's seat, put the car into reverse, and accelerated out into the road. Wrenching the steering wheel around, he headed towards Ladbroke Grove, shooting through a red traffic light.

'Get in the back!' he yelled to Jake. 'Keep that gun on them!'

'What do I do if they try to escape?'

'Hit them! We need to interrogate them. Looks to me as if they were waiting for us.'

Fingering the gun, Jake wondered what on earth he'd let himself in for.

IV

It soon became clear to Frank that he faced an impossible task. Trying to cover the golf course without straying from the rough reminded him of a problem he had once been set at school, to do with an island in the middle of the city and having to cross a set number of bridges. He would, if the hounds picked up a scent, eventually have to bike across the fairway, bringing the wrath of the club secretary down on his head and an end to the day's sport. In other words, he would only get one chance of a kill, and had better make the most of it.

He communicated his worries to Vanessa.

'Relax,' she said. 'If the old fart does lose his temper, it'll make great footage. We'll play some jaunty background music while he chases you with a putter – maybe speed it all up like *The Benny Hill Show*.'

Frank wasn't sure he liked the sound of this: it seemed to him that *Frank Rides Forth* was becoming not so much a useful introduction to foxhunting as entertainment for entertainment's sake. But at this moment he needed Vanessa's backing, so he simply nodded and said nothing.

They drew a blank at the first covert. It looked promising enough to begin with, and the production team watched gleefully as the hounds went to work against a backdrop of sea and fairway with white gulls drifting overhead. But nothing broke from the undergrowth apart from a very alarmed rabbit, and Frank eventually decided to move on.

The second covert was a very different story. No sooner had they reached it than a vixen erupted from the undergrowth in a blaze of red fur and raced in the direction of the first tee, the hounds hard on its trail. Frank and Anna set off in pursuit, giving no thought to the tyre tracks which scarred the fairway behind them.

The fox had a turn of speed such as Frank had rarely seen, and looked at first to be showing the hounds a clean pair of heels. But then something happened which turned the odds against it.

Charging around the edge of the clubhouse came a line of two dozen figures, shouting and blowing horns.

'Antis!' exclaimed Frank. 'That's all we bloody need!'

The fox, however, failed to register the hunt saboteurs as friends. Indeed, it seemed to find them more alarming than the hounds, because it changed course to avoid them, bolting along the side of the building and into the car park.

The events of the next few minutes were so chaotic that even when Frank watched the television footage afterwards he was barely able to make sense of them. To his rage and frustration, the protesters set about neutralising his hounds with pepper spray. With only Anna and an overweight security guard to help him, he had no way of protecting his yelping, increasingly frantic pack. The only thing he could do was keep hunting.

Three of the hounds had broken away from the rest, eluding the saboteurs and continuing their headlong pursuit of the fox as it scurried between rows of parked cars. Raising his horn to his lips, Frank blew a note which cut through the shouts around him like a scythe through grass.

It took the hounds less than a minute to corner the fox in a pile of dustbins. Frank caught up with them just in time for the kill – or so he thought.

The vixen should have been dealt with in an instant, reduced to torn flesh by its larger and more powerful attackers. But it soon became clear that this fox was not like other foxes. Instead of making a last attempt to evade the hounds, it flung itself at them with extraordinary ferocity. Their exultant barking gave way to yelps of pain as one after another they felt the vixen's teeth snapping at their throats.

Napoleon watching his guard retreat at Waterloo was not more astonished than Frank as he saw his hounds recoil; a moment later the fox darted between them towards safety – and as it did so Frank had an awful moment of realisation. He fumbled for his gun, then saw that Anna had hers already drawn.

'Shoot it!' he yelled. 'It's got fox flu!'

But no shot came. The fox vanished from sight with a flash of its bright tail. The saboteurs cheered.

Frank stared at Anna.

'What the f– are you playing at? You had a clear shot.'

'No I didn't. All those people –' she gestured towards the saboteurs. 'I might have hit one of them.'

'They were well out of the line of fire. And now, thanks to your concern for those idiots, the entire country is at risk from a diseased animal.'

'You don't know for sure that it was diseased.'

'Have you ever see a fox behave like that before?'

He walked across to where the three hounds were sprawled on the ground. They were covered in blood and yowled pitifully. Frank knelt beside them and examined each in turn; then he got to his feet, drew his revolver and fired three shots. The yowling stopped.

'Watchman, Boris and Raskolnikov,' he said. 'Three of my best. And you tell me that fox wasn't diseased.'

There were tears in his eyes.

'I'm sorry.'

'You're sorry. Well, tell that to Nick Llewellyn. Tell that to the government. Tell that to the millions of people whose lives you've put in danger.' He turned to look at the protesters. 'As for that bunch of maniacs . . .'

He was still holding the revolver, and for a terrible moment Anna thought he might use it on his antagonists. But seconds later a police siren sounded in the distance. The antis took to their heels.

'That's right!' Frank shouted after them. 'F– off home. And if you come near my hunt again I'll blow your f–ing heads off.'

He took a deep breath. 'Here's what we do. No one must know about that fox until I've talked to Nick Llewellyn – least of all

Vanessa. I need you to keep her off my back, and get those dead dogs out of here.'

'What are you going to do?'

'What do you think?' He took out three bullets and reloaded his pistol. 'I'm going to hunt a fox.'

V

'*Kidnapped?*' exclaimed the Prime Minister. 'In Westbourne Grove? I don't believe it.'

'I'm afraid it's true. A car rammed the front window. He was bundled into it along with his scientific adviser.'

'What about his bodyguards?'

'Overpowered. It seems to have been an exceptionally well-planned operation.'

'And the police?'

'There weren't any. He just decided to go shopping – a spur-of-the-moment thing, apparently. Didn't wait for his escort.'

'Then it can't have been well-planned.'

'Sorry, Prime Minister?'

'If he decided to go on the spur of the moment, no one could have known in advance. So they must have been watching for an opportunity – and when it came, they grabbed it.'

'Yes, Prime Minister.'

The Prime Minister reached for his glass of water. His hand was shaking.

'Do we have any idea who's behind this?'

'Not as yet.'

'Jesus Christ.'

The Prime Minister had heard, but never had cause to use, the expression 'staring into the abyss'. He murmured it now. A senior government figure abducted while the guest of another nation – wars had started over less. As for Mulberry Tree, he could kiss goodbye to that, barring a miracle.

'Get the Cabinet in here,' he said. 'And the heads of the police and the armed forces. This is a national emergency.'

VI

'This must be the place,' said Jake as the SUV bumped down a narrow track towards a half-derelict farmhouse. 'He said there was a bit of work to do on it.'

If Jake was blessed with one thing, it was an unfailing sense of direction and an ability to read maps. Thus, when Matt had wished him Godspeed from prison with instructions on how to find Stooks Farm, he had not had difficulty in committing them to memory. And when Sammy had asked him, as they sped along the motorway with their prisoners, whether he could think of anywhere they might hide out, his old cellmate's property had instantly suggested itself.

What Jake hadn't reckoned on was finding Matt at home. He stared in astonishment at the figure who walked across the yard to meet them.

'Matt! F– me! I thought you was still banged up.'

Matt laughed. 'Don't look so pleased to see me, Jake. I thought you were the police coming to take me back – so as you can imagine, your ugly mug comes as something of a surprise.'

'You mean you escaped?'

'You could say that – thanks to Selina over there.' He nodded to a figure standing in the entrance of the barn.

Jake whistled. 'You're a dark horse all right. How'd you do it?'

'It's a long story. I'll tell you over a cup of tea. Who's your friend?'

'No names,' hissed Sammy.

'An old mate.'

'Bring him in. The kettle's just boiled.'

'The thing is . . .' Jake glanced at the two men under his feet. 'We brought a couple of people with us.'

Matt peered through the car window. He registered the two figures lying on the floor and the gun in Jake's hand. He frowned.

'I think an explanation is in order,' he said.

VII

Jennifer Pettifer sat parked in a lay-by checking her map. Stooks Farm couldn't be far away now. She traced the route with her finger, then re-started the engine.

Although much of her career had been spent prying into other people's lives, she had hitherto done it at one remove. Her years as a bureaucrat had taught her to sniff her way through the mounds of information held on private individuals, building up a picture of their assets and liabilities, their foibles and their felonies. Medical records, bank records, police records: all were grist to her mill, thanks to the great catch-all known as anti-terrorist legislation. As Jeffrey Crusham had so memorably remarked, 'When we know everything, we can do anything.'

This morning's mission, however, was a new departure; and much as Jennifer loved her computer, the idea of venturing into the field gave her an unexpected frisson. She saw herself as a James Bond heroine on the trail of an international mischief-maker – and she was determined to look the part. So she had bought a pair of dark glasses from Boots and a headscarf from Marks & Spencer, along with a state-of-the-art pocket camera. Her car – a second-hand Skoda – was, perhaps, not of the glamorous variety associated with spies; but she told herself that for her purposes its anonymity was a virtue.

She had done her homework. Over a sandwich lunch, Steve from Planning and Maria from Health & Safety had given her a checklist of common misdemeanours; Steve – a maladroit giant who addressed her chummily as 'Jen' – had even offered to accompany her. But Jennifer was too well versed in inter-departmental politics to take him up on it: she had enemies who would exploit any suggestion that she had misused council resources. She had told neither Steve nor Maria the location of the property in question, and had taken a half-day holiday to pursue a crusade which the malicious might interpret as a personal vendetta.

Before setting off she spent half an hour practising with her new camera. She took photographs of her soft-toy collection, her home filing system and her laptop. Then she checked her map, donned her dark glasses, and accelerated out of her turning with an uncharacteristic disregard for the safety of oncoming vehicles.

The entrance to Stooks Farm was easily missed, and Jennifer had to execute a three-point turn in a narrow gateway to set herself right. The track down to the house seemed in good enough repair to begin with, but soon deteriorated. Jennifer abandoned her car and started to walk.

As the house came into view she began to have misgivings. However important her mission, she was technically committing an act of trespass – and for someone who lived and breathed regulations, that was no small matter. If she had not known Matthew Dunstable to be safely behind bars, she would certainly have turned back.

But once she came close enough to see the sorry state of the building, the thrill of the chase entered her blood. It seemed inconceivable that with so much work to be done, corners had not been cut or rules overlooked. Why, the very fact that she – a stranger – had been able to approach this dangerous structure unchallenged betrayed the slipshod nature of the operation. Where were the fences, the 'DANGER' signs, the notices insisting on safety boots and hard hats? Nowhere, she noted gleefully – nowhere!

Perhaps she could even get the building condemned.

Jennifer reached for her camera to record the damning scene. She was still adjusting the settings when a man walked up to her and put a gun to her head.

CHAPTER TWELVE

Dressed in silk pyjamas, Jonty Lo surveyed Eaton Square from his balcony as he cradled his morning cup of tea between delicate fingers. Below him taxis moved along the road like a restless row of dominoes; builders shouted above the noise of a cement mixer; a dog yapped from a basement. It was all too exhausting – and now this news to harass him too. He stepped back into the drawing-room, closing the French windows behind him, and sank on to the Geoffrey Bennison sofa. For a moment he felt almost middle-aged.

'Morning', in Jonty's vocabulary, was a relative term. The important part of his day began while the working man's was coming to a close. A couple of drinks parties or private views, dinner in a comfortably expensive restaurant or a West End mansion belonging to friends, followed by dancing at Annabel's or the newest fashionable club. There were few nights when he and Faye returned home before 2am.

Faye, though, moved to a different rhythm. She would be up again at seven, working out with her personal trainer, doing a little kick-boxing, breakfasting at the gym. After that came what she called her 'beauty time': a facial, a massage, a visit to the hairdresser or manicur-ist. (And Faye was beautiful: few men remained unmoved by the sight of her slim body, disproportionately large breasts, flawless skin and almond eyes as deep as a nymph-haunted pool.) Coffee with a new best friend, some shopping in Knightsbridge, a charity lunch – these were the things that occupied her while Jonty bathed, break-fasted and lingered over the newspapers. Occasionally they met at the front door as she arrived home for her siesta and he set off for a game of backgammon at his club, leaving the coast clear for one of her lovers. Otherwise it was not until the cocktail hour that they came together, exchanging the day's news before setting off once more to join the cavalcade of the rich, ambitious, beautiful, well-connected, vain, self-centred, shallow and sleazy that passed for high society.

Today, though, was different. He had been awoken two hours early by a call from the Embassy; he had forced himself to watch the television reports live from Westbourne Grove; he had received a text from Faye saying that she had cancelled her lunch and was on her way home. Emails arrived minute by minute, reporting, questioning, instructing, before crystallising into the single curt message which now occupied his screen.

He contemplated the room with its eclectic mixture of classical and oriental: the Empire furniture, Liao-dynasty ceramics, hand-printed Florentine wallpaper, marble fireplaces from an Irish castle. How lucky he was, he often told himself, to live in these sumptuous surroundings at his government's expense. Now he was being asked to earn his keep.

He reread the email from Beijing. There was no room for ambi-guity, no pretending that he had decoded it incorrectly.

'Find the revisionist traitor Zhou Zhi,' it said, 'and kill him.'

II

'You mean,' said Matt, 'that you've kidnapped two men and you don't even know who they are?'

'They're the enemy,' said Sammy. 'That's enough for me.'

'And how do you know that? Because they're Chinese?'

'Like I said, they were lying in wait for us.'

'But they weren't armed, and they surrendered at the first opportunity.'

'Stranger things have happened.'

Matt gazed at the two captives. Sammy had tied their hands behind their backs with electrical wire and forced them to kneel in front of a mouldy bale of hay in the far corner of the barn. Their dark suits had patches of dusty white where they had rubbed against the walls.

'So are you going to ask them some questions?' he said.

'As soon as Jake comes back with the gun.'

Matt looked at Selina. 'Let's get out of here,' he said. 'I'm not hanging around to become an accessory to kidnapping and threatening behaviour. Do me a favour and take me back to prison.'

Before she could answer, the door opened and a woman stumbled through it, falling in a heap on the floor. She was thin, middle-aged and bespectacled, and wore a dark blue suit with a red pussycat-bow blouse.

'She was snooping around with a camera,' said Jake. 'I reckon she's a reporter.'

Matt snorted. 'What would a reporter be doing here?'

'Search me. Maybe someone tipped her off.'

'I suppose that's a possibility. There *have* been a lot of dodgy characters around – magpies, squirrels and the like. Maybe it was one of them.'

Jake looked aggrieved. 'Don't take the mick, Matt. We're mates, ain't we?'

Matt sank down on a tea chest and put his head in his hands.

'Sorry, Jake. Yes, we're mates. It's just that when I invited you to drop in any time you were passing, I didn't expect you to show up with a trigger-happy lunatic and three members of the general public being held against their will. But I'll tell you what we're going to do: we're going to start finding out who the bloody hell these people are. You first.' He turned to the new arrival.

Jennifer Pettifer stared up at him. If this man really was Matthew Dunstable, how had he got out of prison? And what would he do if he found out who she was?

'Come on,' he said. 'I'm not going to bite.'

Jennifer gathered her courage. 'My name's Sandra Scott. I'm an estate agent. I work for Greaves & Campbell. I heard there was an interesting property here, so I thought I'd come and introduce myself.'

'I see. And who told you about this "interesting property"?'

'I don't remember. I meet so many people in my line of work.'

'But whoever it was didn't mention that the house was a ruin? Spectacular views of daylight through the roof? Charred floorboards in need of modernisation?'

'I don't remember.'

'She's lying,' said Sammy.

'Have you got a business card?' asked Matt.

'Not on me. I might have one in the car.'

'She's not going anywhere,' said Sammy.

'Then how are we going to check her story?'

'Ring her office.' Sammy turned to her. 'What's the number?'

'I . . .'

'You're wasting your time,' said Matt. 'There's no mobile signal around here.'

'Then let's take a look at this.' Snatching the camera from her hand, Sammy scrolled through the ranks of soft toys. 'I'd say business was a bit on the slow side.'

'It's a new camera. I was experimenting.'

'I'll check her car,' said Matt.

'The lock's a bit tricky. If you let me come with you . . .'

'You're not going anywhere,' said Sammy.

As Matt walked up the track jangling the woman's car keys he considered his options. He could see no advantage in staying at the farm as Sammy and Jake's accomplice – he was in enough trouble as it was. Better to take Sandra Scott's car, drive into town and hand himself in at the police station. It would mean abandoning Selina, of course – but then, her behaviour towards him had not exactly been considerate; and though they'd had amazing sex, he didn't see that as the basis for a lasting relationship. He thought of Nikki and felt consumed by guilt.

There was the car up ahead. He had expected a nippy little Mini with the estate agent's logo on the side – but no, it was a plain Skoda. Not that it made any difference. All he needed in this situation was a set of wheels.

He opened the driver's door and climbed in. As he pushed the seat back, his eye fell on a white square of plastic on the floor beside him. It was an ID card with a photograph of the middle-aged woman, and it bore the name 'Jennifer Pettifer'.

III

'Now your turn.' Sammy hauled the Vice President from his kneeling position and sat him on the bale of hay. 'Who are you?'

The Vice President blinked at him, unable to believe his ears. It didn't make sense. These men had risked their lives to kidnap him and they didn't know who he was?

'Funny joke,' he said. 'Ha ha.'

'It's no joke, sunshine.' Sammy seized him by the lapels. 'You answer the question or you'll be sorry.'

The Vice President thought desperately. If these men hadn't targeted him, what was their reason for attacking the shop? They must be ram-raiders. How would professional criminals with nothing else to show for their operation react to the news that they had an international statesman in their clutches? Demand an enormous ransom? Almost certainly.

'My name is Huang Jun,' he said. 'I am visiting England as an interpreter for a Chinese trade delegation. My colleague here is also an interpreter.'

'I see,' said Sammy. 'Pays well, does it, interpreting?'

'No, not much at all.'

'So how come you was shopping at Gucci?'

'Our delegation is here to promote the sale of Chinese leather goods. It is important for us to see the state of the luxury market.'

He was not prepared for the violence of his interrogator's response. The next thing he knew he was lying on the stone floor with Sammy's hands at his throat.

'You little yellow bastard! I know what you Chinkies are like – you've got no respect for the animal kingdom! Chihuahuas for breakfast, Dalmatians for dinner, anything you f–ing well fancy for tea. Got a cough? Let's shoot a rhino and grind up its horn. Having trouble in the bedroom department? Let's kill a tiger and string its teeth round your pecker! And as for f–ing leather goods – you've got rivers running red with the blood of poor creatures just so you can walk down the street in patent winkle-pickers! You disgust me, you murdering son of a bitch!'

'Oi, Sam, that's enough.' Jake pulled his friend back, but not before he had managed to land two kicks on the Vice President's rump. Zhou lay gasping for breath, his Armani suit covered in straw.

Jennifer Pettifer looked on in horror. If this was how these people treated innocent foreigners, what was in store for her?

IV

'You expect me to believe that, Mr Prime Minister?'

'It's the truth, Mr Ambassador. I wish it wasn't, but it is. We have absolutely no idea who abducted Vice President Zhou and Professor Li. The CCTV footage may yield some clues, but it will take time to examine it properly. Meanwhile, every police-man in the land is looking for them – you have my solemn oath on that.'

'Such a thing has never happened before.'

'No.'

'My government views the situation with extreme concern.'

'Of course, of course. It is a concern that all of us here share. We only ask that your government shows a little patience.' Beneath his grey flannel suit the Prime Minister's shirt was soaked through with sweat.

'It is easy to say that when your man is not at risk.'

'I appreciate that.'

'It is not only our man, but our whole standing in the world that we must think about. There have already been demands for retaliation. Students are demonstrating in the streets. There is talk of trade sanctions, of mobilising the army . . .'

Oh please God, no, thought the Prime Minister.

'However . . .' The ambassador pressed his fingertips together.

'Go on.'

'There is one condition on which my government is prepared to overlook your culpability.'

'Which is?'

'You must announce that this kidnapping is the work of the Brothers of Light.'

The Prime Minister was bemused. 'How do you know that?'

'It is not a question of what I know, it is a question of what the world must be led to believe.'

'It's a bit far-fetched, isn't it?'

'Not if it comes from your security services. Intercepted telephone messages, that sort of thing. I think you know the form.'

'But why would we be intercepting messages from a pacifist organisation run by priests on the other side of the world?'

'Really, Prime Minister, I do not think you are using your imagination. Let us say that you were monitoring an established terrorist group: picture your surprise at finding that it was in communication with the Brothers of Light! Or is this asking too much of you? Would you prefer that diplomats were withdrawn and our cyber experts set about targeting your military bases?'

'No, no,' said the Prime Minister hastily. 'The announcement will be made.'

'Good.' The ambassador smiled.

'But suppose the kidnappers are found and turn out to have nothing to do with the Brothers of Light?'

The ambassador smiled again. 'That, Prime Minister, is your problem.'

V

It was Selina who heard the news on Matt's beaten-up radio. She hurried to tell the others.

'The Vice President of China!' exclaimed Matt. 'I don't bloody believe it!'

'But he told us he was an interpreter,' said Jake. 'Why would he do that?'

Only Sammy was able to find a bright side to the news.

'Don't you see what this means? We have one of the biggest bargaining chips in the world! We can lay down the law to the British government *and* to the Chinese. They can start by empty-ing every zoo and every research laboratory of animals. Then there's the leather industry, the fur trade . . .'

Matt looked at him incredulously. The guy wasn't just a zealot – he was completely off his head.

'But the government doesn't know that you've got him,' said Selina. 'They think it was these guys called the Brothers of Light.'

'Then we'll telephone them and tell them otherwise.'

'They'll trace the call.'

'We'll think of something.'

Matt tried to review the situation calmly and rationally. It wasn't easy. The moment he had realised that the woman poking around his farm was his nemesis from the council, he had become consumed by thoughts of anger and revenge. Oh, the things he would like to do to her! Hang her by her ankles from one of the beams; force her to run naked round the farmyard; play a pressure hose on her in the old pig-sty.

Matt was too moderate a man to put such fantasies into effect, but one thing was certain. He could not bring himself to go meekly back to jail while this scheming, trespassing witch went unpunished; and having failed to slip away while the going was good, he was now implicated in Jake and Sammy's crime, with Jennifer Pettifer ready to play chief witness. Had it not been for her nosiness, he could perhaps have persuaded Sammy to dump the two Chinese in the middle of nowhere, and the police might never have been the wiser. Now the only answer he could see was to flee the country, leaving the Vice President and his sidekick to be found after he and Jake and Sammy were gone. But for a prisoner on the run like himself, any border was a tricky prospect; and even if he managed to escape, what would the future hold? Exile from this beautiful farm – and how Jennifer Pettifer would gloat over that!

He thought again of the news Selina had brought. The Brothers of Light: where did they come into it? Might they provide a way out?

There was only one person he could think of to ask.

VI

In Belgravia, Jonty and Faye Lo were glaring at each other across the kitchen table.

'I don't see why *we* have to do it,' said Jonty.

'It's what we're trained for.'

'So are any number of people in the service, *non*? They could have an assassin fly in from Beijing, do the job and never set foot in England again. Instead they ask us to jeopardise a cover we've spent ten years building. Where else are they going to find two people who can turn up at a drinks party at St James's Palace without alarm bells ringing? Who else knows their way around the Chelsea Flower Show, Royal Ascot, Cowes Week? When I think of the crashing bores I've wined and dined to get membership of the MCC, the Leander Club, White's – and now that's all being risked for the sake of a straightforward hit.'

'There's nothing straightforward about killing Vice President Zhou. It can only be carried out by an operative or operatives who have the total trust of the Politburo. Think of the mileage the counter-revolutionary cadre could get out of this! And how is an assassin from Chongwen going to track the kidnappers through the south of England – if that's where Zhou Zhi still is – without arousing the suspicion of everybody he meets? It's going to be hard enough for us.'

Jonty had to concede that she was right. Still, the timing could hardly have been worse. There was a party on a Russian oligarch's yacht in St Katherine's Dock tomorrow evening, and one at the American Ambassador's residence the night after – both rare opportunities to plant some listening devices.

'Do we have any leads?' he asked. 'Is there a chance they could still be in London?'

'The car the kidnappers used has been identified as a stolen Range Rover. It was caught on traffic-control cameras heading out on the M40.'

'Well, that narrows it down. You take the Midlands and I'll take Wales.'

Faye glared at him again. Of all the sacrifices she'd made for the People's Republic, living as Jonty's wife for ten years had been the greatest. She didn't share his enthusiasm for the high life – indeed, she found it profoundly suspect. But they had been put together by Beijing, and as a former actress she had quickly learnt to play the role of jet-set arm candy. The rows of invitations on their mantelpieces, and the hundreds of reports they had filed on the West's wealthiest and most influential figures, were evidence of the partnership's success.

'We'll have the colour of the car and its registration number from Scotland Yard's computers shortly,' she said. 'Once they've been fed to the surveillance satellites we'll be halfway there.'

'If they haven't abandoned the car at the first opportunity.'

'Even if they have, there will be clues. The important thing is to get to them before the police do. So you'd better get some clothes on.'

Hm, thought Jonty: the green leather driving gloves, or the red?

VII

'Tessa!'

'Hi, Christophe.'

They hugged.

Christophe looked at the tall, neatly turned-out young woman in front of him and struggled to remember the girl who had been Ben's babysitter. That was the most disconcerting thing about growing older – not the gradual slackening and greying of one's own appearance, but the emergence of a new generation doing adult jobs, leading adult lives.

'Come in,' he said. 'Good of you to come over.'

'What, all the way from Drayfield? Well, I suppose it was a bit of an effort – five miles in the car. I'll have to charge you for my petrol.'

She smiled mischievously. You couldn't call Tessa beautiful, but she had plenty of charm, and in a profession like journalism that counted for a good deal.

'How are you?' he asked. 'You're looking well.'

'Great. A bit tired – my editor's a real slave-driver – which was why I decided to come home for a few days. But it's exciting work, so I can't complain.'

'And your parents?'

'Very cross with you. They say you keep disappearing off around the world, and they haven't seen you properly for months.'

'It's true – I've been travelling a lot; China mainly. In fact, that's what I wanted to talk to you about. But first: coffee? I've just made a pot.'

'Great.'

He led the way into the kitchen. The window and back door were open, but it still smelt musty: he'd found a dead mouse in the swing-bin – a victim of misadventure, flipped into a plastic cavern from which there was no escape. The truth was that he didn't use the cottage often enough to justify the rent – or, more importantly, to look after it as it deserved. But he couldn't give it up: it was a place that Ben loved, that Sara had loved. And now and again he just needed to be somewhere where there was no one to watch his comings and goings, without a landline or internet connection or television – somewhere as near as you could get in the 21st century to being off the map.

'Milk? Sugar?'

'Just some milk. You make it by boiling cold water, right?'

'What?'

'I always remember my father telling me – "Christophe's such a purist about coffee that he never uses water from the hot tap, because it's been sitting in the tank too long. That's the French side of him." '

Christophe laughed. 'I suppose so – but it *is* the only way to do it properly.'

They sat at the big table, covered in a pale blue oilcloth of Sara's choosing, now showing unidentified, indelible yellow stains.

'Is this about the Brothers of Light?' asked Tessa.

'Yes. How did you guess?'

'I know you've been involved with them for a long time, and when I heard the news . . .'

'What news?'

'You don't know? The Chinese Vice President was kidnapped in London this morning. They're saying the Brothers of Light were responsible.'

Christophe put down his cup and stared at her. 'Who's saying that?'

'The government.'

'Good God.'

For a moment Christophe felt his life held in freeze-frame. The sunlight on the windowsill, the bright red of the coffee pot, the worn corner of linoleum by the door – these were things that would remain with him for many years.

'Could it be true?'

He shook his head. 'It's utterly impossible. The Brothers have always been opposed to violence. They're a church, for goodness sake!'

'Then why . . .'

'The Chinese government wants the world to think of the Brothers as terrorists so that it can have a free hand in suppressing them. And it looks to me as if it's got our government on its side, for reasons which . . . well, that's why I asked you here.'

She took a tape recorder out of a large bag embroidered with a cartoon cat. Christophe smiled. How many women in a macho newsroom could get away with that?

'Do you mind if I use this?' she asked.

'No, go ahead.'

Christophe related in detail the story of his flight from China. Tessa interrupted him occasionally to ask for the spellings of names and whereabouts of places. Finally, he produced the package containing the syringe.

'Here it is,' he said. 'The key to the Mulberry Tree technology. One jab from that and you can be tracked anywhere – by satellite, by CCTV, via your telephone, through your computer. There will be literally no hiding place.'

Tessa stared at it. 'Fox flu,' she said at last.

'Fox flu? What about it?'

'That will be the government's excuse. It's planning a vaccination programme for the entire country – and the vaccine is coming from China. What's the betting the syringes are as well?'

Suddenly Christophe felt the enormity of what he had become involved in. He shook his head. Thank God he'd found an ally. 'Of course. That's it. So you'll write about this?'

'Will I ever? Christophe, you've just given me the scoop of a lifetime. In fact, I'm going to give you a kiss.' She came round the table and planted one on his forehead. 'My editor will be in seventh heaven. He loathes the surveillance society and the erosion of civil liberties, and he thinks the Prime Minister is a paranoid control freak – which I'd say this pretty much confirms. But he'll want more than allegations. We need an expert to confirm that this syringe does what Professor Li says it does.'

'I've thought about that. There's a guy I know called Patrick Neary – used to be an adviser to the Ministry of Health, now has his own research laboratory in Northumberland. He has the expertise, and the credibility.'

'You need to get it to him as soon as possible. In fact, we should go together. Let me just call the office.'

She went into the garden. When she came back there was disappointment on her face.

'They want me in London. They're short-staffed and they say I'd be more useful to them there. But they're definitely interested in the story, as long as Neary is prepared to go on the record.'

'I don't get it. A story like this . . . surely they should be mobilising a whole team of journalists.'

'I didn't manage to speak to the editor – just my immediate boss, who's always sceptical of conspiracy theories. But don't worry: I'm not going to let this one go. I'll call you when I get to the office.'

'I gave you my new mobile number, didn't I? I've ditched the old one – you can't be too careful.'

'Don't worry, I've got it. Love to Ben.'

After she'd gone he called Patrick Neary: could they meet to discuss an urgent professional matter?

'Of course, Christophe, if you really don't mind coming all the way up here. I'm afraid I just can't leave the place at the moment: we've got something very exciting brewing. Very exciting.'

'That's fine. I'll sort out my travel arrangements and let you know when I'm arriving.'

'Turn up whenever. I'll be here.'

How to get to Northumberland? The easiest thing would probably be to drive to Oxford and take a train north. He could pick up some fresh clothes from his flat along the way.

He gathered his belongings, emptied the fridge and locked up. But when he tried to start his car nothing happened.

'Damn!'

He rang the RAC. They were experiencing a high volume of calls. They would be with him in two to three hours.

Tessa must have gone back to her parents' house to pick up her things; perhaps she was still there. But when he called there was no reply.

As he paced the ground outside the cottage, it occurred to him to call Birendra, his upstairs neighbour in Oxford, just to check the lie of the land. The phone was answered immediately.

'Christophe? Thank goodness you rang. I'm afraid I've got some bad news: there's been a burglary at your flat. I don't what's been taken, but I found the door open and a terrible mess inside. The sooner you can get here the better.'

VIII

Frank felt out of his depth. Hunting a fox through unfamiliar countryside was difficult enough – hunting it through an unfamiliar city was a nightmare.

He had followed this one on horseback to the outskirts of Canterbury with half a dozen hounds. Then, faced with a road system dangerous to animals, he'd called Anna to take care of Dostoevsky and all but one of the dogs. She'd taken an age to get there, and arrived looking as if she expected an apology. Dream on, thought Frank as he exchanged his horse for a mountain bike – if anyone was owed an apology, it was him.

The fact that the centre of the city was pedestrianised made life slightly easier; but the pedestrians themselves were more of a hindrance than a help. In London he'd established his turf – people knew him and deferred to him. Here they just stared and pointed as if they'd never seen a huntsman on a bicycle before.

'Oi, Jorrocks!' shouted one. 'Your nag's got a puncture!'

'Why don't you try the Fox and Geese?' yelled another. 'You might find something in the bar.'

Frank ignored them. Marshal, after several minutes of sniffing round the restaurants on the main street, suddenly gave tongue. Frank changed gear and set off after him.

But it was a busy shopping day, and finding a clear passage was impossible. Forced to get off and push, Frank found himself getting left further and further behind. In desperation he dropped the bicycle and ran.

Rounding a corner, he saw the hound disappearing into the cathedral precincts, scattering a group of alarmed tourists. This was better: an enclosed space. If the diseased fox really was inside, there was a good chance of cornering it. The important thing was to get a clear shot at it before it attacked Marshal.

But as he sprinted towards the ancient gateway, a man stepped out to intercept him. He was large and bald and wore a badly fitting suit.

'Excuse me, sir, is that your dog?'

'It's not a dog. It's a hound.'

'You can call it what you like, sir, but if it's a carnivorous quadruped of the genus *canis*, it's a dog in my book. And dogs, I regret to inform you, are not permitted in the cathedral grounds.'

That's all I need, thought Frank – a comedian.

'It's a hound, OK? A foxhound. A hound that's trained to chase foxes anywhere they bleeding well go, because they are carnivorous quadrupeds which currently pose a threat to public safety. So if you do me the courtesy of shifting your arse I will deal with the hound and the fox to the best of my bleeding ability.'

'This will have to be reported.'

'Then f–ing well report it.'

Frank pushed past and ran in the direction of Marshal's yelping. It echoed against the ancient stone like a hammer striking an anvil.

It was quite a building, the cathedral that rose in front of him. As he raced across the courtyard and in through the great arched doorway, Frank felt that he was entering a labyrinth – one whose intricacies and mind games were not confined to the floor plan, but cobwebbed across the walls and ceilings, reaching to the Gothic pinnacles and filling the high spaces. As a huntsman he had spent his adult life puzzling out hiding places and escape routes, but nothing he had seen compared to this. If a fox could turn to stone it might hide for ever among the vaulting, the tracery, the gargoyles.

There was a commotion at the far end of the nave as Marshal gave tongue again. Chairs were knocked sideways; somebody screamed; figures in gowns hurried forward. Frank sprinted towards the altar, hurdled a rope barrier, rushed up a broad flight of stone steps and through a narrow archway. Now he was among the choir stalls, almost colliding with the lectern, trying to get past a throng of sightseers. Somewhere up ahead Marshal's voice reached a higher pitch and suddenly went quiet.

Panting, Frank made his way through to the final section of the cathedral. There on the flagstones between a great marble column and the railings of a royal tomb lay his hound, dappled by the sunlight falling through the stained-glass windows, so that it was not immediately obvious that blood was seeping from a wound in its throat. Kneeling beside it, Frank saw that this time there was no need for his pistol. Marshal was as lifeless as the marble effigies around him.

Out of the corner of his eye, Frank saw a shadow move.

He was back on his feet in a moment, giving chase along the stone walkways, back through the arches, back through the people shouting and remonstrating with him. He scarcely noticed them as he hurtled down steps, stumbled among scattered chairs, blundered towards the exit.

As he reached it he lost his footing. He fell forwards, landing heavily on his right knee. Gasping with pain, he hauled himself up again. The fox was disappearing to his left, hugging a row of houses opposite the cathedral. Ahead of it lay a small car park – and a way out into the main part of the city.

Frank limped after it. Each step was agony. There was no way he could catch up.

He leaned on a bollard to catch his breath; and as he did so, he saw an extraordinary sight. A man in a chauffeur's uniform was loading a suitcase into the boot of a large, shiny black car; he was about to close it when something distracted him, causing him to look momentarily away – and in that split second the fox jumped inside, hiding itself behind the suitcase. The boot closed; the chauffeur climbed into the driver's seat and started the engine.

'Hey!' shouted Frank. 'Hey, stop!'

But the chauffeur didn't hear him. The car moved off, and as it did so, Frank caught sight of a familiar face in the back seat – the bad-tempered man he had met on the golf course that morning.

CHAPTER THIRTEEN

Christophe's wait for the RAC mechanic was an anxious one. That a burglar should have chosen this moment to ransack his flat could not simply be a matter of chance: someone was after him. Oxford was no longer a safe destination. He would have to head north, in a car that worked.

It was less than an hour after his call for assistance that he heard an approaching engine. What was going on? Had the RAC dispatcher been unduly pessimistic, or was he about to receive a visit from someone he hadn't invited?

He considered his options. There was an orchard at the back and side of the cottage; beyond that, an open field; then woodland. If he locked the cottage door and took up position in the orchard, he would at least have a chance of reaching the wood before anyone realised he had gone.

But there was nothing threatening about the car which finally appeared. It was a red MG driven by a man he recognised. Christophe stepped out of his hiding place to meet him.

'Matt – this is a surprise.'

'Hi Christophe.' Matt Dunstable looked embarrassed. 'I hope you don't mind a surprise visit from your brother-in-law – or ex-brother-in-law, I suppose I should say.'

It was Christophe's turn to feel embarrassed. 'Come in, Matt. It's been quite a while.'

He led the way into the cottage. Matt looked around him.

'No great changes, then.'

'Nothing to speak of. Coffee?'

'Please.'

How long was it since they'd seen each other? Over a year, Christophe reckoned. Ben's 18th – that was it. Matt looked thinner and didn't seem to have shaved.

'Am I right in thinking you've given up your job?' he asked.

'That's right. I decided to do up Great Aunt Dorothy's house instead. Only there've been some unexpected problems.'

He told the story of his imprisonment. Christophe shook his head.

'What bastards those bureaucrats are! I'm sorry, Matt, I should have known. I've been travelling a lot, I'm afraid; haven't really kept track of things here.'

'That's OK – no reason why you should.'

'Sara would have approved. She always admired your high principles.'

There – the name was out. Matt's dead sister. Christophe's dead wife.

'She had pretty high principles herself.'

'That's true.'

There was a pause.

'So,' said Christophe. 'You're on the run, and you've come here because you need somewhere to hide. Is that right?'

'Actually, it's more complicated than that.'

The idea of Matt as a jailbird had been hard enough to take in. The tale he told now left Christophe staring at him with incredulity.

'I didn't know what to do,' Matt concluded. 'But I knew you had a good knowledge of China, and I'd heard you talk about the Brothers of Light, so I thought I'd come over on the off chance that you might be around.'

'And this man who's with the Vice President – you're sure his name is Li?'

'That's what he said. Claimed he was just an academic, of no interest to anyone. But Sammy wasn't convinced.'

'Sammy was absolutely right.'

Christophe told his own story. It was Matt's turn to be astonished.

'So Li is here to set up a British version of Mulberry Tree?'

'Exactly. At the moment all the proof I've got is the syringe – but if I can produce the man who invented it, and get him to explain how the system works, then we can stop Mulberry Tree in its tracks.'

'But why would he spill the beans? Presumably it's more than his life's worth.'

'Once the Chinese work out that I got the syringe through his carelessness, he's not going to be safe anyway. It won't take much to convince him that he'd be better off in another country. What we need to do now is to get him to Northumberland. With his testimony, and Patrick Neary's confirmation that the syringe does what he says it does, the government won't have a leg to stand on.'

As they climbed into the MG, Christophe glanced at his own car. If only the RAC had been quicker off the mark. But there was no time to hang around. Any transport was welcome now.

II

'You have to tell me where he's gone.'

'I don't have to tell you anything.'

Frank and the Archbishop's secretary were well matched. They glared at each other across the desk – he muddy, sweaty, red in the face, she immaculate, severe, pale with indignation. The uniformed security man watched uneasily, wishing that he were somewhere far, far away.

'That fox is a danger not just to him and his driver, but to the entire population,' said Frank. 'Got it? Whoever opens the boot of the car is more than likely to be attacked. Not that I care very much about His Holiness, having seen his behaviour on the golf course, but I reckon the geezer who has the unfortunate duty of driving him from one portcullis to the next deserves a chance. More to the point, if there isn't a reception committee waiting for that four-legged plague carrier, there's no knowing where this could end.'

The Archbishop's secretary returned his glare.

'Really, Mr – Mr –'

'Smith.'

'Mr Smith. First, you let a dog run loose in the cathedral, and now you have the gall to burst in here without so much as a by-your-leave. In terms of manners, there seems little to choose between you and your hound. And yet you expect me to divulge confidential information about the Archbishop's whereabouts. The least I require is an apology.'

Frank took a deep breath. His instinct was to tell this snooty old bitch where to go. But he recognised this as a moment when he must swallow his pride.

'OK. I'm sorry I didn't knock. But this is a matter of life or death, and I would very much appreciate if you could tell me where the Archbishop has gone. I would also appreciate his mobile number.'

The Archbishop's secretary sniffed. 'I will take that as an apology,' she said, 'though not everybody might recognise it as such. If you must know, the Archbishop is on his way to stay with his sister in Tewkesbury. He does not, however, carry a mobile telephone.'

'So how do we get in touch with him? Send an angel?'

The glare returned. 'If you are going to blaspheme, Mr Smith, I must ask you to leave these premises.'

'What about his driver? He must have a mobile.'

'He does, though of course it will not be switched on when he is driving.'

No, of course it won't, thought Frank. He sighed. 'Can I take the number so that I can leave a message?'

The secretary wrote it down.

'And the Archbishop's sister's number?'

The secretary frowned but complied.

'Thanks,' said Frank. 'You've been very helpful.'

Outside he phoned both numbers. There was no reply from either. He left messages asking them to contact him urgently. Then he rang Anna.

'I need you to pick me up,' he said. 'We're going to Tewkesbury.'

III

'You've got to let him go,' said Christophe.

Sammy shook his head. 'No way. The Animal Lovers' Army has got itself a bigger political asset than we ever dreamed of. The Vice President of China has fallen into our lap, and we're keeping him till our demands are met.'

'Think it through. Every policeman in the land must be looking for you. And in the meantime a totally innocent organisation is being held responsible for what you've done. You're putting lives at risk.'

'And what about the lives that are already at risk? What about the cats and dogs on the menu at every takeaway in Shanghai? What about the tigers being hunted for their goolies? This is our chance to change all that.'

'You'll never change all that.'

'Yes, we will. All China has to do is sign the International Accord on Animal Rights. Then they can have their Vice President back.'

Matt had warned Christophe that Sammy was a difficult character, but nothing had prepared him for this. There seemed no limit to the guy's delusions.

'And what about his mate?' Sammy went on. 'You're not planning to let *him* go.'

'Professor Li has agreed to come with us of his own free will.'

'Only because he's as pissed as a newt.'

There was no answer to that. How Li had gained access to a keg of cider despite having his hands tied behind his back was a conundrum for Houdini. At any rate, he had taken full advantage of it.

'Let's go, Christophe,' said Matt. 'We've got a long drive. The sooner we hit the road the better.'

'In what?' asked Selina. 'We're not all going to fit in the MG.'

Neither Matt nor Christophe had thought about this.

'We could go and pick up my car,' said Matt.

'And suppose the police are watching your house?' Selina objected.

She was right, of course – too risky.

'What about the council woman's car?' suggested Christophe.

'They'll be looking for that the moment she's reported missing.'

'The Range Rover, then.'

'No way,' said Sammy.

'I need some fresh air,' said Matt.

He walked up the track, trying to suppress a sense of panic. It was bad enough that the police were after him to take him back to prison; now he had become an accomplice in an act of kidnapping as well. There was no getaway vehicle available, and the question of what to do with Jennifer Pettifer remained unresolved. With every moment the manhunt must be becoming more intense.

Again he felt tempted to cut loose from all of them. But there was his country to think of, and the freedom of his fellow citizens to go about their business without the interference of Mulberry Tree. He imagined Jennifer Pettifer in control of it, binding the limbs of honest Englishmen with its silken strands.

Suddenly he became aware that someone was watching him. Just ahead, in a gap in the hedgerow, there had been a slight movement. Matt walked warily forward, peered around the corner, and found himself staring at a small boy. He wore the kind of clothes that Matt associated with children of the 1950s: a tweed jacket, grey flannel shorts, Fairisle jumper, pink tie. He had sandals on his feet and socks which were furled around his ankles. A red and white cricket cap sat on his head. But for his face, which was Asian in appearance, he might have been a character out of Enid Blyton.

'I say,' he said.

'I say?' Matt was bemused.

'Is this your farm?'

'Yes.'

'I think it's absolutely ripping.'

Even in Matt's schooldays such language had been laughably old-fashioned. He wondered whether someone was playing a practical joke on him.

'It is rather nice, isn't it?' he said, looking around for a hidden television crew. 'What's your name?'

'Yu major.'

'Is Yu minor with you?'

'No.' The boy shook his head emphatically. 'He's with the mater.'

'And where's the mater?'

'She bolted with some frightful bounder. They're living in Welwyn Garden City.'

'And the pater?'

'He's up the road struggling with the B.U.M. He's in a fearful bate.'

'You'll have to tell me what the B.U.M. is.'

'The Bloody Unreliable Machine. If you put the initials together they spell "bum".' He giggled.

'What's your first name?'

'Frederick. But you can call me Freddie.'

'Hello, Freddie. I'm Matt.'

'Hello, Matt. Here's the pater now.'

Matt followed his glance, expecting to see a figure in plus-fours striding down the track. Instead there was a thickset man wearing jeans and a beaten-up leather jacket.

'Frederick!' shouted the new arrival. 'How many times I bloody told you not to wander off on your own? Maybe you meet a homicidal maniac!'

'This is Matt,' said the boy. 'He's not a homicidal maniac.'

'I could be,' said Matt. 'You're father's right. You can't be too careful.'

'Thank you,' said Mr Yu.

Matt looked at him carefully. It seemed rather too much of a coincidence that someone Chinese should arrive at Stooks Farm just when two of his compatriots were being held prisoner there.

'I gather you're having some trouble with your car,' he said.

'Not car. Mobile Catering Unit. Nothing but bloody trouble since the day I bought it. Now the GPS is acting up too. Brought me down these bloody country lanes and got me stuck in your bloody gate.'

Matt didn't like the sound of this at all.

'I'd better take a look,' he said.

Frederick ran ahead of them.

'That's a remarkable boy you've got,' said Matt.

'Thank you. He makes his father very proud. All A* grades at school. Fine singing voice. Also a useful slow left-arm bowler.'

'His language is rather unusual.'

'I know. Precocious! Yes, sir! Let me tell you something, Matt: when I arrived in this country, I spoke ten words of English. I knew nothing of British culture. That was a big problem for me. So when Frederick was born I thought to myself, "What advantage can I give my son that I never had?" I think about this very much, and at last I realise one thing is more important than any amount of money: to be a proper British gentleman.

'Now, many people today laugh at this idea. They think, "Umbrella, bowler hat, post-colonial power, yesterday's news!" But I know better. I meet people from all over the world, and they still believe in the British gent, even if British people don't. So I say to my wife, "We are going to bring our boy up by the book. He is going to dress like a little gentleman, and also speak like one. OK, we don't have money to send him to expensive private school, but we can do it ourselves." So I raise him on G.A. Henty, R.M. Ballantyne, John Buchan, P.G. Wodehouse, all the classic English authors. And you see the results! Maybe one day he will win a scholarship to a major public school – Eton, Harrow, Winchester. But for now we are doing bloody well without them.'

They reached the top of the track. The Mobile Catering Unit was larger than Matt had anticipated – closer to a lorry than a van. It was light blue in colour, and the words 'Pu Dong Pudding Company' were painted on the side.

'Pu Dong Pudding Company?'

'Good name, don't you think? My family is from Pu Dong in Shanghai. Well, not Shanghai back then, just farmland next to it, but now prime real estate. Not that it has done my family any bloody good.' He spat on the ground. 'You want to look inside?'

'Perhaps when we've sorted this out. It's doing a good job of blocking the road.' Not much traffic came this way, but the last thing Matt wanted was attention being drawn to his property.

'Take a quick look. Only one minute.'

The inside of the lorry was unexpectedly luxurious. At one end was a battery of cookers, fridges and freezers, and an array of immaculate work surfaces. At the other a sofa was bolted to the linoleum floor, along with an ancient school desk, chipped away at and tattooed by generations of penknives and ballpoint pens. In one corner stood a shower and lavatory cubicle.

'Home from home!' said Mr Yu proudly.

'Very nice.'

How exactly the Mobile Catering Unit had become wedged in Matt's entrance was hard to say, but Yu had made a thorough job of it. The lorry appeared unable to go forward without demolishing the gatepost or backwards without wrecking a hedgerow and placing its rear wheels in a ditch. Matt climbed into the cab to see whether any other possibilities suggested themselves. He noticed a figure of St Christopher attached to the dashboard. The radio was on.

There was only one thing to be done: remove the gatepost. Fortunately it was wooden rather than metal and, though driven well into the ground, could probably be eased out by a couple of strong men.

It was harder work than he expected. He and Yu struggled for several minutes, pulling and pushing until they were soaked in sweat – but the amount of give was minimal.

'Let's take a break,' he said at last.

They leant against the side of the truck. Yu produced a bottle of lemonade. Three pips on the radio announced the hourly news.

'A massive police hunt is under way for two senior Chinese officials kidnapped in London earlier today,' said the reader's voice. 'The men, who were on a diplomatic visit to Britain, were visiting a fashion store in the Notting Hill area of the city. Official sources say that a radical Chinese group, the Brothers of Light, is believed to be responsible.'

Yu chuckled. 'Good for Brothers of Light, I say. Show that bunch of crooks in Beijing what's what.'

Matt looked at him with interest. 'So you know about the Brothers of Light?'

'Sure. Every Chinese person in Britain knows they are brave, brave people. If anyone can bring change back home, the Brothers can. All my friends are behind them 100 per cent for certain.'

'And you?'

'Sure. Anyone who can give those Communist bastards a bloody nose, they got my respect.'

'Would you help them?'

'If I had the opportunity, sure.'

They wrestled with the post again. Still it refused to move more than a fraction.

'We're never going to manage this on our own,' said Matt. 'I'll go and get one of my friends.'

Back at the barn, Sammy was in a state of high tension.

'Where the hell have you been?'

Matt explained.

'I think he might be the answer to our problems,' he said. 'He's sympathetic to the cause, and there's plenty of room in his truck – we can sleep in it overnight if necessary.'

Matt and Christophe were chosen to put the question.

Yu frowned. 'If I was on my own, I would help you like a shot. But with Frederick . . .'

'I was going to suggest that Selina could take care of him,' said Matt. 'She could drive him to his mother's if you like.'

'Let me think about this.'

Yu walked away along the edge of the field, where poppies gave colour to the dusty ground. When he came back he said,

'I will help you. I think of what my family have suffered from the Communists, and I cannot refuse.'

'And Frederick?' asked Christophe.

'Many of the restaurant people we deal with are my friends. I will leave him with one of them on our way.'

'Where are you heading?' asked Matt.

'Next stop Cheltenham. But Pu Dong Puddings go anywhere there are Chinese restaurants. Very flexible.'

'We'd better sort out this gate,' said Christophe, 'or no one's going anywhere.'

The battle with the post resumed. Christophe's added strength immediately began to tell. Within a few minutes the truck had room for manoeuvre.

'I can take it from here,' said Yu. 'As soon as you are ready to go, just say the word.'

On their way back down the track, Matt and Christophe formulated a plan.

'We've got to split up,' said Matt. 'You need to get to Northumberland with Professor Li as quickly as possible, and the rest of us would only slow you down. I'll try to persuade Selina to let you take her car.'

'Where will you go?'

'Sammy and Jake have some sympathisers in Herefordshire they reckon they can hole up with. As Mr Yu is heading in that general direction, it should all tie in rather well.'

'And you're sure you want to stick with them? Sammy strikes me as a real liability.'

'That's precisely why I need to keep an eye on him. If he does something stupid that attracts the attention of the police, we'll all be in trouble.'

Christophe smiled ruefully. 'I think you could say we're in trouble already.'

'I suppose you could.'

The two men looked at each other. Matt seemed about to say something, but didn't. He turned and led the way back into the barn.

IV

'A needle in a haystack,' said Jonty Lo.

'Ssh!' Faye was finding it hard enough to monitor the police messages without constant complaints from behind the steering wheel.

'A bottle of Château Lafite in a wine cellar,' complained Jonty. 'A sturgeon's egg in a jar of caviare.'

But the truth was that his mood had mellowed since hitting the motorway. He enjoyed letting the Bentley have its head, and since he considered racing around Knightsbridge in the early hours of the morning an occupation for pathetic showoffs in their first Lamborghinis, an excursion like this was a rare opportunity. The Bentley was not the most beautiful car in the world, but it had all the attributes of a big beast.

Exactly where they were going remained to be seen. The stolen 4x4 had last been picked up by the primitive British motorway tracking system south of Junction 3. It could have turned off towards High Wycombe or Reading; but Jonty's experience of kidnappers was that they either went to ground much closer to the scene of the crime than generally expected, or as far away as they could safely get. It was possible, of course, that these ones had a light aircraft standing by; otherwise their most likely route was north along the motorway towards Birmingham, or west towards Wales.

On this basis he suggested a stop in Oxford, if no further sightings had been reported by the time they reached it: 'That way we'll be ready to go in either direction.'

Faye knew him well enough to discern his true motive. Jonty fancied an afternoon strolling through the picturesque streets, idling among the delicatessens of the covered market, and eyeing up the pretty undergraduates; perhaps he would buy some shirts from the university outfitters or take tea at the Randolph. None of this appealed to Faye; but the logic of the fusty old city as a temporary base could not be denied, and so she gave her assent.

Jonty indulged in a final burst of speed, pushing the Bentley to 120, then peeled off the motorway towards the dreaming spires.

V

It was agreed that none of the cars could be left at Stooks Farm. Selina would drive Jennifer Pettifer's Skoda and leave it in a public car park at least ten miles away, before joining the rest of the party in the truck; Sammy would do the same with the 4x4.

Matt and Christophe made a thorough check of the farm buildings, removing any traces of recent activity. First Zhou and then Jennifer Pettifer was led to the truck wearing the lacy blind-fold which Selina had packed, with a selection of other interesting accessories, in her overnight bag.

'We don't want either of them seeing the outside of the vehicle,' insisted Matt. 'They mustn't be able to identify it.'

'It's going to be a hell of a squash,' said Selina, peering into the driver's cabin. 'How are we all going to fit?'

'Plenty of room,' said Mr Yu cheerfully. 'Three adults and my son up front, the rest in the back.'

Not everyone was happy with this arrangement.

'You can't expect us to travel without safety belts!' exclaimed Jennifer Pettifer. 'Unless one is provided for every passenger, this vehicle cannot be taken on to the public highway.'

'Shut up, skinny lady,' said Yu. 'I take my whole family to Blackpool every summer in this vehicle, and if it's safe enough for them, it's plenty safe enough for you.'

'I think she's got a point,' said Selina. 'My father would insist on them being properly secured.'

She produced a pair of handcuffs.

'Do you always carry those?' asked Matt.

'Of course. I was going to try them on you later. Maybe I'll still get a chance.'

Manacled together and protesting loudly, Zhou and Jennifer Pettifer arranged themselves on the sofa as best they could. Jake was given the gun and left to invigilate them. Sitting at the old school desk, which had been designed for someone half his size, he resembled a collapsed umbrella with its spokes retracted.

The next challenge was to get Li into the MG.

'If he's sick, you're cleaning the whole car with a toothbrush,' said Selina as Christophe and Matt helped the professor up the track.

I'm the hoochie coochie man

Li sang as he veered sideways, pushing Matt into the hedge.
Everybody knows I'm him.

Manoeuvring him into the low passenger seat almost had the three of them sprawling on the ground; but at last he was made comfortable. Wishing Christophe and Matt sweet dreams, he closed his eyes and fell fast asleep.

'He shouldn't be too much trouble,' said Matt. 'Just keep him tanked up.'

'I don't think that's a good idea,' said Christophe. 'A drunk Chinese guy can't be a very common sight where I'm heading – and I'll need him to be completely sober when we arrive.'

He held out his hand. Matt hesitated for a moment before taking it. He felt that an opportunity had been lost. So much needed to be said, but now was not the moment to say it. They had been overtaken by events.

'Good luck, Matt.'

'Good luck, Christophe.'

The noise of engines filled the air, blending like the throaty call of wood pigeons. The 4x4 moved off, the Skoda and the Pu Dong Pudding van following in convoy. Last came the MG, lurching over the dried mud in the gateway and accelerating away on its lonely course, a red silhouette against the pale blue sky.

CHAPTER FOURTEEN

'So how far is Tewkesbury?' asked Anna.

'A hell of a long way.' Frank consulted the dashboard computer. 'One hundred and eighty-two miles to be precise.'

'They've got to stop at some point. Surely the driver will check his messages then.'

'Not necessarily. After all, one should not employ one's mobile at a petrol station for fear of blowing oneself and one's archbishop to kingdom come. We just have to bloody hope that he will – and that he doesn't decide to get something out of the boot first.'

'There should be a strong scent of fox in the car. Maybe they'll stop to investigate.'

'With luck there'll be such a stink that His Holiness will never be able to use his motor again. But in the meantime we need to get after them.'

Though Frank drove without regard for the speed limit, the trailer full of hounds slowed the car down. He'd thought of leaving them behind with the horses, hoping to see to the fox with one shot from his revolver, but decided it was too risky. If the fox was released before he got to it, he would need other options.

He was still furious with Anna. If she'd shown more of a killer instinct, he would have been spared all that aggravation at the cathedral. He'd be on his way home now, to a hot bath, and a cup of tea by the fire with Captain. And he'd have made his reputation once and for all, as the man who'd hunted down the first flu-ridden fox in England. Instead, he was likely to go down in history as the prat who'd missed a golden opportunity.

'That's what comes of making a council-house boy an MFH,' they'd say. 'Of course he was going to f– it up. No breeding, you see.'

Oh yeah? He'd show the bloody lot of them, no two ways about it.

He put his foot on the floor.

II

'How does it work?' asked Matt. 'The Pu Dong Pudding Company?'

Mr Yu grinned. 'You ever been to a Chinese restaurant?'

'Of course.' Matt thought wistfully of chicken with cashew nuts. 'And what do they have for pudding?'

'I don't know . . . there isn't usually much on offer. Toffee bananas, perhaps; and a sort of green jelly-ish thing – but I've never found that very appetising.'

Yu slapped the dashboard. 'Exactly! You hit the nail on the head one hundred per cent. Now let me explain something.

'Chinese people don't eat like English people. A traditional Chinese meal doesn't include pudding at all. That's what I used to serve when I had a restaurant.

'But I had this customer: big, fat guy. He came to the Golden Duck – that was my restaurant – a lot; and every time he got to the end of his meal he said, "Hey, Mr Yu" – actually, he was not as polite as that – "why is there no pudding on the menu? Where is the treacle tart, the spotted dick, the lemon meringue pie?" So that got me thinking maybe there's a gap in the market: maybe I should start a business supplying English puddings to Chinese restaurants. But I had a big problem: I don't have a sweet tooth – so how can I tell if the puddings I make are any bloody good?

'So for a long time I did nothing. But then when Frederick was born I began to think about it again. I said to myself, "If I can teach my son to love puddings like an English gentleman, it will be good for him and good for me!" Right, Frederick?'

'Rather, Pater!' said Frederick, sucking on a gobstopper.

'So I fed him suet pudding, tapioca, apple pie – you name it! But my wife, she didn't like it. She said it was an unhealthy diet for a growing boy, especially a Chinese one. "Why do you want to feed him all this foreign muck?" she asked. She didn't have my vision, you see; and when our second son was born she said, "No way you're going to do the same with him!" Then one day she found me giving him a bowl of rhubarb crumble: that was it – off she went with a bloody IT consultant, and took Danny with her. But Frederick, he wanted to stay with me and eat two good puddings a day.

'So then I had to run the Golden Duck on my own. How to do that and start a new company? Not possible. But one day fate took a hand: the environmental health officer closed the restaurant. "Rats in the garbage," he said. Sure there were rats in the garbage – you show me garbage and I will show you a rat! No one in

London is ever more than ten feet from a rat: well-known statistic. But he would not listen.

'So then I thought, "Maybe this is a blessing in disguise! Maybe this is the moment to launch the Pu Dong Pudding Company!" I also thought, "If I have a mobile catering unit, no more trouble with environmental health, because no one knows where I am!" Three weeks later I bought the truck, fitted it out with pudding-making equipment, and said to Frederick, "Let's get to work, number-one taster!" Now we have more than fifty clients. Every day we stop somewhere different, cook fresh puddings, and deliver them to the local restaurant. And people love it! Turnover is up sixty per cent year on year.'

'I presume that's apple turnover.'

'Apple turnover! Ha!' Yu slapped the dashboard again, almost colliding with a white van coming in the opposite direction. 'Very funny, Matt! Apple turnover! Ha!'

They now were several miles from Stooks Farm. Soon it would be time for Selina and Sammy to abandon their respective vehicles.

'Tell me, Matt,' said Yu. 'The skinny lady – she's not from the environmental health department?'

'No. But you know these petty bureaucrats – they're all as bad as each other.'

He told his story briefly. Yu shook his head sympathetically. 'Same the whole bloody world over. All decent hard-working people want is to be left in peace – but is that possible? No! The skinny lady, the environmental health officer, just put on this planet to drive us mad – and we pay their wages with our taxes! Crazy!'

They had reached the outskirts of Witney. Sammy, who was leading the small convoy with Selina behind him, slowed to 30 miles an hour. Ahead were a set of traffic lights and beyond them, on the left-hand side of the road, a public car park. Glancing in the wing mirror beside him, Matt saw a patrol car.

'Police,' he said. 'Right behind us.'

Mr Yu looked in his own mirror. 'No need to panic,' he said. 'Probably just going home for tea.'

The lights turned red. As the convoy came to halt, Matt realised that the truck must be blocking Sammy and Selina's view of the patrol car. He wondered whether he should warn them. But to climb out of the cab would inevitably attract the attention of the police.

'Flash your lights,' he said.

Yu did so. Sammy waved a hand. Whether he had understood the signal was impossible to say. Perhaps he thought they were simply drawing his attention to the car park.

The traffic lights went green. Sammy moved off in the 4x4, crossed the junction, indicated left and turned into the car park. As he did so, all hell broke loose.

The police car whipped out from behind Yu's truck, lights flashing, siren scissoring the air. It overtook the truck, accelerated past Selina in the Skoda, and swung across her in pursuit of the 4x4. At the same moment a second patrol car came careering towards them from the opposite direction and slewed to a halt, blocking Sammy's exit. Two officers leapt out and sprinted towards him.

'Keep going as if nothing has happened,' said Matt.

Selina had clearly had the same thought. They followed her to the far side of the town, where she left the Skoda in a larger car park.

'You OK?' asked Matt as she climbed in beside him.

'Why wouldn't I be?'

'It's not every day you nearly get run into by a patrol car.'

'It's not every day you get involved in a kidnapping.'

'I suppose not.'

Nobody spoke for the next twenty minutes. Finally Mr Yu broke the silence. 'Tell me, Matt,' he said, 'which do you think is better: Eton or Harrow?'

III

In the boot of the limousine, the fox was attacking the Archbishop's suitcase. She had slept for the first part of the journey, exhausted by her run-in with Frank's hounds, but now the fierce hunger in her stomach reasserted itself. Among the neatly packed vestments, shirts and hosiery she scented a box of Duchy Original shortbread, and it was towards this that she now gnawed her way. First she shredded the case's nylon lid and polyester lining; then she ripped at silk, cotton and wool, before tearing aside the polythene and cardboard packaging to feast on the sugared biscuits. The Archbishop's pyjamas were unwearable, his smalls reduced to tatters; but still her hunger raged.

IV

Jonty Lo had few regrets in life, but one of them was that he had attended neither Oxford nor Cambridge. Beijing National University had given him a good grounding, and Stanford had introduced him to the hedonism of life on the West Coast; but neither could be described as romantic. How elusive that quality was, he reflected, and how much harder to capture as the years passed! Yet he had only to set foot in these streets – the Broad, the Turl, the High – to feel it steal over him like a morning mist rising on Christ Church Meadow. The beauty of the buildings was its essence, but there was something more: the meeting of past and present, of ancient learning and young blood. Year after year new undergraduates arrived, filling the streets and lecture halls with their chatter, gliding past the honeyed walls on quaint bicycles, too busy with their lives to notice half the glory of their surroundings; and when they left, their places were taken by others equally heedless. Only in middle age would they look back and see what they had squandered:

Deep as first love, and wild with all regret;
O Death in Life, the days that are no more!

Tennyson, that master of melancholy! Jonty felt the tears, idle tears gathering to his own eyes.

Curiously, it was in Oxford that Jonty had first killed a man: a dissident computer genius causing trouble with his attempts to penetrate China's firewall. Jonty had followed him to the University Parks, knifed him under a willow on the riverbank, and hidden the body beneath an abandoned punt. Baudelaire had been Jonty's master then, *Les Fleurs du Mal* his bible; indeed, when first posted to London he had lobbied hard for a transfer to Paris. He had even affected a beret, though he blushed to think of it now. Ah, the gaucheries of youth . . .

Come to think of it, there had been some collateral damage that sunny afternoon – a student nurse who had come upon him hauling the punt into position. Fortunately the boat was wide enough to cover her as well; and he had learnt two valuable lessons from the experience. First, that the immediate aftermath of a killing carried as much danger as the act itself; and that additional unrelated killings were a useful means of confusing the police.

A pair of shoes in the window of Ducker's caught his eye. Oxfords from Oxford – what could be more amusing? He pushed open the door.

His fancy had shifted to a pair of tan brogues when his mobile rang. It was Faye.

'Where the hell are you?'

'Where am I? On a very comfortable chair in one of my favourite shops in the epicentre of this ancient city.'

'Well, get your ass in gear. The 4x4 has been found in Witney and the driver's under arrest; no sign of Zhou or the professor. Get back to the car now.'

Jonty sighed. There was no time to be lost.

'I'll take two pairs,' he said.

V

Christophe was in a slow line of traffic approaching Oxford. He'd been stupid to take this route instead of joining the motorway further north, but it was the way he always came, and on another day it might have saved him time. Besides, he kept half thinking about passing by his flat to see what state it was in, even though he knew the idea to be really stupid. Whoever had ransacked the place might easily be waiting for him: he must forget about it until his mission was complete.

Beside him Li was asleep, head lolling. Christophe knew he must keep a close eye on him. If the professor was going to drink himself senseless on any alcohol within reach, he would be precious little help when they got to Patrick Neary's.

Christophe made one stop, to call Tessa; but she wasn't answering. Presumably she was still on the road back to London. He'd try again from a service station once they were on the motorway.

His thoughts turned to another young woman: Amy. Where was she now? Had the medical intervention worked? Would he ever see her again? Perhaps, when this was over, there would be a chance to make enquiries through the Brothers. What a lot of pieces of his life there were to pick up, one way or another.

Seeing Matt had unsettled him. Even though there had been no discussion of the past, Christophe felt reproached. Was he a fit person to be entrusted with a task like this one? True, he had got Amy to safety – but he could have managed things better. Now he had another chance to prove himself and he should be relishing it. Instead he felt tired and daunted.

They finally reached the Wolvercote roundabout. Li sat up in his seat.

'Where are we?'

Concentrating on the traffic coming from the right, Christophe didn't immediately answer. His chance to pull out came; and as he did so, he briefly took in the flashy Bentley that was turning into the road he was leaving. He glimpsed a well-dressed young Chinese man at the wheel; but whether the man saw him, or Li, he couldn't be sure.

VI

Jonty Lo made a mental note of the MG's registration number. He'd been thinking for a while that he'd like an old-fashioned sports car as a run-around – something a bit lighter and more elegant than the Bentley. A Triumph Stag was what he'd had in mind, but the MG looked in exceptionally good condition. He might just track the owner down and check whether it was for sale. Curious, though, that there had been a Chinese guy in the passenger seat.

VII

'Try the driver again,' said Frank.

Anna dialled the number for the umpteenth time. Once again it went to voicemail. There was no point in adding to the three messages she'd already left. She rang off.

'No reply,' she said.

'I don't believe it,' said Frank. 'Sometime, somewhere he's got to stop and turn his phone on.'

'Perhaps he's just not getting a signal.'

Frank said nothing. The speedometer climbed to 110; it had scarcely been below 100 since they hit the motorway. Frank drove with fierce determination, which wasn't unusual in a horseman – fast cars were the next best thing to animals; but there was something about the intensity of his focus that Anna found deeply attractive.

'You can always tell a person's character by the way they drive,' her father had told her – and if anyone was in a position to know, he was. But would his opinion of Frank concur with hers?

The blaring of the horn as Frank tailgated a BMW brought her back to the present. Whether she fancied him was irrelevant, because for now Frank was barely talking to her; and unless they caught up with this wretched fox, that wasn't likely to change.

VIII

'Can we stop, Pater? I need to answer the call of nature.'

'Sure thing.'

Mr Yu pulled in beside an abandoned filling station. Frederick disappeared up a bramble-lined path. His father, Matt and Selina got out to stretch their legs.

'Shall we see how the others are doing?' asked Matt.

Yu undid the rear doors. Zhou and Jennifer Pettifer were lying on the sofa like rag dolls, looking furious and exhausted. Jake was sitting at the school desk looking highly entertained.

'You should have seen them,' he said. 'Getting very chummy they were. All over each other! Lucky they had the handcuffs on, or there'd have been no stopping them.'

'Idiot!' spat Jennifer Pettifer. 'We could have broken every bone in our bodies. You've contravened every regulation governing the transportation of persons. If I suffer any bodily harm, I'll sue – just you wait and see.'

Jake chuckled. 'There's been a lot of that.'

'The lady is right,' said Zhou. 'And it is not just you who will face the music. You insult me, you insult my government. My country will impose the severest sanctions on yours.'

'Your country!' exclaimed Mr Yu. He seized a scrubbing brush and brandished it under Zhou's nose. 'I think you mean *my* country that you and your damn cronies have stolen from honest hardworking people. You call yourselves Communists, but you are bloody oligarchs. I think maybe you need your mouth washed out with soap and water.'

'Let's all cool it,' said Matt, taking the brush from his hand. 'Let's just leave our guests for a few minutes and have a little talk among ourselves.'

'May I guard them, Pater?' asked Frederick, reappearing.

'Sure, why not?' Yu laughed and ruffled his son's hair. 'They give you any trouble, just sing out.'

Frederick took a broom from a corner cupboard and adopted the stance of a Praetorian guard. The four adults climbed down from the truck and walked over to the derelict shop. Selina and Jake lit cigarettes.

'Where's Sammy?' asked Jake.

Matt explained.

'F— me,' said Jake. 'Old Sammy banged up. Still, about time he learned for himself what it's like on the inside.'

'Will he talk?' asked Selina. 'If he tells the pigs that we're riding around in a van marked "Pu Dong Puddings", I'd say our time was very short.'

Jake shook his head. 'Not Sammy. He's no grass. And the Animal Lovers' Army trains you how to withstand torture – even waterboarding. At least, Sammy waterboarded me.'

'This place in Herefordshire,' said Matt. 'You've been there before, haven't you?'

'Once.'

'And you're sure you can find it again?'

'Sort of.'

'What does that mean?'

Jake shrugged. 'Kind of sure.'

'Great.'

'There's a more basic question,' said Matt, 'which is whether it's the best place to head for.'

'Why wouldn't it be?' asked Selina. 'It's not like we've got anywhere else to go.'

'Yes, but it was Sammy's idea, and now he's out of the equation. We could just release Zhou. We're only creating trouble for ourselves by keeping him.'

'You're going to let him go scot-free?' asked Mr Yu indignantly. 'That dirty oligarch? Let him go back to his life of luxury?'

'It's that or face charges of unlawful imprisonment.'

'And the nosy lady? You want to let her go too?'

'No, but . . .'

'OK,' said Selina. 'Let's ask ourselves a question. What is the most important thing here? It's that Christophe gets to Northumberland with the professor and exposes this Mulberry Tree conspiracy, right?'

'Right.'

'And if we release Zhou, does that make it easier for Christophe or more difficult?'

'Well . . . Zhou would be able to tell the police that it wasn't the Brothers of Light who kidnapped him, and that the professor had gone with Christophe of his own free will.'

'But would he? He wants to make as much trouble for the Brothers as possible, and he doesn't want the professor undermining the Mulberry Tree project. So what he'll actually tell the pigs is that Christophe is forcing the professor into it. He'll also be able to give them Christophe's description. Which means we've got to keep him under wraps.'

Matt nodded. 'That makes sense to me. What do you think, Mr Yu?'

'I think the lady is right.'

'Jake?'

'Whatever you say, Matt.'

'OK, so we stay with Sammy's friends tonight. Then we'll see how the land lies tomorrow.'

'Just one more thing,' said Yu. 'I need to make my delivery in Cheltenham.'

'That's on our way. I don't see that it should be a problem.'

'Very good. But the Pu Dong Pudding Company emphasises the freshness of its dishes.'

'Meaning?'

Mr Yu smiled. 'Have you ever made spotted dick?'

IX

At a service station on the M6, Christophe stopped to call Tessa.

'Newsroom,' said a man's voice.

'Tessa Traherne, please.'

There was a moment's hesitation.

'Who's speaking?'

'Christophe Hardy.'

'What's it in connection with?'

'I'm a friend.'

'Right . . . Christophe, I'm afraid Tessa's been in an accident.'

'What? But I saw her just a few hours ago.'

'She was involved in a collision on the motorway. She's been taken to hospital. That's all we know.'

'Is she badly hurt?'

'I don't know. I'm sorry.'

'Can you tell me which hospital?'

'Sorry, no idea.'

Christophe dialled Tessa's parents. A machine answered. He left a message with his mobile number.

He sat down at a table, his head in his hands, wondering what could have happened. Had it really been an accident? Perhaps there were people involved in this that he didn't know about – the people who had ransacked his flat. But how could they have discovered that he'd talked to Tessa? If they'd engineered an accident for her, might they engineer one for him?

He needed to talk the situation over with someone. He thought of ringing her office again, demanding to talk to her editor. Then it occurred to him that it might have been her own call to the office – intercepted by a hostile party – that had sealed Tessa's fate.

If only he hadn't dragged her into it. That was what it came down to. He couldn't bear to think that it was his fault. Again.

CHAPTER FIFTEEN

'Custard? You call that custard? Looks to me like banana-coloured vomit! So here is what I'm going to do – I'm going to throw the whole damn lot out and you are bloody well going to start over again!'

Matt and Selina exchanged glances. Mr Yu had been a pleasant enough companion on the road, but in the kitchen – or at least the part of the truck equipped as one – he was a tyrant. He screamed and cursed and shouted; he brandished ladles and rolling pins; he threw anything that came to hand. They had been cooking for half an hour and already the floor was strewn with broken china.

Jennifer Pettifer was getting the worst of it. She had been put in charge of the apple crumble, and her tentative efforts elicited a merciless tirade of abuse.

'Now I know why you're so thin, skinny lady!' Yu ranted. ''Cos you can't bloody cook to save your life! What did I tell you? More flour! More flour!'

He seized the rest of the packet and emptied it over her head. She spluttered and sobbed as the white powder settled on her hair, her face, her shoulders, until she resembled a madwoman at the court of Marie Antoinette. The humiliation! And the lack of hygiene! What would the environmental health department have made of it? She hadn't even been issued with polythene gloves!

The apples for the crumble were being prepared by Vice President Zhou. Rather than let him get his hands on a knife, Mr Yu had issued him with a potato peeler – an instrument which was clearly new to him. He glowered as he worked.

'Faster! Faster!' shouted Yu, jabbing him in the ribs with a wooden spoon.

Matt and Selina were spared physical assault, but were left in no doubt as to the shortcomings of their bread-and-butter pudding. Only Jake, conjuring up a spotted dick and sherry trifle with unexpected artistry, was beyond criticism.

'Amazing,' said Matt. 'Where'd you learn to cook like that?'

Jake grinned. 'My nan used to clean for Constance Spry. She was always coming home with recipes. You want a *potage de tomate à l'estragon*, you know who to come to. Mind you, that was before I found out what went into her *escalopes de veau à la crème.*'

The final judge of every dish was Frederick, who sat at his school desk with a Latin grammar open in front of him and a row of tasting spoons close to hand. 'Tophole' was his ultimate accolade, 'spazzo' his fiercest put-down. Zhou's fury at being judged by a ten-year-old was plain to see. Finally he exploded.

'Enough!' he yelled. 'I am the Vice President of the People's Republic of China! I will not be treated like this! I demand to be – '

Jake gagged him with a dishcloth and handcuffed him to the oven.

'Another squeak,' he said, 'and you're toast.'

At last the full complement of puddings was ready. Mr Yu surveyed the chaos of the kitchen; then he picked up a packet of floor cleaner and threw it at Jennifer Pettifer.

'OK, skinny lady,' he said. 'Get scrubbing.'

II

An hour later the truck pulled up outside the Golden Palace Cantonese restaurant. Matt and Selina helped to unload the puddings while Jake made sure that the prisoners didn't draw attention to themselves.

'You expanding?' the restaurant owner asked Mr Yu. 'You are doing well if you can employ *gwailos*. Soon you will have a whole fleet of trucks on the road, just like Eddie Stobart!'

'Two friends helping out, that's all,' said Yu. 'With my product you need specialist knowledge. You sure you have enough treacle tart?'

'OK, give me one more. And next time maybe a couple more lemon meringue pies. No disrespect, but can you believe people eat this stuff?'

Yu shrugged. 'You know the old proverb – "Only he who drinks the water knows whether it is cold or warm." '

'True enough. See you next week, then.'

'See you next week.'

The restaurant owner watched the truck move off. Then he hurried indoors to make a telephone call.

III

'The driver of the 4×4 is being taken to London,' said Jonty Lo. 'He's being held under the Prevention of Terrorism Act. White, late thirties, medium height. That's all I've got so far.'

He and Faye were sitting in the bar of the Cotswolds' most elegant boutique hotel, where Jonty rather hoped they would be staying the night. There was a Sancerre on the wine list that he was particularly keen to try.

Faye frowned over her laptop. The arrest was a mixed blessing: it meant they were probably in the right part of the world, but also that the British police might very soon know the whereabouts of Zhou. Her network needed to come up with something fast.

She thought of it as *her* network because, in all honesty, she had put ten times as much work into it as Jonty. Though the word 'loner' was not lightly to be used of a comrade, Jonty had never really been a team player, and for every titbit he brought back from his tours of clubland, she suspected him of hoarding several more. Not only that, but rubbing shoulders with the great and the good had turned him into a snob, reluctant to engage with the foot soldiers of the intelligence world. She wondered whether, once Zhou had been despatched, Beijing would allow her a change of partner.

Her mobile vibrated. As she listened to the voice at the other end, her face became charged with excitement. Jonty felt the bottle of Sancerre receding.

Faye rang off and snapped shut her laptop. 'That was our man in Cheltenham,' she said triumphantly. 'He's just had a delivery from one of his suppliers, and he says there was something very suspicious about the van. It's time to kick ass.'

IV

'Try the archbishop's driver again,' said Frank.

'We're nearly there. He hasn't rung, so we must have overtaken him.'

'I said try him again.'

Anna did so. This time someone answered.

'Hello?'

But the signal was gone immediately.

'Cut out,' she said. 'But he answered – he actually answered!'

They were on the outskirts of Tewkesbury now. Frank shot through a red light, almost colliding with a minibus. It hooted angrily in his wake.

'After fifty yards turn right,' said the satnav. He clipped the kerb as he swung into a street of substantial Victorian houses. 'You have reached your destination.'

A pair of redbrick gateposts; a sweep of gravel. And there it was: the shiny black limousine. Chauffeur and passenger were standing beside it – and the boot was open.

'What happened?' yelled Frank as he pulled up beside them. 'Where's the fox?'

'You!' exclaimed the Archbishop. 'If this is your idea of a practical joke . . .'

'It's my idea of a nightmare. Where's the f–ing fox?'

'I just got your messages,' said the chauffeur apologetically. 'But it was too late: I'd already opened the boot.'

'And who, pray, is going to pay for this?' The Archbishop indicated his tattered suitcase and savaged clothes.

'I'd keep praying, mate,' said Frank. 'You might get some pennies from heaven. In the meantime, if you don't mind, I'll borrow these.' He picked up a pair of purple boxer shorts which had been torn to ribbons. 'The hounds should get a good scent off them.'

The evening sun was softening, outlining in gold the silhouettes of the pack as Frank released them from the trailer. Anna glanced at her watch: there couldn't be more than an hour of daylight left.

Frank pulled his mountain bike from the back of the car, then proffered the remains of the boxer shorts; the hounds inhaled deeply. For a moment it looked as if they might go after the Archbishop; then they gave tongue and disappeared through the gates, with Frank in pursuit. Anna climbed into the car and roared after them.

V

'Here we are,' said Jake.

'Brilliant,' said Matt. 'Who needs a GPS when we've got you? I'm going to patent you when all this is over.'

The entrance to Sammy's hideaway was easy to miss. They had taken a turning without a signpost down a road without markings into a dense wood, where it became a poorly maintained avenue; at last they reached a pair of rusty white gates in a wall weighed down with ivy. Beyond, the trees thinned out, giving way unexpectedly to a trim lawn. On the far side of it stood a modern house of timber and glass, its steeply pitched roof forming a central A.

'Looks comfortable,' said Matt. 'Let's see who's at home. Jake, you come with me.'

The chime of the bell brought a large middle-aged woman to the door. Her grey hair was tied back with an orange silk scarf, and a pair of plastic-framed spectacles hung from a chain on her neck. She was barefoot.

'Can I help you?'

Jake look confused.

'We're looking for the, um, animal-lovers. I was here before. With my mate Sammy.'

The woman frowned. 'That must have been some time ago.'

Jake shrugged. 'A year, maybe.'

'Yes. Well, there have been some changes here since then. The animal kingdom is no longer our main concern, though of course it has its part to play in the Great Scheme.'

'The thing is,' said Matt, 'we were rather hoping that we could stay here for the night.'

'I'm afraid I don't think that will be possible. There are only three of the old community here now, and we have all moved on. Spiritually, I mean. Deeper communion with Mother Earth is our only concern now.' She peered past him. 'What's that written on the side of your van?'

'The Pu Dong Pudding Company,' said Matt, and explained its function. Slowly the woman's face grew less severe. By the time Matt had finished running through the menu, it was suffused with benevolence.

'I think,' she said, 'that you and your friends should come in.'

VI

Frank stopped at the top of the hill, exhausted. There was no sign of the fox. The hounds had lost the scent, and were weaving futile patterns on the grass. Worst of all, the light was draining from the sky and the first stars were beginning to pierce the dusk.

So that was that. He'd hunted all day – on horse, on foot, on a bike and in a car; he'd driven across the breadth of the country. And what did he have to show for it? Nothing. He'd had days without a kill before – plenty of them; but none where the stakes were so high, or which left him so desperately pondering his next move.

He called the hounds to him and led the way back down the hill. Anna was waiting in the road with the car and trailer.

'Any sign?' she asked.

'No.'

The reproach was unspoken.

'Would you like me to drive?' she said when they had loaded the hounds. 'You look all in.'

'Sure.'

She paused as she put the key in the ignition.

'Frank,' she said. 'I'm sorry. I blew it. I should have fired when I had the chance. I just didn't trust myself.'

'It's OK. It's what hunting's all about, isn't it? The thrill lies in taking risks – but you've got to recognise when the risk is too great: the strand of wire on top of the bank, the allotments that end in a railway line.'

Suddenly he started laughing.

'What's so funny?'

'I was just thinking of the tourists in the cathedral – the looks on their faces. There probably hadn't been an animal inside those walls for a thousand years, other than rats and mice.'

She laughed too, with relief.

'Where can I take you to, sir?'

He pulled out his mobile. 'We need to track down the local MFH – see if he can accommodate the hounds, and us. Then tomorrow we have another go at that bloody fox.'

She fired the engine.

VII

'What do you mean, you lost them?' demanded Faye.

'I know Yu Shen's run,' said the restaurant manager. 'After me, he always goes to the Jade Pavilion on the other side of town, near the railway station. I figured I had time to call you, then catch up with him there. Then someone crashed a minibus at the end of my street. By the time I got there, he'd gone.'

Faye slapped his face. 'Idiot,' she said. 'You should never have let them out of your sight.'

They were standing in the kitchen of the Golden Palace. Jonty had found a set of knives and was throwing them across the room one by one, making a gleaming fringe around the edge of the door.

'Where does he go after the Jade Pavilion?' he asked.

'The Silver Temple in Bristol. I just phoned them. They haven't seen him.'

'And after that?'

'Back to High Wycombe.'

'OK, so we put a watch on the road into Bristol and the A40 going east. Also his house. We'll catch up with him soon enough.'

There was a scuffling in the corner. In a single movement Jonty turned on his heels and flung the final knife. A mouse lay skewered on the floor.

'Dead for a ducat,' said Jonty Lo.

VIII

'What about the man they picked up?'

'He's under maximum-security detention, Prime Minister,' said the voice on the telephone. 'Name of Sammy Lipfriend. Claims to be a member of the Animal Lovers' Army.'

'Good grief. What the hell do they want with the Vice President of China?'

'That's not yet clear. Lipfriend is demanding to be treated as a political prisoner. Says he won't answer any questions until that happens.

'So how exactly would we be treating him if he were a political prisoner?'

'At this point, no differently at all.'

'In that case, can't we just tell him that he is one?'

'I'm afraid not, Prime Minister. We'd have Amnesty International all over us like a rash.'

The name was like a red rag to a bull. If there was one thing the Prime Minister couldn't abide, it was bleeding-heart human-rights organisations.

'In that case,' he said, 'I suggest we take a few short cuts. What about some sleep deprivation?'

'I don't think I heard that, sir.'

'You did, but not from me.'

'Well . . . It's a bit early in the evening for that kind of thing, isn't it?'

There was a brief silence on the other end of the telephone.

'All right, here's what we do.' The Prime Minister's voice was rich with sarcasm. 'We wait until midnight, and then – provided his fairy godmother doesn't appear with a coach made out of a pumpkin and spirit him away – we make sure he doesn't sleep a wink for the remainder of the night. I will be breakfasting with the Chinese Ambassador at 8am, and I need to have some good news to tell him over his cornflakes. Are we clear on that?'

'Yes, sir. Clear as daylight.'

The Prime Minister put down the phone with a frown. The more the Mulberry Tree technology threatened to elude him, the more essential it seemed.

IX

Matt and Selina sat in front of an open fire drinking mugs of nettle tea. They would have preferred a glass of wine, but the commune did not approve of alcohol – 'Poison to the chakras,' the large lady called Jeanette had explained. Fortunately she had no objections to the prawn stir-fry Mr Yu was preparing in their kitchen, with Jake and Frederick as his sous-chefs. A selection of desserts would follow. The delicate odours crept into the sitting room and mingled with the wood smoke, bestowing a general sense of wellbeing. Matt smiled, almost forgetting the two prisoners in the back of the van and his status as a fugitive.

The members of the commune – six women and two men – sat in the middle of the floor chanting. Occasionally one of them struck a Tibetan prayer bell. Around them the walls were hung with pictures – all bright, indecipherable whorls – painted from the subconscious.

'Fruitcakes,' Matt had whispered as soon as he saw them.

Jeanette led the incantations.

Gaia, mother goddess, mother earth she intoned.

Birth mother, breath mother, death mother.

'Death mother,' echoed the acolytes.

You are our womb, you are our tomb.

The seed grows to grass. All things must pass.

'All things must pass.'

They were a pasty-faced lot: the earth mother, it seemed, fell short of providing a well-balanced diet. The women were overweight, the men weasel-faced and scrawny. Matt wondered what the sexual dynamics of the group were. The men he imagined as captive mates in an insect colony, drained of their vital juices. But no doubt the arrangement suited them. He found himself humming an old Beach Boys song:

Two girls for every boy
In California!

The thought of Nikki came into his head. How appalled she would be if she could see him now, surrounded by these mad, dowdy matriarchs! What an affront to her sense of style!

She and Matt had had good times together. He remembered their first weekend away, at a grand hotel in Seville; the sailing holiday on her brother's yacht in Greece; their friend Neil's baronial wedding in Scotland. He was still thrilled to think that this beautiful, intelligent, chic woman had chosen him above all the eligible men who came her way. Of course, that had been before he 'dropped out', as she liked to put it; but she'd stuck with him – he had to give her that. Was he really going to trade her in for the impetuous, over-made-up girl sitting next to him?

He realised that he needed to give her a call.

X

Christophe had been driving for five and a half hours by the time he turned off the M6. He needed a good night's sleep, and he didn't see himself getting one at an anonymous motorway hotel with overheated rooms and stains on the carpet. Nor did he like the idea of leaving the MG in an unsecured car park. The possibility of someone stealing it didn't bear contemplating.

Instead he found the River House, a hotel with ambitions it was unlikely ever to fulfil, in a small town he'd never heard of. The 'spa' advertised at reception consisted of a shallow pool in which a short person might manage half a dozen strokes. The 'waterside terrace' was a cramped balcony used only by smokers *in extremis.*

The River Club Bar did not stretch to a barman – though, Christophe reflected, this was just as well given Li's drinking habits.

Still, the rooms were clean and the sheets fresh. Christophe would have liked a room to himself, but he couldn't risk letting Li out of his sight. They took it in turns to wash, then made their way through a labyrinth of fire doors to the Weir Restaurant. They were the only diners.

'They should call it the Weird Restaurant!' said Li, beaming at his joke. 'No customers!'

Their table had a view of the river. The dark water reflected the orange light of the streetlamps which lined the towpath, and carried the shadows of the stone warehouses which overlooked it. A pretty teenage waitress brought menus. The soup of the day and the halibut were off.

When they had ordered, Christophe went into the corridor to call Tessa's parents. After a few rings her father answered.

'Hello?' There was an edge of hysteria to the voice. Christophe's heart sank.

'Jim? It's Christophe. I heard about the accident. How is she?'

'She's out of danger, thank God. Broken collarbone, broken ribs, a bit of concussion, but she'll mend. That's the thing about motorway accidents – the emergency services can usually get to them within the so-called "golden hour". On country roads it takes much longer for an accident to be reported or attended to, so the chances of survival are lower. Sixty per cent of fatal accidents take place on country roads and only six per cent on motorways. Did you know that?'

'No, I didn't.'

'Neither did I until they told me just now. They have some really interesting statistics.'

'It sounds like it. Is Tessa conscious?'

'Heavily sedated. They think she'll be in hospital for at least a week. But she's alive. That's the main thing.'

'Do they know what happened?'

'They say there was another vehicle involved – someone driving very dangerously – but they haven't made an arrest. Tessa was trying to avoid a collision and ended up hitting the crash barrier. They say it's a miracle there wasn't a pile-up.'

'Poor girl.'

'Christophe?'

'Yes?'

'You know Helen and I aren't great church-goers, but . . . will you pray for Tessa?'

'Of course I will.'

'Thanks. I'd better go now.'

'Sure. Take care, Jim.'

Christophe pocketed his phone, then leant against the wall for a minute with his eyes shut. Was it a miracle that Tessa had survived? Perhaps. But if so, why had she needed one? Because of someone else's recklessness or viciousness? Or because of his own stupidity in embroiling her in all this?

He had needed her help; she had been willing to give it. There was more at stake than either of their two lives. He had to remember that.

He returned to the restaurant. Pushing open the door, he saw to his horror that it was empty.

Feeling sick, he wondered why he had been stupid enough to leave Li on his own. But there was no way that Li could have left the room without passing him, unless he'd gone through the kitchens.

Then he realised his mistake. The far end of the restaurant was screened off. There must be another exit on the far side.

He hurried towards it. As he did so, invisible fingers began to play an invisible piano. Rounding the edge of the screen, he found Professor Li seated at a baby grand, picking out the chords of *Boogie-Woogie Bugle Boy*.

He was good – very good. Christophe stood and listened; and as he did so, the stress and fatigue of the day washed away. He imagined the Andrews Sisters singing this song back in the 1940s on a makeshift stage to star-struck young men in uniform. He wondered whether his grandparents had watched them on film in a smoky London picture house. And, to his own surprise, he wondered whether Amy in her provincial Chinese town had ever heard those flawless American harmonies.

Li came to the end of the song. He rested his fingers on the keys for a moment, then rose to his feet and carefully closed the piano lid. Christophe applauded.

Li smiled. 'Thank you, Dr Christo. Do you know, of all the pieces I have ever learned, that is my favourite.'

'Who taught you to play like that?'

'I will tell you over dinner. It is an interesting story.'

The waitress brought potted shrimps for Christophe and scallops for Li.

'My parents were very keen for me to learn the piano,' said Li. 'They had a friend who was an accomplished player, and I was sent to her for lessons. But soon I got bored of playing classical pieces. Then one day I had to take our radio to be mended, and while I was waiting I heard – very, very faintly – a completely different kind of music coming from the back of the shop. So I followed the sound and found a man playing records on an old gramophone.

'I asked him what kind of music it was, and at first he looked very alarmed and didn't want to tell me. But when I told him how much I loved it, he smiled and whispered, "Boogie-woogie!"

'As you probably know, all forms of jazz were disapproved of in China then: it was considered bourgeois music. But boogie-woogie had me under a spell: I went back to the shop whenever I had spare time. The man's name was Mr Deng and he had built up a hardware business, going around the houses with a hand-cart and collecting broken pieces of electrical equipment. Some of them he would mend, some of them he would strip for their components. Before long I started to help him. We would sit side by side listening to his records and working on the repairs – so I got an education in music and technology at the same time.

' "How come you know so much?" I asked him one day. Then he told me that he had been a university lecturer in his younger days, until the Cultural Revolution came and he was sent to work in the countryside. He had a very difficult time there, and though he finally got to come back to the city, he could not get another academic job – so he ended up fixing electrical goods. But one thing kept him going through all of this. "Other people play the blues," he used to say. "I play boogie-woogie. It makes everything OK."

'Meeting Mr Deng was the best thing that ever happened to me, but it was also the worst. Because of him I came top of my class and went to university to study science, and got to be where I am today. But what I really wanted to be was a pianist. I dreamed of touring the world and playing at Ronnie Scott's in London and Bourbon Street in New Orleans. Instead I had to work in a laboratory late into the night. Sometimes I feel very sad and maybe I drink a little bit too much because of that.'

'Perhaps when all this is over you can change your life and play piano full-time.'

Li smiled. 'Perhaps.'

How soon would it be over? All being well, Christophe thought, they would reach Neary's by lunchtime tomorrow. Neary would need some time to examine and test the syringe and discuss it with Li – but with luck no more than a few hours. The question was what to do then. With Tessa on board, the breaking of the story had seemed straightforward. Now he didn't know who to trust – or who would listen to him.

XI

Through Nick Llewellyn, Frank and Anna found lodgings for the night at Headlam Hall. The elegant, dilapidated Georgian house belonged to Horry Pine MFH, described by Llewellyn as 'a good sort, though a little odd'. Oddness ran in the family, and over the past two centuries several of Horry's ancestors had been committed to the county asylum. The house, inevitably, had come to be known as Bedlam Hall – though things had been quiet enough since Horry had inherited it. Only his after-dinner rat hunts with a Jack Russell and a First World War revolver disturbed the ghosts of Pines past.

'We'll stow the hounds and then show you your quarters,' he said.

He was a short, stout man with very bad teeth and a reluctance to look his guests in the eye. His head moved constantly up and down and from side to side, like that of a reptile waiting to catch an insect on its tongue.

'Do you know anything about poetry?' he asked as he led the way to the kennels.

'I used to be able to recite *Grief* by Elizabeth Barrett Browning,' said Anna. 'But it was a bit gloomy.'

'My nan read *Eugene Onegin* to me once,' said Frank. 'That wasn't a bundle of laughs either.'

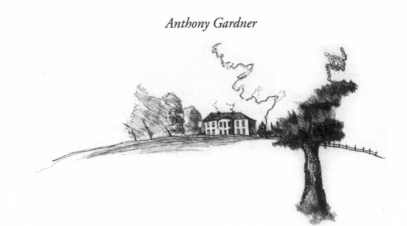

'I like something a bit more compact,' said Pine. 'The sonnet is my preferred form. Eight lines to warm the thing up, then kick 'em in the sestina. Here we are. My pack lives up the road with my huntsman in the new kennels, but this place is still fit for purpose. You'll find food in that bin over there if the rodents haven't devoured it all.'

The kennels were cold and musty, but the hounds bayed with excitement at their new surroundings and the prospect of dinner. Once fed, they stretched out on the straw, grateful for any kind of respite after their long odyssey. Frank thought of their four dead companions and the fox which had savaged them. Would tomorrow bring revenge?

Horry Pine's house was only fractionally warmer than the kennels. The window of Frank's room sat uneasily in its frame, leaving a steady draught to ruffle the thin curtains. The single bed sagged in the middle, and the carpet was gnawed at the edges. Half a dozen pictures – topographical prints and faded watercolours – were stacked in a corner. It was, Frank thought, the most inhospitable lodging he had ever found.

A bath in tepid water did nothing to raise his spirits. Descending the stairs for dinner past a line of lugubrious portraits, he felt

Horry's ancestors deploring his upstart presence. Anna, of course, must be used to this kind of thing. The three of them might all carry the letters MFH after their names, but a gulf divided him from the other two.

He found his host sitting at the kitchen table with a sheet of paper in front of him and a pair of half-moon spectacles on his nose. A cat was asleep in front of the Aga.

'I'm trying to think of a rhyme for "incantatory". Any ideas?'

'Sorry,' said Frank. 'It's not really my line.'

'Not really my line!' Horry chuckled. 'Oh, that's good – that's very good! I wish it wasn't my line, but it is: I've written it and now I'm stuck with it.'

'What about "bakery"?'

'Bakery! That's a thought. I wouldn't have come up with that in a thousand years. But it's hard to put the two together. "Incantatory" is sort of high-flown, and "bakery" is rather down-to-earth. Byron might have managed it, I suppose, but it's a bit beyond old Horry. What about a drink?'

Dinner was served in an oak-panelled dining room. A tall, thin young woman in jeans banged the food down on the table, cursing in a language Frank didn't recognise.

'That's Katerina,' said Horry when the door had slammed behind her. 'She's got a filthy temper, as you may have noticed. She calls herself a cook, but her food's pretty filthy as well, so she can't get a job anywhere else. And as no one else wants to come and work in an old ruin like this, we just have to rub along as best we can.'

The dinner was indeed disgusting – a lukewarm, peppery vegetable soup followed by a gristly joint of pork. Horry passed most of his food to a skinny black spaniel which sat looking up at him with imploring eyes. Frank wondered how Horry managed to remain so fat and the dog so thin.

Afterwards Horry produced a worn and much-Sellotaped map. It did not take him long to establish the exact spot where Frank and his hounds had lost the fox.

'There are two sizeable earths in the vicinity, here and here. That's where we'll start in the morning. To the best of my knowledge only one has been in recent use. So let's pray that your fox has gone to ground in the other – or God knows how many infected animals we could have on our hands.'

XII

Stretched out in the darkness of the Pu Dong Pudding truck, Jennifer Pettifer was trying to sleep. Her body was exhausted, but her mind kept running over the misadventures of the day. One moment she had been a free woman, a senior council executive with the power to meddle in the lives of thousands; the next she had become a helpless prisoner, hauled across the country against her will and forced into slave labour. Now, handcuffed on the sofa, she dwelt on thoughts of revenge. Not only would her captors be charged with false imprisonment, but every Chinese restaurant within the council's jurisdiction would have the book thrown at it – environmental health, fire precautions, noise pollution, the lot. There would be a wholesale crackdown on mobile catering units. Immigration officers would bring terror to the hearts of illegal aliens.

It would be wrong to say, though, that Jennifer had conceived a hatred of all things Chinese. Indeed, for the man who shared her predicament she felt nothing but awe and respect. To think that he had held sway over a bureaucracy thousands of times larger than hers – well, what could a girl feel but a shiver of excitement? And though he had barely spoken a word since the two of them had been forced together, there was an aura about Zhou that reminded her unmistakably of Jeffrey Crusham.

Now Zhou, like her, was confined to the sofa for the night. A blanket thrown on top of them increased the sense of intimacy. A loud snoring from an unseen corner told her that their guard, Jake, was oblivious to their activities.

Suddenly Jennifer felt a hand exploring her thigh.

Although Zhou had limited room for manoeuvre, he put it to expert use. Within a few minutes, those parts of Jennifer's body that had been long starved of male attention had been unveiled, caressed, primed for nirvana. But for Jake's sleeping presence, she would have screamed her gratitude.

'Empower me,' she moaned. 'Empower me!'

XIII

Try as he might, Frank couldn't get comfortable in his sagging single bed. He had just turned over for the twentieth time when he heard a tap on the door. It was Anna.

'I can't sleep,' she said.

'Me neither.'

She was wearing a silk dressing gown borrowed from their host. It smelt of tobacco and the cuffs were frayed. Frank wasn't sure whether she had anything on underneath.

She sat down on the end of the bed.

'I can't believe how close we got to it,' she said. 'At the golf club, when I could have shot it. And then in the Archbishop's car – if the driver had only answered his phone sooner. Now we've got to start all over again, and there's no guarantee that we'll find it at all.'

'There never is, is there?'

'No, but in day-to-day hunting it doesn't matter, does it? There's always tomorrow or next week. This time so much depends on it. But at least Horry seems to know what he's doing.'

Frank snorted. 'I wouldn't be too sure of that. I think he's a bleeding head case – all that poetry nonsense.'

'You think poetry is nonsense? What happened to Mr Russian literature?'

'I'm not saying all poetry is nonsense – I'm saying that his is.'

'He's just a bit eccentric, like Nick Llewellyn said. And he took us in at a moment's notice. Tell me you're grateful for his hospitality at least.'

'You call this hospitality? No hot water, a pig-awful meal, and as for this room . . . You may have a gorgeous suite in the west wing, but I wouldn't put my hounds in here. That might be eccentric where you come from, but to me it's f–ing rude.'

'So we're back to class, are we?'

'I'm only saying . . .'

'You think he's given you the worst room in the house, and it's because you're not as posh as he is.'

'Maybe.'

'Well, let me tell you this, Frank Smith – my room is no more comfortable than this, and I bet you a thousand pounds Horry's isn't either. It's just the way he lives. He's a kind soul who's doing his best to help us, and if you can't see that, you're not the gutsy, intelligent self-made man I took you for – you're just a sad, chippy bastard.'

She got to her feet.

'Wait,' said Frank. 'I'm sorry. I'm knackered, and so much depends on catching that fox, and . . . I guess you're right. It's good of the bloke to put us up, and I haven't seen anything in the house that could be called luxurious.'

'So you'll be nice and friendly to him in the morning?'

'Yeah.'

'Good.' She unfastened the dressing-gown and let it slip from her shoulders. 'Then I'll be nice and friendly to you.'

XIV

It was in the deadest part of the night that Sammy cracked, after several hours of being doused with cold water at thirty-minute intervals. He revealed that Vice President Zhou's probable destination was a private house in Herefordshire, and that Professor Li was heading elsewhere in a red MG. But when asked to locate his comrades' house on a map, he was unable to do so.

'It's somewhere around here,' he said desperately, running his finger over a network of country roads. 'I'd know the place if I saw it.'

'Right,' said the officer in charge with an exasperated sigh. 'Find him some dry clothes, put him in a car, and get him down there ASAP. And make sure we've got plenty of back-up.'

CHAPTER SIXTEEN

The sky was paling into morning above the surrounding woods when Matt stole out of the house. Waking birds were making tentative calls from unseen branches; a rabbit hopped across the lawn leaving small marks in the dew.

Morning has broken, like the first mor-or-orning
Matt sang quietly to himself.
Blackbird has spoken, like the first bird.

Nikki, he knew, was at a conference in Singapore, which meant that he had a chance of catching her during the break for lunch. He felt deeply guilty about ringing her while his imprint was still warm on the bed he'd shared with another woman, and he certainly wasn't going to borrow Selina's mobile for the call. But he could borrow Jake's, if he was up and about.

There was no sign of life from the van. Matt was debating whether to rap on the back door when he noticed something lying between the back wheels. It was a smartphone. This must be his lucky day.

The phone was turned off and demanded a PIN code when he activated it. But he knew that most people kept their PINs basic. He punched in '1-2-3-4'. The phone came to life.

He dialled Nikki's number.

'Hello?' The voice at the other end sounded befuddled. The connection was better than he expected.

'Hi, darling.'

'Matt? Jesus, what time is it?'

'I'm guessing it's about 2pm your time.'

'My time? Where the hell do you think I am?'

'You're in Singapore, aren't you?'

'You know perfectly well that my trip was cancelled. At least, you would do if you'd bothered to pick up any of the messages I left on your answerphone last week.'

'Why were you leaving me messages when you knew I was stuck in prison?'

'You're not in prison.'

'Well, no, but . . .'

'You're not in prison because, in case you've forgotten, I paid your fine.'

'You did what? When?'

There was a sigh at the other end. 'You're pissed, aren't you? I'm guessing that you've been arseholed since last week when I paid your fine and they let you out. Because I can't think of any other reason why you haven't rung to thank me, or apologise for making me look a complete and utter tit by not turning up to the welcome-home party I organised for you. When I think what I went through to get that private room at Rivera . . .'

'Nikki, I . . .'

'Forget it, Matt. I'm tired of having a boyfriend who's a total loser and has absolutely no respect for my feelings. It's over.'

She rang off.

Matt went back to the house in a daze.

'What's up?' asked Selina sleepily. Her dark hair was spread against the pillow like seaweed upon the ocean floor.

'I'm not supposed to be in prison.'

'What do you mean?'

'I just discovered. My fine was paid last week, which means that I should have been released. So this running away has been for nothing. Now I'm going to be had up for absconding and kidnapping, whereas if I'd stayed put I'd be a free man.'

'Oh, sweetheart, no.' She reached out for him. 'It's all my fault for luring you away. I'm so sorry.'

'There must have been a mix-up.'

'I suppose so.'

'Why don't you come back to bed?'

Matt did so, reflecting that being on the run, even by mistake, had compensations.

II

Jonty Lo had spent an unexpectedly agreeable night at the Beau Regard guest house. It looked nothing from the road, and under normal circumstances he would not have deigned to set foot in it. But with every hotel in the vicinity filled with delegates to an agricultural convention, he and Faye were left with no choice.

'You're in luck,' said Mrs Herrick, its white-haired owner, brightly. 'I have an unexpected vacancy on account of a gentleman being taking ill in the cakes and preserves tent.'

They followed her upstairs. Not since his student days had Jonty stayed in a B&B, but he had vivid memories of nylon sheets, corn dollies and bars of soap barely visible to the naked eye. If it was too awful, he might just sleep in the car.

But Mrs Herrick proved to have excellent taste. The sheets were Egyptian cotton, the knick-knacks Swarovski, the soap and hand cream Roger & Gallet. The furniture was repro but superior in its finishing, and the prints on the walls were of lesser-known Old Masters from the Rijksmuseum in Amsterdam. Whether travellers en route to agricultural shows appreciated these things, Jonty wasn't sure, but he himself was deeply grateful.

What was more, he and Faye had had excellent, high-octane sex. This was not a regular feature of their relationship, for both preferred to take their pleasures elsewhere; nor was it accompanied by any pretence of affection. But both subscribed to the belief – popular among big-game hunters and professional assassins – that carnal knowledge on the eve of a killing steadied the hand and improved the eye; and since both had a sadistic streak, their congress involved excitements largely unknown to more conventional couples.

Lying on his duck-down pillow listening to the dawn chorus, Jonty felt more than ready for the task in hand. What Vice President Zhou had done to fall foul of his colleagues in Beijing was no concern of his; nor was the fact that his death was to be attributed to that ruthless terrorist organisation the Brothers of Light. All Jonty's professional pride demanded was that he should do the job with a single bullet – though of course further ammunition might be needed if anyone were stupid enough to get in the way.

He must have drifted off again, because the beeping of Faye's BlackBerry brought him to himself with an unpleasant jolt. She turned to him with a look of glee.

'Beijing has picked up a signal from Zhou's phone. He's less than ten miles away. We're out of here.'

III

Frank, Anna and Horry had risen while it was still dark. Frank was well used to early starts, but it was one thing to assemble a handful of hounds for an urban hunt and quite another to get a real pack into a lorry and an unfamiliar horse into a trailer by the light of a feeble yard lamp. On top of everything else, Horry's huntsman and whipper-in had been taken ill.

'There's this wretched Indian place down the road called the Hungry Swami,' he sighed. 'I warned them about the saag gosht, but would they listen? We'll just have to take fewer hounds.'

But Frank had no complaints: wasn't this the real thing, the sport his father had raised him to? His heart thrilled at the prospect of a chase across open countryside. Add to that the memory of his night with Anna, and – well, Frank felt ready for anything.

Horry went about his business with more energy and efficiency than Frank could have believed him capable of. He had picked out horses for Frank and Anna without a moment's hesitation, and chivvied the hounds with a stream of good-humoured banter.

At last the loading was completed. The convoy moved off, Horry and Anna leading with the horses, Frank following with the hounds. They met no other traffic as they brushed along hedgerows still black and indistinct.

They parked on the stretch of road where the previous day's hunt had ended. The hounds spilled out like schoolchildren beginning their holidays. They lolloped away down the tarmac and clambered on the bank to sniff the long grass; then, called to order by the cracking of whips, they allowed themselves to be diverted into the nearest field.

Frank swung up on to his borrowed horse. It was a young chestnut with a mischievous look in its eye, but nothing he couldn't handle. The way it cantered up the hillside made a mock-ery of his laborious ascent by mountain bike the day before.

They paused at the summit, three riders with a flood of hounds swirling around their horses' legs. Frank wondered whether Napoleon and his marshals had felt the same sense of anticipation on the battlefield of Borodino.

'Right,' said Horry. 'Let's go.'

The flood broke and streamed down the hill.

IV

'Her!' Matt sat up suddenly in bed.

'Who?' asked Selina sleepily.

'Jennifer bloody Pettifer!'

'What about her?'

'She must have known. Think about it. She's the superbureau-crat: she must have been informed that my fine had been paid. Yet there she was, snooping around the farm, quite sure that she wouldn't be caught. Which means only one thing: she fixed it so that the payment got lost in the system. Just wait till I get my hands on her!'

He pulled on his clothes. In the sitting-room the commune's members, some still in pyjamas and dressing gowns, had gathered for pre-breakfast chanting. The men looked more wan than ever.

There was no sign of the others. Mr Yu and Frederick, he assumed, were still asleep in the other guest room.

Outside, the world had changed from grey to gold, but Matt in his fury barely noticed. He strode across the gravel and flung open the doors of the truck. A figure lay stretched out, gagged and handcuffed, on the sofa. But it wasn't Zhou or Jennifer Pettifer. It was Jake.

V

'Jesus, Jake! What happened?'

Fortunately the key to the handcuffs had been left on the draining board. Jake pulled off the gag and rubbed his wrists.

'It was Zhou,' he said. 'Somehow he'd trousered that potato peeler he was using yesterday. The kid comes in bright and early looking for his breakfast, and suddenly Zhou grabs him and puts the peeler to his throat: says he'll rip him open unless I free him and the bitch from the council. Makes me hand over the gun as well. Then they scarper.'

'When was this?'

'Half an hour ago.'

'And they took Frederick with them?'

'Yes. Said he was their insurance.'

'Jesus.'

They found Mr Yu shaving in one of the washrooms. He listened to the news in horror, his face half lathered.

'My son,' he whispered. 'My son.'

For a moment Matt felt as if he were looking at a ghost. But before he knew it, Yu's fighting spirit had returned.

'They'll be sorry!' he shouted, brandishing his razor. 'I'll cut them into little pieces! I'll stir-fry them with noodles! They'll wish they never heard of the Pu Dong Pudding Company!'

It took Selina and Jeanette to calm him. Selina sat him down in the kitchen with a cigarette while Jeanette brewed caffeine-free coffee and shooed away inquisitive members of the commune.

'We need a plan,' said Matt. 'Obviously we have to get after them as soon as possible, but there are any number of ways they could have gone, so we have to be methodical. We need to ask ourselves what we would do in their position.'

'I'd head down the avenue,' said Selina.

'Right. But they might well realise that that's what we'd expect them to do, and take the opposite direction. What about the fields behind the house, Jeanette – any possibilities there?'

'If they go west they'll come to the river. I doubt they'd try to cross that; and it's very boggy to the south, so I can't see them going that way.' She spoke as if an atavistic feeling for the chase had banished all thoughts of the goddess's tranquil ministry. 'But that still leaves a wide area to be covered.'

'Would your people be prepared to help?'

'Oh, yes. It's all for the greater good, isn't it?'

'Then here's what we do. Mr Yu takes the truck and drives down the avenue. Everybody else divides into pairs and fans out across country. If anyone sees anything, they call me on my mobile.'

'What happens then?' asked Selina. 'Zhou's got a gun, remember.'

'He has. However, it doesn't contain any bullets.'

'What?' said Jake.

'I took them out yesterday while everyone was busy cooking.'

'If I'd known that –'

'Zhou wouldn't have been able to overpower you. I realise that, and I'm sorry. I just didn't want there to be any accidents.'

'Accidents! There I was, tied up like a bleeding chicken . . .'

'Please,' said Mr Yu. 'No arguments. I need you to help me find my son.'

VI

Mr Yu climbed into the cabin of his truck and turned on the engine. How many times he had set out in it with Frederick by his side! It was more of a home to them, all things considered, than the small house in High Wycombe. There was something at once cosy and exciting about sitting on this high seat with the road before them while Frederick chattered in his schoolboy English. Another adjective came to mind: companionable. But now – that villain, that devil Zhou! Yu trembled with fear and outrage as he thought of his child in the hands of such a man. There was not a moment to lose.

And yet, he told himself as the truck jolted along the avenue, he mustn't go too fast: if he did, he might miss them altogether. The moment they heard him coming, they would head for cover. The engine must run as quietly as possible.

He reached the rusty gates. Now the search became more challenging. So many trees on either side: more, it seemed, than when he had driven along here yesterday. Scores – no, hundreds – of hiding places.

At last the wood began to thin out. Around the corner, a road sign warned, was a junction. Which way should he go?

He was still deliberating when a blue light penetrated the surrounding trees. He turned the corner to see a line of police vehicles filling the road ahead.

VII

Frank's excitement had given way to anxiety. They had made a good start, finding almost immediately; but now, after an exhilarating run – three miles at least, he reckoned – the hounds had lost the scent. Instead of the gung-ho pack that had charged over walls and ditches, they snuffled around in twos and threes like punters at a car-boot sale.

The weather too had changed for the worse: gone was the early sunshine, to be replaced by low cloud and light rain. But there was still a couple of hundred yards' visibility, and as he crested a small hill Frank came upon a baffling sight. Strung out across the fields in front of him were a dozen men and women on foot, some of them wearing pink dressing gowns.

'Take a butcher's at this,' he called to Horry and Anna. 'What do you make of it?

They rode up beside him.

'Looks like a sleep-walkers' convention,' said Horry. 'But perhaps they've seen something. Let's go and ask them.'

He urged his horse forward.

VIII

Mr Yu hesitated. Had the police spotted him? Perhaps it was a godsend that they had come now, with the resources to find his kidnapped son; but if he himself was identified as a kidnapper, would they even listen to him?

He was spared the decision. One of the cars surged forward to meet him and two uniformed men got out.

'Good morning, officers. Pu Dong Pudding Company at your service.' Yu gave them his brightest smile. 'What can I offer you – a nice sherry trifle? Matron's leg?'

The policemen looked bemused.

'A bit early in the day for me,' said one. 'What about you, Morton?'

'I had a full English, Sarge.' There was a note of regret in his voice. 'I knew I should have gone easy on the chipolatas, but the wife was very insistent.'

The sergeant turned back to Yu. 'If you wouldn't mind stepping down from your cab, sir, we need to ask you a few questions.'

Yu gave a fine performance. The commune, he explained, was a new stop on his delivery run. No, he hadn't seen any other gentlemen of Asian appearance. In fact, he hadn't seen anyone except the lady who'd placed the order – lemon meringue pies, treacle tarts and sticky toffee puddings enough to feed a small army. He had an idea that she and her friends went out for a walk at this time of day.

'Do you mind if we take a look in the back of your vehicle, sir?'

Yu racked his brains – was there anything incriminating inside? He wasn't sure. But he could hardly refuse their request.

He opened the rear doors. Everything looked spick and span.

The sergeant climbed in and glanced around. 'Very nice,' he said. 'Very well-appointed.'

'All passed by the environmental health officers,' lied Yu. But inside he was bursting to end the charade – to sink on his knees and implore them, 'Find my boy!'

Something glinted in the corner. The sergeant stooped to pick it up.

'What's this?'

Mr Yu was speechless. From the policeman's hand dangled the handcuffs that had been used to secure Zhou and Jennifer Pettifer. The game was surely up.

Suddenly there was a loud bang and the truck lurched under him, throwing him to the floor.

IX

Jonty Lo watched with satisfaction through his telescopic sight as the police scrambled for cover, ducking behind their cars and vans. He and Faye had got here in the nick of time. By shooting out the tyres of the Pu Dong Pudding Company's truck, he had effectively blocked the approach to the house: if the police wanted to get to it they would have to make their way on foot through the woods – and past him. Given the British obsession with health and safety regulations, they were unlikely to be going anywhere soon; by the time they did, he would have slipped away and Faye would have visual contact with their target – who, according to her monitor, was proceeding at walking pace across the open fields. Faye, fit as a fiddle from her daily sessions at Belgravia's Bio Logical gym, had hit the ground running and was gaining on Zhou by the minute. It saddened Jonty that he wouldn't be in on the kill, but as he was the better marksman and Faye the faster runner, the division of responsibilities had been obvious enough.

One of the policemen was venturing out. 'Naughty, naughty!' thought Jonty. He squeezed the trigger and a windscreen shattered into a spider's web of glass. The policeman threw himself to the ground and stayed there.

X

'Foxhunters! Wait till I get my hands on them!'

Jake started towards the mounted figures coming down the hill. Matt grabbed him by the shoulder.

'Leave it, Jake.'

'Leave it? Why should I leave it? You think I'm going to stand by and let those bloodthirsty toffs chase a poor helpless animal to its grave?'

'This is not the time.'

'Then when is? Look at them in their fancy get-ups – like they were going to a bleeding party.'

'Think about why we're here.' Matt was restraining him with both arms now. 'If we don't rescue Frederick, we could all be going to a funeral. These people can help us.'

'I'd rather be helped by Saddam Hussein and Osama bin f–ing Laden.'

'Handy though they might be in tracking down a ten-year-old boy through a field of cow pats, they are unfortunately both dead. This lot are alive and kicking, presumably know the lie of the land, and can cover the ground far more quickly than we can. So do me a favour and put a lid on your undying hatred of them for five minutes. Can you do that?'

Jake shook himself free. 'I suppose so.'

The leader of the hunt was a fat man in a red coat. Behind him came a younger man who looked vaguely familiar, and a very pretty woman – blonde, pink-cheeked and well-groomed.

'Morning,' said the fat man. 'You look as if you've lost something.'

'Some*one*, actually.'

Matt explained about Frederick's abduction, without mentioning Zhou or Jennifer Pettifer's identities, or the fact that both had until recently been prisoners themselves.

'We were hoping you could help,' he concluded.

The hunting party exchanged anxious glances.

'We'll have to split up,' said the familiar-looking one. 'We can't give up on the fox at this stage.'

'You see!' Jake erupted. 'I told you they were callous bastards! And I know who he is too: that cocky git from the telly. Frank bloody Smith – class traitor!'

He launched himself at Frank, trying to pull him from the saddle. Frank's horse reared, twisting sideways and colliding with Horry's mount. Somehow Frank managed to stay on; it was Horry who fell heavily to the ground, giving a cry of pain. Jake looked astonished and delighted.

Now it was Matt's turn to lose his temper. He grabbed Jake and shoved him backwards.

'You idiot!' he shouted. 'I ask you to do one simple thing, and can you do it? No! This is all your bloody fault. If you hadn't brought that half-witted crony of yours to the farm, we wouldn't be in this f–ing mess, would we?'

Jake had never seen his friend so furious.

'I'm sorry, Matt. I just thought . . .'

'I don't care what you thought. Get lost. Do you hear me? Get the hell out of it.'

Jake searched for something to say, but found nothing. He turned and walked slowly away across the field.

'I'm really sorry,' said Matt. Horry was still on the ground, with Anna tending to him while Frank held their horses. 'He's basically a nice guy, but he has a thing about foxhunting. Are you OK?'

'I think so. No bones broken anyway.'

But when he tried to stand up, he was back on the ground in a moment.

'Bloody knee's gone,' he said. 'It's happened before. I was on crutches for six weeks last time.'

'We'd better get you to a doctor,' said Matt.

'Forget that – you've got bigger fish to fry. Do you have anything with the boy's scent on it?'

Matt shook his head. 'His father would have something in his truck, but that's back there.' He gestured over his shoulder. 'I've got this, though, belonging to the guy who kidnapped him.' He produced Zhou's mobile.

'Not ideal,' said Frank. 'But better than nothing.' He turned to Anna. 'I'll take half the pack and look for the boy. You go after the fox.'

'What about Horry? We can't just leave him lying here.'

'I'll get Jeanette and her friends to help him back to the house,' said Matt. He waved to a woman approaching from the far side of the field. She was accompanied by two figures in pink dressing-gowns and wellington boots.

'You're sure they're not barmy?' asked Horry. 'My family's had enough dealings with lunatics.'

'Just a little eccentric,' said Matt.

'We'd better get moving,' said Frank. 'Can you ride?'

This was not something Matt had bargained for. 'I used to a bit, years ago.'

'Good. You can take the other horse. That OK by you, Horry?'

'Fine by me.'

'Then let's go.'

XI

Faye stopped by a gate to catch her breath and stared in bewilderment at her monitor. The movement of the pulsing dot marking Zhou's phone made no sense at all. No longer was it travelling at uniform speed in a straight line; it alternated between standing still and moving incomprehensibly faster than it had before, sometimes forwards and sometimes sideways – occasionally even back on its tracks. What was he up to?

There was nothing for it. She adjusted her shoulder holster and ran on.

XII

Jennifer Pettifer was not looking her best. The rain had combined with the remnants of Mr Yu's flour to make her hair a mass of sticky globules; her shoes and tights were covered in mud. There was, nonetheless, a radiance about her. She was a woman in love.

Her natural inclination was to do things by the book. Not in a million years would her younger self have imagined hauling a ten-year-old boy across the countryside against his will. But Jeffrey Crusham had taught her that those who make the rules can also break them, and in Vice President Zhou she had found for the first time a man who could compare to Crusham. She saw him as a mandarin in silken robes, commanding the furthest corners of a huge empire from a jade throne in the Forbidden City . . . So when she questioned the wisdom of taking the boy with them, and Zhou replied 'For insurance', she told herself that he knew best.

Certainly Frederick was slowing them down, but not by much. Zhou had him under his arm in an effective hold – one hand on his collar, the other on his ear – and dragged him determinedly along, cursing him in Chinese. To begin with Frederick had responded in the language of Billy Bunter – 'You rotter! Leggo, you fearful cad!' But now he only gasped and snivelled, with the occasional cry of pain.

As for where they were going – Jennifer didn't care. Every moment spent in the company of this masterful man was precious; every new challenge brought them closer together. She dared to hope that he felt the same about her – that this English rain was the prelude to the sunshine of Beijing, where she would rule alongside him, a bureaucrat commanding the lives of a billion people.

They reached the top of a gully. The ground dropped steeply before them in a grey scar of scree punctuated by medium-sized rocks. At the bottom it flattened out into an empty field, beyond which lay a thick wood.

'Come on!' cried Zhou. 'In the wood we will be safe!'

They scrambled down, Frederick crying out in fear as the stones slid away under his feet and Zhou shouted at him to keep quiet. More than once Jennifer lost her balance and had to grab at a rock to steady herself. But in the end they reached the bottom, dishevelled but unharmed.

Then they saw the fox.

XIII

The fox was in a clump of bushes on the edge of the field. It was clearly agitated, but instead of running off as the three approached, it stood its ground.

Not until they were within ten yards of it did they discover why. Its leg was caught in a steel trap.

It was clear to Zhou that this was not the animal's only problem. He had been fully briefed on the effects of fox flu. The purple stain on its muzzle and wild look in its eye told him that this was a victim. The disease had reached Britain!

What should he do? There might be other carriers in the country, but he couldn't be sure of it. He must act on the assumption that this was the only one.

'What's wrong with it?' asked Frederick, his misery giving way to fascination.

'Nothing wrong with it!' said Zhou. 'We must help this poor dumb animal.'

It didn't take him long to find a long, stout stick. He handed it to Jennifer Pettifer.

'Here. Use it to prise open the trap.'

Jennifer hesitated. 'Are you sure that's a good idea?'

'Sure, no problem.' He smiled.

'Only it looks . . . rather bad-tempered.'

'Wouldn't you be? But when it's free, everything will be OK. And anyway, I have this.' He brandished the revolver. 'Any trouble, I will shoot it. Come on, Jennifer – or perhaps you are not the feisty lady I think you are.'

Now she saw: it was a test – the kind devised for heroines in fairy tales. Was Jennifer going to shirk the chance to prove her devotion to her lover? No. She grasped the stick, positioned it carefully in the jaws of the trap, and pulled. The fox jumped free.

For a moment it stared at the three humans with furious eyes. Then it turned and ran across the field they had come from. Despite its injured leg, it covered the ground with remarkable speed.

'Well done, Jennifer!' said Zhou. 'We have done our good deed for the day.'

XIV

Anna watched the hounds anxiously as they hoovered the ground for a scent. This was a challenge she hadn't bargained for – hunting the fox alone on unfamiliar territory with an unfamiliar pack. It had been hard enough with Frank beside her, knowing how much was at stake; now it was all down to her.

She couldn't help feeling that the odds were stacked against her. Just when Frank seemed to have forgiven her for the incident at the golf club; just when a blissful night together had left her dreaming of a future with him – just at this crucial moment there had to be another complication. She was thrilled, of course, that he had trusted her with these hounds, this mission. But what if she failed?

She realised now that she'd played her hand badly with Frank. She'd let him make false assumptions about her, teased him in a way he only pretended not to mind. But she'd never before seen any harm in flirting; and she hadn't, to begin with, considered him a serious prospect. All along there'd been the thought of what her father would say: Daddy, who'd brought her up alone after her mother had run off; who'd bought her the best that money could buy; who'd dismissed all her boyfriends to date as presumptuous fortune-hunters . . .

But a moment later Daddy was forgotten because there, suddenly, it was, darting across an open field in front of her.

The hounds gave voice and raced towards it. Sounding her horn, Anna galloped after them.

The fox stopped in its tracks, turned, and raced back in the direction it had come from.

Anna rode for all she was worth. The asphalt of Birmingham belonged to a different lifetime: she was part of another landscape now, part of ancient England, at one with the fields and trees and rivers, as the rain whipped her face and the earth flew under her horse's hoofs.

Ahead the fox reached a high bank and disappeared over it. The hounds followed. Anna braced herself to jump it, not knowing what lay on the other side.

She realised her mistake too late. The ground dropped dramatically; her horse almost lost its footing as it landed, and it was all she could do to hang on. As she pulled herself back into an upright position, she realised that the fox had outsmarted her.

She and the hounds were in a kind of pen – though what it had been devised for she couldn't tell. There were high timber walls on three sides; the fourth consisted of a pair of steel gates. Half a dozen brand-new quad bikes were parked along one side; perhaps the owner was afraid of having them stolen. It was a miracle she hadn't landed on one of them.

As for the fox, there was no sign of it. It must have jumped to one side while the hounds' sight was obscured, leaving them to pour into this prison. Leaning from the saddle, she tried the gates; they were locked from the outside.

The walls were obviously too high for the hounds to jump – but a horse?

Anna hesitated. The horse wasn't hers; they were both lucky to be in one piece. On another day she wouldn't have attempted it. But this wasn't another day. If she lost the fox now, it would be gone for good.

She cracked her whip to clear the hounds away, faced her horse to the far wall, and charged towards it.

'Please God,' she prayed, 'let me get over.'

The world blurred. She was airborne. There was a bang as the horse's hoofs hit the wooden parapet, but it was only a glancing blow on the way down. Then they were back on firm ground.

She scanned the field ahead of her. The fox was two hundred yards away, heading for a wood – and in front of the fox were three figures.

XV

The fox didn't recognise Zhou and Jennifer as the people who had just done it a favour. All it registered was a group of humans standing between it and freedom. It went for Zhou.

The Vice President was comfortable with firearms and didn't hesitate. He raised the pistol and fired.

The hammer clicked against an empty chamber. The fox kept coming.

Zhou tried again, with the same result. In desperation he dropped the gun and grabbed the only shield that came to hand: Frederick.

The boy screamed as the fox's teeth closed on his arm. He and Zhou tumbled backwards, sprawling in the mud, the fox on top of them. Anna, galloping towards them, watched in horror.

'Shoot it, Anna! Shoot it!'

It was Frank's voice, coming from somewhere behind her. Glancing over her shoulder, she saw two horsemen and a scattering of hounds, still a long way off.

There was no time to think about what she was doing – just to jump from her horse, draw her revolver, try to angle a shot that wouldn't hit man or child, but would hit the flailing animal.

She fired.

The boy was still screaming, the man shouting. The bedraggled woman standing next to them seemed frozen to the spot. The fox twitched and lay still.

Anna lowered the gun. But Frank was still shouting at her.

'Don't let the hounds touch the fox!'

She turned. The hounds were almost upon her. The diseased carcase was at her feet. She bent and snatched it from the ground just ahead of the hungry pack.

Frank took the dead fox from her hand and secured it to his saddle. Their eyes locked.

He smiled. 'Bloody good shot, girl.'

There was a whimper from the wounded boy. The other horseman jumped down and knelt beside him.

'The bally fox,' said the boy. 'It bit my bally arm.'

'Do you know anything about first aid?' Matt asked Frank.

'A bit. Let's have a look.'

The wound was not deep. Frank was able to bandage it with Anna's stock.

'There,' he said. 'That should keep you going until we get you to a doctor.'

But he knew that Anna was thinking the same thing as he was. What could a doctor do about the virus that had entered the boy's bloodstream?

Jennifer Pettifer had helped Zhou to his feet. 'If you've quite finished,' she said, 'this man needs attention too.'

Matt opened his mouth to speak; but before he could do so, another gunshot sounded nearby. With a strange sideways jerk, Zhou fell back to the ground.

CHAPTER SEVENTEEN

Christophe caught the breaking news on television after breakfast. There had been a siege at a remote property in Herefordshire; one man had been shot. Police looking for the kidnapped Chinese Vice President had been involved. Nothing more was known at present.

Who was the victim – Matt? Zhou? Jake? Mr Yu? Above all, Christophe prayed that it wasn't Matt. The only person whose mobile number he had was Selina; he rang it, but there was no reply.

He gave Li a shake. 'We'd better get going.'

Li was not a morning person. Today he bore a close resemblance to a zombie, but with rather less colour in his cheeks. He gathered his few belongings as if in a trance and followed Christophe downstairs with slow steps. A young man with spectacles was on duty at the front desk.

'We'd like to check out, please.'

'That's fine. Can I have your room number?'

As he waited for his bill to be printed, Christophe glanced at the screen behind the desk. It showed four images streamed from the hotel's security cameras. There was the lobby, the dining-room, the pool, the back door.

'It'll just take a moment, sir. The system's a bit slow this morning.'

The pictures changed. There was the bar; there was the entrance to the garage; and there were two men examining a red MG.

Who the hell were they? Thieves? Classic-car enthusiasts? Plain-clothes policemen?

'There you go, sir.'

Christophe paid in cash. Then he laid an extra £20 note on the desk.

'I want you to do something for me. There are two friends of mine from the MG owners' club in your garage, and I'd like to play a bit of a joke on them. I need you to go and ask them if they're the men who are meeting Christophe Hardy, because if so he's been taken to the local hospital with alcoholic poisoning. They'll think that's very funny. Tell them I'm in Ward 7 if they want to pay me a visit.'

The receptionist was doubtful. 'I'm not really supposed to leave the desk,' he said. But he eyed the £20 note with the look of a man who thought he could usefully do something with it.

'It'll only take you two minutes. We'll mind the shop.' Christophe gave him a wink.

'Well . . . OK.'

'Good man.'

As soon as he had gone, Christophe led the way out through the back door. There was a small garden at the rear of the hotel, and beyond it an area for deliveries. This opened on to a residential street which came out, Christophe calculated, some twenty or thirty yards beyond the garage.

As he and Li entered the street, he realised that he'd forgotten to ask which way the hospital was. How could he have been so stupid? If it was past the entrance to the hotel, the chances of meeting the two strangers were small. But if their route took them in the opposite direction, the situation was much trickier.

He reached the end of the street and peered around the corner. There was no one to be seen. Had the men already gone?

He waited for five minutes. The road remained deserted apart from an old lady with a tartan shopping trolley. It seemed safe enough.

'Come on.'

Li groaned. 'I don't feel well. I think perhaps those scallops were no good.'

That's all I need, thought Christophe: a passenger with food poisoning.

'It's not far,' he said. 'You'll feel better when we're on the road. Nothing like an open-top sports car to blow the cobwebs away.'

He could see the entrance to the garage now. Keeping close to the wall, he moved towards it.

In the doorway he paused to let his eyes grow used to the dimness. There was no sign of life. He could see the nose of the MG at the far end of the first row of cars. Thank God it hadn't been stolen.

Behind him Li was bent over with his head between his knees.

'You stay there,' said Christophe. 'I'll bring the car out.'

He stepped into the gloom. The cavernous space was silent apart from the sound of dripping in a far corner. He was just feeling in his pocket for the car keys when a hand seized him by the collar. The next thing he knew his feet had been kicked from under him.

He landed face down on the concrete floor. For a moment he felt too shocked to move. His hands had broken his fall but his left wrist felt as if it had been broken too. He groaned.

'Atishoo, atishoo, we all fall down.'

The voice was strangely high and thin. The man was even heftier than he had looked on CCTV – almost obese. How had he materialised so silently from the shadows?

'Who are you?' Christophe gasped.

'I'll give you a clue: my name's not Christophe Hardy. I know it isn't Christophe Hardy, because Christophe Hardy has got what I want. He's got a very unusual syringe, and he needs to hand it over unless he wants to be seriously incommoded.'

'What makes you think I've got this syringe?'

'My information is that your colleague Professor Li was working on it. My information is that you met him on a train from Beijing to Hong Kong. My information is that you got it off him while he was a drunk as a skunk.'

'Who is this man?' Christophe wondered. 'How does he know so much?' He tried to think through the pain, to make a plan.

'You're right,' he said. 'The only thing is that I left it in Hong Kong.'

The man placed his foot on Christophe's injured wrist and applied pressure until Christophe cried out.

'No you didn't. You travelled back from HK by sea and land, when it would have been a bloody lot easier to fly. Conclusion: you were carrying sharps.'

'How do you know all this?'

'I know it because I'm in the information business.'

'I haven't got it any more.'

The man stepped on his wrist again.

'Yes you have. No other reason to take off down the motorway in someone else's car. No other reason not to go home to your very comfortable flat.'

'Which you trashed.'

'We made a thorough inspection of it. But we didn't find anything, because you were carrying the syringe with you. Probably in your jacket, where it probably still is.'

As he leaned down, Christophe kicked out at his ankles. The man gave a cry of surprise and pain, and for a moment seemed to lose his balance; but then he steadied himself and, with a stream of curses, began to kick Christophe with his heavy boots – in the back, the ribs, the head. Christophe tried in vain to ward off the blows; tried to shield his head, to curl into a protective ball, to shut out the explosions of agony . . .

And then they stopped. His attacker fell silent, and a moment later crashed to the floor beside him. Twisting round, Christophe saw Li standing over them with a thick length of wood in his hand.

'You OK, Dr Christo?'

'I don't think there's anything broken. But I wouldn't go any further than that.'

Li helped him up. Feeling too dizzy and nauseous to stand, Christophe leant against the bonnet of a Mercedes. There was no movement from his attacker.

'Thank you,' he said.

'A great pleasure, Dr Christo. Suddenly I feel a whole lot better.'

'Do me a favour. See what you can find in his pockets.'

Li knelt down. His search revealed a wallet, a mobile phone and a revolver.

'I'd better look after that,' said Christophe, taking the gun. 'What's he got in his wallet?'

Li opened it. 'A lot of bank notes. Three credit cards. One health-club membership card. Nothing else.'

'And the name on the cards?'

'Thomas Warry.'

'Which health club?'

'Barbican Fitness, London.'

'Not very revealing.'

'Maybe the phone will tell us more.'

He handed it to Christophe.

'We'll look at it later,' said Christophe. 'Right now I think we should get out of here. We don't know when his friend will be back.' He felt his head tentatively. A large bump was forming on the back of it. 'Can you drive? I'm not sure I feel up to it.'

'Sure thing. I always wanted to drive a sports car.'

As the MG nosed its way out of the garage, Thomas Warry remained motionless on the concrete floor.

II

'This is a fine mess.'

'Indeed, Prime Minister.'

'Can you explain to me, Mr Ambassador, how it is that Vice President Zhou is undergoing emergency surgery for a gunshot wound while the two Chinese nationals arrested for trying to kill him are claiming diplomatic immunity?'

The ambassador spread his hands in a gesture indicative of destiny's inscrutable nature.

'It is true that Mr and Mrs Lo are accredited to the Embassy. I am not, however, in a position to comment on their involvement in this matter. I can only insist that the protection afforded by their status be respected.'

'We'll have to put out some sort of statement. The worst of it is this media fox-hunter getting involved. That means all the tabloids making a meal of it as well.'

'That was certainly unfortunate. But I am instructed to inform you that my government's views on the situation have not changed. As far as we are concerned, the abduction and attempted murder of Vice President Zhou were incontrovertibly the work of the Brothers of Light.'

'But Mr Ambassador!' The Prime Minister searched for words to express his frustration. 'How can that possibly be made to stack up? We have two members of the Animal Lovers' Army in custody who admit to the kidnapping.'

'There is another part of the equation: Professor Li. According to the kidnappers' testimony, he left the farm where he was being held in the company of a man called Christophe, who has links with the Brothers of Light.'

'They also say that he left of his own free will.'

'That is not the point. We believe that this man is Dr Christophe Hardy, the Brothers of Light's representative in the UK. Not only that, but he is in possession of a syringe stolen from the Mulberry Tree Project.'

'How the hell did he get hold of that?'

'Through his friend Professor Li. In short, we are looking at a conspiracy with repercussions for both our governments.'

The Prime Minister was aghast. 'What do you suggest?'

'Release the animal lovers. Mr and Mrs Lo will be recalled to Beijing, where they too will be discovered to have connections with the Brothers of Light. You will inform the world that Professor Li, far from being a victim of the kidnapping, was one of its perpetrators – and that he and Dr Hardy, as dangerous terrorists, must be found and stopped at all costs.'

Prime Minister looked doubtful. 'I suppose that might keep the press quiet.'

The ambassador smiled. 'Excellent. And now I have good news for you. Your consignment of syringes and vaccine has been assembled sooner than expected. You will be able to start your immunisation programme within the next few days.'

III

'Thank God,' said Matt. 'I thought you were never going to come.'

'Sorry, mate,' said Frank. 'The Old Bill had a lot of questions they wanted answered. Luckily the chief copper was a fan of the show, otherwise I'd still be there. Hop in.'

Matt and Selina climbed into the back of Frank's car. Anna smiled from the front seat. 'Hi, guys. Hope you didn't get too wet in that wood.'

'I've known worse,' said Matt. 'What's the news on the Chinese?'

'The kid and that old sod of a Vice President have been airlifted to hospital,' said Frank. 'You probably saw the chopper.'

'We did. We kept our heads down – thought it might be looking for us.'

'Whether the doctors can do anything for them is another question. As you know, there's no recognised treatment for fox flu. Add a bullet in the neck, and I'd say Zhou won't be long for this world. Not that he'll be missed.'

'And the woman who shot him?'

'Hauled off under armed guard with her lover boy. There's a strange pair – you'd think from their kit they were off to the Chelsea bleeding Flower Show. But she's obviously China's answer to Annie Oakley and he managed to pin down half the cops in Herefordshire single-handed. If that horse hadn't taken off and knocked her for six she'd probably have got away.'

'What about your fellow huntsman?'

'Horry? He'll be OK, no thanks to that friend of yours. You should keep him on a leash.'

'Easier said than done. I never knew anybody with Jake's knack of getting into trouble.'

'We should hit the road,' said Selina.

The car moved off.

'Are you sure about this, Matt?' asked Frank. 'You don't reckon it would be better to hand yourself in? Zhou and the woman from the council aren't exactly in a position to press charges, and if you're already supposed to be out of the nick . . .'

Matt shook his head. 'There's no knowing how long it could take to sort out. And in the meantime Christophe may need our help.'

'Any idea where he is?'

'If all's gone according to plan, he should be a good way north of here.'

'We're headed for Birmingham, if that's any use to you. I'm taking Anna back to hers.'

'That would be a good start. Thanks.'

Anna said nothing. She'd thought that this journey would give her a chance to tell Frank the truth about herself. But it rather looked as if that would have to wait.

IV

Christophe soon regretted asking Li to drive. Being thrown from side to side as they sped along a winding country road towards the motorway only aggravated the pain in his head and ribs. Keen as he was to put miles between himself and their pursuers, he was relieved when the MG halted in a queue of traffic.

Who were their pursuers? He pulled out Warry's mobile. Perhaps it would yield some clues.

First he checked the message file. It was empty. Either the phone was new or its owner made a point of deleting every message as soon as he read it. He surely wouldn't do that unless he had something to hide.

The logs of calls made and received were similarly blank. But the address book did contain a few entries.

Most were Christian names. The exceptions came under H ('HQ') and 'J' ('Journalist'). The second number looked familiar. Christophe checked his own phone, and there it was: Tessa.

He shuddered. The only possible conclusion was that the men chasing him were the ones who had almost killed his friends' daughter.

He hesitated to ring 'HQ'. He was afraid of giving himself away. But he had to know who he was dealing with.

The phone at the other end rang three times, then went through to a machine. The voice on the recorded message was male, authoritative, with a slight Scottish accent.

'This is Chief Inspector Herries of the Anti-Terrorism Unit. Please leave your name and number and I'll get back to you as soon as possible.'

Christophe rang off. Why was the Anti-Terrorism Unit after him? And why hadn't Warry identified himself as a policeman instead of attacking him?

One thing was clear: nobody in a position of authority could be trusted. Apart from a boogie-woogie piano player with alcoholic tendencies, Christophe was on his own.

V

'You f–d up,' said Jonty Lo.

Faye gave him a furious look. 'That's easy for you to say. You didn't have to shoot from ground level through a crowd of people, horses and dogs. I had one second for a clear shot and I got Zhou in the throat. I call that pretty damn good.'

'What they did they teach us at training camp? A clean kill. The true marksman settles for nothing less.'

'And what about you? Letting yourself be captured by the British police: where does that come in the training manual?'

'If the branch of the tree hadn't given way they wouldn't have got anywhere near me.'

'And if you'd given me proper cover, they wouldn't have got anywhere near *me*.'

Jonty turned his back on her and walked over to the window. It was locked, of course. Down on the pavement was the usual group of protesters demanding religious freedom within China. He could think of no more futile occupation.

Aesthetically, the Embassy had the edge over Paddington Green police station, but not by much. Jonty longed to be back in their Eaton Square apartment, sinking into the free-standing lion-clawed bathtub, a bar of sandalwood soap to hand. It was hard to believe that he had set off on this misconceived adventure less than twenty-four hours ago.

Officially, he and Faye were free. The British authorities had not so much as suggested charging them with attempted murder, possessing illegal firearms or damage to police property. But from the inside of a locked room with armed Embassy guards patrolling the adjacent corridor, Jonty felt his options to be uncomfortably limited.

Whatever happened now, he and Faye were finished as a partnership. Neither was used to failure, and each held the other entirely to blame for their predicament. Given the choice, Jonty saw himself enjoying a bachelor life in Paris. But would there be a choice?

The door opened. It was the Defence Attaché, the Embassy's senior spy.

'Good news, comrades.' He gave a thin smile. 'The British government has decided not to challenge your diplomatic immunity. However, for your own safety it has been decided to recall you to Beijing. Your flight is at 10pm tonight. In the meantime, you are to remain under the protection of the embassy. We will arrange for your personal effects to be sent on.'

He smiled again and closed the door.

'What do you think?' asked Faye.

'I think,' said Jonty, 'that we're f–d.'

VI

The traffic finally dispersed. With a schoolboy grin, Li put his foot on the floor. Christophe groaned as he was forced back into his seat.

'Sorry, Dr Christo,' said Li. 'But this baby sure flies. Difficult to clip her wings.'

Christophe's phone rang. It was Matt, wanting to know where they were.

'On the M6, heading for Penrith.'

'Everything OK?'

Christophe gave him an account of the attack in the garage. Matt described the events in Herefordshire.

'The Chinese woman must have been a professional killer,' he said. 'But how she followed us to a field in the middle of nowhere is beyond me.'

Christophe said nothing. He felt as if he were walking into a forest whose trees became thicker with every step.

'Christophe? Are you still there?'

'Yes, sorry. Just trying to get a handle on it all.'

'Selina and I were wondering whether there was anything we could do to help you. Maybe we could meet up – safety in numbers and all that.'

'That's very kind, Matt, but I think we're better off keeping clear of each other. You've got the police after you, and the people who are after me seem happy to kill anyone who gets in their way. I'd rather you lay low and left me to deal with things at this end.'

'How much further have you got to go?'

'It's a couple of hours on from here. We should be there by lunchtime.'

'Well, call me if there's anything I can do.'

'I'll do that.'

'Good luck.'

'I'll talk to you later, Matt.'

Even pocketing the phone brought back the pain in Christophe's ribs. He grimaced.

'Matt is your brother?' said Li.

'My brother-in-law.'

'So he married your sister?'

'No, I married his.'

'I didn't know you had a wife, Dr Christo. She must miss you when you are in China.'

'She died.' Christophe tried to sound matter-of-fact about it. 'Five years ago.'

'Oh, Dr Christo.' Li gave him a sympathetic glance. A lorry coming in the opposite direction hooted as the MG swerved out of its way. 'What a terrible thing. How did it happen?'

'I'd rather not talk about it' was what Christophe almost said. It was his habitual response. There was no reason to give a different one now.

And yet he found that he did want to talk about it. Perhaps it was the situation in which he found himself – as if the hazardous task that had fallen to him required an unburdening of his conscience. And perhaps it was because Li knew him from a different life, lived on the far side of the world, and in all probability would never see him again.

'It should never have happened.' The sound of his voice framing those words sounded strange to him. 'She'd been in hospital for a routine operation, which seemed to have gone well: all she needed was a bit of time in bed to recover.

'For the first two days I stayed at home to look after her. But on the third day there was a conference in Manchester that I was supposed to be talking at. So I arranged for a nurse from an agency to come and take care of Sara.

'I had to leave at seven in the morning to catch my train, and the nurse couldn't be at our house until eight. It wasn't ideal – I would have liked to meet her in person – but it couldn't be helped. Sara told me not to worry: she didn't think that she needed the nurse at all.

'She was dozing when I left. She looked a bit pale, I thought, but that was hardly surprising. I decided to ring her from the train.

'Well, it turned out to be one of those journeys where you couldn't get a signal for any length of time. When I finally got through, there was no reply. But I didn't want to keep ringing in case she was asleep, so I told myself I'd leave it till I arrived at Manchester.

'There was still no answer. I rang the agency to check that the nurse had got there. They said that they hadn't heard anything to the contrary, so they assumed she had. I asked if they could ring her and see; they said they didn't have a mobile number for her, but their staff were very reliable. There was no need to feel anxious.

'I gave my lecture and took part in the Q&A, but I couldn't stop thinking about Sara. At lunchtime I rang a neighbour and asked him to check on her. He found her alone and feverish. I asked him to call an ambulance.

'By the time I got to the hospital she was unconscious. I sat beside her all through the night, but she didn't come round. At dawn she died. It turned out that she'd contracted an infection as a result of the operation. And that was that. No chance to tell her that I loved her. No chance to say goodbye.

'I never discovered why the nurse hadn't turned up. There didn't seem any point in holding a witch hunt. But of course I thought of all the things I could have done differently. I should never have left Sara on her own; should have insisted that the agency send someone to check; should have called the neighbour sooner. Perhaps none of those things would have made a difference – but "perhaps" was no consolation. I kept thinking of her lying there alone, wondering why nobody came, wondering why I had deserted her.

'And then there was Matt, her adored younger brother. How could I persuade him that it wasn't my fault, when I couldn't persuade myself? Not that he reproached me; he just listened to what I had to say and nodded his head. But I could see what he was thinking: that I'd promised to look after her in sickness and in health, and I'd failed – completely failed.'

'You cannot be sure of that.'

'No, but –'

Christophe shrugged and turned his head away. He should have kept his mouth shut. How was poor Li supposed to respond? He watched a hay barn flash by – a group of horses – a half-flooded field – and wondered how he could have given a thought to another woman.

'You are a Christian, right, Dr Christo?' said Li at last.

'Yes.'

'So you believe in life after death.'

'It goes with the territory.'

'That is unusual for a scientist.'

275

'Today, perhaps. But some of the greatest scientists in history have shared that belief. Take Sir Isaac Newton.'

'We have learnt a lot since then. Stephen Hawking and Richard Dawkins are gods now.'

'And yet so much of what Newton wrote still holds good.'

'He did not prove the existence of God. As a scientist, I require proof.'

'But nor has it been proved that God doesn't exist.'

'That is true; which is why I am – what is the English word? – an agnostic.'

'A very respectable position. But I always go back to the first laws of physics. When Mayer says that energy is not dissipated, it simply changes form, I think of the great, unmeasurable energy which runs through our lives: love. Is that an exception to the rule? When we die, does it just disappear? I don't think so. I believe that it moves – that we move, since energy is our essence – into a different realm.'

'So you believe that you will meet your wife again.'

'Yes. And of course that thought should be consolation enough. But sometimes it just isn't.'

'I find your views very interesting. But tell me one more thing: as a Christian, you believe in forgiveness?'

'Yes.'

'So why do you refuse to forgive yourself?'

Christophe had no answer to that.

VII

Matt was restless and dissatisfied. Having come this far on his unexpected adventure, he wanted to see it through to the finish.

He understood his brother-in-law's thinking. If Christophe was to get through to his destination, he needed to draw as little attention to himself as possible. A wanted man was not an ideal companion – but then, nor was a Chinese scientist who had been completely drunk when Matt last saw him. And while Christophe was as resourceful as anyone he knew, he was up against some ruthless characters. Matt felt sure he could have helped.

Anna seemed to read his thoughts.

'I think you guys should come back to my place,' she said. 'We've all been through a lot this morning, and it isn't over yet. We should stick together.'

Anna's place looked ordinary enough from the outside: a tradi-tional, rather ugly Victorian vicarage on the edge of a well-kept village just beyond the girdle of motorways surrounding Birmingham. But to step through the front door was to enter another dimension. The whole of the ground floor was an open space; the back wall had been removed to create an enormous window. White sofas and white rugs marked out the sitting area in a manner not readily associated with a Master of Foxhounds. Steel-framed chairs with ikat seats guarded the glass dining table; zinc surfaces and cherrywood cupboards stretched away along the side of the kitchen.

The garden was equally deceptive: in immediate view, a modest lawn bounded by beech hedges; beyond it a swimming pool, tennis court, vegetable garden, stables and paddocks.

Matt smiled. If he had to kick his heels somewhere, this was as good as it got. He put his arm around Selina's waist.

'What about a swim?'

'I didn't bring my costume. You wouldn't want me getting into that pool naked, would you?'

They kissed.

Frank, however, looked around him with a sinking heart. He'd known Anna was well off, but this . . . The girl was out of his league, and he might as well accept it.

VIII

Christophe's hopes of reaching their destination by lunch-time proved misplaced. First there was the rain, heavier than any he'd ever experienced. It hammered against the car's windscreen and bodywork like an army of tiny panel-beaters; it drummed on the roof until the soft top seemed sure to split beneath the weight of water. Clouds of spray from the vehicles in front enveloped them. The windscreen wipers, flinging themselves from side to side, opened up only glimpses of the road ahead. Li moved over to the inside lane, slowing to 50, then 40. When a service station loomed through the storm he pulled off the motorway.

'Sorry, Dr Christo,' he said. 'I couldn't see a bloody thing.'

They waited in the café for the downpour to ease. Christophe bought a cappuccino and a newspaper. The abduction of the Chinese Vice President was a front-page story; inside, a Far East correspondent speculated as to why the Brothers of Light might have turned to terrorism.

Suddenly he realised that it was Tessa's paper he was reading. He wondered how she was; wished that she was on the end of a telephone, ready to write the truth. But Warry and his friends had tracked her down, just as he had been tracked. He would have to find someone else to tell the story.

First, though, he had to get to Patrick Neary.

After twenty minutes the rain began to slacken. It was still heavy – too heavy for safe driving; but the alternative didn't seem any safer. Christophe imagined Warry at the wheel, pressing on towards them.

'I'll drive,' he said. 'Let's go.'

The fuel gauge showed three-quarters empty. Best to stop at the petrol forecourt.

Perhaps he was thinking too much about the rest of the journey, or concentrating too hard on the numbers reeling up on the face of the pump. For whatever reason, it wasn't until he stepped through the doors of the shop that he saw the two policemen. They were wearing reflective waterproofs and flirting with the pretty girl at the counter.

'See you've got a new coffee machine, love. About time too. God, the last one made a horrible espresso. Could have been drinking sump oil.'

'You probably were,' said the girl. 'Very big on recycling we are. Nothing gets wasted around here.'

'So he's not wasting his time chatting you up?' said the second policeman.

'If that's what you call chatting up, I pity your girlfriend. Must be dying of boredom, her.'

Turn around, walk straight to the car and drive off, Christophe told himself. But there was no surer way of attracting attention than to leave without paying.

'Number four,' he said to the dopey-looking boy at the second till.

'Thirty pounds?'

'That's it.'

'Better get going,' said the first policemen. 'Lots of villains out there waiting to be nicked.'

'Anyone in particular?' asked the girl.

'Just been asked to look out for two males in a red MG. One Caucasian, midforties, the other Chinese, slightly younger.'

Christophe almost dropped his wallet.

'Dangerous, are they?' said the girl.

'Members of the public are advised not to approach them.'

'A change from grannies going the wrong way down the motorway, then.'

Christophe turned and walked towards the exit, his heart pounding. Had they noticed this particular Caucasian? Thank God Li hadn't come in with him.

But the car . . .

There had been a Range Rover in front of it when he was filling up. Now that had gone. Not particularly noticeable, perhaps, an MG seen through a plate-glass window with a dark grey sky behind. But policemen were trained to notice things.

He prayed they'd keep on looking at the girl.

Perhaps he should have thrown himself on their mercy: explained that he was on a vital errand, had two killers after him, needed an escort.

Perhaps not.

He walked to the car as quickly as he dared, opened the door, slid in. Turned on the engine as quietly as he could. Turned out of the forecourt and on to the roundabout. Took the exit for the slip road – and at every moment expected the police car to come after him, lights flashing, looming in the rear-view mirror.

It didn't. As he accelerated down the motorway he thanked God for their escape, and for the protection of the rain, wrapping them round, reducing their visibility. Then he wondered how many other police patrols were looking for them, and what lay ahead.

IX

Frank's producer rang him on his mobile for the sixth time that morning. Once again she was put through to voicemail.

'Frank, this is Vanessa. Why the f– aren't you answering? Every journalist in the country wants to talk to you. My boss is asking why we're not there on the spot doing a *Frank Rides Forth* special

– and do you know what? I've had to tell him that I don't have f–ing clue where you are. Jesus, Frank, this could be the biggest thing in both our careers and you decide to go AWOL. If you f– me over on this one, so help me I'll –'

An electronic beep, indifferent to her dilemma, brought her message abruptly to an end.

X

Jennifer Pettifer was feeling a bit better. She had found a hairdresser near the hospital, where the congealed remains of the flour Yu had thrown over her had been washed away and she had dozed in the leather chair. She had bought a change of clothes at Marks & Spencer and relegated her muddy suit to a carrier bag. Restored to respectability, she felt able to deal with the hospital staff on equal terms.

Not that the situation was easy. Zhou was under police guard in intensive care. A number of Chinese men in suits, presumably from the Embassy, were also in evidence. But emboldened by the afterglow of last night's love-making, and drawing on all her own experience as a bureaucrat, Jennifer had already managed to negotiate the first layers of red tape. She had persuaded several junior members of the medical staff – so young that their faces seemed to reflect the linoleum's gleam – that she was Zhou's girlfriend; and although she had not been admitted to his bedside, they had agreed to let her wait nearby and keep her informed of his progress.

He must recover. They had been through so much together, she and Zhou, that separation could not be contemplated. That he might simply be an old lecher who had taken advantage of their enforced intimacy did not occur to her.

The one person she had been careful to avoid was Yu, who was watching Frederick in a different part of the hospital. She hated him for her humiliation in the Pu Dong Pudding Company van, and no doubt he held her responsible for his son's condition; but there was nothing to be gained from a confrontation. That she had been falsely imprisoned was beyond doubt; and she could fairly argue that Zhou, not she, had kidnapped Frederick. But she was not about to betray her lover – and she knew that any investigation would establish that she had delayed Matthew Dunstable's release from prison. So far the police had only questioned her as a witness to Zhou's shooting. With luck it would stay that way.

She had telephoned her line manager, Mr Lambert, to say that she needed a few days off. He had grudgingly agreed, noting that she had failed to give the correct amount of notice. But meeting Zhou had made her realise that the council's many-layered bureaucracy was puny by his standards. Beyond the stained concrete towers of the 1970s fortress she worked in lay a great, unexplored world of officialdom that she could scarcely allow herself to imagine. With Zhou as her lover, the sky would be the limit.

XI

'Thank God,' thought Christophe as he turned off the motorway at Penrith. They had seen only one police car since the service station, hurtling along in the opposite direction, but he felt far safer on a minor road.

'Neary's house is about thirty miles from here if I remember rightly,' he said. 'A rather beautiful drive when it isn't raining.'

'I think it's stopping now,' said Li. 'Maybe we'll be lucky.'

He was right. As they headed east Christophe was able to switch the windscreen wipers to low; their frenetic shuttling became an occasional lazy swipe as a tentative rainbow took shape against the light blue sky.

The road ran past walls green with moss and through dark tunnels of overhanging branches; beside steep banks and between unkempt hedgerows. It crossed an iron bridge over a picturesque river, climbed through a village of redbrick houses, then flattened itself before the great line of hills which spanned the horizon. How different, Christophe thought, from the landscape he and Li had seen from the Beijing-Hong Kong train. Who would have thought then that they would be sharing this second journey?

The road wound sharply upwards as they approached the hills. Suddenly the engine started to vibrate with a noise like a tumble dryer full of stones.

No, thought Christophe – not when we're this close.

He needed to stop and look under the bonnet, but it was hard to find a safe spot among the succession of blind corners. The engine was running on ever decreasing power; putting his foot on the accelerator was like pushing into sand. A 4×4 behind them flashed its lights, then roared contemptuously past as a straight stretch of road finally opened up.

Christophe pulled over. Together he and Li examined the engine.

'I think maybe it is a spark plug broken loose,' said Li. 'Very difficult to repair.'

Christophe frowned. 'It can't be too long until we reach the summit,' he said. 'If we can make it that far we should be able to freewheel most of the way down on the other side. I reckon –'

A ringtone from the pocket of his jacket interrupted him. It was Warry's phone.

Christophe hesitated. Should he answer or not? At the last moment he pressed the receive button.

'Warry?' said a man's voice. 'We've picked up the MG on the traffic cameras near Penrith. It's heading east along the A686. I want you and Cooper to maintain pursuit. Their likely destination is Newcastle, so I'm despatching Team B from there. Between you this should be wrapped up before they reach the A69. Understood?'

Christophe switched off the phone.

He tried to think calmly. Warry – assuming that he had recovered from his blow to the head – must still be some distance behind them, probably on the motorway. His boss, if he'd smelt a rat, would now be on the phone to Warry's companion Cooper. Even if the pair had reached Penrith, Christophe and Li still had a lead of a dozen miles, with only fifteen or so more to their destination. As for Team B, Newcastle must be twenty miles the other side of Neary's house. All he and Li had to do was drive as fast as the road through these hills would allow, and they would have every chance of reaching safety.

But they couldn't drive as fast as the road would allow, because the MG was about to give up the ghost. At its present rate of progress Warry and Cooper could overtake them within twenty minutes. There was only one thing for it: to get off the road, hide the car, and head across country on foot.

He looked around. Down to his left was a panoramic view back to Penrith and the western peaks of the Lake District. To the north, where grey clouds gave way to a stretch of blue, he could make out a low landmass that he reckoned to be Scotland. But it was the closer terrain that concerned him. Looking down on the rough fields marked out by stone walls, he could see nowhere that a bright red sports car would not stick out like a sore thumb. They would have to drive on.

Perhaps the engine had just needed a rest. Perhaps when he turned the key in the ignition it would come to glorious, high-revving life, and they'd be on their way, outpacing every pursuer.

But as they moved off the car settled into what sounded like a death rattle. Labouring uphill, the speedometer barely touched 30 mph. At any moment the loose spark plug might wreck the engine completely. He wondered what he would say to Matt's girlfriend if he ever saw her again.

At last he saw an opportunity: a minor road curling down to the left.

'Let's try this,' he said.

It worked out better than he could have hoped. The road led down to a disused quarry. There, among an array of ancient, rusting machines standing like toys beside a giant's sandpit, they found a tattered tarpaulin just large enough to cover the MG. By the time Christophe and Li had finished wrapping it, the car looked part of the post-industrial landscape. It might have been there for years.

As they climbed back towards the main road, Christophe considered the challenge ahead. The countryside took on a different character now that they were on foot, its contours more dramatic, its distances greater. The journey ahead of them – some fifteen miles – would take several hours. He had no hope of finding Neary's house except by following the road, but to stand on it even for a minute was to risk being spotted. Trying to hitch a lift was out of the question. All they could do was make their way across the fields, keeping the road in sight but making sure that they were invisible from it. The ground was sodden and the going wouldn't be easy.

It occurred to him to ring Matt. If he and Li could lie low for however long it took Matt to reach them, that might be the safest option. But when he checked his phone, he found it had no network coverage.

'I hope you like walking,' he said to Li, 'because we've got a lot of it ahead of us.'

XII

At that moment a telephone was ringing in the wreckage of Christophe's flat. Eventually the answering machine cut in.

'Christophe . . .' The voice sounded distant, tentative. 'Christophe, this is Amy. They're sending me to Paris for treatment. I wonder if we could meet up there. I need to talk to you about what you found on the train. We've just heard from one of our people in government that there's more to it than Li told you – much more. Will you call me?'

She left a number. The machine clicked off. Silence repossessed the flat.

CHAPTER EIGHTEEN

It was obvious, as Christophe and Li approached the main road, that they were on the wrong side of it. Behind them the landscape dropped down wide and exposed; ahead, across the tarmac, it rose to a slight ridge.

'We need to get up there.' Christophe scanned the road for traffic. 'Quick as we can.'

They scrambled up the rough grass. Christophe wished he was wearing shoes with better grip. He wished, too, that he was carrying at least a small supply of food and water.

The only sign of life was a small flock of sheep which surged away over the hillside. Christophe told himself he had to be more careful. Any sudden movement could attract attention.

The grazing looked meagre even for sheep. Who could make a living from farming around here? There was only one house to be seen, a small, grey dwelling off to the left which betrayed no sign of life, the windows shuttered, the driveway empty.

Ahead a line of telegraph poles marched towards the summit. Christophe's eyes followed them to the road: in the distance, a building took shape which gave him sudden hope. It looked like a café – which meant food, drink and a public telephone from which to call Matt or a local taxi. But it was also an obvious stopping point for whoever was looking for him. He and Li needed to get there quickly, and approach it with caution.

It was a single-storey building of grey brick, with a row of trestle tables on a small terrace looking back over the valley towards Penrith. Also facing the valley was a single car – a blue Volkswagen Polo. Not the kind of car, Christophe thought, that Warry or his friends would drive. Edging nearer, he saw that it contained a greyhaired couple eating sandwiches.

As for the café, there was no sign of life. Rounding the corner, they found a sign saying 'CLOSED' hanging in the window.

Li sat down on a low wall, looking like a man whose horse has come in first without its jockey.

'No drink,' he said.

'No.'

'No food.'

'No.'

'No telephone.'

'No.'

Li nodded. He began to croon softly to himself as he stared at the ground.

Yes, we have no bananas,
We have no bananas today.

Christophe tried to hide his own disappointment. 'There's bound to be another place like this further on. We just need to keep going.'

An idea struck him. He walked across to the car and knocked on the window with a smile.

'Sorry to bother you. We're in a bit of a fix – my car's broken down. I don't know if you're heading in the direction of Alston: we'd be very grateful for a lift.'

'Sorry, son, we've just come from there,' said the old man. He spoke with a local accent. 'We're on our way to Kendal. We can drop you in Melmerby if you like, or Penrith. Plenty of garages there.'

'That's very kind, but I think we'll keep heading in this direction.'

'If you're sure. You've a fair old walk ahead of you.'

'The exercise will do us good. Thank you anyway.'

'Would you and your friend like a sandwich?' asked the woman. 'I always make too many. We've got egg and watercress, cheese and tomato, or fish paste.'

'That sounds too good to refuse. Cheese and tomato for me, please.'

Li chose egg and watercress.

'Could I ask you a great favour?' Christophe asked. 'I'm supposed to be meeting my brother-in-law at a friend's house, and I need to give him the address, but I can't get a signal for my mobile. Do you think you might possibly give him a call for me if you find yourselves near a telephone?'

'I'll see what we can do,' said the old man.

Christophe took out his wallet. He wrote Selina's mobile number and Neary's address on the back of one of his business cards and handed it through the window.

'Thank you so much,' he said.

'Right-oh. We'd best be going. Good luck.'

The car moved off. As Christophe watched it disappear down the winding road towards the distant mountains, a sharp gust of wind blew up suddenly from the valley. He wondered whether his message would get through.

II

'Hartside Summit,' said a road sign. 'Altitude 1903 feet.' A little further on was another: 'Welcome to Alston Moor.' Now the lie of the land was reversed, so that the open country spread out to Christophe and Li's right while the hills rose to their left. They crossed the road and again scrambled up to a point where they could look down without being seen.

The view ahead was impressive. The landscape was brightened by patches of sunlight which brought the heather-covered hillsides to life; the peaks of the Pennines rose in the distance, their silhouettes blue beneath a bank of grey cloud, as if they had been smelted from the sky and plunged into the liquid horizon to cool. The road below twisted downwards, its borders marked by tumbled-down stone walls. By following a straight line across country, Christophe reckoned they were saving several miles; but the terrain was rough and their progress was slow. They were barely a mile from the café when they saw two cars approach from opposite directions and stop side by side some fifty yards down to their right.

'Get down and stay down,' said Christophe.

He wriggled forwards on his stomach to the edge of the ridge.

The car which had come from the road behind them was a black Range Rover. Two men got out: Thomas Warry and Cooper. The second car was a red Toyota containing two more men – presumably Team B from Newcastle. One was lanky and fair-haired; the other, short and swarthy with a black pony tail. Christophe noticed that he walked with a slight limp.

Though Christophe had a clear view, he was too far off to hear their conversation. But it wasn't hard to guess its starting point. If neither team had seen the MG, where was it?

Warry laid a map out on the bonnet of the Range Rover. The lanky man drew his finger across it and seemed to lead the discussion with a local knowledge the others lacked.

There were only two conclusions that they could come to: either Christophe and Li had already reached their destination, or they had turned off on to a minor road.

Christophe realised that the MG's breakdown might work to his advantage. If his pursuers believed that he had taken another route, they would follow that and leave a clear run to Neary's house. He didn't know how many turnings lay ahead on the A686, but he guessed a fair few. Warry and Co could spend the rest of the day exploring them. They might even give up.

Warry started to fold up the map. Christophe turned to check on Li. As he did so, there was a sudden commotion behind him; a shout from the road; a gunshot; and something warm, wet and red spattering his arm.

It took him a moment to work out what had happened. A pheasant, startled by Li, had flown up from the moor behind him; one of the men on the road had seen it, pulled out a gun and shot it just as it passed over Christophe's head. It lay now in the long grass, a short distance in front of him, feebly flapping its wings, with dark blood staining its beautiful plumage. And the man with the pony tail was climbing up the hill to collect his prize.

'You all right, Dr Christo?' called Li.

God! Li obviously couldn't see Pony Tail heading towards them. Christophe signalled frantically for him to be quiet. He prayed that the sound of Li's voice had been carried away on the wind.

Pony Tail kept climbing. His face was weather-beaten and grizzled; his tied-back hair gave him a piratical look.

Christophe had a choice. He could stay where he was and hope that Pony Tail was too focussed on the pheasant to notice him; or he could risk drawing attention to himself by scrambling back to the greater safety of Li's position.

He decided to stay put.

He felt in his jacket for Warry's gun. Holding it in his hand did little to reassure him. He didn't want to shoot Pony Tail, and if he did, he would immediately have the other three on his trail.

Pony Tail climbed with surprising swiftness. Christophe pressed himself into the grass.

As Pony Tail came nearer, Christophe could see him grimacing with every step. That he was taking the hill so fast despite the obvious pain involved – and all for the sake of a dead bird – showed a frightening determination.

He was twenty yards away; ten. Christophe could see his gun tucked into his belt. Pony Tail wouldn't be expecting to use it, which meant Christophe would have a couple of seconds' advantage. If it came to that.

Pony Tail stopped and reached for the pheasant. As he picked it up an arc of blood splashed across his boots. Pony Tail stared at them for a moment; then he looked up and fixed Christophe with his eyes.

At least, that was how it seemed to Christophe. Later he realised that Pony Tail's gaze had been caught by something else – a tall cairn at the top of the hill. Pony Tail considered the pile of stones and grunted. Then he turned and started to make his way back down the slope.

Christophe remained motionless, his heart thudding, until the diminishing figure reached the road. Warry was clearly not pleased that his manhunt had been turned into a shooting party: he gesticulated angrily, then turned his back on Pony Tail and climbed into the Range Rover.

Which way would they go? The Toyota made a three-point turn and headed back towards Newcastle. Christophe expected the Range Rover to follow it – but it didn't. It too turned round, taking the road towards the deserted café.

Christophe rose to his feet, trying to make sense of it all. No policeman, not even a member of the Anti-Terrorism Unit, should be so trigger-happy. But if they weren't policemen, who were they?

'Have they gone, Dr Christo?'

'For the time being. But we can't assume that we've seen the last of them.'

'It gave me a big shock, when they shot that bird.'

'Yes,' said Christophe. 'Me too.'

III

'Penny for your thoughts,' said Anna.

Frank shrugged. 'Nothing in particular.'

'Come on – ever since you came in the front door you've been looking as if a hound had eaten your dinner.'

He couldn't deny it. 'The thing is, Anna . . . all this.' He looked around the white, immaculate room. 'I feel like a round peg in a square hole.'

'Oh dear. You are hard to please.' She had changed into jeans and was stretched out on the sofa. 'What are we going to do about you, Frankie? You don't like Horry's, you don't like mine . . . I could make you up a kennel round the back if you like.'

'Leave it out, Anna. It's all right for you: you grew up with all this. I'm from an armpit of an estate in Essex. To the manor born, right?'

'Don't give me that. You're a national TV star and you live at one of the best addresses in London. You could call in an interior designer tomorrow and turn it into the swankiest pad in town.'

'I'm not made of money. Everything I earn from the telly goes into looking after the hounds. And even if I could give the place the glossy-magazine treatment, I wouldn't feel comfortable with it. It's not who I am.'

'So who are you, Frank?' Anna got to her feet and glared at him. 'Are you an Essex boy who's going to go through the whole of life thinking that the world is against him because he's not posh? Or are you a grown-up who's very good at what he does and thinks it's enough that people respect him for that? Come on, grab your coat. We're going for a little outing.'

'Where to?'

'I'll tell you in the car.'

The car was a white open-top Mercedes. Frank didn't feel at home in that either.

'I'm taking you to meet my father,' said Anna. 'Think of it as a little test. He's as posh as they come. If you can deal with him, you can deal with anybody.'

'Give me a break! It's been a long day, yeah? I really don't need this.'

'Relax. He can be a bit gruff at first, but he's a sweetheart underneath.'

'And what kind of house does he live in?'

'A great Victorian pile – it goes on for ever. But I'm not taking you there. Like most aristocrats, he has an eccentric side. His favourite thing in life is poking around scrap-metal yards looking for bits of classic cars that he can stick back together. Today's his Auto Reclaim day.'

The scrap yard lay in the shadow of a flyover, flanked by a self-storage depot and a furniture warehouse. The skeletons of cars piled up on each other in myriad shapes, sizes and colours reminded Frank of the big tin of sweets his grandmother used to keep, gleaming with gold and purple foil. Columns of tyres teetered; shiny chrome bumpers sat cheek by jowl with crumpled, rusting doors. Machinery growled in the background as cranes swung back and forth, delivering metal carcasses to an enormous crusher; there was a regular shattering of glass and grinding of steel on steel. Frank wondered how many foxes had found a home in this wilderness of wreckage. Anna's Mercedes looked as out of place as an Olympic hopeful in an old people's home.

'There's Daddy,' she said.

A thickset man was standing talking to two others in boiler suits. He wore a well-cut tweed jacket and corduroy trousers with an open-neck white shirt and highly polished brogues. His hair was cut to a military shortness and his face was bright red, as though fine burgundy from an ancestral cellar flowed through his veins.

'I'm afraid he rather stands on ceremony,' said Anna. 'He likes to be addressed as "Your lordship".'

'He's not the first one I've met,' said Frank, gritting his teeth.

'Daddy!'

Anna's father turned, his face breaking into a smile.

'Hello, princess!'

To Frank's surprise, he spoke with a broad Birmingham accent. Was this another side of his upper-class eccentricity?

'Daddy, this is Frank.'

'Good afternoon, your lordship.'

He father looked at him for a moment, then burst into a great peal of laughter.

Frank stared at him in bemusement. 'What's so funny?'

Anna's father exploded again. He clutched his sides and laughed till he was gasping for breath. Anna giggled beside him.

'Sorry, son. I'm afraid this disgraceful daughter of mine has been having one of her jokes. So I'm a lord, now, am I? Well, I hate to disappoint you, Frank, but I'm plain Mick McCormack and this is my manor.' He opened his arms and indicated the mountains of scrap. 'Any car that's reached the end of its useful life – and there's no shortage of them in this town – can find a home in one of my yards. The pity is that I can't do the same for people. Come on, Frank, I'll give you a guided tour.'

Frank was too bewildered to speak. He followed silently as Anna's father picked his way between the hills of debris, explaining an organising principle that no outsider could have guessed at. For every make and model of car, Mick McCormack knew the spare parts most in demand: a newly arrived saloon would instantly be stripped of its side mirrors, a 4x4 of its bumpers.

'A chap came in the other day wanting a wing for a Ford Fiesta. Told me he was taking it all the way to Slovakia on his roof rack as a present for his father-in-law. "That's a big present," I said. And he said, "Oh, I always take something like that. Last year it was a new bonnet and the year before that it was two doors." So I said, "Sounds like he has a lot of accidents, your father-in-law." And he said, "Oh no, he's never so much as scratched the car. But he says that if he did have an accident, the replacement parts would take a long time to come, so he wants to collect them in advance." How about that? The old chap must have a whole spare car by now. If only every customer was like that, I could retire tomorrow. "All in advance" – oh my!'

He started to laugh again – such an infectious laugh that soon Frank too was spluttering and reaching for his handkerchief. The story seemed the funniest thing ever told.

'So, Frank,' said Mr McCormack at last. 'I hear you're on the telly. I don't watch it much, I'm afraid, so I haven't seen you, but Anna tells me you're very good. What always puzzles me is how people like you can keep so relaxed. I'd be stood there thinking, "My sister's watching this – and my mates – and everyone that works for me – and everyone in the street where I grew up. How can I not make a fool of myself in front of them all?"'

'That's how I felt to begin with,' said Frank. 'But after a while you think, "It's just me and the camera crew." Then eventually you forget the camera crew as well.'

'Still, you've obviously got a talent for it, or they wouldn't stick with you.'

'I'm only on for half an hour twice a week. The truth is I'm just an ordinary huntsman.'

'No, you're not,' said Anna. 'You're a Master of Foxhounds.'

'That's a fine thing,' said Mr McCormack. 'A great achievement. It wasn't easy for Anna, and I don't suppose it was easy for you.'

'No,' said Frank. 'It wasn't.'

'A few toffee-nosed types, I should think.'

Frank looked at him suspiciously. Had Anna put him up to this?

'One or two,' he said.

'We've had our share of those, haven't we, Anna? Some of those headmistresses when we were looking round posh boarding schools.'

'Horrible,' said Anna.

Frank tried to imagine her feeling out of her depth. He couldn't.

'But what I said to her was this,' her father went on: 'people are really very simple. If you go through life expecting them to like you – and why shouldn't they, after all? – then most of them will. But if you go around thinking, "This lot won't give me the time of day," like as not you'll be proved right. That's how I see it, anyhow. And if someone manages to wind me up, I just think of that crusher over there' – he indicated a machine labouring noisily on the far side of the yard – 'and imagine all their mean-spiritedness being pulverised inside it. Come on, I'll show you how it works.'

IV

No one else was out walking that afternoon. Christophe couldn't blame them: the sky was overcast, the ground sodden underfoot. A lone cyclist in bright Lycra skimmed past on the road below; occasional cars broke the silence, but none that he recognised. The only other signs of life were a herd of cows which stared at them over a broken wall, and a scattering of sheep on the slope down to his left, grazing among clumps of rushes and the conical shake holes which pitted the surface of the ground.

'I think maybe you could bury somebody in one of those,' said Li.

It would be easier, Christophe reflected, to throw a body down one of the many disused mine shafts in these hills. But he kept the thought to himself.

They passed a rackety farm building with a sagging roof and an ancient, rusty horsebox parked beside it. A little further, a minor road peeled off to the right. Christophe wondered whether it offered a safer route. But he knew only one way to Neary's house, and that was along the road they were following. Besides which, the simple fact was that no road was safe.

The ground began to flatten out. They couldn't be more than a mile or two from the river which bisected the valley they were now crossing. But flat ground meant exposure. They had to keep more than a hundred yards from the road to use the cover of the ridge. As they followed it a red car came suddenly into view, driving at such speed that Christophe pulled Li to the ground beside him; but it wasn't the Toyota. They got to their feet, even wetter than before.

Soon there were signs of human habitation: the entrance to an estate; neater fields; a plant nursery. They must be approaching Alston.

Christophe's first feeling was one of huge relief. The town, as far as he remembered, was a good size. There would almost certainly be a taxi to take them the rest of the way.

Those were the positives. But as he strained to remember the lay-out of the town, he realised that it also had dangerous disadvantages.

The main problem was the bridges. There were two of them – one on this side of the town, the other on the way out of it. The fact that a pair of rivers met here, and there were no other crossing points nearby, gave the town its importance – and also made it an obvious place to keep a look-out for fugitives. Christophe knew what he would do if he were Warry: post one man on each bridge while he and the fourth member of the team patrolled the town centre.

But then, Warry didn't know that the MG had broken down. In fact, he had every reason to believe that Christophe and Li had passed through the town two hours ago, and that it would be a waste of time to post anyone there at all. Trouble was, you couldn't tell what he'd done without walking into the place – by which time it might be too late.

What was the alternative? To wait until darkness, perhaps. That was still hours away – too long to hang around feeling cold and wet and hungry; and the bridges, lit by streetlamps, would still be a problem. Or you could follow one of the rivers north or south in search of another crossing – but there was no knowing where you'd find one, or how you'd get back on the right road.

In other words, there wasn't an alternative.

They had kept their distance from the road for so long that setting foot on it seemed like a violation. As they descended the hill towards the first bridge, Christophe felt painfully exposed – a feeling which the tall, overgrown wall on their left only aggravated. It was the kind of wall, he thought, that people got shot against.

He wondered if he should take the lead: go down to the bridge first, see if it was clear, signal to Li to follow him. Walking into town together, the two men were bound to attract attention. But then, so was a Chinese guy on his own.

'Walk right behind me,' he said to Li. 'Stay close.'

As the bridge came into view, he was surprised at how small it was. It looked insignificant, almost an afterthought. It also looked deserted.

They crossed quickly. On the far side the road curved. They passed signs to a hospital and a youth hostel. Then they were in the town centre.

It had seen better days. On one side of the road was a cluster of workshops, now shut up and dilapidated, their paint peeling, their windows opaque with grime. Several Union Jacks decorated the skyline, suggesting that patriotism was the last refuge of the locals. But a road climbing up a hill to their right brought more promising façades – one of them painted with the words 'Coffee-Tea-Sandwiches-Hot Food'.

It was the answer to their prayers. Christophe and Li found a table by the open fire where they could dry out. A friendly young waitress took their orders for a pot of tea and a fry-up. The only other customers were two old ladies comparing photographs of their grandchildren.

'Would you have the number of a local taxi?' Christophe asked the waitress.

'I can ring one for you if you like.' She smiled. 'Where are you going?'

'It's a house about seven miles from here, on the road to Whitfield.'

She came back to say that the taxi would be there in twenty minutes. 'Is that OK?'

'That's fine.'

The fry-up – spicy sausages, bacon, tomatoes and baked beans – was excellent. As he ate, Christophe felt his strength returning. The taxi journey shouldn't take more than fifteen minutes; their journey was almost over.

Then the door opened and a man with a pony tail walked in.

He obviously wasn't expecting to see Christophe and Li there, because he did a double take. Perhaps he wasn't even sure that they were the pair he was looking for. But whatever the reason, his hesitation gave Christophe a chance. He picked up the pot of hot tea and threw it in Pony Tail's face. Then he picked up a chair and knocked him to the floor. The waitress screamed; the old ladies stared open-mouthed.

'Come on!' Christophe called to Li, heading for the door. Pony Tail groaned, trying to pick himself up.

There was no sign of his partner outside – or of the taxi. But at the bottom of the hill Christophe spotted a bus. He shouted to Li to run for it.

They raced down the hill, wet shoes slipping on the stone underfoot, almost colliding with a girl pushing a buggy. The bus had already left the stop, but was caught behind a double-parked car. Christophe signalled frantically to the uniformed driver, who shrugged his shoulders and activated the doors. Christophe and Li climbed aboard. The car in front moved off; so did the bus. Glancing back up the hill, Christophe saw Pony Tail limping in pursuit. The bus gathered speed. Pony Tail disappeared from view.

There hadn't been time to think about where the bus might be going. Now Christophe realised that it was following exactly the road that they wanted. They couldn't have been luckier.

'Do you stop at Whitfield?' he asked.

'If someone asks me to.'

'Great. Two singles, please.'

He reached for his wallet. But his wallet wasn't there.

He went through his pockets. No sign of it. He must have dropped it in the café, or stumbling down the hill.

He told himself to calm down. All he needed at this moment was the bus fare – only a few pounds. But all he had was a handful of coppers.

'Li, have you got any money on you?'

Li shook his head.

The bus had crossed the second bridge and was climbing up out of the town. Just outside the speed limit a young man carrying a shovel flagged it down.

The driver glared at Christophe. 'If you haven't got the fare, you'll have to get off.'

Christophe looked back down the road. Perhaps Pony Tail was already in his car, already in pursuit.

'Look,' he said, 'we just need to get to Whitfield – not even that far. It's urgent. Here –' He pulled out Warry's mobile. 'I'll give you this.'

The driver shook his head. 'This is a bus, mate, not a pawn shop. Off you get. You're holding up the other passengers.'

Christophe looked at the faces behind him. There were half a dozen, all showing different degrees of irritability.

'Anyone want to buy a mobile for £10?' he asked.

They looked at him as if he were mad.

'You heard me,' said the driver. 'Off the bus.'

Christophe felt Warry's gun tucked into his pocket. He could put it to the driver's head and make him take them to Whitfield – but he didn't want the whole of the local police force after them. Nor did he trust the guy with the shovel not to have a go.

'Come on,' he said to Li. 'Looks like we'll have to walk it.'

V

As the bus moved off, the driver revelled in his gift for repartee.

'A bus not a pawn shop – that's what I told him!' he called over his shoulder to his passengers, though none of them could hear him above the noise of the engine.

A moment later the look on his face turned from self-delight to alarm as a red Toyota came racing up behind him, lights flashing. It overtook him, then screeched to a halt a hundred yards down the road. He barely had time to put on the brakes before two men jumped out and waved him down. Bemused, he opened the automatic doors.

A small man with a pony tail climbed aboard, waving his open wallet.

'Police,' he said, his eyes scanning the passengers. 'The two men you picked up in Alston – one English, one Chinese. Where are they?'

'I put them off a mile back.'

'You what?'

'They didn't have any money for the fare. One of them tried to pay with a mobile. I told him . . .'

'Where did he ask to go to?'

'Whitfield. What've they done?'

But the man had already turned his back on him. He stepped off the bus and ran back to the car to talk to his companion. The bus driver closed the doors and revved his engine.

'What do you make of that, then?' he called over his shoulder. But his passengers could hear nothing.

VI

'That's funny,' said the old man to his wife. 'I can't find that piece of paper.'

'Which piece of paper?'

'The one that chap gave me at Hartside Top, with his brother's number on it.'

'Brother-in-law's.'

'Pardon?'

'I said it wasn't his brother's number. It was his brother-in-law's.'

'Oh.'

'Time you put a new battery in that hearing aid.'

'That's as maybe. But where's that piece of paper gone? I could swear I put it in the pocket of my waterproof.'

'Maybe it fell out. Maybe it fell on the floor of the car.'

'I've looked there. I hope it's not important. I don't want to let the lad down.'

'It didn't sound very important.'

'It didn't, did it? Still, I would have liked to help.'

'Don't worry, love. It'll sort itself out.'

VII

Christophe and Li had lost no time in scrambling for the higher ground. The bus had dropped them on the edge of a thick copse which afforded good cover to begin with, but then gave way to open fields. A more substantial plantation spread across the side of the hill to their right. If they could reach that, Christophe reckoned, they would be safe for the time being. But first they had to cross two hundred yards of sparse terrain in clear sight of any passing car.

The going was treacherous – the ground uneven, the grass slippery. Twice Li slithered and fell in the mud; Christophe, helping him to his feet, cursed him silently for slowing them down, then rebuked himself. It was amazing what Li had put up with in the last 24 hours, never complaining or questioning what was asked of him. True, he'd been pie-eyed when he agreed to the adventure; but sobriety seemed to have done nothing to change his mind. His tenure at the university in Beijing, his privileged existence under the Party leadership's protection – all this had been left behind for a dream of playing piano in a Harlem speakeasy.

They were halfway to the trees when Christophe looked down towards the road and saw the red Toyota. He could just make out two small figures climbing out to flag down the bus. A glance up the hillside would be enough to tell them what had become of their quarry.

But for the time being they were focussed on the bus and its passengers. Christophe and Li stumbled on. The ground seemed more sodden with every step; the faster they tried to go, the harder it was to keep their balance. They reached the wood just as Pony Tail stepped off the bus and back on to the road.

Christophe leant against a tree trunk gasping for breath. Down below, the bus resumed its journey. Their pursuers must have discovered that he and Li were heading for Whitfield. What they didn't know was that Neary's house was two miles this side of it: with luck they would stake out the village and wait in vain for the fugitives to show up.

But to his dismay the Toyota turned round and headed back towards Alston. Pony Tail and Lanky must have decided to take up the chase on foot from where he and Li had left the bus – a point which was still too close for comfort.

'We'd better get going,' he said.

Almost at once the trees thinned out and they found themselves standing on another road – narrow, and by all appearances not much used. Where did it go?

He soon saw that it ran almost parallel to the one they had come from – and there, coming into view below them, was the red Toyota, containing only one man.

There was no doubting the driver's plan. When he reached the next junction he would turn and follow this road, with an unobstructed view of the fields. As long as Christophe and Li remained among the trees, he couldn't see them; but meanwhile, his partner would be coming up the hill behind them, hoping to flush them out.

'Quick,' he said to Li. 'This way.'

Someone had been at work clearing the wood, but instead of making their progress easier, it made it more difficult. There were piles of stripped trunks to clamber over; newly felled trees with splayed branches blocking their way; clearings in which the human form was only too visible to a pursuer. Christophe remembered the speed with which Pony Tail had scaled the hillside to retrieve the dead pheasant, and tried not to imagine him coming after them.

At the end of the plantation they paused for breath. They were a good height above the upper road now, but not high enough for comfort. To their right rose the summit of the hill, reachable only via an open expanse of rough grassland. Ahead and to the left ran two more roads, with the ground in between offering only slightly more cover. Christophe didn't fancy their chances in either direction.

On the other hand, they couldn't stay where they were.

Or could they?

'Where next, Dr Christo?'

'This used to be mining country – there are disused mine shafts all over it. There –' he pointed '– and there, and there. So we're going to do what a fox does: go to ground.'

VIII

It was a *Marie Celeste* of a mine. There was nothing surprising in the shaft itself being abandoned: presumably it had simply run out of whatever it produced, or become too expensive to maintain. But what about the machinery? Half a dozen rusting hulks stood by the entrance, their functions unidentifiable. Why hadn't the owners sold them off? Why leave them here as if they might start work again tomorrow?

Whoever was responsible for shutting the shaft off had made a poor fist of it. It was clear that Christophe and Li were not the first people to pass the signs saying 'DANGER – DO NOT ENTER'.

The mud at the mouth had been thoroughly churned up – recently, from the look of it.

Daylight penetrated only a few yards inside. But it was not the dark or the damp which most struck the visitors as they felt their way forward: it was the smell – a heavy stench which lay on the air like a blanket and brought Christophe close to retching.

'I think there is something dead in here,' said Li.

Christophe thought so too. The sheep that grazed these hills must sometimes fall ill or meet with accidents; perhaps one of them had limped in here and never come out again.

He turned back to take stock of their situation. From the entrance he could see past the forgotten machines to the edge of the plantation – to the silhouette of a man: Pony Tail, looking straight towards them.

Coming straight towards them.

But whether he had actually seen them wasn't clear. They couldn't be sure. All they could do was retreat into the fetid darkness and hope.

They felt their way along the rough wall inch by inch. There were some darknesses so dark, Christophe thought, that your eyes never got used to them. This was one.

His right foot knocked against something. It was hard, but not as hard as the rockface, and it shifted slightly. Bending down, he felt a length of wood: a pickaxe handle by the shape and size of it. He picked it up. It might come in useful.

The floor of the pit sloped gradually. What he feared was a great hole opening up suddenly in front of his feet – a fall in the darkness, a broken limb, helplessness. He used the pickaxe handle to test the ground in front of him like a blind man with a white stick.

The next thing his foot touched was soft. This time he leant down and felt ragged wool – wool and bare bone. He had been right about a sheep crawling in to die.

Or had he? The bone beneath hand was dry, picked clean of meat; the terrible smell was coming not from this carcase, but from something else. What were the chances of two dead animals ending up here through simple misadventure?

He thought of the newspaper stories that appeared from time to time about a great beast roaming Exmoor, preying on local livestock. Was it possible that a creature of that sort had made this mineshaft its lair?

No, that was ridiculous. The Beast of Bodmin was a myth; he had never heard of a similar story attached to the North Pennines.

'There's no way out, you know.' Christophe felt Li clutch his arm as Pony Tail's voice echoed along the dark passageway. 'You've reached the end of the road. Best thing you can do now is come out with your hands in plain view. Do that and you won't be harmed.'

Christophe and Li were silent.

'All we want is the syringe,' the voice continued. 'Just hand it over and you can go free.'

'Do you believe him?' whispered Li.

'No.'

'It's up to you,' Pony Tail shouted. 'We can wait all day. Isn't that right, Mike?'

'That's right.'

Two of them. Lanky must have left the car and joined the hunt on foot.

It's an impasse, thought Christophe. He and Li could not hope to get past the men at the mouth of the cave. But equally, the pursuers weren't going to come down the mine knowing he had Warry's gun.

Time was the problem. The enemy could call for reinforcements, take shifts, stock up with food and drink while he and Li became hungrier and thirstier and colder.

Not that Pony Tail and his friends would want to stay there for ever. Perhaps if they were given the syringe, they might just disappear. But had he carried this vital evidence halfway round the world just to hand it over? No way.

'Go to hell!' he shouted.

'To hell, to hell!' his voice echoed – and then a gunshot rang through the shaft, its detonation gathering force with every second until the noise seemed a flood, assaulting them, battering them, engulfing them. Christophe pressed himself against the rockface, waiting for it to die away.

But it didn't. Or at least, it gave way to something else: a deeper noise, coming not from the mouth of the tunnel this time, but from somewhere far beneath him. It began as a low rumbling, as if the earth itself were speaking – and yet so unearthly was its effect that Christophe felt the hairs rise on the back of his neck.

'What was that, Dr Christo?'

'I have absolutely no idea.'

The sound came again: louder this time, and more insistent, penetrating their bodies at such a pitch that it seemed to shake their bones.

'A dragon!' exclaimed Li.

'There are no such things as dragons.'

'A dragon! A dragon!'

The next thing Christophe knew, Li was scrambling towards the mouth of the tunnel. He tried to grab him, but missed his footing and tumbled to the ground. Pulling himself up, he tried again, this time managing to catch Li's ankle. Li struggled for a moment, then stopped. The noise had died away, but in its place was a new one, coming closer; a noise of something moving across rock, gathering speed, breathing heavily.

What it was, Christophe could not possibly have said. He had an impression of bulk, of speed, of awful power – but only a momentary one, because instead of attacking him the shape rushed past him and towards the daylight. A moment later he heard a terrified scream.

He hauled Li to his feet. 'Come on!'

The two men rushed for the open air.

Reaching the entrance, they paused for a second. There was no sign of their enemies, or of whatever had lurked in the shaft.

'What was it?' asked Li.

'I don't know,' said Christophe, 'but I'm not waiting around to find out.'

They set off across the hillside at a run.

IX

Mr Yu sat in the hospital watching his sleeping son. His fingers had grown stiff from holding Frederick's hand, so for now he just looked at the boy. But it seemed wrong not to be touching him, or at least something that belonged to him, so he picked up the muddy school cap which lay on the bedside table and started to twist and turn it in his hands.

It was a good hospital. The wards and corridors were spotless, the nurses solicitous. But they had not been able to assure him of his son's wellbeing. Frederick had been infected with a disease for which there was no known cure. He had suffered a severe shock. They were doing their best for him.

So Yu sat beside the well-made bed contemplating the end not only of Frederick's life but of his own. He had always worked hard – long hours, few holidays. He had built up first his restaurant and then his pudding business. He was proud of what he had achieved, but that was not to say that he attached enormous importance to it in the great scheme of things. Catering was something he happened to be good at, that was all. What mattered to him in the end was his children: in particular, Frederick.

It was a terrible thing for a parent to have a favourite; perhaps he was being punished for it now. His own mother and father had been scrupulously impartial. 'Which of us is best at making pancakes?' he had asked once, knowing that on all the available evidence the answer had to be him. But his mother had managed to find equal merit in his brother and sister's less orthodox efforts. He had been disappointed, but came to understand their wisdom. Too many problems in too many families, in too many hearts, came down to that uncertainty: 'Am I as well loved as he or she is?'

And here he was, a transgressor. But how could it be otherwise? His wife had kept their younger child from him; his peripatetic business had made it hard to keep in touch. He saw the little boy perhaps once a month, and like other absent fathers asked the question, 'Am I just disrupting his life? Would it be better for him not to see me at all?' Whereas Frederick – well, he saw Frederick every day, gave him breakfast in the morning, put him to bed at night. Frederick was the lantern that illuminated his life: a lantern now, perhaps, about to be snuffed out, leaving only cold starlight to guide him on his stumbling, pointless way.

He would change his ways if fate gave him a chance. He would cherish little Danny, make up for neglecting him. He smiled to himself: it would be a joyful penance. But what if fate turned its back on him? How could he ever look on Danny without thinking of the boy's lost, beloved brother?

'Why don't you take a break, Mr Yu?'

He looked up at the sound of the nurse's voice, but couldn't make out her face.

Embarrassed, he reached for his handkerchief to wipe away the tears.

'He's heavily sedated,' she went on. 'He won't wake for hours. You should get some fresh air.'

'No,' he said. 'Thank you.'

There was a story he'd been told about a man put in a cell with a lunatic. As long as he was able to keep awake, he could quell the madman with his gaze; but should he lose concentration or fall asleep, those hands would be at his throat. And now, it seemed to Yu, he himself was locked in a similar vigil. As long as he sat here at Frederick's side, facing down death, his son had a chance of survival. He was not about to abandon him.

Besides, he didn't trust himself to roam the hospital corridors. He knew that Zhou was being treated here as well. The sight of an Embassy official or anyone associated with that son of a snake would be enough to send him into a fury which would almost certainly end in violence.

Those very people were the reason he'd done it. Easy enough, with hindsight, to say that he should never have got Frederick mixed up in such a thing. But Yu was a man who believed that everyone had a responsibility to history. His parents – Frederick's grandparents – had suffered terrible things during the Cultural Revolution, exiled to a dirt-poor mountain village for 'education through labour'; his cousin was suffering even now in Beijing Detention Centre Number One. The younger generation must not be allowed to forget the sins committed against their family in the name of a perverted ideology; or to think that an opportunity to strike back at it could be shirked. Frederick, his Anglo-Chinese boy, must grow up knowing the value and splendour of British democracy, and be prepared to die for it.

But surely, thought Yu, staring at the small, worn cap in his hands, he could not be meant to die for it yet.

CHAPTER NINETEEN

'Why the f– hasn't he rung?' said Selina. 'He must have got there by now.'

She was sitting on the white sofa with Matt's head on her lap.

'That's Christophe for you,' he said. 'Mr Loner. The cat who walks by himself.'

'He married your sister.'

'Yes.'

'If he's so much as scratched my car . . .'

'Christophe's a careful driver.'

'What is it with you two?'

'Which two?' he said, though he knew perfectly well what she meant.

'You and your brother-in-law. You always seem like you've got something you want to say, but you never come out with it.'

He didn't reply.

'Well?'

'He's my brother-in-law. That's it.'

'And you didn't like him marrying your sister?'

'Quite the opposite. I thought he was a great guy – intelligent, interesting, enterprising. He was perfect for her.'

'But . . .'

'She died.'

'And you blame him.'

'Not at all. What happened wasn't Christophe's fault. It was just that . . .'

'What?'

She watched his body start to contract, moving towards the foetal position. But instead he pulled himself up and sat staring at the floor.

'He pushed me away. OK, we're both British – at least, Christophe's half British, though also half French. But Sara meant so much to me, and when she died, I wanted to talk to the only person who was as close to her as I was. Only I couldn't. Whenever I was with him I felt this wall between us, as if the whole subject was off limits. And gradually I began to realise that he didn't want me around, because I reminded him of her. So I kept my distance. I wouldn't have seen him at all if I hadn't been determined to keep in touch with my nephew. And I wouldn't have dreamed of visiting him yesterday if it hadn't been such a desperate situation. But it was. And when I spoke to him this morning it was the same old thing. I thought we should be working together, but he didn't want to know.'

'You can't be sure of that. Maybe he genuinely thought it was the right thing to do. And maybe all this will give you an opportunity, when it's over, to put things right between you.'

'Except that I might be back in prison.'

She frowned. 'I think you're in prison already. I see it in my dad, and I see it in you – all you men. You're just locked away inside yourselves. And I'm not sure that you really want to be let out.'

II

The rain returned, moving across the hills in a silver shimmer. It was lighter this time, but heavy enough to leave Christophe and Li sodden.

Still, there wasn't much further to go. They had crossed the Northumbrian border and begun the descent into the valley beyond, shadowing the road as it twisted and turned. Now it ran straight, parallel with the river where Christophe had fished two summers before with Patrick Neary.

A black Range Rover – possibly Warry's – had raced along the road below them an hour ago. It hadn't come back. Since then the only thing to give them pause had been a hare following its mesmerising figure-of-eight course across the moor.

The question of what had rushed past them in the mine continued to baffle Christophe. A wild animal which had made the shaft its lair was the only possible explanation. But no wild animal he had come across was capable of making such a noise. He thought of the lines in the Bible describing the wind that passed by Elijah. But he wasn't about to bracket himself with an Old Testament prophet.

The light was beginning to slip from the sky. He reckoned that they had half an hour before it vanished entirely. That should be long enough.

'We should see Neary's place soon,' he said, 'down there on the right.'

'And you are one hundred per cent sure Professor Neary will be able to help us?'

'Yes.'

That much at least was clear in Christophe's mind. He gave Li a brief outline of Neary's career: his early brilliance; his academic achievements, culminating in a chair at Harvard; his run-in with a medical company whose work he had discredited, and the failure of certain colleagues to stand by him; his return to Britain, vindicated but disillusioned; his consequent determination to pursue his own path.

'I can't think of anyone,' Christophe concluded, 'who's more likely to stick his neck out for what he believes in. And there' – he pointed towards the river – 'is his house.'

At the foot of the hill below them stood a cluster of buildings: a farmhouse with smoke rising from the chimney; a smaller cottage; two large outbuildings, their curved metal roofs glinting in the last rays of the sun. An owl hooted as the two men made their way down the grassy slope towards it. In his mind's eye Christophe could see the kitchen lit with butter-yellow light.

They crossed the farmyard, past hay bales wrapped in heavy black plastic. Christophe knocked on the door. A moment later it opened, and he found himself looking into the eyes of Thomas Warry.

III

The demonstrators opposite the Chinese Embassy took it in turns to mount an overnight vigil. Theirs was a token presence, but the fact that they had been there for over a year despite legal challenges and intimidation by the Embassy's security staff was an undeniable achievement. They had a small tent for shelter, with a field stove, collapsible chairs, sleeping bags, and a discreet chemical lavatory; mobile phones and a video camera were always at the ready in case of a surprise attempt to evict them.

Not much tended to happen after dark. The police occasionally stopped to look them up and down, but had long ago decided that they were no threat to public order. One or two other members of their church might drop by; a well-wisher who ran a restaurant in Soho made a welcome delivery of hot food towards midnight. Otherwise they just sat in the tent, talking, praying and dozing until the morning shift came to relieve them. So it was quite an event when they saw Jonty and Faye Lo abseil on curtain cords from a first-floor window and hurry down the street before climbing into a passing taxi.

'That was easy,' said Jonty, sinking into his seat.

'They need a new head of security,' said Faye.

'Zheng Guang was a pushover. I thought he'd be a real handful, a big guy like that. But he went down like a ninepin.'

They both smiled. For a moment the tensions of the past two days were forgotten. They were a team again. 'Do you think there'll be someone watching the flat?' asked Jonty.

'I doubt it. If they'd thought there was a chance we'd escape, they would have guarded us a bit better. But let's go in the back way just in case.'

As it turned out, the flat was deserted. They collected their back-up laptops and phones, and all the ordnance on the premises, which they loaded into the back of Faye's Mercedes. In addition, Jonty packed a handful of silk shirts, his collection of Lanvin ties and the contents of their safe, consisting principally of bundles of banknotes and fake IDs. Faye added the kitchen knives. Before driving off they put new number plates on the car. Faye took the wheel while Jonty opened up his laptop.

'You're sure that Li is the key to this?' asked Faye.

'Absolutely. If we can track him down and recover the stolen prototype, we'll be heroes in Beijing. If we can't, we're dead meat.'

'Have the British police got anything?'

'I'm just checking. Hack-hack-hack. Here we are: they're looking for two males, one British, one Chinese, in connection with the kidnapping of Vice President Zhou, travelling in . . . a red MG. Now that *is* interesting.'

'Why?'

'Because yesterday I saw two men – one British, one Chinese – in a red MG on the road out of Oxford. And because the car rather took my fancy, I memorised the registration number – which is something the British police do not have. So now I just have to go into their motorway surveillance system to see if that number shows up anywhere, and . . . bingo! Caught by a mobile speed camera heading north on the M6 at lunchtime today, just outside Penrith. I wonder if I can access an image . . . yes, here we go . . . and yes, I have to say it looks very like our two friends.'

'But that was hours ago. They could be in the north of Scotland by now.'

'They would have shown up on another camera. No, my hunch is that they're still in the area – unless they left the car in Penrith and caught a train. Let me just check that image against the CCTV records from the local station.' He tapped again. 'No, nothing. Which means that with luck they're there for the night, and we've got plenty of time to catch up with them.'

IV

Christophe reached for the gun in his jacket pocket but Warry was too quick for him and grasped his wrist, forcing him to drop it. Twisting loose, Christophe turned and sprinted for the far side of the farmyard. A security lamp snapped on, washing the ground in front of him with light. To his left was one of the metal-roofed buildings, but no visible entrance; to his right, a high wall. The only place of refuge was a timber lean-to – and that was clearly a dead end.

There was nothing else for it. He darted into the lean-to, slammed the door shut behind him, felt for a key or a bolt. There wasn't one. He braced himself against it just in time to feel the weight of Warry's body on the other side.

He knew he didn't have long. He reached for his mobile, praying that there would be a signal. There was, thank God. He speed-dialled Selina's number as Warry's shoulder crashed against the door.

'Selina? This is Christophe. We're at Neary's but we're in serious trouble –'

He got no further. The door burst open, knocking him to the concrete floor. The phone spun from his hand. When he looked up, there was a gun pointing at his head.

V

'Where was he calling from?' asked Matt.

'Neary's,' said Selina. 'Which would be very helpful if we knew where Neary's was.'

'Did he say what kind of trouble he was in?'

'No, I told you. That's all there was.'

'Let me see what I can find on the internet. Maybe Neary has a company registered at his home address.'

The search drew a blank.

'We've got to do something,' said Selina.

'Give the police your phone – get them to trace the call.'

'Perhaps by trouble he meant the police.'

Matt sighed. 'Then what do you suggest?'

VI

Patrick Neary's kitchen was much as Christophe remembered it: the Aga with its grimy twin steel lids, the scuffed linoleum floor, the crockery-stuffed dresser – 'All rather a relief,' Neary used to say, 'after a lifetime in immaculate laboratories.' The only thing that seemed out of place was Neary himself. It took Christophe a moment to recognise the old man – normally so full of life – sitting silently at the table. There was a large bruise on the left-hand side of his face.

'Patrick! What the hell have they done to you?'

'Shut up and sit down.' Warry's gun was aimed at his chest now. On the far side of the room, Cooper was pointing another one at Li.

They did as they were told.

'Professor Neary has been helping us with our enquiries,' said Warry. The high, thin voice was as disconcerting as ever. 'And very helpful he's been.'

'Patrick, are you OK?'

Cooper moved to hit Christophe, but Warry shook his head.

'I'll live,' said Neary. Then he added, 'They shot my dog. Can you believe it? He didn't even bark at them.' He sounded close to tears.

Cooper chuckled. 'Tom's never got on with dogs. Have you, Tom?'

'Shut up,' said Warry.

Christophe studied him. 'You're not an anti-terrorism officer at all, are you?'

'I never said I was.'

'But your phone . . .'

'Rang "HQ", did you? It's nice that people still fall for that. An answering machine in an empty office – it's amazing what you can get away with.'

'So who are you?'

'We are employees of – what shall I call it? – an international security consultancy. You need protection for your staff in a war zone, or someone to take out a rival firm's computer system, we sort it. In this case we have been engaged by a private individual with a strong interest in the medical-supply industry. We came to hear – through our highly developed network of informants – that Professor Li had developed a new syringe with marketable properties. The question was how to obtain a prototype. So imagine our interest when it came to our ears that you'd done that very thing and were heading back to England with it.

'Unfortunately, you didn't do what you were supposed to. You didn't arrive in London by Eurostar as scheduled. Nor did you put your head down in your cosy flat in Oxford. In fact you led us quite a merry dance.'

'So how did you know I was coming here?'

'Our analysts put two and two together. They've managed to compile quite a dossier on you, including a list of friends and colleagues. Once we'd narrowed down your probable destination to this area, it became obvious that you were planning to meet up with the professor. Of course, it's a matter of regret that the information wasn't processed sooner – it would have saved us a lot of foot-slogging. Anyway, all's well that ends well, because here we are. We've got the syringe – '

He gestured with his gun. Christophe unzipped his jacket and laid the packet on the table.

'– and we've got Professor Li for good measure. On top of that, we arrive to find that Professor Neary has just developed something of great interest to our client: an antidote to fox flu.'

Christophe looked at Neary in amazement. 'Is this true?'

Neary nodded. 'I thought you and I might be opening a bottle of champagne tonight to celebrate. But at that point I saw my discovery as a blessing for all mankind rather than a get-rich-quick scheme for some greedy criminal.'

'There's a batch in production across the yard as we speak,' said Warry. 'As soon as it's ready, we'll be spirited out of here. All except you, Christophe – the general feeling is that you're more trouble than you're worth.'

'Was that the general feeling about Tessa Traherne?'

'You're absolutely right.'

'And that's why you tried kill her?'

'Ms Traherne had been making enquiries about our company that weren't particularly welcome. But as it happens, we didn't try to kill her. A teenage driver who'd had too much to drink did that for us. I gather she'll be out of action for some time.'

Christophe shook his head. He couldn't believe how badly everything had gone wrong. He might not be to blame for Tessa's injuries, but he was certainly to blame for dragging Patrick into this – Patrick, whose invention could have stopped the Mulberry Tree vaccination project before it started. Now Patrick faced abduction, and he himself . . .

'When will the batch be ready?' he asked Neary.

'First thing in the morning.'

'Will the condemned man eat a hearty breakfast?' said Warry. 'We'll have to wait and see. In the meantime, let's make you all comfortable.'

VII

Warry chose Neary's utility room as their prison. It was a narrow space with a heavy door and a single window too small for a man to squeeze through; off it was a cloakroom whose window was even smaller. The fixtures consisted of a washing machine, a tumble dryer and a sink; there were also half a dozen coats which could be piled on top of each other for a makeshift bed. Before locking the door, Warry and Cooper searched their prisoners for mobile phones and left them a miserable meal of bread and cheese. Water had to be drunk from the tap.

'Patrick, I'm sorry,' said Christophe. 'If I'd thought it would come to this, I'd have stayed well away.'

'You weren't to know. To be honest, I thought everything was going a bit too smoothly. If there's one thing I've learnt in my career, it's that to be left to get on with one's work in peace is more than anyone can hope for. Is that your experience, Professor Li?'

'You're darn tootin'.'

'I don't suppose there's another way out of here,' said Christophe.

'You mean a secret tunnel or some such? I'm afraid not. What you see is what you get.'

'We could signal: turn the light on and off. Morse code.'

'We could try. The switch for this light is outside the door, but we have control of the one in the toilet. Unfortunately the window looks out on to the yard, and if the outside light is on, there isn't very much chance of getting noticed.'

'Worth a try, though.'

'Yes, worth a try.'

Christophe set to work. The response came quicker than he expected. The door opened and Warry marched in, gun in hand; Cooper stood guard behind him. Warry took a hand towel from beside the sink and removed the bulb from its socket.

'There,' he said. 'Now you can piss in the dark.'

VIII

Jonty and Faye's reconciliation hadn't lasted long. In fact, they had barely reached the M1 before they started squabbling.

'Any news?' said Faye.

'Not as such.'

'What does that mean?'

'It means I'm working on it.'

'Maybe you should do the driving and let me do the thinking.'

'I have several more leads to follow.'

'I'm glad to hear it. Because the idea of driving 300 miles through the night to Penrith and then not having a clue what to do next does not amuse me at all.'

'Do you have a better idea? Shall we just turn round and catch the death plane to Beijing?'

Faye slowed as traffic cones signalled yet another lane closure. Jonty's smartphone vibrated. Suddenly he brightened up.

'Now we've got something.'

'What?'

'A text from my friend in the Industrial Espionage division. It turns out that someone close to Professor Li at the university has been sending information to a private security firm in Jersey called Janissary.'

'Do they know who?'

'Not yet. But what's the betting it's Christophe Hardy?'

'Even if it is, I don't see how that helps us.'

'The boys in Beijing are at work on Janissary's computer system. Once they're in, they can tell us what there is on Professor Li and Hardy. And with luck it will lead us right to them.'

CHAPTER TWENTY

It was Christophe's turn to stretch out on the pile of coats on the floor, but he insisted that Neary take it. He knew he wouldn't be able to sleep himself, and Neary would need all his strength for whatever lay ahead.

He was worried about his old friend. It wasn't just the bruise on his face – there was a hollow look in his eye which Christophe hadn't seen before. It was as if the living man had moved a degree closer to death.

Perhaps it wasn't surprising. He had reached the culmination of his life's work, something that should have compensated for all his earlier reverses – and now it was to be snatched away from him. The loss of his dog had clearly shaken him too: he'd had the animal for years. Why had Warry inflicted that on him?

Christophe looked again for a way out. The door of the utility room was solid, the windows were impassable. The three scientists had tried the Apollo 13 procedure: laid out everything at their disposal on the floor and racked their brains for anything they could improvise with it. The only weapon they'd identified was the plate containing their supper, and that hardly seemed adequate for tackling two armed men.

So Christophe considered the prospect of death.

He knew that, as a Christian, it shouldn't frighten him. He thought about the reading he'd heard at so many funerals about merely going into another room. But of course, what it didn't mention was the slamming of the door – a door that opened in only one direction.

He thought of his mother's funeral – carrying the coffin, extraordinarily heavy for one so light, across the slippery grass of the country churchyard. There'd been rainwater at the bottom of the grave, reflecting the slate-grey sky, and the glint of it had brought home like nothing else the finality of that resting place.

I know that my Redeemer liveth
he sang softly to himself.

How could he know?

He thought of space – the planets he'd watched with such excitement through his father's telescope. And the stars, the way they went on and on for ever, more of them even than the cells that made up his body; more of them than all the people who had been born and lived and died since the beginning of mankind. What could he, in his minuteness, set against that? Why would he not vanish like the drop of rain that he was, falling from a leaf into eternity?

It seemed to him that his life had been very short. He wasn't someone who'd achieved great things at a young age: he'd just progressed at a reasonable pace, and now he was finally coming into his own, only to be stopped in his tracks.

He wondered what he could have done differently in the past forty-eight hours, and realised that it was his body that had let him down. In his younger days he could have driven through the night, been here early yesterday morning, sorted everything out before Warry & Co got anywhere close to him. But not now. He'd tried to be a hero, and he'd ended up doing more harm than good. Maybe he deserved to be shot at dawn. The world wouldn't miss him.

Except . . . Ben. If there was anything in his life that Christophe was proud of, it was his son. He was a fine young man: clever, competent, affectionate. But he had lost his mother too young, and now he was about to lose his father as well. Christophe felt a sob well up in his chest. He should have done better for Ben, just as he should have done better for Sara.

For the grass is withered,
And the flower thereof is fallen . . .

The Brahms *Requiem*. He remembered Matt singing it with his school choir, and how proud Sara had been of her younger brother. It seemed a lifetime away. It *was* a lifetime away.

But that language – so beautiful. The flower thereof: what could be more majestic? And the voices, the massed human voices, dropping into the quietness of those two lines, and then – exultantly, filling the whole chapel –

But His name liveth for evermore.

That was something he could set against the darkness of space: the elegance of those words, the beauty of that music. Tiny, of course, but that was the wonder of them – the fact that something so small and fragile could not only be laid in the balance against something so enormous, but hold its own. That, and the love that lingered after death, and the look of compassion in the eyes of the crucified Christ.

He thought of Amy – her bravery, her certainty of faith. She at least was someone he hadn't failed. He'd brought her safely from Beijing to Hong Kong, and carried her in his arms across that faraway island, and over his shoulder across that rickety pontoon, so that she could escape her persecutors and be treated for her sickness. He remembered her face as she lay asleep, and felt suddenly saddened that he would never see her again.

II

'So what now?' said Faye.

'We wait,' said Jonty. 'The hackers will get through.'

'You said that two hours ago.'

'These guys are the best. It just happens that Janissary has a particularly challenging system – not surprisingly, given that it's a security company. We have to be patient.'

The Mercedes was parked outside a supermarket on the outskirts of Penrith. Dawn was still an hour away.

'This is a wild goose chase,' said Faye.

'Do we have an alternative?'

'We should never have accepted the assignment to hit Zhou Zhi. Getting involved in Politburo infighting is always a disaster.'

'If you remember, you were the one who was so keen to take it. "Get them to send someone from Beijing," I said. But would you listen? No. Because you never do listen, do you? You always have to have it your own bloody way.'

'That's it! Enough!' Suddenly she was pointing a handgun at his head. 'Get out of the car.'

'You don't mean that.'

'Try me.'

'Look, I don't like this situation any more than you do. But we're far more likely to get through it in one piece if we stick together.'

'I'll take my chances.'

'Faye, come on. We'll finish this and then we need never see each other again.'

'I'm counting to five and then I'll blow your head off. I can't tell you how much pleasure that will give me. One – '

'Faye, please.'

'Two – '

With a sigh, Jonty opened the door and climbed out. He had a full loaded automatic in his shoulder holster and didn't doubt his ability to take her out as she drove away. But he couldn't see that it would help his situation. If the car crashed, the explosives in the boot would bring every policeman in the county down on him.

The tail lights of the Mercedes disappeared on to the dual carriageway. He wished he'd had the presence of mind to grab his Lanvin ties.

III

As the first sunlight touched the farmhouse windows, Thomas Warry pushed back his chair and downed his cup of coffee.

'Take him outside and shoot him,' he said. 'There's an old pigsty on the other side of the laboratory. Do it there.'

Christophe felt a lurching in his stomach, as if a lift had gone into free fall and been caught by its safety mechanism.

'For God's sake,' said Neary. 'Why can't you just let him go?'

'What, to tell the police everything he knows? No chance.'

'If you kill him, your masters won't get any help from me.'

'Not my problem, Professor. Our assignment is to deliver you and the syringe safely: once that's done, you can sit on your arse until doomsday for all I care.'

'Breakfast,' said Christophe.

'What?'

'You promised me a hearty breakfast. The condemned man, remember?' Warry stared at him, then burst out laughing.

'I don't think I actually promised you that,' he said. 'But I like to see the fearless Christophe Hardy grovelling for a few extra minutes of life. Cooper, see what's in the fridge, will you?'

IV

Leaning on the bonnet of a stolen Volvo, Jonty surveyed the farmhouse through his pocket binoculars. The layout looked simple enough, but he could have done with someone to cover the back door. Damn that bloody woman.

If only Faye had hung on for another fifteen minutes, which was all it had taken for his friend in Beijing to breach Janissary's security wall. The discovery that Christophe Hardy wasn't the mole at the university was a surprise; but the rest of the file made straightforward reading. Janissary had two operatives on Neary's property; the prototype syringe was there awaiting collection, along with two prisoners. A helicopter, despatched to take them to the Channel Islands, was due in half an hour. That gave Jonty time enough to get in and out of the farmhouse.

He unholstered his handgun and started to make his way down the hill.

V

Christophe spun his breakfast out for as long as he could, making a show of savouring each slice of toast and forkful of scrambled egg. To begin with, Warry watched him with amusement, even pretending to be Mr Bumble from *Oliver Twist* as he ladled porridge from a large saucepan. But after a while his patience grew thin.

'Right, that's it. Get him out of here.'

'On your feet,' said Cooper. 'You go in front, hands on your head.' Christophe did as he was told. Stepping out into the sunshine, he had a moment to wonder at the beauty of the morning – the eager chatter of birds, the gleam of gossamer on the grass. Then there was a strange sound, halfway between a breath and a sigh, as Cooper fell to the ground behind him with a bullet through his temple.

Thomas Warry was lucky enough not to have a gun in his hand. Jonty Lo landed two blows, one to the solar plexus and the other to the jaw, leaving him semiconscious but alive.

The three prisoners stared at their elegantly dressed rescuer in astonishment. Ignoring Christophe and Neary, he addressed himself to Li.

'Professor, I have been sent to take you back to the People's Republic. Where is the prototype syringe?'

Li glanced at Christophe, but Jonty Lo had already spotted the package on the kitchen dresser. He picked it up, checked the contents, and tucked it into his jacket pocket. Christophe watched him in bewilderment and despair.

'You're Dr Hardy?'

'Yes. I suppose I should thank you for saving my life.'

Jonty Lo smiled. 'Oh, I didn't come here to do that,' he said. 'I came here to kill you.'

VI

Christophe wondered whether he had actually woken up that morning. This couldn't be anything but a nightmare.

'Why?' was all he could manage.

'Because you've aided and abetted the Brothers of Light. Because you stole the syringe from Professor Li. Because you threaten the sale of the Mulberry Tree Project to the UK. And because those are my orders.'

'I don't get it. Why is your government so keen to sell this technology? If I were the head of your security services, I'd want to keep it to myself.'

Jonty smiled. 'For an academic, you're very slow off the mark, aren't you? Yes, we're selling our top-secret, state-of-the-art technology to a country which is far less advanced. But the beauty of it is that (a) we get very well paid and (b) – though your government isn't aware of this – we retain control of the entire system.'

'What?'

'All the information picked up by your computers will be copied automatically to Beijing. Whatever your government knows, we will know. And if we want to override the system – to hide something from them, or give them false information, or do some extra investigating of our own – we can. We will be able to track anyone in your country at any time. And that's not all. The device implanted by the syringe is being adapted for export with a destructive capability. If we want to kill somebody – or lots of people for that matter – we just have to press a button.'

Christophe turned to Li. 'Did you know this?'

'No,' said Li miserably. 'We discussed a destructive capability, but I said I would have nothing to do with it. I thought the British system would be just the same as ours.'

'Not that you need to worry, Dr Hardy.' Jonty Lo raised his gun. 'You can be dealt with in the old-fashioned way.'

'Gaaaargh!'

The bellowing noise came from the corner in which Warry had been slumped. Still dazed, but conscious, he lunged across the floor at Jonty Lo's legs.

It took Lo only a moment to sidestep the attack, but that was enough. Christophe seized the saucepan of porridge on the Aga and flung it his head. It caught him full on the forehead and sent him crashing to the floor. The gun spun from his hand, coming to a halt just beside Warry, who snatched it up and got unsteadily to his feet.

'Now,' he said. 'Where were we?'

As he spoke, Christophe became aware of a distant thrumming, becoming steadily louder: the sound of a helicopter.

VIII

Christophe, Neary and Li filed out into the sunshine. Warry followed, gun in hand, and leaned against the porch. All four gazed up at the great machine as it slowed and halted above the farm buildings and then began its descent, its shadow falling deep across the yard, the noise of its rotors battering their eardrums. As the downdraft enveloped him, Christophe found himself thinking of the parable of the threshing floor, the wheat being separated from the chaff. Was this his moment to be cast into the fire?

The helicopter settled; the rotors slurred into visibility and a door opened. But what came out of it was not what any of them expected.

With a hideous yowling, four large black-and-tan foxhounds leapt on to the ground and charged towards the house. An obscure instinct seemed to tell them that Thomas Warry was their enemy; or perhaps they detected a spattering of dog's blood on his shoes. Whatever the reason, they hurled themselves upon him, knocking him backwards and trampling on his chest as he cried out in terror.

Behind them came Frank, Anna, Matt, Selina and a plump woman with a clipboard.

'Matt!' Christophe embraced his brother-in-law. 'We thought you were . . . well, the enemy. How did you find us? Where on earth did you get hold of this helicopter?'

'Selina got a call in the middle of the night from an old man who said that you'd asked him to give me this address – seems he'd lost the piece of paper and had only just found it. As for the helicopter, that was Frank's doing. Frank, this is Christophe.'

They shook hands.

'Outside broadcasting,' said Frank with a grin. 'There's more on the way.' He pointed to two large vans with satellite dishes bumping down the farm track. 'We're flavour of the month after yesterday's bit of hunting, so I persuaded Vanessa here that her company should splash out a bit.'

The woman with the clipboard gave a half smile. 'We need to get filming, Frank. You can catch up with your friends later.'

Frank winked. 'A bit of a slave-driver, our Van. I'd better get those hounds under control. Excuse me a mo.'

'You OK, Christophe?' asked Matt.

'Yes, thanks. At least, I think so. It's been quite a morning. There's another man in the house – he, well, tried to kill me. I may have killed him. And there's another man who's definitely dead.'

'Let's go and take a look.'

'And Matt – '

'Yes?'

'There's something I need to talk to you about. Something I need to explain.'

Matt smiled. 'I think we should sort out the casualties first. Then we can talk. OK?'

'Yes,' said Christophe. 'That's fine.'

He gazed in wonder at the fields behind the house. The grass was new; the sky was new; the leaves on the trees were new. He had been granted a new life.

High above him, a second helicopter came into view, hovered indecisively, and then turned away again, vanishing into the southern horizon.

CHAPTER TWENTY-ONE

Jennifer Pettifer had been nursing a dream. In it, Zhou made a full recovery and was granted political asylum on the grounds that his enemies in China would kill him if he returned. At this stage she intervened, suggesting that his administrative experience could be immensely valuable to local government – provided he was prepared to grace the town hall with his presence. A meteoric rise followed, resulting in his appointment as leader of the County Council with Jennifer as helpmate. Granted, Oxfordshire was not quite Beijing, but there would still be meetings and memorandums and by-laws and fast-track prosecutions. That, and their sexual chemistry, would be enough to make them happy.

For now, though, the dream had faded, eclipsed by the news headlines. In the wake of the Mulberry Tree scandal, the Prime Minister had stepped down; so had the Archbishop of Canterbury elect. The Brothers of Light had received an apology from the British Government, and an arms deal with China had been cancelled. In other news, a woman driving a Mercedes full of arms and explosives had been detained at Stranraer.

But Jennifer didn't take in the other news. Instead, through a blur of tears, she stared at the red banner on the bottom of her television screen, and the terrible words running across it again and again: 'JEFFREY CRUSHAM RESIGNS AS PRIME MINISTER.'

II

'Is it working, doctor?'

The woman in the white coat pursed her lips. 'It's too early to say. His pulse is certainly stronger. But with a new treatment like this . . . I'd be happier if he'd woken up. Then we'd know he was on the mend.'

When she had gone, Mr Yu resumed his seat beside Frederick's bed. With an unsteady hand he reached out and touched the boy's cheek.

'My son,' he said quietly. 'What kind of father have I been to you? Not much of one. I've tried to make you into something you're not. I never asked you if you wanted to be British: I just made up my mind that it was the best thing for you – for us. You could have had a normal childhood like your brother, instead of having to eat those strange puddings, to wear those strange clothes . . .'

He stopped. There were no words that could express all he wanted to say. He took the small hand beside him and pressed his forehead against it.

As he did so, he felt a slight movement. Looking up, he saw

Frederick watching him through open eyes with a smile on his face.

'But Pater,' he said, 'I think they're absolutely ripping.'

III

'Where?' said Jonty Lo.

'Milton Keynes. A new eco-housing estate. I'm told it's very nice. Close to the countryside – good for walking.'

'You're joking.'

The man in the pinstriped suit shook his head. 'You can hardly go back to living the high life in Belgravia, you know. A new identity means exactly that.'

'But all the information I've been giving you – don't tell me it isn't worth more than that.'

'What about me?' Faye interrupted. 'Where am I going?'

The man looked bemused. 'Surely it's been explained to you that you'll be staying together?'

Jonty and Faye exchanged looks of sheer hatred.

'No,' said Faye.

'Absolutely no way,' said Jonty.

The man sighed. 'Those are my instructions. If you accept HMG's hospitality, it's on our terms. If you don't, we reckon you'll be dead within forty-eight hours. The choice is yours.'

IV

'They caught the bear,' said Sammy.

'What bear?' asked Jake.

'The one we liberated from the zoo.'

'Where was it?'

'Northumberland. Living in a mine shaft, apparently.'

'That's a shame.'

'It's not a shame, it's a bloody insult. After everything we went through to rescue it.'

'Can't be helped, can it?'

Sammy frowned. 'Oh yes it can. We're not going to sit back and let people think that the forces of oppression have got the better of us.'

'What you going to do then?'

'We are going to rescue it again.'

Jake looked dubious. 'I don't know, Sam. Remember what happened last time?'

Sammy put an arm round his shoulder. 'This negative attitude, Jake, is not worthy of you. The great thing about life is that you learn from your mistakes. This time the plan is going to be flawless. Trust me.'

V

'You're not serious.'

'I am, Van – straight up. Sorry.'

'But you're the biggest thing on TV. Think how many people watched the *Frank Rides Forth* special: twelve million. That's a fifth of the population. Every time the Mulberry Tree scandal comes on the news on there's footage of you at Neary's farmhouse. And I'm not just talking about the UK. We've got an American station wanting to film you hunting coyotes in Texas, Bollywood is pitching a musical about renegade tigers . . .'

Frank put down the rifle he was cleaning.

'You don't get it, do you, Van? I never set out to be a star on the telly. All I've ever wanted to do is hunt foxes – preferably in the open countryside, not down some poxy alleyway off the Edgware Road. And now I've got the opportunity. The urban fox cull has been downgraded to level three; Horry's asked me to be his joint master, hunting over some of the most gorgeous countryside in Britain, just down the motorway from my equally gorgeous girlfriend and her hunt. So you can keep your coyotes and your Bollywood musical, because this Essex boy's got everything his heart desires.'

Vanessa drove out of the park in a rage. She didn't need Frank; her reputation as a producer was made. But his attitude galled her nonetheless. How bloody selfish could one man be?

VI

Matt stood in the ruins of his great aunt's house drinking a cup of coffee. He and Selina had been at work since dawn, anxious to make the most of the good weather. They'd agreed on a tea break at 9.30, but Selina was still up on the roof fitting slates. What an amazing girl she was: there didn't seem to be anything she couldn't put her hand to.

He'd quite enjoyed all the fuss. The apologies from the prison service and the council – with a waiving of tax on Stooks Farm – had been deeply satisfying. He'd even had an embarrassed phone call from Selina's father. But he was glad to be able to put it all behind him and work with his hands again.

He studied the wooden tea chests beside him. Where had they come from: India? Ceylon? China?

'Penny for them.'

Selina took the mug from his hand and settled herself on his knee.

'I was wondering how many tea leaves you could fit in one of those chests,' he said. 'What do you think? Hundreds of thousands? A million? It must be equivalent to the population of an entire city – maybe a small country.

'Anyway, the thing is – that's us, isn't it? You and me, and Christophe, and Frank, and Anna, and Professor Li, and Mr Yu – we're just leaves in the great tea chest of life. And yet we've managed to bring down the Prime Minister and give the Chinese government a bloody nose. There's this bizarre thing of all these entirely different individuals working for the common good, and the common good depending on respect for the individual. And maybe the whole history of mankind should be seen like that: the relationship of the individual to the community. What do you think?'

'I think,' she said, putting down the mug, 'that I'm only interested in two people, and that's you and me.'

She started to sing in her delicate soprano:
Our house is a very, very, very fine house
With two cats in the yard.
Life used to be so hard –
Now everything is easy 'cos of you.
She stopped and looked at him with her dark eyes.

'Is it?' he asked.

'Yes.'

They kissed.

VII

'And Professor Li?'

'He sent me this photograph.'

Christophe handed Ben his smartphone. The screen showed Li sitting at a piano with a broad grin on his face. Next to him was a girl in a low-cut top who looked equally happy.

'Where was it taken?'

'New Orleans. He's having a holiday down there before he starts work at MIT. And this –' Christophe scrolled through the photo library – 'is Patrick Neary's new dog.'

'Sweet. What kind is it?'

'A Spitz, I think: some name like that. MIT wanted him too – Neary, not the dog – but he says he'd rather stay put. After so many years in the wilderness, he feels the world can come to him.'

'Good for him.'

'And one more – Matt and Selina.'

'She looks scary.'

'She's actually a very nice girl underneath it all. I think they're well matched.'

'I'm glad you've made it up with him.'

'We didn't really ever fall out: it was more of a misunderstanding. But yes, it's good.'

'I had a text from Tessa, Dad. She's back home, convalescing. She says she's the hero of the hour on the paper: exclusive interview with Christophe Hardy filed from her hospital bed – lots of brownie points.'

'It was the least I could do.'

Christophe took another sip of wine. It was good to be in a Parisian bar: for most of his life he had lived as an Englishman, but it was a relief, every now and again, to open the door to the other half of himself. It felt like going on holiday – or rather, like going home.

'You're sure it's OK for me to stay another couple of nights?' he asked. 'Your landlady won't mind?'

'No, Dad. I think she's rather thrilled, having an action hero around.'

Christophe laughed. 'Hardly. If I'm in the way, you must say – I can go to a hotel. It's just until Amy comes out of hospital.'

'So she's doing OK?'

'That's what they tell me.'

'I'm glad. She's a great woman, Dad.'

'You think so?'

'Yes, really.'

'You don't mind that . . .'

'What? That you've got a girlfriend?'

'I wasn't going to put it like that.'

Ben reached out and put his hand on his father's shoulder.

'I want you to be happy,' he said. 'And that's what Mum would have wanted too.'

Christophe nodded. He put his hand on top of his son's, and for a moment they sat like that in silence while the waiter cleared the table behind them and the rush-hour traffic of Saint-Germain-des-Prés blared past the open door, heedless of the strange journey that had just reached its end.

ACKNOWLEDGEMENTS

I would like to thank Jean Findlay and all her team at Scotland Street Press; Nicola and Rosanna Reed for their wonderful illustrations; Derek Westwood for his excellent cover design; Jean Tsang Earle for her guidance on Chinese culture and cuisine; Sue Gaisford, Linda Kelly, Pauline Kang Fiennes, Josa Young, Johnny de Falbe and Arabella von Friesen for their encouragement and advice; and above all my wife Rosanna – to whom this book is dedicated – for her moral support and ever-acute editing.

I acknowledge with gratitude the authors of three splendid songs quoted in the text: *Raining in My Heart* by Buddy Holly; *Joe Hill* by Alfred Hayes and Earl Robinson; and *Our House* by Graham Nash.

The songs from which Professor Li and Matt sing snatches:

My Very Good Friend the Milkman by Harold Spina and Johnny Burke; *Stormy Weather* by Harold Arlen and Ted Koehler; *Don't Sit Under the Apple Tree* (*With Anyone Else But Me*) by Sam H.Stept, Lew Brown and Charles Tobias; *Hoochie Coochie Man* by Willie Dixon; *Morning Has Broken* by Eleanor Farjeon; and *Yes! We Have No Bananas* by Frank Silver and Irving Cohn.

Also from Scotland Street Press

Non-fiction

Freedom Found by Sara Trevelyan

"Sara Trevelyan did not set out to have one of the most notorious marriages of the twentieth century."

Sunday Times

She was independent, clever and privileged: a doctor who campaigned for penal reform. Then she fell in love and married Jimmy Boyle, a convicted murderer who became a famous writer and sculptor. He was in jail and their lives lived under the scrutiny of the media. In this intimate memoir we learn why Jimmy admits, "If it hadn't been for Sara's courage, I would still be in prison."

Paperback with colour photographs 321 pages. ISBN 9781910895078. £10.99

A Land Girl's Tale by Mona McLeod

"I can see the disgust on the face of one neighbor when Jack, the farmer, asked to lend a man, produced a land girl."

Mona Macleod worked in Kirkubrightshire during the second World War, providing the skilled labour needed on farms before mechanization. The girls were given heavy agricultural work in fields, with animals, carrying hundred weight sacks, sawing wood, felling trees, filling up rat holes. It was a tough way to grow up, but this illustrated memoir provides a record of a time when women faced the rigorous physical challenges involved in winning the war at home.

'A significant contribution both to the annals of Scottish Social history and to the advancement of women's rights in Britain. It is also immensely readable and a typically stylish Scotland Street Press production with delightful illustrations.'

Drummond Place News

Paperback with colour photographs 150 pages £9.99 ISBN 9781910895115

Nine Months in Tibet by Rupert Wolfe Murray

'His combination of derring do and naivety produce some unusually funny scenarios . . . Reading this engrossing memoir, I was reminded of Paul Theroux's philosophy of travel.'

The Herald

9 Months in Tibet is about overcoming the fear of travelling alone, getting a job in Llasa, riding a horse through Eastern Tibet, witnessing a violent protest between Buddhist monks and the Chinese police, and getting expelled from Tibet.

Paperback 380 pages. £12.99 ISBN 9781910895030

The Sweet Pea Man – the life and times of the Victorian plant hybridist Henry Eckford 1823–1905 by Graham Martin

'Fascinating biography . . . a wonderful testament to a remarkable man.'
Garden News Magazine

Taking you on a journey through nineteenth century British gardens, a minutely researched biography of the breeder of the famous Grandiflora Sweet Pea.

Hardback with colour illustrations 480 pages. £24.99 ISBN 9781910895184

A Large Czeslaw Milosz with a dash of Elvis Presley
By Tania Skarynkina

'She writes as if penning a letter to a close friend, loosely, intimately, but never less than engagingly.'
Alan Taylor in *The Herald*

A collection of essays from a forgotten town in a forgotten country in an unsupported language. Translated from the Belarusian by Jim Dingley, a cocktail of world literature seen from a small town in Belarus.
'This collection exists at the very edge of the imagination'
Country Life

Paperback 260 pages £9.99 ISBN 9781910895221

The First Novel from Scotland Street Press

Errant Blood by C.F. Peterson

'Superbly constructed literary thriller.'

Undiscovered Scotland

'Reminiscent of Iain Banks, and I do not say this lightly."

Alastair Braidwood in *Scots Whay Hae*

'It's a crime for a debut to be this good.'

Criminal Minds

A boy has been murdered in the local village and the people investigating are not the police. Eamon Ansgar the reluctant laird of Duncul Castle, recently returned from active war service, is woken from his self imposed retirement. His curiosity and sense of duty take him on a trail leading to big science and international conspiracy all set in a rain soaked winter in the Scottish Highlands today.

Paperback with illustrations 236 pages £9.99 ISBN 9781910895061

The First Young Adult Novel from Scotland Street Press

Black Snow Falling by L.J. MacWhirter

'A powerful new mythology'

Anna Claybourne

In 1592, a girl with spirit is a threat. Ruth has secrets. An old book of heresy belonging to her long-absent father. A dream that haunts her. And love that she and Silas hide from the world. When she is robbed of all she holds true, her friends from Crowbury slide into terrible danger. Hope is as faint as a moonbow. Dare Ruth trust the shadowy one who could destroy them all?

'Capacious imagination, a deep sense of history and complex characterization. Its rare to find all three at once in YA ficion, and in all my time . . . I don't think I ever have. I recommend it highly.'

David Robinson Books Editor, the *Scotsman* 2000–15

Hardback 250 pages £12.99 ISBN 9781910895214